New Age

Advanced Praise

UFO Symphonic is an entirely unique and revitalizing contribution to UFO literature, a tantalizing must read about the universal language of music.

—Martin Willis, host of *Podcast UFO Live*

Mike Fiorito's *UFO Symphonic* explores the relationship between music, synesthesia, and UFOs. This is a fresh and welcomed contribution to ufology. As far as I know there is no other study quite like this. I was once asked if aliens enjoy music. I've thought about this quite a bit, being a musician myself. In my work as a ufologist, I've personally investigated numerous cases where UFOs and music have intertwined. In 2016, an all-girl punk band were taking a cigarette break outside of the Hollywood venue they'd just played at, when they observed an anomalous craft, a "flying saucer, all lit-up like Christmas," hovering near the venue. I closed the case as an "unknown". There was no prosaic explanation for what they observed. Another case I investigated was that of a bassist coming home from band rehearsal. As she drove home on the Pacific Coast Highway, a giant black triangle, lights on each corner, swooped out of the fog, flew over her car, and nearly caused her to hit the Meridian wall. Another case I investigated happened over the main stage of the Coachella music festival. A mathematician had been dragged to the event by his girlfriend, he wasn't a fan of that sort of event. As he watched the concert, a 50 foot triangular craft hovered directly over the main stage. People weren't really reacting to it. Perhaps they thought it was a holographic special effect, and part of the show. It wasn't. But the most amazing account, and one of the reasons I became a UFO investigator in the first place, was a late-night conversation I had with my dear old friend, the late great Chris Squire. Chris was an English musician, singer and songwriter best known as the bassist and backing vocalist of the progressive rock band Yes. In 2005, I was visiting with Chris in his hotel room. He was in town, recording a new album. Chris knew of my interest in UFOs, and he told me this account: "We were touring the United Kingdom in 1977 and while driving through a particularly rural area I asked my driver to pull over, so I could use nature's bathroom. I got out, and I was peeing on a rock, when suddenly, I felt watched. I looked up, and not 30 feet away from me was a hovering UFO. It was a metallic flying saucer with a dome on top, right out of a movie! It had large garish purple lights spinning around the bottom, like you'd see on a carnival ride. I zipped-up, and watched the disc defy gravity. It hung there for a few moments, then tilted to its side. Without a sound, it accelerated from stand-still and shot-off so quickly, if I hadn't been watching, I would've thought it had disappeared. I've pondered this for years. Now who the hell do you think could have piloted that thing, Earl?" I thought about it for a moment.

"Perhaps it was a musicologist from the future, Chris. Jacques Vallée proposed that aliens might be us from the future." Chris looked shocked. Not generally an emotionally demonstrable man, Chris lifted me up in a great bear-hug (the only time he ever did that!). He grabbed a pen, and a post-it. "Earl. Please repeat what you just said." I said, "aliens might just be us from the future."

A year or so later, Yes premiered a new, unrecorded song in San Diego. It was Chris's new composition. It was titled, "Aliens (Are Only Us from the Future)." After the show, we were invited backstage, and Chris didn't say a word about the song. He simply grinned and winked at me. And we never did speak about it. Musical notes are messengers, just like UFOs. They are the connective tissue between us and the ineffable. They hover anomalously above us in the ether, beyond conscious thought and expression. And if we are blessed, we get little glimmers of this great Other, of which this world is but a shadow. Music is a key to that starry vault and Mike Fiorito knows this well.

> —Earl Grey Anderson, MUFON State Director of Southern California

"*UFO Symphonic* manages to be both a concerto - bridging and contrasting themes and ideas - as well as a sort of "On The Road" narrative of Mike Fiorito's journey through the many-faceted jewel of the UFO experience. The stories of scientists, artists, and musicians whose lives have been suffused with the phenomenon and altered irrevocably by it, reveals fresh methods to perceive and understand the UFO issue with the heart and intuition, rather than endless processions of data that don't explain the emotional rollercoaster and life changes that are often experienced by witnesses."

> — Greg Bishop, author of *It Defies Language! & Project Beta: The Story of Paul Bennewitz, National Security, and the Creation of a Modern UFO Myth*. Greg is also the host of *Radio Misterioso*

How does one articulate the unfathomable? How does one give voice to that which defies conventional understanding? These questions often arise in the context of experiences that stretch the limits of our perception—anomalies that challenge our grasp on reality. My time observing the Tic Tac encounters left an indelible mark on my worldview, illuminating the intersection of the extraordinary and the everyday. In moments of profound realization, we often find ourselves grappling with feelings that seem ineffable. This is where art becomes essential. It serves as a bridge, connecting our personal experiences to the universal truths that bind us all. Mike Fiorito's work, *UFO Symphonic—Journeys into Sound*, embodies this connection, exploring how music transcends boundaries and encapsulates the complexities of human existence. As someone who has witnessed the inexplicable, I resonate deeply with Mike's assertion that "music is a language." It is more than mere communication; it is a visceral experience, a conduit for the ineffable. In the cacophony of our daily lives, music emerges as a soothing balm, a way to navigate the chaos and find coherence amidst uncertainty. Noise may dominate our surroundings, but it is the intentional arrangement of sound that offers us clarity. The way we organize these sonic experiences can illuminate some of life's most profound mysteries. In this way, music is not merely an art form; it is a means of connection that draws us into a shared human narrative. Mike's exploration is not just about UFOs; it's about what those encounters evoke in us as individuals and as a society. Each chapter invites us to reflect on our relationship with the unknown, urging us to find meaning in the extraordinary. It is a testament to the power of creativity and imagination in the face of phenomena that often elude rational explanation. What struck me most during my own experiences was the realization that we are part of a continuum that extends beyond our immediate understanding. As we seek to comprehend the "Other," we must also acknowledge our place within the broader tapestry of existence. This duality is beautifully captured in *UFO Symphonic*, where the threads of music and the unknown weave together to form a compelling narrative. This work resonates on multiple levels, much like a symphony, where each note contributes to a greater composition. Mike seamlessly intertwines personal anecdotes with broader themes, creating a rich tapestry that encourages us to explore the depths of our own experiences. It is this balance between the personal and the universal that transforms the narrative into something truly impactful. In a world that often prioritizes the empirical, *UFO Symphonic* invites us to consider the value of introspection and emotional resonance. It reminds us that our encounters with the extraordinary can enrich our understanding of what it means to be human. Just as music has the power to heal and inspire, so too can our encounters with the unknown provoke profound shifts in our perception. As we delve into Mike's exploration, we are reminded that while the technological aspects of UFOs can fascinate, it is our human experience that breathes life into the discussion. Just as a skilled musician navigates the complexities of their craft, we must navigate the interplay between the known and the unknown, allowing the mystery to guide our inquiry. Thank you, Mike, for illuminating this journey and reminding us of the beauty and complexity that exists within and around us. Your work serves as a beacon, encouraging us to embrace the inexplicable and to find our own voices within this grand symphony of existence.

> — Kevin M. Day USN (Ret.), M.Ed. in Educational Technology TIC TAC Radar Operator and Air Traffic Controller

UFO SYMPHONIC

Copyright © 2025 by Mike Fiorito

All rights reserved. No part of this book may be reproduced or transmitted in any form or by any means, electronic or mechanical, including photocopy, recording, or any information storage and retrieval system, without prior permission from the publisher (except by reviewers who may quote brief passages).

First Edition

Casebound ISBN: 978-1-62720-605-1
Paperback ISBN: 978-1-62720-606-8
Ebook ISBN: 978-1-62720-607-5

Book cover art by Pat Singer
Book design by Adam Robinson
Promotion Development by Olivia DiTroia

Published by Apprentice House Press

Apprentice House Press
Loyola University Maryland

Loyola University Maryland
4501 N. Charles Street, Baltimore, MD 21210
410.617.5265
www.ApprenticeHouse.com
info@ApprenticeHouse.com

UFO
SYMPHONIC
Journeys into Sound

Mike Fiorito

"All art constantly aspires to the condition of music."
—Walter Pater

"Coltrane played life. John Coltrane's sound rearranges molecular structure."
—Carlos Santana

"Magic is what we do. Music is how we do it."
—Jerry Garcia

"One day it will have to be officially admitted that what we have christened reality is an even greater illusion than the world of dreams."
—Salvador Dalí

"Don't cry for me, for I go where music is born"
—Johann Sebastian Bach
[*said to his wife as he lay on his deathbed*]

To Pete Rowan, my friend and mentor. Thank you for the journey. As Bill Monroe said, "Don't ever give up, Pete, don't ever give up!"

Peter Rowan and the Magic Flute. Frank Serio: Photo Credit.

CONTENTS

UFO Symphonic	v
Foreword by Joshua Cutchin	xvii
Prelude by Kevin Cann	xxi
A Note on Polyphonic Music	xxix

KYRIE   1

Preface	3
Introduction	9
Overture	21
Alien Gnosis	23
Beings of the Bush	32
Altered States and Music Sound Effects *Dana Larocca's Story*	38
The Angel of Light	43
Twelve Notes in Three Seconds	46
Dreaming UFOs	49
When He Reached Down His Hand For Me	53
The Many Voices of Palestrina	58

GLORIA   63

Two Miles from Fermilab *Lauren Crisanti's Story*	65

The Holy Spirit Healed During A Praise and Worship Song *Gloria Hass's Story*	67
The Day of the Crows—Myron Dyal	69
My Only True Friend—Scott Sharrard	80

SANCTUS/BENEDICTUS — 85

Lightning Striking *Leigh Ann's Story*	87
UFOs in Mexico, 1974 *Becky Johnson's Story*	101
Duets in Lockdown	104
Spookiness at a Distance *James Faulk's Story*	106
San Pedro	108
Aliens Like Bluegrass *Mark Turner's Story*	113
UFO Visions *Massimo Teordorani's Story*	128
Music as a Form of Telepathy *Joshua Cutchin's Story*	139
Making Music is Paranormal Activity in Public View *Sebastiano De Filippi's Story*	156
York Cathedral	169

CREDO — 173

Angel Voices *Julie A. Colton's Story*	175
Spaces of Otherness *Tim Bragg's Story*	180

Thin Lizzy & Freda *Another Tim Bragg Story*	187
Fluting Consciousness— *Tim Bragg*	189
Music is a Language— *Tim Bragg*	190
Doorways to Other Realities *Tim Kaney's Story*	192
Yungchen Lhamo	196
Mescalito Riding His White Horse—Peter Rowan	202
The Goddess (Also) Lives on Tinder *Christopher Henry's Story*	209
The Magic Flute *Frank Serio's Story*	216
See You Tomorrow *Andrea Tarquini's Story*	224
The Bron-Yr-Aur Song	229
American Psychic *Marla Frees's Story*	233
Gong Yoga	239
The Ground Will Protect You	249
Call Me Guido	255
Just a Gigolo	260

AGNUS DEI   **263**

Music Matters Even If Mum Can't Sing *Dianne Porter's Story*	265
The Angelic Orchestra *James Iandoli's Story*	268

Questions on Scraps of Paper *Christina Marrocco's Story*	273
Bands! *Janice Aubrey's Story*	279
While My Guitar Gently Weeps *Marilyn Brannon's Story*	285
Visions of Truth *Max Wareham's Stories*	287
Seasons That Pass You By	292
King Diamond	296
Sounds in the Sky	300
From Language to Singing	302

ENCORE   **307**

Paul's Dreams of John	309
Bibliography	313
Acknowledgements	315
About the Author	317

FOREWORD BY JOSHUA CUTCHIN

How does one articulate that which cannot be put into words? How does one quantify the infinite?

It seems like an impossible mandate. I would argue that such expressions are exceedingly rare, perhaps solely restricted to two domains. The first is the numinous, those anomalous moments verging on the divine, the transcendent, the supernatural, the Other. The second—much more common, but no less miraculous—is in art. Mike Fiorito realizes this, and the concept has never been presented more thoughtfully than in *UFO Symphonic—Journeys into Sound*.

While all art touches us in personal, ineffable ways, music holds a special spot for many of us. "Music is a language," Mike writes. But it often seems like so much more than that. Music isn't just *a* language…it might be *the* language, the music of the spheres, the motor of existence.

Noise represents the natural state of our existence on Earth, of our reality. Even the most remote locales on the planet, places relatively devoid of flora and fauna like Antarctica, are subject to the incessant drone of the wind, the thunderous *fortissimo* of calving glaciers. To order sound into coherence harnesses what may perhaps be the greatest mysteries known to humankind.

To that end, as Mike suggests, music may also represent our *oldest* art. The implication is clear: being a musician places one on a continuum of humanity, stretching back before we were even *Homo sapiens*.

We cannot escape this impulse if we try; we are *all* inherently musical. As Henry Van Dyke observed, "The woods would be very silent if no birds sang except those who sang best," or, more pragmatically, as Diane Porter, one of the contributing writers in this book, says, "Music matters even if mum can't sing."

Contradictorily, by taking our place within this human continuum, we gain insight into what it means to be *more* than human. It holds the potential to bring us into contact with our second expression of the inexpressible: the supernatural.

This is the recurring refrain of *UFO Symphonic*. Reading Mike's intimate look at the interplay of music and the unknown—not only in his own life, but also in the lives of others—is akin to attending the premiere of a grand opus.

Think of it as a duet between two aspects of existence, seemingly unrelated but both fundamental to the human condition, intertwining in a contrapuntal dance, a reciprocal dialogue where music nurtures the Other, and vice versa. Although UFOs constitute the central leitmotif, Mike regularly modulates to the closely related tonalities of other inexplicable phenomena: synchronicities, spiritual revelation, psychic abilities, and more, all using music as a unifying framework.

Like any artfully executed performance, Mike seems to have pulled off the impossible. In the interest of full disclosure, I once thought about writing a book on anomalous music myself, or music and the Phenomenon[1] writ large. I would have written something grand, something academic, full of endnotes and music theory and endless scholarly commentary.

But it wouldn't have meant as much as Mike's work. It wouldn't have included an ounce of *who I am* or what music means to *me*. Despite how much I'd pat myself on the back, it would have been absolutely the *wrong* approach.

---

1 The Phenomenon or phenomena (plural) will be used throughout this book to describe experiences and objects, both unusual and ordinary, that people characterize as spiritual, paranormal, magical, occult and/or supernatural.

Thankfully, Mike realizes that while there's value to be gleaned from an academic line of thought—he includes just the right amount in *UFO Symphonic*—music demands a much more personal touch. It's not solely, or even mostly, about sweeping statements. It's about our own individual connections, those small, meaningful moments juxtaposed against our greatest mysteries. For these reasons, I am *so* glad that a project like this found its way to him first, rather than me.

This means that *UFO Symphonic* offers insights not only into UFOs, music, researchers, and experiencers, but also into Mike as well. It would have been easy to just present an endless string of interviews, but he manages to let his personal experiences shine through, a *cantus firmus* undergirding the themes and variations he plays for us along the way. Mike elegantly balances the words of his subjects with the context of music and the Phenomenon in his own life.

It is the age-old dance of composer and performer, the art of creation and the art of interpretation. They need each other to create a holistic picture, to bring the composition to life. To be featured in Mike's work myself, alongside so much depth and intimacy, is an honor.

Music, as Mike notes, can save lives. So can the Other. If I were speaking of the Other specifically, I might say it re-enchants life, but this is a misnomer. Life is already enchanted. Always has been, always will be.

There exists no greater proof of that statement than music itself. It's a perspective that Mike presents clearly and is perhaps the greatest strength of this book. *UFO Symphonic* reaffirms life, reminding us that we are embedded within a miraculous reality—whether the rapture that holds us originates from a rock concert or from a UFO.

But maybe that's splitting hairs. As Mike points out, even musicians can be UFOs. Forces that can enter our lives for but a moment, yet completely transcend time and space, changing our perspectives forever.

The ufological discussion has ebbed and flowed over the years, oscillating between pragmatic analyses of propulsion systems or antigravity technology and loftier examinations of humanity's role in the universe. Recent developments have firmly swung the pendulum back in the direction of the technological, the scientific.

UFO Symphonic offers a realignment of sorts, a complementary perspective essential to the "nuts-and-bolts" approach that Ufology fetishizes. Mike realizes that, while it's all fine and good to look *out there*—at the UFO itself—we have to realize it may not make complete sense unless we also turn our attention inward.

Put another way, you can buy the world's finest guitar, show up to the gig with fifty pedals, plug into the most expensive amps... but there's no guarantee that you'll make *music*. You have to put in the time to learn the instrument. You have to navigate things like harmonies, rhythms, and form. Above all, you have to be *human*.

In music, there's art alongside the *craft*. The same can be said of Ufology: there's a human *art* that, if absent, renders the structured *craft* of UFOs meaningless.

I will champion the need to discuss UFOs in the context of the arts and humanities until my last breath. It's good to know I'm not alone. *UFO Symphonic* is filled with others who feel the exact same way, including its author.

Thanks, Mike, for reminding us what it means to be human.

PRELUDE BY KEVIN CANN

This is really pretty funny. I recently met Mr. Mike Fiorito at a class I was teaching for a book I co-authored with Jeffrey K. Kripal. I liked him immediately. I bought his previous book, *For All We Know: A UFO Manifesto* and left it a nice Amazon review, as he deserved it. After the class was over, Mike contacted me, and mentioned that he was writing this book, and that it was going to be submitted for final approval in just two weeks. I quipped, "Hey! I'll write you a Prelude!" Little did I know for what I was volunteering. I was really just joking. It was a joke and a gesture of supporting a promising author.

I am one of the least musical people on Earth. I'm a high-functioning autistic with extreme sensory overload symptoms. I try my best to minimize both visual and auditory sensory inputs, as it always feels like the world (people and otherwise) is 'shouting at me'.

I tend to avoid music as much as possible, while some of it is beautiful (not much beautiful in the past 40 years mind you, per my taste at least), the problem with music for me, is that it disrupts the 'song within me'.

Now, as a non-musical person, it's not my first instinct to use music as a metaphor, but really, Mike's book has really opened my being to a new metaphor. I think that I already knew most of this stuff, but Mike is so eloquent, and he has found so many amazing, and extremely cogent musical references.

When we first started collaborating, I said to Mike, "Hey! Have you read *The Silmarillion*?" (Written by J.R.R Tolken and edited by Christoper Tolkien, published by William Morrow in

2012, and earlier editions.)

In this majestic story, the head divine guy Illuvatar, in concert with his many assistants the valar and maiar literally 'sing the universe or world at least into existence.' There is also trouble in paradise of course, what with the evil valar Morgoth, singing a negative and conflicting story to create dramatic conflict so that a story could be told!

Sound like a familiar story? Shades of Lucifer you know, even though of course in our world, Lucifer never existed but was a reference to King Nebuchadnezzar II and even earlier historical and semi-historical/mythological (or even full on mythological) figures. Really, who existed and who didn't is always hard to determine, and generally doesn't matter in the least. There are modern religions of course, that are more than ninety percent pure lies and confabulations, but still have billions of followers. What matters is that we tell each other good, no GREAT stories, and stop hating each other and fighting each other over nonsensical quibbles that at the end of the day matter exactly zero. Well, that's my take on it.

It turns out Mike hadn't read it. Seems like a missed opportunity to me, given that Mike LOVES music. I would imagine he'll get around to reading it, but I imagine his 'tbr' (to be read) stacks are pretty significant. Mike loves all forms of stories and arts, not just music.

Let's talk a bit about Mike and his book a bit more specifically.

Mike has done a very beautiful thing; he has found all these lovely musical references and stories, some 'mystical' and some rather ordinary (at least on the surface).

From the proposed anthropology of singing apes, and singing Neanderthals, and how singing may have contributed to the great leap forward of human intelligence and creativity, to the effects of music on neural plasticity (the brain is a living organ, constantly changing through use), I'm simply blown-away by what a great job Mike has done with his central thesis, and I'm summarizing, 'Music is at the core of everything; every harmony of interacting voices (informational data inputs to someone like me), the weaving together, and later perhaps unweavings (life and death you know), it's all very ambitious and enrapturing.'

I myself 'worship' if that's even an appropriate word, truth and beauty, and venerate all true storytellers, from viruses, to amoeba, to folks like Mike and all the other authors and musicians all the way up and past the physical universe, to what lays beyond it, in my observation. I call that something POTENTIALITY and its closely related aspect called "Awareness". Think of POTENTIALITY as the pan-universal field (beyond universes, space and time) of all potentials that could exist, and all the possibly interactions, and the premise is that all those potentials, both 'data bits' and how they interact, 'the data algorithms' all are occurring, right here, right now, simultaneously and forever.

If one becomes a citizen of all worlds, by realizing their true nature, from outside of space and time, then you come to realize that POTENTIALITY, as Mike might put it, is the 'primal song' and it's playing right here and now and everywhere else.

THIS is where Mike and I come together, where a sensory-avoidant autistic comes to realize, that a primal and eternal song, the very one he 'hears' in his own way, is the very essence of what Mike is writing about in this book.

In Platonic Surrealism, the philosophical framework that I write from, there are a transfinite number of 'pre-sung songs', that others call 'universes' but which I call "read-only data archives from the past," as from a timeless perspective (in the mystics' perspective) everything exists in the past, as it's all visible before the inner eye. Well, those parts that aren't pure bullshit confabulation, not a newly developing ability for humans, at least. Who knows how much is special, and how much is truly bull shit. I don't know either.

And THAT is the question of our age, where science is grinding to a semi-halt in many areas, due to (in my view) ignoring the potentials of autistics, special folks of other neural configurations, and artists whose primary language need not be verbal, but a product of the very special right brain hemisphere, which is the mediating part of the brain, in conjunction with the left brain hemisphere to bind it into words and art and even the 'third brain' the enteric nervous system of the 'gut' which contains twenty to thirty percent of the bodies total neurons, which generates or remembers our most special stories and songs.

Yes, gentle readers, humans have three different 'brains', all seeking to 'sing to each other', in harmony as much as possible, and our societies of this very irreverent age, where we are destroying our 'mother' the Earth, at the most rapid rate in human history, due to the greed for money and power. At this rate, we are soon to make mother childless, as the Earth may survive, but maybe humans may not, unless they turn themselves into cyborgs and head into space. Now there is a very interesting story to be told there, I have watched it, but that is for another book and another day.

To start wrapping this up, in a very real sense, 'our' Universe is a collaborative effort of many songs (beings/nodes and information transfer vectors; call it physics if you must, but that only captures part of it).

While no 'God' created the Universe, in a sense a massive collection of future beings ('us') did come together to form it. If you really must believe in a 'God' rather like a pacifier against fear, there most certainly is a 'Primary storyteller' of this Universe, and the billions of collaborators ('us')—everything is 'us'.

The thing about this actual Storyteller, not the human created 'gods', is that one of the primary functions of the Primary Storyteller is to hide Himself/Herself, to quiet down the infinite chaos of all possibilities executing all interactions at once, (in a multiverse of block universes, a nod to physics), to allow all the collaborators from before time and space ('us') to have a place to come together, to be co-creators, and to just have crazy fun. We owe the Primary Storyteller much; without Him/Her we would have no place to meet each other, His/Her co-equals, to become acquainted, and to learn how to value love, more than money and power.

THIS is what I see when I look at Mike's book. I hope that you enjoy it as much as I have.

"May your reality be as pleasant"; Star Trek the Cage, the original Star Trek pilot from 1965, first released in 1988. Or as Mike would say it, "May your song be as pleasant."

— Kevin Cann, named contributor for Chapter 3 of *How to Think Impossibly: About Souls, UFOs, Time, Belief, and Everything Else* by Jeffrey J. Kripal, University of Chicago Press [2024]

"I often think in music. I live my daydreams in music. I see my life in terms of music."

—Albert Einstein

"Everything in Life is Vibration."

—Albert Einstein

"There are things known and there are things unknown, and in between are the doors of perception."

—Aldous Huxley

A NOTE ON POLYPHONIC MUSIC

"The idea is distributed in space. It isn't only in one part; one part can't express the idea any longer, only the union of parts can completely express the idea. The idea found it necessary to be presented by several parts. After that, there was a rapid flowering of polyphony."

—Anton Webern

KYRIE

PREFACE

UFO Symphonic: Journeys into Sound is an invitation to explore the mystery of music. Music reinterprets history and presents it as a point in time. When listening to music, we hear a condensed chronicle of migrations, wars, inventions, personal and collective memories, etc., expressed in symbolic forms. These symbols contain information that is both conscious and unconscious. There is more information in the making and listening of music than we recall in everyday reality. Musician and novelist Amit Chaudhuri wrote that he *knew* that he had listened to *more* than he could consciously remember. Car horns, sea breezes, and songs by the Who, can be heard anew, or, as if, for the first time, in a given context. Inspired listening invites you to hear at a deeper level. These moments of "discovery" or "mishearing," as Chaudhuri referred to it, can offer profound insights. Listening provokes memories, correspondences, or revelations. In some cases, this is where music composition happens.[2] The Italian composer, Ennio Morricone said that he was inspired to write the main theme of the song "Se telefonando[3]" by the siren of a police car he had heard when visiting Marseilles[4].

More than math or language, music is a ready form of communication, which can be either understood on a simple level, or on a vastly more sophisticated one. Whether beating rhythmically on

---

[2] Chaudhuri, Amit. *Finding the Raga, An Improvisation on Indian Music.* New York: New York Review of Books, 2021
[3] Transl, "If, by calling on the telephone"
[4] https://en.wikipedia.org/wiki/Se_telefonando

a drum, or singing gospel hymns, we use music to commune with the unknown. To reach beyond. As Jaques Vallée wrote, "I believe that the UFO phenomenon is one of the ways through which an alien form of intelligence of incredible complexity is communicating with us symbolically.[5]" Like the UFO, music opens a portal. Through the navigation of its symbols, it is possible to bridge to another reality, another time and place. Sometimes into the realm of "high strangeness."[6]

In *Flying Saucers, A Modern Myth of Things Seen in the Sky*, Carl G. Jung stated that the Phenomenon is woven into the fabric of our psyche. It speaks to us in a primitive or symbolic language. And while I've long been interested in Jung's alchemical writings, I had never understood them until I delved deeper into ufology. Like the alchemical images Jung presents in his books, UFO experiences lead us into a labyrinth of questions. Those who have a UFO encounter or spirit visitation can't always sufficiently explain it to others, or even themselves, when they return to everyday reality. It is fleeting, like a dream. But it is also an initiation. *A passport to the cosmos.*

As Jung wrote, "Only by discovering alchemy have I clearly understood that the unconscious is a process and that ego's rapport with the unconscious and its contents initiate an evolution, more precisely, a real metamorphosis of the psyche."[7]

According to Jeff Kripal, the Phenomena speaks to us through "symbol and story and because that's the only way it *can* speak to us." Therefore, it "is always going to be relative, it's always going to be local. We can always reduce that symbol in story to something social or something historical but that doesn't mean that what's speaking to us is social and historical; it just means that's the only

---

5 Vallée, Jacques, *Dimensions: A Casebook of Alien Contact*. Anomalist Books, 2008
6 Introduced by the astronomer Dr. J. Allen Hynek in the 1970s. A quality of being peculiar, bizarre, or utterly absurd. Psychic element often associated with UFOs.
7 Jung, Carl. G. *Memories, Dreams, Reflections*. Vintage Books Edition, 1989

way it can."[8]

In his groundbreaking research, psychologist Dr. John Mack observed that people who report an abduction experience are often contacted in a symbolic form that they can't immediately understand. It could be in the form of an image, or in the script of an unfamiliar language.[9] Sometimes it is presented as unusual sounds, or as music.

This symbolic language surpasses our conscious understanding and interfaces with our collective unconscious. With the symbolism of dreams.

And while music touches the deepest parts of the psyche and can be universal, the context is often very specific. I've long appreciated the raga[10] as a musical form. However, I wasn't aware, until reading Chaudhuri's *Finding the Raga,* that ragas were written to be listened to at specific times of the day. Yet I could appreciate ragas in the way that I heard them.

In the same manner, the R&B songs that my sisters played when I was a kid have a powerful contextual specificity to me. They evoke a time, place and emotions relative to my experience.

My wife has only recently begun to appreciate my love of seventies Philadelphia R&B songs. At first, they sounded like bubblegum hits to her. Over time, however, she began to hear them anew after years of listening.

Music has that malleability. Songs are stories. We come to each song with our version of that story. And that story can change over time.

Former epidemiologist Leigh Ann, whom I met after writing the book *For All We Know: A UFO Manifesto,* described how her

---

8 https://youtu.be/4HIELWKbKSw?si=_ChdVKHEb_frzu7z
9 Mack, John E, M.D. *Passport to the Cosmos.* United Kingdom: White Crow Books, 1989
10 Melodies in Indian music are classified by an ancient system of ragas. A raga (pronounced RAH-guh) is a collection of pitches, kind of like a scale or mode in Western music. Each raga is defined, however, not only by the pitches themselves, but also by specific formulas for using them

back patio becomes a starship that takes her to other places and times in the universe. In these instances, she receives instructions from the "Others" to sing songs that provide healing to beings she doesn't know. Songs are also given to her that communicate information from the Others. Another experiencer, Mark Turner, told me how he encountered a UFO at a bluegrass show in Raleigh, North Carolina, which seemed to be connected to other numinous events. Sebastiano De Filipi, a conductor from Argentina, conveyed his story about how he enters the minds of deceased conductors to bring their works to life.

I'll leave the rest of the accounts to the chapters in which they are featured. They are as varied as the people who relayed them. They reflect the many voices of the Phenomenon.

Some of the stories were conveyed to me on web calls while others were written and sent. I wanted to give people a comfortable way to tell me their story. Some experiencers became very emotional and even cried during our conversations. In these moments, I felt enormous gratitude for their trust in me. In some cases, this was the first time they had publicly shared their stories. I thank everyone for their bravery and honesty in conveying their tales.

And while I talked to people from the United States, England, Italy, Australia, and Argentina, this book does not purport to represent the full spectrum of voices, cultures, genders, etc. *UFO Symphonic* is a snapshot as seen from my limited frame of reference. My hope is that others will continue this work, adding new voices and perspectives.

"No matter [if] you write it or play it, you still listen to it. Listening is the big thing in music."

—Duke Ellington

"Like the UFO, music is a transport system."

—Mike Fiorito

INTRODUCTION

In the grip of music, we are plunged into the deeper places of consciousness. We relive the past, conjure those we have lost, fantasize about a love, or imagine altogether different times and places. Music allows us to bypass the ego, opening us to a vastly larger world of experience.

Beyond the personal realm, music connects us to transpersonal experience, or what Jung called the collective unconscious.

Hearing national anthems, we experience being part of a unit. We might even feel a swell of emotion in our throats. Rhythms get us moving, sometimes tapping or dancing. They can lull us into a joyful feeling of togetherness or launch us into a collective frenzy. We become something bigger than ourselves.

It takes time to learn the languages that enable us to understand people from different countries; however, music is instantaneous. All people have the capacity to appreciate, and sometimes deeply understand, music from any culture and time. Music connects. It is a universal language. There is also music beyond the human realm: insects, birds, imploding stars, pulsars, and oceans. The wind.

Research suggests that music has its origins in our primate ancestry. Researcher Eva Maria Luef of the Max Planck Institute for Ornithology sought to create the first scientific and detailed analysis of food-associated calling among gorillas. She observed that "Music might have served many functions for early humans. Music could have been used for courtship, territorial claims, and uniting social groups, much as calls and songs are used by whales, birds, and apes. Music might have helped soothe infants or unify groups before a hunt, battles, or ceremony. A biological capacity for music evolved early in our species. Gorillas: they hum and even sing during mealtime." In her research, "Luef and her team identified two different types of sound that gorillas in the Congo made when eating. One of them was humming—a consistent low-frequency tone akin to the 'mmm' that humans make. The other was singing—random mismatched notes, like someone singing an improvised ditty. 'They don't sing the same song over and over,' said Luef. 'It seems like they are composing their little food songs.'" Luef added that gorillas sing loudest while eating their favorite foods.[11]

British archeologist Steven Mithen coined the term "singing Neanderthals," suggesting that Neanderthals evolved vocal and singing abilities enabling them, among other things, to meet the challenges of the Ice Age.

In the book *Human Evolution*, Robin Dunbar argues that the anatomy involved in singing is related to the anatomy that facilitates laughter. Dunbar adds, "Wordless singing (or humming) also shares with both laughter and speech a number of properties, including segmentation, articulation, phrasing and synchrony."[12] If the anatomy of laughter is related to singing, would singing also be related to crying, moaning, and the groaning sounds of joy? Perhaps music is bound up with our deepest emotions, connecting to prelingual layers of human consciousness. As such, it speaks to our most primal urges and emotions.

Dunbar found that geladas, among the most vocal of all primates, utilize a repertoire of loud and complex vocal sounds. While grooming one another, they employ finely timed calls and replies in the way that humans use speech. These call-and-reply duets are also used to communicate to other members of the group the business of the day—feeding or traveling, for instance. Not only are these calls and replies functional, but they also demonstrate sing-

---

11 One Earth (Oneearth.org)
12 Dunbar, Robin. *Human Evolution*. New York: Penguin Group, 2014

song qualities and the complex use of lips, tongue, and mouth cavity among nonhuman primates. Moreover, imagine how the brain and the mouth cavity conspired to evolve these capabilities.

Dunbar also showed that, while using vocalization during grooming, geladas register an endorphin surge. Creating and hearing music, as with us, make geladas feel good, and this good feeling enhances their social bonding, again, as it does in humans.

As if this isn't mind blowing enough, neurophysiologists Karel F. and Heda Jindrak hypothesized that vocalization catalyzes cleaning of the cerebrospinal fluid in the skull. Early humans might have sung the detritus out of their skulls, removing chemical waste, thereby making the skull work more efficiently.[13]

Perhaps early humans began using a simple form of singing: call and response within a group. At some point, maybe this was accompanied by drumming and even dancing. All of this, as Karel F. and Heda Jindrak have suggested, allowed for further evolution of the brain. In the alchemical process of transformation, the creation of music became an artifact of culture. Perhaps, in time, there were particular kinds of music in different sub-groups. Subgenres specific to different regions may have developed. These styles and techniques then passed from generation to generation. Perhaps first used to support the business of living, music evolved into something early humans just did. A combination of fun and necessity, like sex and eating.

According to Sufi master Hazrat Inayat Khan, music harmonizes the mind and body. Making or listening to music, Khan asserts, soothes and calms the body. The result is that music makes us more balanced, and hence more functional. More likable. "This is why in ancient times the greatest prophets were great musicians. For instance, in the lives of the Hindu prophets one finds Narada,

---

13 Karel F. and Heda Jindrak. *Sing, Clean Your Brain and Stay Sound and Sane: Postulate of Mechanical Effect of Vocalization on the Brain*. City: K F Jindrak, 1986

the great prophet who was at the same time a great musician, and Shiva, a godlike prophet who was the inventor of the sacred Vina. Krishna is always pictured with a flute."[14]

Khan adds that in addition to the "natural charm that music has, it also has magical power." He claims that while we became out of touch with the magic of science, the magic of music is still prevalent. I think it's fair to say that humans around the globe either listen to music or play music in some form. Music is a socially acceptable way to explore the Phenomenon.

Khan continues, "The deeper we penetrate the mystery of sound, the more we are able to trace the link that connects all sounds. This link is what the musicians call harmony, and it is in harmony that hides the secret of joy and peace."[15] Or as Wynton Marsalis said, "Music is the art of the invisible. When you get so deep inside of a human being the superficial differences are not there."

In her book *Encounters*, Diana Pasulka discusses the pioneering work of space psychologist Dr. Iya Whiteley, who designed spaceship interiors for astronauts. Additionally, Whiteley is working on research to train infants to "hear" the sounds of Earth: animals, insects, etc. She asks the question, "How can we expect animals to learn our language, when we don't endeavor to learn theirs?" I have often listened to the twittering of birds and felt that it might just be physics put to patterns and melodies. But, in general, we do not stop to listen, or better, to understand. Some cultures have long listened to the language of nature, but in modern Western Civilization, some think that animals, trees, birds, and oceans have nothing to say.

Consider the importance of music in film. Music evokes all emotions—fear, joy, surprise, sadness—and elevates the visuals

---

14 Khan, Inayat Hazrat. *The Mysticism of Sound and Music*. Boulder: Shambhala Publications, Inc., 2022
15 *The Mysticism of Sound and Music*, Page 29

INTRODUCTION

immensely. It is no wonder that in *2001: A Space Odyssey*, the discovery that a bone can be used as a tool is accompanied by Richard Strauss's *Thus Sprach Zarathustra*. The ape's revelation seems to be expressed through the rising crescendo of the music. In an essay entitled "Alsop Sprach Zarathustra," conductor Marin Alsop wrote that *Thus Sprach Zarathustra* is "a 'song' in the key of everything, employing a musical form—the fanfare—that has been traced back to the 14th century, when it was used to signal the start of a hunt."

Interestingly, in the movie *Close Encounters of the Third Kind*, the aliens communicate through musical tones. The character Lacombe, who is based on the ufologist Jacques Vallée, uses Curwen hand signs that correspond to the five-note extraterrestrial tonal phrase. The extraterrestrial replies with the same gestures, then returns to its ship, which disappears into the sky in a flash.

Perhaps buried in the matrix of those notes are millennia of scientific knowledge. A simple melody could be a way to express a staggeringly complex physics formula or theory. A code. According to Stephan V. Beyer in his book *Signing to the Plants*, "Users of DMT [N, N-Dimethyltryptamine] report hearing 'alien music' and 'alien language.'" American ethnobotanist Terrence McKenna reported that he heard *a language of alien meaning that conveyed alien information* while on an ayahuasca trip. Meaning that evaded rendering. Like a dream.

In his highly imaginative book *Alien Information Theory*, Andrew Gallimore writes, "Communication between humans and distant alien species doesn't depend upon interstellar travel, but only on the transmission of code. And, as we direct our pulses of electromagnetic radiation into the glistening night sky, we hope that one day, perhaps millennia in the future, the messages encoded in these pulses will reach the brain of an alien intelligence."[16]

Perhaps the transmission of code is embedded in music. Could

---

16 *Alien Information Theory, Psychedelic Drug Technologies and the Cosmic Game,* Andrew Gallimore

the complex vibrations of sound be carriers of some extraterrestrial messages?

As a parent, I remember singing to my sons before I could speak to them. I sang lullabies, rhymes, and songs, sometimes performing them on the guitar and singing. Similarly, as already stated, some primates sing when grooming, or to signal that it's time for the troop to eat. Perhaps the ability to sing expresses a sense of the "Other" in both primate and human consciousness. Music connects us to others, and to a deeper sense of ourselves. Chasing down the origins of the singing mind may confront us with an, as yet, unknown aspect of consciousness. When we sing, we are not alone. When we hear music, we connect across time and space. You can lose your mind when singing and, in doing so, find yourself. It is this aspect of music that brings it into the realm of the Phenomena.

The Phenomena engages us to grasp at the Other. Our pathway to the Other can include mystical visions, UFO sightings, telepathy, precognition, bilocation, and time travel. It can also involve synchronicity, cryptozoology, psychedelic experiences, dreams, near-death experiences, visits from nonhuman intelligences, and more. The Phenomena are rarely amenable to human logic. Perhaps because elements of the Phenomena are beyond the range of current human comprehension. As philosopher Dr. James Madden wrote in his book *Unidentified Flying Hyperobjects,* "The UFO stretches us to—and maybe even beyond—the limits of what humans can understand. Thus, as we approach the Phenomenon, we should mistrust ourselves simultaneously as we try to make sense of it."

I think it is important to add thoughts from Robert Salas, retired US Air Force captain, here. "The Phenomena is not a simple mystery that can be solved once you have some key evidence. It is not a separate and distinct puzzle. This involves a complex series of puzzles that we have to confront since we looked up at the night sky and wondered. We are both cause and effect for this mystery.

Introduction

What we perceive as something that has evolved from our sightings of unidentified flying objects, something from 'out there' is really about us and our relationship with the 'out there.'"

Music is likewise a hyperobject. We don't really understand it. Moreover, the definition of music goes beyond singing or playing instruments. Underlying what we call music are vibrations, sounds that emanate from atoms, planets, pulsars, crystals, stones, even stalks of corn. These vibrations have the ability to change or focus human consciousness, to bring us to the Phenomena. According to Khan, "Someday music will be the means of expressing a universal religion."[17]

In his book *The World Is Sound,* jazz writer and philosopher Joachim-Ernst Berendt borrowed the term *Nada Brahma,* a Sanskrit expression (with roots in Indian Vedic spirituality), which he translated as *the world is sound.* "Nowadays we know that the ocean, especially in the deep sea, is filled with sound. There is whistling and grunting, rattling and snoring and ringing, sawing and creaking and electronic noises, snapping and snipping and crackling, the beating of bass drums and tom-toms and tambourines, screaming and howling, groaning and moaning,"[18] he writes.

Why is nature so noisy?

Berendt suggests that "Just like the dancing mosquitoes, trumpeting elephants, and singing birds... including of course the concerts put on by human beings... None of these phenomena is necessary for the perpetuation of the species, but they create a framework in which procreation can be differentiated—becoming richer, easier, more joyous and livelier."[19]

In other words, the buzzing, chopping, thundering, and whooshing of nature is built into its very fabric. The entire universe is alive with sound. And humans have long attempted to recreate

---

17 *The Mysticism of Sound and Music,* Page 10
18 *The World Is Sound,* Page 76
19 *On Listening to the World,* Joachim-Ernst Berendt, Page 199

the sounds of nature in music. The field of study dedicated to this topic is called zoomusicology.

There are numerous examples of music imitating nature. Ralph Vaughan Williams's "The Lark Ascending," Jean Sibelius's "The Swan of Tuonela," and Antonio Vivaldi's "The Four Seasons" immediately come to mind.

There is also a list of instruments with the ability to mimic the sounds of nature: the recorder imitating the sound of the cuckoo, flutes imitating birdsong, and the double bass, which sounds like a raging thunderstorm. Or the rain stick, which imitates the sound of falling rain. Or the xequerê (shekere), which originated in Africa and arrived in Brazil through the slave trade, made from a variety of gourds such as the calabash, wrapped in a mesh of seeds, shells, or beads. When shaken or struck on the hand the xequerê provides a rhythm reminiscent of fluttering wind or crickets scraping their limbs together.

As Fritjof Capra noted in the foreword to *The World Is Sound*, "The nature of reality is much closer to music than it is to a machine."[20]

The chapters that follow convey the incredible web of synchronicities and relationships that have developed from my writing projects. These relationships are examples of the magic of music. How music projects our sense of self across the world. How my father's obsession, for example, with Neapolitan music is like a message sent to me from the beyond as an inspiration to write a series of articles, short stories, and books. How interviewing and meeting bluegrass legend Peter Rowan initiated a rocket launch of writing, including this book you're reading now. What's especially thrilling is how this project combines various subjects I've written about—Neapolitan music, bluegrass, psychedelics, science fiction, ufology—and brings them together in a single narrative. If that's

---

20 Berendt, Joachim-Ernst. *The World Is Sound, Nada Brahma*. Rochester: Inner Traditions, 1983

not magic, I don't know what is.

Introduction

"One day your life is a stone in you, and the next, a star."
—Rainer Maria Rilke

"Music is probably the only real magic I have encountered in my life. There's not some trick involved with it. It's pure and it's real. It moves, it heals, it communicates and does all these incredible things."
—Tom Petty

"Visionaries open doorways. And those doorways are not just open for themselves. The doorways are open for everyone."
—Herbie Hancock in "Wayne Shorter: Zero Gravity"

"The most important thing I look for in a musician is whether he knows how to listen."
—Duke Ellington

OVERTURE

Perhaps you are in a conversation. First there is talking, using words. Maybe you want to be more dramatic, transitioning to poetry, or rhyme, elevating the words. When we have moved to singing, then using rhythm, something new happens.

Music doesn't take a month to read or translate. It is instant telepathy. Like it or not, when Taylor Swift is singing on television, half the world is singing with her, connecting, being in each other's head, sharing a multidimensional hallucination that is also real.

Music provides a way for us to visit ourselves at different times in our lives. It also provides a means for us to connect with other people, those we know and those we don't. Music can be the sound of me singing in my head, or the sound of an entire stadium shouting "We Will Rock You." Through song I can be drawn into the mind of its composer. Songs create new worlds. Revolutions are launched with melodies. Coronations, births, and deaths are accompanied by music. It travels with us from the beginning to the very end.

And yet, a song can be sung silently in a cosmos of countless minds. Many minds, many voices, like a million saints in heaven. Who knows how often that happens?

Music is the first thing our baby minds perceive, making us coo and smile. Some say chants guide us across to the other realm when we have shuffled off this mortal coil.

Like a spore, music transcends the ground we stand on. The music we have made and the music we have heard lives beyond our death. It becomes the possession of others. Which is fine because it was never fully ours. It lives on in the minds and in the thoughts of those who have left this Earth. It gathers and floats. Rolls and tumbles. Seeps and crackles.

Music is the groan of earthquakes, the symphony of birds, and the sweet patter of the rain.

ALIEN GNOSIS

I first heard Terence McKenna's term "heroic dosage" in 1984 when I was eighteen years old. I had learned it from friends who had drunk the Kool-Aid, as they say. Ivan was about seven years older. He'd taken acid, according to his own count, hundreds of times. John, also about seven years older, had taken acid innumerable times. Both were crazy, to be honest.

At eighteen, about to start college, Ivan handed me six hits of green blotter acid, which I readily consumed. Six hits. That dosage blew my skull wide open. I described the trip in my story "Tom Turkey's Tie Dye." It was profound and frightening. However, I'm glad I did it. If I had known what I was getting into, I wouldn't have done it. My first acid trip produced in me what Dr. John Mack called an ontological shock: I crossed the threshold into a different reality.

The next time I tripped, exercising (slightly) better judgment, I took three hits of blotter acid—still considered a "heroic dosage" by some. Even considered an insane dosage by others.

One thing I distinctly remember from this second trip was listening to the Allman Brothers song "Blue Sky," letting the notes take me on a journey down a river of pure consciousness and watching Ivan's room become a cartoonish reality. As Ivan lit up his pipe to smoke weed, he transformed into a cosmic Popeye. While this was all bizarre, it was definitely more manageable than what transpired with the six-hit dosage.

When I initially met Ivan, he was a jerk with an attitude. When my friend Lan and I saw him on the street in the neighborhood, we thought he was just trying to scam us for weed or money. Over time, he grew on me.

Despite Ivan's orneriness, he was an avid reader and interested in learning. Together we read works by Aleister Crowley, McKenna, Starhawk, and other writers of esoterica. Our mutual interest in books and learning developed into a friendship. A friendship that would sadly come to an end many years later. But that's a story for another time.

Fast forward to roughly 1991. I was twenty-five years old, living in Oakland, California. I had gone there to visit my friend Felicia and then decided to stay. The Bay Area drew me in, first because it was beautiful— the skies were bluer, the trees were bigger, more stunning. Along with the ocean brine, was the cloying scent of jasmine and eucalyptus. And I was fascinated by the interesting lives that people were living "out there" on the westernmost edge of the country. Where you'd eventually fall into the Pacific if you kept going. I met young people dressed like woodland fairies, playing music in jamming circles, singing and holding hands. I was invited to saunas where hippies hung out naked together, not to have sex, but to be naked together in public.

Driving down the coast north of the Golden Gate Bridge, breathing in the lush mountains and vistas of the oceans was intoxicating. There was an openness in the Bay Area that didn't quite exist in New York City. In the late '80s and early '90s, New York City was too fashion conscious, too old-school intellectual and even conservative. There was Greenwich Village downtown, where I went to New York University, which had a similar vibe to the Bay Area, but was still grittier. In New York City, if people didn't want to listen to your shit, they just shut you up. They didn't have time for accounts of UFO abductions.

The point is, while the Bay Area was concentrated with progressive hippie types, New York City in this period was a melting pot of conflicting ideas, with room for tough guys, ethnic neighborhoods, street fights, gangs, and the Mafia.

In the Bay Area I had only one friend, Felicia, the aforementioned ex-girlfriend, if I can even call her that. We were more like friends. When I arrived, Felicia had a boyfriend and a full life. She was an environmental scientist, doing field work, testing contaminated soil.

During my first few months there, I saw a sign in a bookstore announcing that Terence McKenna's book *Archaic Revival* had been published and that he was coming to Oakland to do a reading. Although I had stopped smoking pot or doing any other kind of drug, I remained deeply interested in the philosophy of psychedelics.

During the reading, McKenna was hilarious—not only a brilliant writer and original thinker but decidedly funny. McKenna's idea that psychedelic mushrooms triggered the development of consciousness in primates was not an easy pill to swallow as he was well aware. McKenna sometimes described himself as loony and crazy. This self-deprecation gave him a great deal of latitude to express his fringe ideas. And while a self-professed nutjob, he was a serious researcher and intellectual. And no one to date, I believe, has disproved his idea of primate evolution.

Recall that I didn't discover McKenna in Greenwich Village, or at New York University, or in the Bay Area. No, my route to finding him started in New York City, in Queens. On the streets, as we used to say.

Serendipitously, while researching another chapter in this book, I came across a footnote in *Singing to the Plants* by Stephen Beyer. In this footnote, Beyer refers to McKenna's connecting the UFO Phenomenon to music and singing. Of course, I had read *True Hallucinations*, *Archaic Revival*, and *Food of the Gods* years ago, but I had forgotten the link between music and the Phenomena. It was buried in my subconscious, waiting for me to remember.

The footnote said, "Users of DMT report hearing 'alien music' and 'alien languages' which may or may not be comprehensible. Terrence McKenna speaks of hearing 'a language of alien meaning that is conveying alien information.'"[21]

Although these ideas are scattered throughout his oeuvre, in his book *True Hallucinations* McKenna recounts the exotic expedition that he made. He, along with his brother, Dennis, and other companions ventured to Amazonian Colombia to find and consume ayahuasca and other hallucinogens. He tells of flying saucer visions and encounters with mythical beings. While his tale is off the wall and often hysterical, it is profoundly interesting and comports with other accounts in shamanic literature, of which McKenna was a scholar.

Like John Lilly, Robert Monroe, and others before him, not to mention the thousands of indigenous shamans throughout history, McKenna embarked on a research project in which he was the main subject. The specimen. While reading the book, I was curious to know who financed the plane rides, the hotels, and the cash needed to secure the help of the local Colombians. Did he have a trust fund? That aside, McKenna's courage and tenacity of spirit cannot be underestimated.

True Hallucinations details the search for the aboriginal DMT, of which McKenna and his crew were in pursuit. Referred to as *Oo-Koo-Hi* by the native shamans, it was known to be severely restricted in usage and difficult to obtain. The Witoto tribe of the Upper Amazon, it was said, used *Oo-Koo-Hi* to obtain knowledge and to talk to "little men." The description of this DMT reminded McKenna of the DMT he had taken in Berkeley which had him "bursting into a space inhabited by merry elfins, self-transforming, machine creatures."[22] McKenna goes on to say that their language was "transmuted from a thing heard to a thing seen."

---

21 Beyer, Stephen. *Singing to the Plants*. Albuquerque: University of New Mexico Press, 2009
22 McKenna, Terence. *True Hallucinations*. New York: Harper Collins, 1993

While in the Amazonian jungle, the exploits of McKenna and the crew were nothing short of incredible. Taking various hallucinogens, including *Amanita Muscaria*, and smoking marijuana, the travelers experienced the jungle as a rich field of imaginary play. In the account there is an element of the white conqueror taming the jungle, but I forgive McKenna to a degree because we learned so much as a result of his earnestness and brilliance. It can be argued that we owe a great debt to him. He was a visionary.

McKenna reported that, while consuming mushrooms, Dennis heard a sound, distant and faint, but audible. "A sound almost like a signal, or a very, very faint transmission of radio, buzzing from somewhere, something like tingling chimes at first, but gradually becoming amplified into a snapping, popping, gurgling, crackling electrical sound."[23]

Dennis tried to replicate the sound with his mouth, saying that it recalled a giant insect. While this sounds funny in everyday consensus-reality talk, someone buzzing like an insect, while you're in a psychedelic state, might not actually be a laughing matter.

Afterwards, Dennis and Terence shared rapid-fire theories on what the sound was and how they could use it to manipulate spacetime. Dennis recounted something Michael Harner, an anthropologist, had written about in *Natural History*. Harner had implied that *ayahuasqueros* whom he was studying with Ecuador had vomited a magical substance that enabled them to transmute spacetime.

Harner wrote that when the Jívaro shamans consumed ayahuasca, they vomited a deep blue bubbly liquid which they then spread on the ground. Like scryers, the shamans could see other times and places in the puddled liquid, which they said was made of "space/time or mind."

Apparently, Harner wasn't the only one to report this finding. There have long been rumors and unconfirmed reports of "magi-

---

[23] McKenna, Terence. *True Hallucinations*. New York: Harper Collins, 1993

cally empowered psychophysical objects generated out of the human body using hallucinogens and song."[24] According to alchemical observation, the secret hides in the feces.

After some experimentation, Dennis thought that by using sound, he could create this liquid on demand. And because it was made of the imagination, it had infinite applications. By making this sound, he surmised, he could make worlds, traverse other dimensions, travel time. In other words, he could implement the galactic engineering capabilities of an Advanced Level III Civilization.[25]

Interestingly, in a recent interview on the *Third Eye Drops* podcast, Neuroscientist and N, N-Dimethyltryptamine (DMT) researcher, Dr. Andrew Gallimore stated that an alternative version of the Kardashev model was proposed by astronomer Dr. John Barrow about ten years ago. Named "micro-dimensional mastering," Barrow theorized that advanced civilizations retreat into smaller and smaller scales, where they can manipulate spacetime. To the point where they are invisible. And can be both everywhere and nowhere simultaneously.[26] In fact, Gallimore suggests that Amazonian (and other) mystics have understood communicating with beings in these realms long before scientists in the West have even considered the possibility.

Having once again eaten mushrooms and smoked grass, Dennis was able to make the sound. He was certain, he wrote in his journal, that he could now produce the sound without the use of hallucinogens.

While Terence and Dennis launched into exuberant and insane conversations, the others watched them skeptically. Surely, the

---

24 McKenna, Terence. *True Hallucinations.* New York: Harper Collins, 1993
25 A Type III civilization is a civilization that can harness and utilize the energy of an entire galaxy, typically through the use of a Dyson Swarm, a hypothetical mega structure that would encompass all the stars in a galaxy and capture their energy. This notion is referred to as the Kardashev Model.
26 https://www.youtube.com/watch?v=pgFuV_ej-dU&t=2118s

brothers had lost their minds out there in the thick of the jungle, recalling the madness of Mr. Kurtz from Conrad's *Heart of Darkness*. Terence observed that, "There seems to be a parallel mental dimension in which everything is made of the stuff of visible language, a kind of universe next door inhabited by elves that sing themselves into existence and invite those who encounter them to do the same."[27]

Terence later realized that the psychedelics, weed smoking, and isolation in the jungle may have affected his observations and theories. Dennis recounted Terence's behavior and his response to it in his book *Brotherhood of the Screaming Abyss: My Life with Terence McKenna,* saying that Terence loaded him up with psychedelics and pummeled him with big brother exuberance. Anyone who has an older brother would recognize this situation. I spent many an hour pinned to the floor, while my older brother, a college champion wrestler, lorded it over me, sometimes threatening with a string of spit that he would dangle from his to my face before sucking it back up into his mouth. Disgusting. Dennis also adds that Terence, like my older brother, Frank, was a powerful influence on him. Minus the spit. Perhaps.

Despite the craziness of the McKenna brothers' experiences and experiments, there is much to be valued. Professor Jeff Kripal referred me to his book, *Esalen: America and the Religion of No Religion,* for more on what he called their "alien gnosis."

Kripal writes that Terence and Dennis encountered an "invisible landscape" or "world of gnosis." In their psychedelic-induced trance states, they came into contact with an alien Other who communicated to them in "elaborate conversations in an effort to reveal an entire hyperdimensional reality that overlaps with or suffuses our own. In religious language, they were receiving a revelation."[28]

I can attest, along with countless others, to this notion of re-

---

27 McKenna, Terence. *True Hallucinations.* New York: Harper Collins, 1993
28 Kripal, Jeffery, *Esalen.* Chicago: The University of Chicago Press, 2007

ceiving a revelation during a psychedelic experience. When we have a psychedelic experience, we are not hallucinating. We are seeing something that is buried in the matrix of consciousness. Whose consciousness? That I'm not certain. I know that I have encountered a world of intelligence which was organic and earthly, yet intergalactic. A cosmos that was beyond anything my Queens, New York City teenage mind could have conjured. I am reminded of the concept of Mind at Large proposed by Aldous Huxley.[29] Huxley maintained that the human mind filters reality so that we can go about our everyday lives, obtaining food, safety and procreating. According to Huxley, psychedelic substances remove the filter, exposing ordinary consciousness to the Mind at Large. In this state, we encounter "high strangeness" events and have extraordinary visions. I have spent the last forty years integrating these "high-strangeness" experiences into my comprehension, or lack of comprehension, of life, of existence.

Kripal writes that, in a 1983 address at Esalen, McKenna stated that the human soul is so disconnected in our present culture that we see the soul as an extraterrestrial. McKenna added that, "The UFO, in other words, is the human soul exteriorized into three-dimensional space as a religious experience. We will only overcome our own alienation when we realize that we ourselves are the alien, and that there is nothing more marvelous and bizarre in the entire cosmos than what is going on in our upper cortex, right now, right here, quite beyond the three extended dimensions of space and the fourth of time, that of mere ordinary history."[30]

Are these theories the deluded machinations of deranged minds, addled by psychedelic substances? If that's the case, why are institutes like John Hopkins, New York University, UC Berkeley, and other psychedelic research centers asking for volunteers

---

29 Huxley, Aldous, *The Doors of Perception & Heaven and Hell.* New York City: Harper Perennial, 1956
30 Kripal, Jeffery, *Esalen.* Chicago: The University of Chicago Press, 2007

who've had extraterrestrial experiences to participate in research studies? I've participated in those studies as a volunteer subject.

In my naivete and ignorance, in taking psychedelics, I stumbled upon something, it seems, that the world is now very interested in. I was just looking for an experience. I didn't realize I was going to plunge into the depths of existence itself, into the shockwave of eschatology. Into the Phenomena.

I leave you with this quote from McKenna's book *Archaic Revival*:

"History is the shockwave of eschatology. In other words, we are living in a very unique moment, ten or twenty thousand years long, where an immense transition is happening. The object at the end of and beyond history is the human species fused into eternal tantric union with the superconducting Overmind/UFO. It is that mystery that casts its shadow back through time. All religion, all philosophy, all wars, pogroms, and persecutions happen because people do not get the message right. There is both the forward-flowing casuistry of being, causal determinism, and the interference pattern that is formed against that by the backward-flowing fact of this eschatological hyperobject throwing its shadow across the temporal landscape."[31]

---

31 McKenna, Terence. *The Archaic Revival: Speculations on Psychedelic Mushrooms, the Amazon, Virtual Reality, UFOs, Evolution, Shamanism, the Rebirth of the Goddess, and the End of History*. New York: Harper Collins, 1993

BEINGS OF THE BUSH

Although I call myself a guitar player, I've always been drumming in one way or another. Once, as a kid in Catholic School, I was called out for banging out a drum rhythm on the school desk with my hands. While I was off in a fantasy, tapping out a beat, Brother McGrath, my ninth-grade math teacher, stopped talking during class, and asked, "Are you finished?" I caught on a few embarrassing moments later. "OK, we can go on," he said, after getting my attention.

There has always been a beat in my head. My best friend, Lan, has the same affliction, except that he is an actual drummer. We've been playing together since we were twelve, when we entered a talent contest, performing Elvis's "Blue Suede Shoes." I sang and he played drums—just the two of us, no guitar or piano. For the record, we came in second place, falling behind two girls disco dancing.

Whether it's vocal beatboxing, or body percussion with my hands and feet, there's a steady tap-tap and ticking in the deepest layers of my mind that finds its way out.

Aside from classical music, most modern music, particularly American music, is very drum beat oriented. This includes disco (four to the floor), bluegrass & rock-n-roll (backbeat, on the two and the four), and funk, specifically James Brown (on the one).

The Ravenswood Projects, where I grew up, were next to the Queensbridge Projects, one of the epicenters of rap music. Nas's 1994 *Illmatic*, considered by some to be the greatest hip-hop album of all time, describes, in a brutally honest language, his experiences in Queensbridge. Other notable artists associated with the Queensbridge hip-hop scene include Cormega, Tragedy Khadafi, Nature, Screwball, Capone, and Big Noyd.

I didn't listen to rap when I was younger; it wasn't geared toward me. Some white kids in the projects at that time felt that rap music, like a weapon, was pointed directly at them. This is a complex issue. Now I hear rap music in a totally different way. In songs like "Fight The Power," I hear the urgent demand for justice. For equality. I hear the disgust of four hundred years of racial tyranny.

Rap is a music of revolution. Of oppression.

On the streets, I heard kids doing complex beats, cupping their hands over their faces, finding creative ways to change pitch and tone.

One time in the '80s, standing in the Queensbridge station, I remember watching a group of teenagers compete to see who could improvise a rap of the longest duration. They each took turns, some were able to conjure rhymes longer. Some were more gifted in devising unique beats. There was one kid who towered above them all, cleverly rhyming "conniption" with "Egyptian," coughing into his closed fist, making a dramatic pause, then firing off creative beatbox sounds.

I heard Latin music growing up as well. The basic rhythmic pattern in Latin music is called the clave [CLAH-ve] rhythm. The two main varieties of the clave rhythm are son clave and rumba clave. There are many varieties of Latin rhythm and dance, including salsa, rumba, and cha-cha-cha.

The clave pattern originated in sub-Saharan African music traditions, where it served essentially the same function as it does in Cuban music. The influence of the clave and Latin rhythms has become infused in American music.

While jazz rhythms swing, most Latin jazz tunes have a straight eighth-note feel. Latin jazz rarely employs a backbeat, using a form of the clave instead. Most jazz rhythms emphasize beats two and four. Latin jazz tunes rely more on various clave rhythms, depending on regional style.

In many cultures, drumming is key to religious practices and daily ceremonies. In the Manianka villages of Mali, musicians, particularly drummers, are seen as healers. The word for musician is related to the word for healer. Whereas in the West, musicians are often seen as entertainers, in Manianka the healing power of music is well recognized.

"In Minianka," write the co-authors, Yaya Diallo and Mitchell Hall, in *The Healing Drum*, "the musicians are expected to live by high standards of morality and self-restraint. Music is powerful. By their example, the musicians will influence the youth for better or worse... The fundamental principle of Minianka musical training is devotion to music in the service of the cosmos, the environment, and the community."[32]

Diallo and Hall describe the relationship between teacher and student, emphasizing that it is not taken lightly. The student does chores for their teacher: cleaning their house, gathering firewood and tending to their chickens. The teacher is expected to impart moral training to the student. The musician is learning more than just their instrument, they are also undergoing a moral education.

Yaya Diallo tells a story of a student who approached an older musician to receive training. The teacher invited the young student to stay and work with his family. He made the student labor in the fields every day. The teacher never once talked about music or showed the student anything on the drum.

After three years the teacher said, "Why did you come to my house?"

The student replied, "To learn how to play the drums."

"So, go play the drums," said the teacher.

The student played the drums exceptionally. The teacher said,

---

[32] Diallo, Yaya and Hall, Mitchell, *The Healing Drum: African Wisdom*. Destiny Books, 1989

"You hear that? You don't need me to teach you."

While this tale is humorous, the point is understood. Music is not only about notes and beats. It is, in Minianka, as much about the services the musician offers their community.

Diallo writes that, in Africa, traditional dances are related to work chores. Even when people dance at festivals or celebrations, their movements mimic the gestures of work.

"When women wash clothes on the riverbank, they make music slapping the clothes against the calabashes. To pound grain into the daily cereal, four women stand around a large mortar carved out of a portion of a tree trunk. Their pestles rise and fall like pistons. If one woman loses the beat, it will break the rhythm of the others."[33]

Villagers swap services with musicians so that they accompany them during their daily labors. It is believed that the productivity of the group is influenced by the sensitivity of these musicians.

Each job has a different rhythm. A sensitive and gifted musician knows how to use the appropriate music for the right chore or activity.

Therefore, the musician bears a lot of responsibility. The music must express feelings or even supernatural forces. According to Diallo, when musicians play, they harmonize the visible world with the invisible world, to pacify spirits that can be lurking but not seen.

The presence of spirits is often signaled by trance. During trance, the spirits possess the bodies of villagers.

"Trance phenomena among the Minianka are complex and not well understood. They are not amusements. Humans in trance are subjected to forces beyond their control. I saw a man jump into a well and leap back out as if propelled by springs. He was not just playing around with an abundance of energy—something beyond

---

[33] Diallo, Yaya and Hall, Mitchell, *The Healing Drum: African Wisdom*. Destiny Books, 1989

him was playing with his body."[34]

Diallo describes people known as *djinambori* who possess spirits and can perform extraordinary things, for good or bad. *Djinambori* claim that, using music, they can make lions, snakes and elephants appear in the wink of an eye, like the Arabic or Islamic Jinn.

Extraordinary things happen regularly in the villages of Minianka. Diallo writes that strange lights appear around the village, which no one can explain. "Points of light float in the air, suddenly becoming very strong, shining on people's bodies, and going from tree to tree. Just as suddenly, they disappear, then reappear, and disappear again. The entire village is surrounded by these mobile, floating balls of light, appearing unpredictably. All who have encountered them report that the lights become increasingly bright and give off heat."[35]

In Minianka, spirits are also known as beings of the bush. According to the villagers, there was a time when there was no distinction between the humans and the beings of the bush, though they each kept their distance. They even spoke the same language. According to folklore, after a conflict between the humans and beings of the bush, the Creator decided to keep them in separate realms. Since that time, when beings of the bush encounter human weakness, they tease and haunt that person.

The musician-healers of Minianka are charged with creating harmony with the village spirits, who are attracted to the dancing and music.

Diallo tells of a friend who played the talking drum and could "foretell the time of death of fellow villagers. Even though he spoke of what was true, most people preferred not to know. Once I was there with him when he fell asleep for about three minutes. During the sleep, he said, he saw some images like a little nightmare. When

---

34 Diallo, Yaya and Hall, Mitchell, *The Healing Drum: African Wisdom*. Destiny Books, 1989

35 Diallo, Yaya and Hall, Mitchell, *The Healing Drum: African Wisdom*. Destiny Books, 1989

he awoke, he spoke the name of a man who it turned out had just died. Another time, I was going to invite an orchestra to come to the village to join in a celebration. He told me not to do it because a death had occurred that would prevent the celebration."[36]

Through dreams, Diallo says, the man learned how to treat illness. He was never trained. It was an unexplainable gift. Maybe even supernatural.

Diallo adds that since a child, music would come to him in dreams. He would awake from these dreams and quickly write them down.

---

36 Diallo, Yaya and Hall, Mitchell, *The Healing Drum: African Wisdom*. Destiny Books, 1989

ALTERED STATES AND MUSIC SOUND EFFECTS

Dana Larocca's Story

Dana Larocca, PhD, is founder and CEO of Further Biotechnologies, LLC, and a consultant for the biotechnology industry. She is a parent, scientist, inventor, entrepreneur, and author. She is currently working on a scientific memoir that recalls her life as a transgender woman scientist and longevity advocate. In her memoir she describes her coming of age in an unwelcoming world, her quest for authenticity and her pursuit of scientific advances that will enable us to live longer, healthier, and more authentic lives. She is also an experiencer and explorer of the UFO/UAP phenomenon. Her career spans over twenty-five years of leadership positions in regenerative medicine and longevity biotechnology companies. Dana has given talks at various regenerative medicine and longevity conferences. She has authored over forty-six scientific publications and holds twenty-one issued patents. Dana earned her Ph.D. in Molecular and Cellular Biology from the University of Southern California and a B.S. in Biology from Ithaca College. She did her post-doctoral training at Harvard University.

I met Dana in James Madden's online "Unidentified Flying Hyperobject" class in early 2024. In this class we discussed James's book *Unidentified Flying Hyperobject: UFOs, Philosophy, and the End of the World*. And while the class material and presentation was excellent, the people taking the class were also extraordinary. I was thoroughly impressed with the quality and depth of the questions asked. This was a group of intellectuals devoted to the UFO topic. During the last class, some people elected to give testimonials about their experiences of the phenomenon. Dana's story was powerful and moving. After the class, I wrote to her and asked her if she'd like to have a chapter in the book I was working on.

This is Dana's story.

My encounter with non-human intelligence began when I was in graduate school in the Fall of 1980. I had been experimenting with self-hypnosis for self-improvement. I had always been reserved and shy and saw this as a way to become more assertive. However, I had no idea about what I was getting into. I was like a child reaching for the box of matches in the kitchen cupboard. I did not realize how alluring and addictive the hypnotic state could be or what doors within me it could possibly open. At first, I used pre-recorded cassette tapes but later learned to induce these states on my own, sometimes with the help of a metronome. A ticking metronome at 40 beats per second will facilitate the process of hypnosis. I came out of these sessions feeling elated and refreshed. But I wanted more, so I began doing sessions at least three times per day. I started not only to sleep less but I began to feel I had so much energy that I only needed 2 or 3 hours of sleep a night. I eventually fell into an altered state that lasted 24/7 and continued for about three weeks culminating in my encounter with non-human intelligence.

Many perceptual changes occurred during this time. First, I noticed a general heightening of all my senses. Colors seemed brighter than usual, especially the color blue which would take on a magical glow. My tastes in food and personal care products changed radically. I switched brands of juice, cereal, toothpaste, soap, and other products to suit my new sensations. My hearing became enhanced in various ways, particularly when I was listening to music. I felt an exceptional sense of dimension and clarity in music, whether on the radio or from a vinyl record. There was an extraordinary emotional depth in every note played by each instrument. My sense of time became distorted as well. There were moments when time seemed to stop entirely. Everyone around me became frozen in time like in an old Twilight Zone episode.

I began to think these odd events were a window into another reality that can at times be perceived in altered states. It seemed like I could experience biological time accelerating as I watched a person's face advance to old age and then back again to youth. I could see objects advance in time as well like a piece of white paper becoming yellow and worn with age as if burnt. Although I would not read the book until years later, this type of world where things begin to age and decay is described in detail by Philip K. Dick in his novel, "Ubik." In addition to my altered senses there was a new sense that I could feel another person's "vibe" as I stood or walked next to them. I would feel a literal negative vibe when I was near a person I felt uneasy about.

Sometimes, late at night in my apartment, I heard music. It was incredibly beautiful and sounded like some kind of celestial piano but not like one I had ever heard before. It seemed to come from above and I thought it might be someone in the apartment above me. However, I had never heard the music before my three week journey, nor at any time afterwards. Another odd auditory change was that background noises could at times move into the foreground and become incredibly intense. I would be at a meeting talking with someone and the hum of an air vent or the ticking of a clock became the dominant sound. Loud sounds like a gas-powered leaf-blower engulfed my entire being, making them difficult to tolerate. I became very tuned into the subtleties of language with regard to tone and intonation.

The unconscious cues that we normally aren't aware of were amped up in a way that I could not ignore. This was part of my opening up to a very different way of seeing the world. My bland everyday world was suddenly brought to life with intense clarity and emotion. While much of my journey involved the joy of discovery and elation of feeling connected to an intensely alive universe, it was not all rainbows and unicorns. There was also a dark side to the awakening. I was now vulnerable to my own internal emotions. I had suppressed much of my internal emotional pain over the years in my pursuit of the rational and safe world of science. As a result, at times, I would also experience periods of intense regret and sadness.

There was another curious auditory phenomenon that felt like a type of internal censoring. I had been experimenting with the idea of using the metronome to induce the hypnotic state while watching television. The result was some interesting visual and auditory perceptions. Again, there was an enhanced emotional intensity to conversations occurring within various TV shows. But I also experienced gaps in the soundtrack as if some of the words were edited out. This was not uncommon in movies shown on TV that contained R rated language, but it occurred on shows that would not normally have this sort of editing. A striking example was the show, "Cosmos: A Personal Voyage," by Carl Sagan. I briefly entertained the idea that Sagan was an emissary of a non-human intelligence that had been sent to teach us about the heavens. But the blank spaces only left me puzzled. They were clearly misperceptions. Viewing the program now, I can safely say that no such gaps in the soundtrack exist. But if my unconscious was censoring, what was the meaning of it? What was it trying to tell me?

I felt like I was seeing a parallel world, one that overlaps our own world but is normally occluded. It was kind of like in the 1988 movie, "They Live" where the protagonist puts on a pair of sunglasses and can see aliens all around him, cohabiting with humans. I did not directly see any aliens like in the movie, but I did try to contact them and got an answer. I had been having many paranormal experiences including multiple occurrences of clairvoyance, telepathy, and synchronicities. I had read about Carl G. Jung's theory about synchronicity and the mysterious repetition of the number twenty-three. I dialed the numbers two and three on my rotary landline just to see what would happen in this new magical world I seemed to have entered. To my surprise, I heard ringing and then a voice pronouncing, "You have reached the spaceship twenty-three!" I was so alarmed that I slammed down the receiver not wanting to know more.[37]

---

37 Decades later, I would learn that the quantum physicist, Jack Sarfatti, had a very similar experience. Sarfatti claims that the Department of Defense recruited him to research consciousness and UFO propulsion.

Was I losing my mind? I thought it was possible but unlike a psychosis where there is a loss of rationality, my rational mind was always there observing and taking notes. As a scientist, I did not latch on to any one belief about what was happening but stood back and collected data. I tried different ways to control my conscious state and observed the results. As intoxicating as much of this was, it could not go on forever. Eventually I began to burn out and wanted it to end. One night I tried taking a sleeping pill with the idea that I just needed to get back to having a full night's sleep. However, the next thing I knew I felt like my body was shutting down. I panicked and called 911. I wound up in the emergency room of a local hospital. Once there I did finally get to sleep while waiting to be checked out. I woke up though in a lucid dream where I was in Vietnam getting ready to parachute down into the jungle. I remember thinking, "this isn't my life, I don't belong here!" Then I woke up in the hospital and ran for the exit, not looking back. Walking home, I felt an energy beam from the sky penetrate my brain.

When I got home and into bed, I looked up and saw five golden stars shining through my ceiling. I heard celestial music once again. I felt a sense of calm and connectedness to the entire universe; past, present, and future. That is when the download started. I experienced intense flash cut images of abstract colors and shapes that were interspersed with a sense of hovering over alien landscapes. It lasted for much of the night. When I awoke, I felt refreshed and renewed. As I headed for the bathroom, I stopped and stood in my room motionless staring up at the ceiling. That is when I felt a message come through. It was a clear telepathic message in English that read as follows. "We want humanity to work on extending its lifespan. We need molecular biologists to join this cause. We want you to participate." I thought it was odd that this higher power or non-human intelligence would ask me to do what I was already planning anyway. But I have since realized that it was an affirmation, an invitation to make a strong commitment and not waiver from the cause.

THE ANGEL OF LIGHT

In *Flying Saucers, A Modern Myth of Things Seen in the Sky*, Carl G. Jung introduces the psychic element into ufology. Jung asserts that, while the UFO is a thing in the sky, it also emerges from deep within the collective unconscious. Jacques Vallée's *Passport to Magonia* builds on Jung's idea that the Phenomena has been with us even before human beings began painting on cave walls, and has adapted itself to specific cultural contexts. It reflects back how a given culture sees itself. From Vallée, we can draw a line to the great John Keel, who threw all logic out-the-window. To frame the Phenomena, Keel felt that the future scientist would be an oracle. Or a shaman.

In the current time, Diana Pasulka, Bernardo Kastrup and Jeff Kripal have extended upon Jung's initial idea that the UFO is perhaps us looking at ourselves in a mirror. And like a mirror, what is observed may not be faithful to the observer. Jung writes that "UFOs can appear suddenly and vanish equally suddenly. They can be tracked by radar but remain invisible to the eye, and conversely, can be seen by the eye but not detected by radar."[38] As already stated, the Phenomena evades logical analysis. We may see a UFO, or a Marian apparition, or an angel, but we are not likely to capture it on video, or even take a quality photograph of the experience. Even when we have evidence, we can't see the Phenomena. The New York Times[39] published the 'tic-tac' radar video, along with the ex-

---

38 Jung, Carl. G. *Flying Saucers, A Modern Myth of Things Seen in the Sky.* Princeton University Press, 1978
39 https://www.nytimes.com/2019/05/26/us/politics/ufo-sightings-navy-pilots.html

pert eye-witness accounts of pilots, and the world mostly ignored it. Congress is discussing the testimonies of pilots, scientists, and others who have had encounters, and still the public, in general, is silent on the subject.

In the epilogue of *Flying Saucers, A Modern Myth of Things Seen in the Sky,* Jung recounts the story of Orfeo Angelucci, whose career as a prophet began with the sighting of a UFO on August 4, 1946.

Interestingly, in Greek mythology, Orpheus, from which the name Orfeo derives, was a Thracian bard, legendary musician and prophet.

During the encounter on August 4, Orfeo was informed by the beings he encountered that the UFOs were remote controlled by a mothership. In his book *The Secret of the Saucers*, Orfeo explained that, while the occupants of the UFOs didn't need the vessels, they used the UFO likeness only to present themselves to humans. To be recognized. Understood in a way they thought we could comprehend.

Orfeo said that he detected the "electro-magnetic force of the saucers." He felt the heart and power emanating from the alien spaceship.

On July 23, 1952, not feeling very well, in a state where psychic phenomena may occur, as Jung says, Orfeo had another encounter.

"Suddenly he saw a luminous object on the ground before him, like an 'igloo' or a huge, misty soap bubble."[40] Orfeo discerned a doorway leading to a brightly lit chamber. The walls of the interior were made of ethereal mother-of-pearl.

"He sat down and had the feeling that he was suspended in the air...Then he heard a humming, a rhythmical sound like a vibration, which put him into a semi-dream state. The room grew dark and music came from the walls." The sound poured out around

---

40 Jung, Carl. G. *Flying Saucers, A Modern Myth of Things Seen in the Sky.* Princeton University Press, 1978

him. He couldn't believe his ears when he recognized the melody of his favorite song "Fools Rush In."[41]

Jung continues, saying that Orfeo was carried away into space, until he saw the earth from a distance. He was overwhelmed with emotion. The beings assured him that they would look after the earthlings. Recognizing our foibles, they prayed for human salvation. Welled with emotion, tears began to pour down Orfeo's face. "The voice said, 'Weep, Orfeo. Let tears unblind your eyes. For at this moment we weep with you for Earth and all her children.'"[42]

Then the craft moved into deep cosmic space. Through a window, Ofeo saw a UFO made of crystalline substance. Music rang from it. "I listened to music that I had never heard or could imagine. It was beyond description, for it was not music as we know it, nor was it played to our musical scale. It was strange, haunting drifts of melody that brought visions of star galaxies and planets spinning in notes of perfect harmony."[43] In the thunder of sound, a voice sang to him that all humans were divinely created. He heard strains of the "Lord's Prayer," played "as though by a thousand violins." He saw that the voice and music emanated from a huge spaceship. Orfeo noticed that at both ends of the spaceship "voices of flames" propelled the ship forward. The "voices of flames" were also instruments for telepathic communication. The sole purpose of human experience, the voices said, was to attain reunion with the "immortal consciousness." Hearing this, Orfeo wept. Tears rolled down his face to the accompaniment of music.

Orfeo describes his experience as a spiritual path. The beings regard Earth as "the accursed planet" and "home of the reprobate, fallen ones."[44] They come to Orfeo, communicating telepathically, and with great compassion, to plant a seed that he can carry forward. To save humankind and the Earth.

41 Angelucci, Orfeo. *The Secret of the Saucers*. Zinc Read, 2023
42 Angelucci, Orfeo. *The Secret of the Saucers*. Zinc Read, 2023
43 Angelucci, Orfeo. *The Secret of the Saucers*. Zinc Read, 2023
44 Angelucci, Orfeo. *The Secret of the Saucers*. Zinc Read, 2023

TWELVE NOTES IN THREE SECONDS

In the early nineties, I moved back from California to New York City.

Living on the Upper East Side of Manhattan, I was single, playing with musicians, going to literary events, and, in general, enjoying a creative and productive life.

One summer day, the sun shining down from an ocean blue sky, I was walking on Ninetieth Street, between First and Second Avenues. Out of the corner of my eye, I saw two younger guys, maybe in their twenties, playing guitars on the front stoop of an apartment building.

As I walked past, I took a quick glance at the two young men. They looked like typical younger dudes. One had a big mop of curly golden blond hair. The other had shorter hair, looked Asian. They were sharing guitar licks.

After a few seconds, having walked past them, I heard a fiery riff explode from the blond kid's fingers. It was not a typical pentatonic blues run. At that moment, I couldn't categorize it. I just knew it was different, interesting. It sounded something like Rachmaninoff playing guitar.

I stopped, turned around and walked back to listen more closely.

Now standing near them, listening, I drew the gaze of the blond kid.

"Do you play guitar?" he asked in an accent I couldn't immediately identify.

"I do," I said. The other guy handed me his guitar and I jammed with the blond kid, who was way better than I was.

Soon after we exchanged phone numbers and met a few times to play.

I don't remember the Asian guy's name, but Peter Evgenev and I became friends. Peter was about nineteen at the time. He lived around the corner from me with his brother. Originally from St. Petersburg, Russia, the two of them had moved to New York City. I didn't know it until years later, but Peter is the son of Ludmila Ulitskaya, a well-known Russian author, whose work has been translated into many languages.

Over the next few years, Peter and I played a lot of guitar. During these sessions, it wasn't unusual for Peter to reach over and move my fingers, showing me different positions.

"Play F♭ with your thumb while playing the D. It's more interesting," said Peter one time.

"Do you hear it?" Peter asked.

I still nodded in agreement, annoyed that he rearranged my fingers.

It was very intrusive, even rude. But the result was that I played more interesting chords.

While I fed him, let him stay at my apartment sometimes, sleeping on the couch, he schooled me in guitar playing. This was very humbling, as I was about ten years older than Peter.

After about a year of this, Peter moved to another apartment a few blocks away. He invited me to a New Year's party at his place. When I arrived at the party, I noticed that the guests there were mostly Russians. One of his roommates, named Sophie, was from St. Petersburg, but grew up in Tallinn, Estonia. She was thin, had long legs and short blonde hair. She giggled at my jokes.

We drank, ate, and had fun. Sophie went to bed early.

I thought that would be the last time I saw Sophie, or Sonya as the Russians called her.

A year later, Peter called me one night and said I must go see this Russian folk singer and guitarist, whose name I can't remember.

"This guy is, like, totally amazing," said Peter, his Russian accent coloring his use of American idioms. I agreed to go.

In a few minutes, he called me back. "Do you remember my roommate Sophie?"

"Yes."

"Is it OK if she comes?"

"Sure," I said.

When we got to the venue, only Sophie was there, waiting on the street.

"Where's Peter?" I asked.

"He's going to meet us inside."

We proceeded in. I couldn't understand the Russian lyrics, but the emotions were evocative, and the guitar playing was spectacular. The performer was very expressive. Introducing the songs, sometimes in English, Sophie explained that the lyrics were mostly political, critical of the Russian government. These songs would have been dangerous to play in Russia even during *perestroika*.

Peter never showed up. Sophie and I wound up having a romantic night. Over the next few weeks and months, we saw a lot of each other.

About three months later, Sophie was pregnant. I was not ready to be a father.

But in those three notes, I can still remember them, played in roughly twelve seconds, the promise of my son Thelonious was born.

DREAMING UFOS

Note the title to this chapter "Dreaming UFOs." I intended the title to have double meaning. Do we dream of UFOs or do UFOs dream us into being?

I often have UFO dreams. I've had them all my life, but in the past few years I've gotten in the habit of writing them down.

In one dream I saw a long string of UFOs that were connected and moving together horizontally like a cigar shaped galaxy. The first in the line of the UFOs looked like an array of bright white lamp bulbs. This was followed by a string of long pine trees lying sideways. All of this was moving across the sky slowly and powerfully. I said aloud "This is a UFO" to my wife, Arielle, who was suddenly standing next to me. While I glared up at the sky, I thought that the Phenomenon was reflecting back to me the way it thinks I see it.[45]

As my friend, Sev Tok, experiencer advocate and ufologist, said "I've had 'encounter dreams' nearly all my life. I knew they were different from traditional dreams but denied their significance out of fear and confusion. When I had a dream that resulted in red X marks burned into my back, I knew these were not traditional dreams. Encounter dreams have a hazy, multi-dimensional feeling to them. Here are a few signs of an Encounter Dream: You cannot forget the 'dream' (for decades or for the rest of your life) because it feels intensely real—some say more real than this reality. You receive information you have no way of normally knowing. And the "dream" catapults a profound spiritual shift. Much ET Contact

---

45 Fiorito, Mike. *For All We Know*. Baltimore, MD: Loya Press, 2024

happens in an inter-dimensional state, when we are focused on the multi-dimensions, as we are asleep or in meditation."

UFO experiences are dreamlike because they *are* dreams. I don't mean dreams in a deprecated reality sense. Dreams are *real* too. Perhaps this is why experiencers feel sleepy sometimes during encounters and can't distinguish between what they saw and whether it was a *real* UFO sighting. People I've talked to will often say, "I'm not sure if I was dreaming when I had the encounter. I had just woken up or wasn't sure if I was definitely awake." I've watched UFO documentaries and become sleepy. Not because they were boring but because some of the resonance rubbed off on me.

Interesting too that UFO and apparition sightings are accompanied by dazzling lights. As are psychedelic visions. Light seems to be central to these experiences. Sometimes the beings, including angels and extraterrestrials, are made of nothing but light. Can this be related to the special phenomenon of light, particularly the speed of light? That there is an uncanny relationship between energy, mass, and the speed of light? That without light we would die? That we are drawn to light when we die?

Jacque Vallée wrote that miracle events have stunning similarities to UFO encounters. They "involve luminous spheres, lights with strange colors, a feeling of 'heat-waves'—all physical characteristics commonly associated with UFOs. They even include the typical falling-leaf motion of the saucer zig-zagging through the air. They also encompass prophecy and a loss of ordinary consciousness on the part of the witnesses—what we have called the psychic component of UFO sightings."[46] Vallée also noted that spectators report buzzing sounds and sometimes music. Interestingly, psychedelic researcher Rick Strassman wrote that many participants in his Dimethyltryptamine (DMT) studies remarked that colors became more intense, and reported hearing unusual sounds, such as an oscillating "wa-wa" noise, a ringing, or a crackling. Later in the

---

46 Vallée, Jacques, *Dimensions: A Casebook of Alien Contact*. Anomalist Books, 2008

experience, some reported hearing musical or "heavenly" sounds, and others reported spoken voices and even a cartoonish *"sproing"* sound.[47]

In dreams, psychedelic visions, and UFO sightings, there is a breakdown of the laws of physics. The material world in these situations becomes more fluid, we progress through a continually shifting space, being one moment in our kitchen, then in another, perhaps, on a spaceship. People's faces morph: my brother Frank becomes my friend Lan. We have conversations with the dead.

When lucid dreaming,[48] we can become more conscious of our dreaming selves and can direct actions. For instance, when I've lucidly dreamed, I've become conscious and was able to "take the wheel," intentionally jumping off a mountain to fly in the sky. Not an expert lucid dreamer, the excitement I felt snapped me out of the dream.

The practice of Tibetan dream yoga is a form of lucid dreaming. Learning how to master your dream state, in this practice, is thought to enhance your everyday awareness. In Tibetan dream yoga, it is believed that we are dreaming even when we are awake. By becoming aware that we are continuously "making up reality," Tibetan yogis believe that we thus move closer to enlightenment. Is it significant to note that the word "Buddha" translated from Sanskrit into English means "Awakened One."

Here is another dream that I recently had. The description also reads like a spirit visitation or psychedelic trip.

I traveled to another city to see Peter Rowan play. I think it was in Massachusetts, but I'm not certain. The venue was in a hotel, with a small stage.

I saw Peter playing on the stage and stood in the audience lis-

---

[47] Strassman, Rick. *DMT: The Spirit Molecule: A Doctor's Revolutionary Research into the Biology of Near-Death and Mystical Experiences*. Rochester, Vermont: Park Street Press, 2001

[48] Lucid dreaming practice involves learning to remain aware during the states of dreaming.

tening. At some point, Peter sauntered off the stage as I was talking to him. Then I found myself having wandered away or steered away from Peter. I was now talking to friends who I knew from a bar back home. I placed my hands on my friend Taylor's shoulders and levitated until I was planking parallel to the floor. Taylor allowed me to playfully trail her floating in the air. I wondered if Peter found this amusing but could no longer see him.

I then meandered from the area where the stage was, like you do in a dream, or when whisked away by extraterrestrials. As much as I tried to find my way back to the stage, I only moved further away from it. I found myself outside now, wandering from the hotel, unable to locate it.

Walking near a dock, I saw a private boat with an enormous bow, which was about thirty feet high above the water line. Looking up I noticed a man at the helm. To the west I saw in the distance what might have been the hotel. Before I could say "Do you know how I can get to the hotel?" I beheld a light flash in the night sky to the east. To my surprise, the light was a purplish translucent UFO that pulsed and glimmered. It was brilliantly lit. My eyes widened to take in the grandeur of what I was seeing. I said to myself, like I often do in UFO dreams, "That's a UFO." The glowing saucer then changed into a different shape. It now looked more like a 1950s style UFO, less symmetrical and rounder at the top like a cup. It started moving to the east. I noticed that patches of sky, containing undulating galaxies, were moving in formation with the UFO. There were other sky portals which moved east in unison with the UFO. They moved slowly, like a falling leaf. Exhilarated by this prophetic vision, I woke up.

WHEN HE REACHED DOWN HIS HAND FOR ME

This was a dream. Wait, no, this wasn't a dream. This happened. But don't dreams also *happen*? Aren't dreams real? Yes, dreams are real, yet different. Different to someone at my level of self-realization. I haven't learned to, as the Tibetan Yogis say, penetrate the veil of dreams. Nor have I learned to fully discern what the Buddhist call māyā,[49] the delusions of everyday reality. However, dreams can offer glimpses into the Mind at Large. As Jung said in an interview on the BBC in 1959, "There are these peculiar faculties of the psyche; that it isn't entirely confined to space and time; you can have dreams, or visions of the future; you can see around corners, and such things."

Driving in my car to Winchester, Massachusetts, Peter Rowan was in the passenger seat. I had driven from Brooklyn, New York to see him perform at a venue in Northampton, Massachusetts. Earlier in the week Peter said there would be a bed for me where he was sleeping that night. He was staying with his cousin Max Wareham, the banjo player in his group. Max was housesitting a place in Winchester, located in 'Greater Boston.'

Let me backup a minute.

When I arrived at the venue in Northampton to see Peter and the band play, I had joined them in the green room while they

---

49 In Buddhist philosophy, māyā is a mental factor that can lead to deceit or concealment about the illusory nature of things. It can also refer to the lack of knowledge (avidyā) of the real Self, Atman-Brahman, when someone mistakenly identifies with their body-mind complex.

waited for the show to begin. I sat next to Peter, noticing that he was reading *Finding the Raga*, by Amit Chaudhuri. Surprised, I told him I was reading it too.

"I was a little turned off by the haughtiness of his writing," I said.

"Keep reading it," suggested Peter. "The second half of the book gets more personal. Humbler. And more interesting."

Peter showed me the list of songs he was listening to, having found them in the book. Songs by Banani Ghosh, Subinoy Roy. Debabrata Biswas and others.

Flash back to after the show in Winchester.

"Max is going to drop off Chris Sartori [who played bass that night]. I can drive with you, to keep you company," said Peter.

A Friday night in early May, it was about 11:30 p.m. The sky was pitch dark.

Not yet on the main highway, I drove down winding roads, following the GPS, but not exactly sure whether I should go straight, turn left or right. Driving slowly, I felt like a blind person using a walking cane to find the right way.

Noticing my hesitancy, Peter said, "These roads were made for farm animals. Farm animals don't walk in straight lines. They walk in curves. Massachusetts has many of these kinds of roads."

Finally on the main highway, trucks and cars tearing by us, I hit shuffle on my iPhone, playing music randomly from my massive catalog of songs.

As if on request "Foggy Mountain Top," by Doc Watson and Bill Monroe, popped on the speakers, blaring. The song was included on a Smithsonian Folkways collection of live performances by Bill Monroe and Doc Watson from 1964-1980.

Peter listened to the song intently, leaning forward.

"I have a collection of live recordings by Bill Monroe and the Bluegrass Boys from 1959-1969. You're on some of those tunes," I said. "I can play that."

"Whatever you want to listen to," said Peter, nonchalantly.

With my glasses on I can't see too well close-up, but I can't drive without them. I needed to stop to make the change.

"Let me just pull over here," I said.

Having driven with me a few times, I wondered if Peter thought that I was a horrible driver. I've made a few precarious turns here and there with him in the car.

I pulled over to the side of the road, as twelve-wheel trucks roared by, spraying dirt from the road on the windshield.

I put the playlist of songs on. Loudly. At a level my wife would scream "turn it down, you're making me go deaf."

Peter didn't say anything. He held onto the car handle, perhaps for dear life, leaning into the dashboard even further.

Since I had the playlist on shuffle, the songs played out of order. I didn't want to pull over again.

"Isn't the quality of the recording amazing?" I said. "This was recorded by Ralph Rinzler. He also wrote the liner notes."

"Ralph had great equipment," said Peter. "He made pristine recordings because he had the best technology available at the time."

We sat listening, not talking. Just the two of us in the car.

After a few songs, I said, "Doesn't it feel like they're playing right here and now?" The sound was so crisp and visceral. I could feel Monroe's mandolin chops thudding on my chest.

Peter agreed.

"Have you heard this album before?" I asked.

"No, but I was at some of these performances," said Peter.

At this point, I didn't feel like I was driving to Winchester. It was like I was traveling through time, as if on a river boat canal.

The song "When He Reached Down His Hand For Me," came on. It's a haunting tune. The gospel harmonies are beautifully mournful, like tears raining down from Heaven.

"Who's doing the high part?" I asked.

"That's Bill Monroe," said Peter.

I couldn't believe it. It was so ghostly and piercing. It didn't sound like Bill Monroe.

"He learned how to sing from his mother," said Peter. "She taught him how to hit those falsetto notes."

When the intro to "Walls of Time" came on, I said, "That's you, Pete. We always know it's you. You played more guitar than the other Bluegrass Boys. No disrespect to them. You stepped out, playing those Doc Watson inspired bass note intros."

Peter was quiet. He just looked straight out the front window of the car, staring at the oncoming traffic. Like he was seeing the faces of the voices he was hearing. People he hadn't seen for over sixty years. Most of whom were no longer alive.

We drove along into the night, listening to the album. It was like I had magically projected sounds and visions onto the car walls from an enchanted ring. I had conjured a piece of history. A history that Peter helped create. And here I was somehow revisiting that history *with him*.

We arrived at the house in Winchester about 1:00 a.m..

Peter showed me my room on the second floor. After we got settled, we met on the first floor of the house.

I took out my Martin-00028 guitar and offered it to Peter.

He looked at it, played it a bit and gave it back to me.

I felt nervous playing in front of Peter. Not that he made me feel nervous. He sat back, his hands behind his head, ready to listen.

My fingers freezing a bit, I mustered the courage to play my arrangement of "Midnight-Moonlight."

He didn't wince. He looked over at me pensively as I sang.

"Do you play that song live?" he asked.

I nodded affirmatively.

"Do people recognize it?" he asked.

"The people I hang with do. They know music."

Max arrived after about thirty minutes. We all passed the guitar back and forth, taking turns playing.

At about 2:00 a.m. we decided to call it a night.

I went to sleep, dreaming that I was playing guitars and singing with Peter Rowan.

"Man, when the music's right you feel like you're flying! You got to love it, so's the peoples will love it the same way!"

—Bill Monroe, 1965 to Peter Rowan

THE MANY VOICES OF PALESTRINA

When my ex-wife Sophie and I separated, I began having panic attacks and became deeply depressed, chiefly due to the uncertainty of how the separation would impact my then six-year-old son, Thelonious.

Of course, our broken marriage saddened me. When I had met Sophie, she seemed mainly interested in getting a Green Card. She was born in St. Petersburg, Russia and grew up in Tallinn, Estonia. She came to the United States on a temporary visa. After a month of being together, she asked me to marry her.

"I can't do that," I said. "We don't really know each other." She started crying. I held her hand, feeling the weight of her situation.

"I want to stay in the United States and pursue my PhD," she said. "But I can't do that without a Green Card."

I thought that was the end of our relationship.

But we kept seeing each other.

The desperation of it all made our meetings hot and urgent.

Then, within about a month or so, she was pregnant.

"You have to marry me," she said. "Either that, or I have to leave the United States and go back to Estonia."

I didn't know what to do.

After we got married, Sophie started her PhD at the City University of New York. She was six months pregnant.

The fact was I never really believed that Sophie was in love with me. Nowadays, we love each other, like family. But back then, it seemed like she merely liked me a lot. We had a good partnership, studying together, and reading each other's papers. And we laughed a lot together. But, during our marriage, I never felt an abiding love from her. And consequently, this blunted my love for her.

When Sophie was pregnant, I had started a technology company while working for another firm. While Sophie answered the phones, I trained her to do some of the work, keeping my day job until I could one day quit. In a strange twist of fate, the company did exceedingly well. Fear had propelled me to work extremely hard, doing the four or five jobs it took to run a company.

The company we founded was a burden to Sophie. She didn't want to do the work. Eventually, I found another company to partner with which relieved her from any responsibilities. She could focus entirely on her PhD.

Sophie and I broke up while she was in Russia, doing research at the archives in St. Petersburg and the city of Vologda for her doctoral thesis. I remained at home in New York City. Our son, Thelonious, was with her.

"I love you like salt, no more, no less," she said, quoting Shakespeare, perhaps thinking that was clever and funny. It wasn't funny to me.

After we broke up, the panic feelings emerged suddenly and randomly. Outrageous jokes I had laughed at previously weren't funny anymore. Songs, especially love songs, were scary and weird. I couldn't listen to them. Having been mostly a cerebral or imaginative type my whole life, I had never felt this kind of panic or depression.

Anything could make me cry.

Lying in bed, I felt like the floor had dropped and I was tumbling down an endless shaft. I got nervous and had to get up and walk around my apartment. I was bloated with fear.

Prior to my separation from Sophie I had heard the choral music of Renaissance composer Giovanni Pierluigi da Palestrina. One of the hallmarks of Palestrina's music is that dissonances are typically relegated to the "weak"[50] beats in a measure. The effect is a smoother and more consonant type of polyphony.[51] Palestrina's style is now considered to be representative of late Renaissance music. Palestrina was extremely famous in his day, and if anything, his reputation and influence increased after his death. His impact on J. S. Bach is notable. Bach studied and hand-copied Palestrina's *First Book of Masses*, and in 1742 wrote his own adaptation of the Kyrie and Gloria of the *Missa sine nomine*.

In my depressed state, Palestrina's music took on new meaning. I became lost in the ocean of many voices and layering of choral parts. Palestrina's masses and motets calmed my panic. When listening to Palestrina, I was delivered to a different world, held in the bosom of those voices. It was as if the many voices, some ancient, some modern, some nonhuman, were made of consciousness. Some had faces, others were ensouled in song only. Faceless beings consuming my every thought.

Ironically, what was soothing to me was considered extravagant and overly complex to the Catholic Church in the 1500s. This had a lot to do with the politics of the Northern European church, which embraced polyphony. The intricate counterpoints, to some, made the religious text, when it was sung, unintelligible. The Roman Catholic Church preferred the monophonic austerity of Gregorian chants, with their lack of complex counterpoint and polyphony.

According to legend, Palestrina's *Missa Papae Marcelli* was responsible for "saving" music. Agostino Agazzari related the story in 1607:

> Music of the older kind is no longer in use, both because of the confusion and babel of the words, arising from the long and in-

---

50 https://en.wikipedia.org/wiki/Beat_(music)#On-beat_and_off-beat
51 Polyphony (/pəˈlɪfəni/ pə-LIF-ə-nee) is a type of musical texture consisting of two or more simultaneous lines of independent melody, as opposed to a musical texture with just one voice (monophony) or a texture with one dominant melodic voice accompanied by chords (homophony).

tricate imitations, and because it has no grace, for, with all the voices singing, one hears neither period nor sense, these being infected with and covered up by imitations; indeed, at every moment, each voice has different words, a thing displeasing to men of competence and judgment. And on this account music would have come very near to being banished from the Holy Church by a sovereign pontiff, had not Giovanni Palestrina found the remedy, showing that the fault and error lay, not with the music, but with the composers, and composing in confirmation of this the Mass entitled *Missa Papae Marcelli*.

By 1828, the story had become more elaborate. Giuseppe Bardi writes:

> Summoning Palestrina before him, Cardinal Borromeo told him face to face to compose a Mass in the desired manner, enjoining on him all possible effort to prevent that the Pope and Congregation of Cardinals might be encouraged to ban music from the apostolic chapel and the church. Poor Pierluigi! He was placed in the hardest straits of his career. The fate of the church hung from his pen, and so did his own career, at the height of his fame.
>
> On Saturday, 28 April 1565, by order of Cardinal Vitellozzi, all the singers of the papal chapel were gathered together at his residence. Cardinal Borromeo was already there, together with the other six cardinals of the papal commission. Palestrina was there as well; he handed out the parts to the singers, and they sang three Masses, of which the "Pope Marcellus Mass" was the last. The most eminent audience enjoyed them very much. But the greatest and most incessant praise was given to the third, which was extraordinarily acclaimed and, by virtue of its entirely novel character, astonished even the performers themselves. Their Eminences heaped their congratulations on the composer, recommending to him to go on writing in that style and to communicate it to his pupils.

While Palestrina, through *Missa Papae Marcelli*, may be responsible for saving music, he definitely saved me. I guess you could say that, deep in my unconscious mind, was the church music I had grown up hearing. Somehow, the long legato notes, blended with different voices and counterpoints, became a steady ground for me. Many voices. Manifesting out of the ocean of sound was the Other. Waiting to be heard, finally, as if it concealed the hidden history of all sentience buried in the sound, dwelling behind the curtain of everyday reality. A history of all woes and joys, not just human ones.

When Palestrina comes on my shuffle, I get comments like "listening to church music now?"

I listen to all kinds of music, including church music.

GLORIA

TWO MILES FROM FERMILAB
Lauren Crisanti's Story

Lauren Crisanti, PhD, is a clinical neuropsychologist who specializes in working with patients with brain injuries. Lauren reached out to me via my website when I was a guest on Whitley Streiber's *Dreamland* podcast. After I received an email from her, we spoke on the phone, then Lauren sent me the following account of her experience.

> I started practicing meditation in the summer of 2023, after conducting comprehensive research of the evidenced-based benefits of natural methods to improve various aspects of daily stressors and anxiety. As a neuropsychologist, I have a personal, professional, and intellectual curiosity in the spectrum of human experience and how to expand and utilize consciousness to our advantage. There are many different types, forms, and approaches to meditation, but music, sounds, tones, and frequencies are ubiquitously associated with it. As such, I initially experimented with binaural beats with different Hertz strength and waves (e.g., gamma, theta, delta), both voice-guided and without. I noticed, almost immediately, that I was able to remain mentally alert while my body "went to sleep." During this phase, I would often lose conscious awareness of my body and it would start to vibrate vigorously. I would sometimes experience a dissociation or separation from it. Sometimes, these physical sensations are accompanied by sparks of light or shifting colors behind my closed eyes.
>
> One Saturday night, on March 9, 2024, I completed a guided, body-scan meditation with binaural beats and background mu-

sic. I went to sleep about an hour later and was awakened in the middle of the night by a very loud, strong, and continuous vibrational tone in my bedroom. It sounded like someone was in my bedroom hitting a tuning fork. I wasn't able to discern the spatial source of the sound, as it sounded as though it was all around me and coming from everywhere. It was a pleasant sound and reminded me of the tones I hear in my meditation tracks. I was not disturbed by it, and as I turned over in my bed to lie on my left side, a very strong "whoosh" of energy moved down my right leg. It was fast, yet warm and gentle. It felt as though it was associated with the tone, which stopped after I turned over.

The next day, my oldest son, Jack, told me he was also awakened to the loud tone and was too scared to get out of bed. I don't know what to make of this experience. As a social scientist, I am inclined to apply logic and rational explanations to it. I live about two miles from Fermilab. Maybe they were conducting an experiment in the middle of the night that generated a loud tone in my house? Maybe it was a jet? Maybe I have nerve damage in my right leg that acted up at this exact moment and never again? Or perhaps I'm unlocking channels in my consciousness otherwise inaccessible to the daily grind of life distractions. I have had many other unique experiences with practicing meditation, and I find them comforting and validating. Consciousness is the new frontier, and I think that meditation with binaural beats is one of the keys to unlocking it.

THE HOLY SPIRIT HEALED DURING A PRAISE AND WORSHIP SONG

Gloria Hass's Story

I met Gloria Hass through the network of friends and colleagues I've encountered through the UFO community. When *For All We Know* was announced Gloria invited me on her podcast. We had a great conversation. What follows is Gloria's story.

> I played the flute from fifth grade through my senior year of high school. I started singing in my school's chorus when I was nine-years-old and continued through my senior year of high school. Later, during my first year of college, I auditioned and was in madrigals. I was eleven when I started singing in the children's choir at church. I didn't start singing in the adult church choir until I was in my thirties. When I was in my forties, I was trained in a charismatic church regarding how to bring the congregation into the Holy of Holies when they sing. This helps bring the Holy Spirit into the service with everyone being in one accord in their mind.
>
> For nine years, I was a traveling evangelist in the United States. During this time, my home base was in Bullhead City, Arizona. While I had a home church, where I would speak or sing special music from time to time, I would frequent area revival meetings. At one revival meeting, I was asked to sing with the praise and worship team. This was a wonderful experience as I hadn't done this before. After the meeting had concluded, a pastor from another church asked me to attend his place of

worship one Sunday morning. After this service was over the pastor asked me if I would help lead praise and worship as he was looking for someone. I prayed about it and spoke with my pastor at my church. I finally accepted the position. One Sunday, something miraculous happened that I hadn't experienced before. As I led the congregation in singing "Days of Elijah," a highly anointed song, the presence of the Holy Spirit fell over the entire congregation. People were weeping and others were healed of their burdens and illnesses.

THE DAY OF THE CROWS— MYRON DYAL

I first learned of Myron Dyal by reading Anthony Peake's *The Hidden Universe*, which discusses Myron's temporal lobe epilepsy and how it related to his visions. I came across Anthony's book after reading Jeff Kripal's *The Flip*, which launched a reading frenzy—still in progress—on the subject of the Phenomena. We subsequently began corresponding. When I went to England in 2023, I met with Anthony at the Southbank Centre in London, along with Rob Dickins, the founder of the *Psychedelic Press*. After spending an afternoon chatting by the water at the Southbank Center, we went to Watkins Bookshop, London's oldest esoteric bookstore. We were joined by another friend who prefers to remain anonymous. This other friend runs a podcast called *Perceptions Today*, based in the United Kingdom.

Fascinated by his story, I wrote to Myron and fell in love with his artwork. Although trained as a musician, Myron uses the canvas as a conduit for his visions. The result is a stunning body of work that continues to grow. Myron and I have since spoken many times on the phone and remain in contact. He's become a dear friend.

Here is Myron's story.

> I am a mystic, artist, musician, and I have visions that are connected to my Temporal Lobe Epilepsy, which is the catalyst for my art! Each piece is a record of a vision that has occurred during some event, and I have over 5,000 drawings, paintings, and sculptures. I was in a coma when I was four-years-old and when

I awoke my mind was erased and my visions began continuing to the present day/this very day. I am a musician and music was all I had to express my inner being until I began creating art in the late 1970s. I began with my journals and then later began to draw, paint and sculpt. When I created, I also "danced." In other words, I conducted a ceremony around all the works in order to internalize their contents. I would spend a great deal of time in the mountains where I was living at the time.

I had to pull myself up out of the stifling pit of Christianity I had experienced. It was a very primitive backwoods form of it, and due to the offbeat personal values of my family, I needed a cornerstone upon which to build some sort of foundation for childhood sanity. That's where music came in; my creative endeavors which long preceded my involvement with the visual arts. I spent a great deal of time writing and playing music. It was my Zen practice, and the only thing that could absorb me in the moment. For me, music had a unique reality; sound itself stimulated my imagination and I was ready and more than willing to travel wherever the music decided to take me. As did my visions, music had the power to carry me into other worlds, other dimensions of being and feeling. While not visions, these musical sojourns had their own very special quality; they formed a sort of counterpoint, a balance, to the visions themselves. They existed in harmony with one another with their own push and pull. I was captivated by the idea of the purity of sound and its lack of restrictions and forms.

Nonmaterial is created out of physical implements, going forth in absolute freedom to the ends of the universe; the sound waves travel onward and upward, unhampered, and unchanged, forever. I was able to wander just as freely through these abstract landscapes of free tonalities, possessing nothing external unto itself, a place where I could climb the mountain of unified reality and see all the way home. Although as you will see, my childhood encounters with the unconscious were few and far between, yet they were always deeply meaningful. There are many obvious differences between the behavior of the elements of the outer world and their inner world counterparts. A storm, for example, in the physical world, will brew, spew its fury, move on, dissipate, and then come to an end.

In the interior world of thought and emotion, storms can rage an entire lifetime, and this was certainly true with me. The severe disturbance of my emotional nature not only continued to churn but would appear and reappear in myriad guises. In the mid to late 1960s I had developed some type of continuous shaking with no discernible physical causes, which only recently was diagnosed as a symptom of chronic PTSD (Post Traumatic Stress Disorder). Living with the constant uncertainty of the sudden appearance of a seizure was bad enough, but the tremors were unceasing. The need to tie down the source of this tremor was imperative, as I could not even write my own name or play the violin. After explaining this new condition to my physician, he prescribed one of those wonderful new miracle drugs, which somehow almost invariably wind up creating a new condition as bad or worse than the one they are intended to cure. The one my doctor recommended for me was a hot little item called Valium. I was told Valium would calm my nerves, which it certainly did, bringing with the relief unexpected bonuses, such as addiction. By the time I was able to sever my relationship with it, my original dosage of 2 milligrams per day had grown to 30 plus milligrams.

The Day of the Crows—October 1963. It was 2:30 a.m., past the witching hour but in my life all bets had been called off and anything was possible at any hour of the day or night. I had a melody playing between my ears for hours, struggling for rulership of my head with the headache accompanying it as an underlying bass line. It was obvious I wouldn't be getting any sleep before dawn. I heard a slight scratching sound from the hallway outside my bedroom. A rat sharpening its evil little claws? Who knew? Or cared? I had been battling recurring dizzy spells for the past few days and there had been no let-up. It had been another long and difficult night overcharged with anger, rage, and physical discomfort that just wouldn't release me from its grip. I was also experiencing pain in my legs, situated just beneath the skin of the lower limbs, like an itch that couldn't be scratched. The pain was increasing in intensity and all my attempted remedies had yielded zero results. Having tried everything else, I placed my large green pillow beneath my knees, hoping the elevation would do whatever it is supposed to do for the blood circulation and bring a little relief. It did very little.

As the minutes ticked by, I grew noticeably more comfortable and even my headache was receding. Then, the music in my head started up again. I had no choice but to succumb to the wooing of the muses, get up from my bed, and plop myself down at the piano, picking out the tune on the black-and-whites and scribbling down notes and chords. The room was cold, so my old robe was a necessity; no replacement for a concert pianist's stylish tuxedo, but at least it was warm and fit the setting. It was ancient and in tatters, the kind of garment you don't throw away until it is condemned by the health department. But it added a sort of classical music feeling of antiquity as I sketched out the melody line on stained yellow music paper. A tattered ghost at the piano ruled by the whims and melodies of my mind. I had been devoting myself to the composition of a new mass, which had been posing problems ever since its original conception, presenting difficulties that continued to plague my progress. Any composer will tell you that the nuts-and-bolts of composition are as far removed as possible from the lilting rhythms of the finished product. Indeed, it is a minefield thickly studded with pitfalls, hazards, and almost irreconcilable conflicts, all of which must be solved in order to produce the final product.

From the beginning I had been uncertain as to the proper tonal center of the piece, but oddly, this night of aches and pains had made the decision for me: B minor juxtaposed with elements of free material, which lent an aura of transcendent freedom and spontaneity. Most composers would have selected B minor after Bach's famous mass, but when it came to me, the decision was made based upon physical infirmities, dizzy spells, and the strange sounds in the night.

This particular composition had displayed a life of its own ever since I wrote the first notes of the opening melodic structure. The music's complex resonance seemed to fill my very being, and its rich sonority made its way from my soul, through my mind, then through my hands and out into the world. Interestingly, the mass was quite eloquent of new life and optimistic faith, which are usually reserved only for the "resurrection" moments of a mass, focusing as they do on the great drama of the "passion" of Christ, the crucifixion, and other more somber themes. The music had taken possession of me and I continued working on the first movement until daybreak. It might have been a trifle manic, but for the first time in weeks the mass was beginning to assume a definite shape and I did not want to stop in mid surge of inspiration. The light of the newly emerging day stealthily sneaked around the shades and penetrated my study, its rays coming to rest atop the piano in a stunning kaleidoscope of colors.

Exhilarated with the uplifting vibration of creativity, I turned to greet the new day as a welcome friend, only to be blinded by the sun's rays. In an all-too-familiar fashion of dizziness, I fell from the piano bench onto the hardwood floor. Suddenly I was adrift in a sea of blue, and eventually, I was able to see more than just color. Off in the distance, were dark-blue mountains girdled by deep green meadows. A mild breeze blew over me while jet-black crows flew unerringly towards me. I sensed a deep connection between the crows and my inner consciousness. Crows have been with me since the beginning of my visions. When I was young and couldn't be more than eight or nine, there would be multitudes of crows landing *en masse* on the tree in our backyard, sounding their reveries in loud cries, which were music and comfort to my ears.

As they gathered, I thought I was a part of their gathering; some of them would swoop down and touch my body, and later would even land on my shoulders. Their beautiful black and blue wings permeated my mind appearing over and over again in my visions. Sometimes in my youth I would say "the crows are flying again," my way of telling people I was in an altered state of consciousness in which the birds and their wings were playing an important part. The crows continued to fly toward me; the flapping of their wings produced a strange music that was reassuring and seemed to have a relationship with the mass. The sound wound itself about me, cloaking me in a cocoon of mystery. I felt impregnated with light and healing energy, and on the wings of the melody I was transported into the heavens, the only suitable place for such sounds. The light was all encompassing and bathed me in a divine radiance, its omnipresence crowding out all impressions of blue mountains and black crows.

The next thing I knew, I was waking up on the floor of my study, surrounded not by healing warmth but freezing cold morning air. Once again, it was time to lift myself up off the floor after yet another seizure, but now my body refused to obey my will, an inconvenient disconnect when one is shivering mightily. I fell back down, the impact of the floor leaving a bruise on my arm, and my leg pinned beneath me. I felt completely inert and probably looked like a broken doll sprawled across the wooden planks. A few minutes before I had been the brilliantly inspired composer, bending recalcitrant notes to my will as I ironed out one musical problem after another. Now I was as helpless as a newborn baby whose only command of sound was to issue forth precious little moans and gurgles. But still lingering around the fringes of my thoughts was that optimism I had brought back from the vision. A feeling that all was as well as when I had been aloft on the wings of my crows soaring through the clear blue skies of my higher mind.

Foggy Beach in My Study—Summer 1974. In the summer of 1974, I received an offer from a local theater company to compose a score for their production of Shakespeare's *The Tempest*. Although I appreciated the offer and their confidence in my compositional abilities, the downside was that their budget contained almost no funds for a conventional score. I told them I would have to approach the score from an unconventional aspect in order to make it work. They gave me the green light and I went to work immediately. I decided to compose it entirely for the piano. Reaching into my past, I turned the inside of my piano into a magic box, not with roadkill and plastic monsters, but materials that would produce interesting sounds: sticks, cardboard, glass, soft timpani sticks of varied sizes, and just about anything else I could think of that would produce distinctive and unusual sounds.

One morning during composing, I was placing glass rods in the piano, when all of a sudden I lost my grip, sending them tumbling to the soundboard beneath the strings. What I thought was ordinary clumsiness or the difficulty of working in the cramped interior of a piano, instead was the paralysis of my left arm. Needless to say, I was more than a little concerned. Deciding that this was a one-time-only event, I didn't think it worth mentioning to anyone. I replaced the rods and continued writing the musical score.

One night while being up late working on the structure of one of the movements intended to duplicate the sound of a storm, I fell, with my arm and shoulder sharply striking the side of the piano. Once more I played diagnostician and wrote the spill-off to fatigue, and once more I continued working and told no one. The next morning there appeared to be no lingering after-effects of my impromptu collision with the piano. I arose at 6 a.m., feeling great. I dressed, made coffee, and rode my bicycle down to the fog-enshrouded beachfront without so much as a slight dizzy spell. The earliness of the hour gave me free run of the streets. The only forms visible seemed to be growing right out of the fog, and they were not easily identifiable. A bank of fog spawning creatures was rather unusual, even for me, but I was now firmly in the habit of shrugging these things off, so I just concentrated on my cycling. Yet within moments I was forced to deal with it, as the fog began to thicken, turn green, and emit a strange aroma. The smell was a musty, outdoorsy scent, reminiscent of old leaves, and I was unable to determine its source. I had more than enough experience with the ocean to know it can send forth all manner of odors, and I was also aware that fog can play more than a few tricks on one's senses. I again ignored what was happening right in front of my eyes and nose, continuing to pedal. The fog quickly thickened to the point that riding became dangerous, so I stopped somewhere along the boardwalk to get my bearings. Pushing the bike beside me, I walked cautiously, squinting while slowly feeling my way forward.

At one point I inadvertently stepped off the boardwalk and onto the sand. Perhaps it was the feeling of being slightly startled by the sudden change of footing that caused me to realize I could no longer hear the sound of the waves, which led to the realization everything had gone silent. Not having the least idea of where I was nor what direction I should take; I took what seemed the safest course of action: none. I merely sat down in the damp sand, laid the bicycle next to me, and hunkered down to wait for the sun to dissipate the fog. A check of my watch showed the time to be 7 a.m.. This may have been a little on the early side for the workaday world just wrenching itself out of warm comfortable beds, but this was the beach. There should have been a pretty good amount of movement by now; surfers, swimmers, fishermen, lifeguards, joggers, restaurant patrons, and other beachgoers. They could not have all been swallowed up by the fog. Even my most bizarre adventures had never found me feeling so lost and alone, disconnected from the rest of the world.

The first vibration of civilization that penetrated the fog was the faint sound of music. I was unsure whether it was external to me or being produced by my own mind. Either way, it was the only sound I could hear. I strained my ears trying to localize the origin of the noise, but that proved impossible. I rose, and started walking randomly, hoping to find a portal out of this madness. I hadn't gone far when I heard a voice, my first contact with humanity that morning. The disembodied voice was calling my name, but yet again I was not successful in putting a location to the sound.

Meanwhile, the fog continued to thicken and felt as though it was closing in on me. Now I began to feel very uneasy, or, truthfully, just plain scared. The moment had a strange timelessness about it, as though I were dwelling outside the confines of the three-dimensional world. I had even begun to forget what it was like to be in the actual world, though it had not been that long since I had been cycling along and enjoying the morning. A soft wind began to move through the fog, surrounding me, hovering above me, then insinuating itself into my being. The heavy green mist gave way to the authority of the wind, yet I still remained caught in its ethereal cloak. I was entrapped by it, being engulfed, pulled in, and dragged down. I screamed into the fog.

Before the scream had been completely carried off on the wings of the wind, I found myself at home seated on the piano bench. My head was reeling with the familiar dizziness, and nausea was dragging my stomach into the act. On the edge of the piano sat my cup of cold coffee, the one I thought I had drunk before heading out on my bike. Unrestrained tears rolled down my face. I gingerly rose from the bench and slowly tried to walk towards the door of the study. My legs were putty; I was unable to maintain my balance. I plopped down on a small chair near the sliding door, trying to get a grip on myself. I threw a glance down at my watch. 10:30 a.m. Where had the morning gone? What on earth had happened to me? As I had so many times before, I tried to assemble a jigsaw puzzle without the benefit of looking at a guiding picture. Not only was there the typical paucity of pieces, but also, they did not seem willing to fit together into even the beginning of a coherent whole.

The morning remained as broken fragments of my mind unwilling to piece together the mystery of the fog. I would have much preferred to have remembered nothing than mere fragments, and then not be certain of what was real and what imaginary. I headed towards the kitchen to make a fresh cup of coffee, check on Susan [Myron's daughter], and to somehow plug myself back into the world. The motion triggered another dizzy spell, the room began to spin madly, elongate into infinity, and once more, consciousness was eluding me. I retreated toward the study, but slipped on the back steps, falling backwards. I was able to break the fall with my right arm, pulling a muscle in the process and sending the coffee cup careening off the stairs. "Damn it!" I cried. "Damn it to hell!" I was able to regain my balance and get myself back into the study room. I sat back down on the piano bench and slammed my fist against the top of the lid covering the keyboard. "Goddamn it!" I bellowed as my anger at the situation overtook my fear. I knew that the trouble, whatever it was, was not minor, but I preferred to remain in a spirit of comforting ignorance when it came to causes; it seemed so much easier to deal with things by ignoring. The need to finish my musical score suddenly pressed itself to the fore, giving me a reasonable, businesslike excuse for not paying attention to my physical woes.

Weeks later, while editing the tapes of my score for *The Tempest*, my inner world made itself manifest. I was listening intently to the score when the music took an additional texture, becoming part of me in ways other than what a musician expects and welcomes. The sound whirled around me as I was losing control of my consciousness. The room began to enlarge, undermining my balance and adding to the dizziness and confusion. All of a sudden, I felt as if I was in the middle of a tornado, and my study was blown off into the distance. The next thing I knew, I was on the floor.

The following day I called a friend of many years who had acted in the capacity of a spiritual mentor. I filled him in on the events of the last few days, hoping he would say something reassuring, or at least reasonably logical. I was to be vastly disappointed. Not only did I find his advice as befuddling as my experience, but his confusion only added bulk to my own. I listened attentively, thanked him, then hung up, no closer to a solution than before. He had been no help and I realized no one could really be of assistance. My seeking of counsel was nothing more than an excuse to avoid dealing with my own problem. I would have to journey into my own psyche and find out what was going on with me. It was then my thoughts turned to the one I would later name Charon.

It had been years since I had encountered my childhood friend and I was frankly unsure as to whether or not I still believed in his existence, at least as an entity separate from my own inner self. Although I was continuously aware of a presence, energy if you will, that accompanied me, or was part of me, I had long since ceased to affix to it a particular persona. I switched on the tape recorder and went back to my work editing the Tempest score. The room had taken on a feeling that I can only describe as lovely in terms of the ambience that had made itself felt when I began to think of Charon. The feeling was one of love, emanating from every corner of the room. I had no doubt of the reality of the presence of another entity that had joined me in the study. I was not alone; indeed, I might have never really been alone throughout those long years. There was no voice, no physical manifestation of any kind, undoubtedly because none was needed. But for the first time in, I could not estimate how long I had the feeling I was part of something greater than myself. And I was at peace.

MY ONLY TRUE FRIEND— SCOTT SHARRARD

Nowadays, my oldest friend Lan comes to New York City about once a year. He has lived in Orlando, Florida, for the past twenty years. One night, six or so years ago, during one of these visits, he insisted that we go out.

"It's late. I'm tired," I said, feeling lame.

It was a cool summer night in Brooklyn. He didn't come all the way from swampy Orlando just to sit in my air-conditioning.

"Let's just go for a walk," Lan demanded, nicely. What kind of friend would I be if I said no?

"Let's go grab a beer at Bar Chord."

"Is this some kind of hipster bar?" he asked, making a face.

Laughing I say, "Shut up, man. You'll like it."

Now closed, Bar Chord was a local bar and music venue on Cortelyou Road in Ditmas Park, my neighborhood. They had music several nights a week featuring terrific jazz ensembles, blues bands, and acoustic acts. I would go there just to have a few beers by myself and listen to the music. It was nice to be able to pop in.

When we got to Bar Chord, the band was on a break. I was almost glad they weren't playing. I was begrudgingly pulling myself through this. After we ordered beers, the music started up again. I didn't know who was playing, but I could hear it was a blues band. Within a few notes, it was clear that this was a great band, and that the guitar player was amazing. Not just good. It was like he had taken off on a rocket ship with his solos. Then he launched into "Two Steps from the Blues," a Bobby Bland song. Not only can he rip the shit out of his guitar, I thought, he can sing, too.

I put my drink down and looked over at Lan. He was also impressed. More than impressed, we were stunned. This guy was just too good. He tore up his guitar, playing soulful blues licks, sometimes pulling on long notes with his slide, as he was dialing in guitar phrases that I had heard before: B. B. King, Duane Allman, and Lowell George. The bell tones. Slide riffs thick and slow like molasses, hanging low like weeping willows. I felt like a radar signal had gone up my spine and turned my brain on highline mode. Lan and I shook our heads in disbelief.

"You see," he said. "I told you we should have gone out." Lan's eyes were watery. It had him too.

"I know, I know," I said. It was like someone had awoken Duane Allman from the dead and put him up there on that stage with those screaming slide notes and blues riffs packed with tears and pain.

"Now I'm going to play something from my new album," said the guitar player, during a brief pause between songs. The drummer trotted into an R&B rhythm; the band followed. The song was funky and soulful. Some people started dancing to the tune. The small crowd at Bar Chord was totally into it. Then the guitar player started singing. He had long hair, like a real rock star. But he didn't just look the part. This guy did it all.

Who the fuck is this guy?

I looked his name up on my iPhone. I could not believe it. It was Scott Sharrard, musical director, co-writer, and guitarist for Gregg Allman. I'm afraid to admit that I didn't know who he was. But things were beginning to make sense. Bar Chord was a great place, but this guy was Greg Allman's fucking guitar player! Greg Allman could have had anyone as his guitar player. He'd played with some of the best electric blues guitar players of our time.

After it had pitched us up and down a rollercoaster of joys and sorrows, the set ended on Sharrard's version of "Melissa" by the Allman Brothers. Motherfucker.

Lan and I were blown away. We weren't even stoned. This was simply miraculous.

I now know that the R&B song Sharrard had played is on his 2018 album, "Saving Grace," and that it was recorded at Muscle Shoals. About half the songs feature Howard Grimes (percussion), Reverend Charles Hodges (keyboards), and Leroy Hodges (bass)—musicians who've been producing hit records since playing with Al Green and Ann Peebles in the 70s. The other cuts feature David Hood (bass), Spooner Oldham (keys), and Chad Gamble (drums), prime movers in the Muscle Shoals sound. Also making guest appearances are Taj Mahal and legendary drummer Bernard Purdie. And, to channel Duane Allman, Sharrard played Duane's storied 1957 Les Paul Gold Top on the album. This was the first time the guitar had been heard since Duane's death. "Saving Grace" also features "My Only True Friend," which Sharrard co-wrote with Gregg Allman. It is Allman's last known original song. Originally planned for his *Southern Blood* album, Allman's health prevented him from recording it. Their song now lives in Sharrard. In fact, so much of the Allman Brothers lives in Sharrard.

Sharrard's playing called to mind the first time Lan's older brother, Lester, played *Eat a Peach* for us. Stereo on full volume making every organ in my body shudder, I listened as Lester talked about how much he loved this album. Though at that time he was a born-again Christian, Lester told us that the Allman Brothers had to be listened to while tripping on acid to get the full impact. He didn't realize it, but I heard him saying *you need to do acid and listen to this record now.*

Because he was passionate about the music and the myths surrounding it, Lester essentially established our musical taste. And because we venerated the ground he walked on, we listened to his favorite records, trying to hear them like he heard them.

Years later, when our friend Paul and I listened to *Mountain Jam* on LSD, in fulfillment of Lester's prescription, our minds became one. We became eternal. This music spoke to me about the history of the cosmos, about love and friendship.

In 2001, Paul, a firefighter, was taken from us in the World Trade Center tragedy.

A few years later we lost Lester to a sudden stroke.

As Sharrard was playing, Lan and I shared a space where Lester and Paul continued to exist. They were in the music, in the notes.

Crossroads, will you ever let him go? The gypsy flies from coast to coast.

It dawned on me that Paul was always the gypsy of that song; that while he lived in an infinite blue sky, the rest of us were growing old and gray. That we would never let him go and yet he must forever fly away.

And Sharrard's music, his playing, his singing, was bound up with all of this. He knew what he was doing. As he leaned forward with fresh ideas, incorporating new styles in his playing, his music brimmed with the past.

The song "My Only True Friend" was written from the perspective of Duane Allman, as if Duane had written it for Gregg. I was so moved that night by Sharrard's playing because he embodied the spirit and the abiding love that brothers have for each other.

> *I hope you're haunted by the music of my soul*
> *When I'm gone*
> *Please don't fly away and find you a new love*
> *I can't face living this life alone*
> *I can't bear to think this might be the end*
> *But you and I both know the road is my only true friend*

Lan and I headed home in shocked silence. Lester's and Paul's spirits were there with us saying, *Hey, remember when we listened to this music.*

People, can you feel it, love is everywhere. The love that keeps you going on this road we call life, the love of true friends.

SANCTUS/BENEDICTUS

LIGHTNING STRIKING
Leigh Ann's Story

I met Leigh Ann through Lorilei Potvin, who hosts a podcast called *The Angel Rock With Lorilei Potvin*. She interviewed me on the podcast about the strands of research I was doing for *UFO Symphonic,* and she said, "You have to meet my friend Leigh Ann; she has a special connection to music."

I felt privileged to receive Leigh Ann's powerful and intimate story. The fact that I hadn't known her previously made our conversations all the more precious. Leigh Ann was prepared; she read from her detailed journals and poured her heart out like we were old friends. I admire her courage and integrity. What follows is a transcription of our video call.

> **Leigh Ann**
> My professional background is [in] infectious disease epidemiology. Currently, I am unemployed, and that's by choice. But my last profession was an infectious disease epidemiologist in the state of Georgia and other institutions, rubbing elbows with all kinds of people. I have a master's in public health, and I decided I wanted to stop.
>
> I don't want to go back to school anymore. Somehow there was a change in me, and I just decided I wanted to do something else. That's when it just went sideways with music and crystals and meditation. And here I am. It's so weird, even ten years later. It's almost like I cannot walk the walk or talk the talk of public health anymore. It's almost foreign to me. It served its purpose. I am where I'm at for a reason, so I know that. I can see every step

in my life that brought me where I am today.

Now I'm an Akashic records and a crystal practitioner. If somebody were to say I don't believe you, then okay, fine. I get it. No, totally. I really get it. This is just where I'm at and I've really learned to go with the flow more, instead of forcing something and having to be a certain way. Learning to be more like that, rather than constrictive, controlling, demanding, anxious and whatever.

Mike
Was there a specific event that changed things for you?

Leigh Ann
From 1999 to the year 2000, I was in a very tumultuous relationship. I am no longer with that person. Narcissistic, codependent, awful. We were splitting ways like it was the beginning of the end. I was very upset and felt like I didn't know which way I was going to go. What was I going to do next? I had to find another place to live, and all of that. At that time, I was working at Emory University Hospital as a medical technologist working in the blood bank department. I'm talking to one of my coworkers about how I'm reading these books on infectious disease, like a detective basically, which were books about epidemiology, and I was like, "Oh my God, this is so fascinating. This is what I want to do." She said, "You know that Emory University has a whole program in public health which includes infectious disease."

I hauled ass that afternoon and got the hell out of work fast. I couldn't go fast enough to find some information and it was like, "Hell, this is what I'm doing." I applied and started studying to take the GRE test for the first time in 2000. In the midst of all this turmoil at home, September 11, 2001, happens. I know this because I made copious notes in my journal. I record everything because I'm looking for connections. For example, I am looking at my journal now. I just want to show you the date so you can see this date. Do you see September 6?

Mike
Yes.

Leigh Ann
The title is: *That's the Importance of a Life* and I wrote this as if I am talking to someone who is interviewing me about my life.

Mike
Well, you're doing that now. Synchronicities abound once you notice them.

Leigh Ann
I'm going to start with this story. This is my journal entry, September 6, 2023. *That's the Importance of a Life*. I'm shown my lifetime here now on everyday reality Earth in my mind's eye. In a vision I see swirling fractals, which I see as an expression of music. My mother read my diaries and journals when I was a kid, so I stopped writing about anything other than school notes and homework. But now, I'm writing about the importance of music and tones. Vibration and frequency, sound comes first, then it can become light. In the Bible, Genesis one through four, it says:

"In the beginning, God created the heavens and the earth, and the earth was without form and void, and darkness was upon the face of the deep and the spirit of God moved upon the face of the waters, and God said, "Let there be light," and there was light, and God saw that the light was good, and God divided the light from the darkness."

On September 7, 2023, I looked at five or six Bibles before continuing to ponder this statement. There is sound before light. I wanted to be clear on the point of sound. The vibration in frequency is creation. Sound and light are produced from vibration and frequencies. Somehow, I want to say sound came first, then light. Music and tones can be very expressive, cathartic, and absolutely healing. I incorporated the music I had available: jazz, classical, orchestral, big band, forties, and fifties to the present. Hip hop, rap, opera, cellos, violins, double bass. I could go on about high school band, marching band, concert band, the bond of music and people.

I learned to study by playing music, and it helped it stick or sink in, rather than just by memory or sight, as if I was lecturing or teaching an auditorium of people on whatever subject. I did this technique in high school, college, and somewhat in graduate school. Music had messages for me in many ways and many events throughout my life. I think while I studied this way, I felt the importance of music. I really noticed music speaking to me. I was struck by a song I found on a 9/11 tribute CD. The song is "Bridge Over Troubled Water" by Simon and Garfunkel. This was before I became an epidemiologist. Initially, it was the first half of that song that was important to me. I was essentially kicked out of my fiancé's home. Basically, my boyfriend/fiancé was a complete *****. I was working full time as a medical technologist and discovered that I could not exist this way for the rest of my life, which is why I started taking graduate-level classes. I had not yet declared a major of study at Rollins School of Public Health at Emory University in Atlanta, GA. The first class I took was in the summer of 2000.

I've recognized my part in that horrible, codependent relationship. I was excited to study, learn, and eventually professionally be an infectious disease epidemiologist and walk the same hallways as my CDC [Centers for Disease Control and Prevention] rock stars. I was taught by, met many, and collaborated with a few CDC scientists. I graduated in May of 2004 with a master's in public health with an emphasis in infectious disease. I didn't write this here in this journal entry, but "Bridge Over Troubled Water" and "Amazing Grace" sung by Tremaine Hawkins are heavy hitters for me. I've known "Amazing Grace" my whole life, but nothing compares to that version. And then "Bridge Over Troubled Water," which I don't think I'd ever heard before finding it on the 9/11 tribute CD.

Moving on to the spring of 2002, with the intention of enrolling full time as a graduate student, I took the GRE in March of 2002 and scored a 1410. The cut off was 1400. I studied, I self-tested for the GRE. I worked full time and nothing else. I took the GRE test again a week before Easter and my score came up two hundred and fifty points to 1660. I got so excited, but for a minute I thought I had no one to call and to share this information with. I took the test in a testing center in a room full of cubicles. As soon as you finish the test, the number pops up on your screen. I got a 1660! I took it on a weekday, and I was sitting in my car early in the afternoon, and I thought, who can I call? Normally it would be your partner, your spouse, your love. But no, not this time—we had split up. I called a coworker. I'll leave him nameless for now. He is very religious, and he was so happy for me, and I told him about how music stays with me, and he said "Oh, I know." I remember him saying, "You don't have to tell me that." I told him that song wakes me up in the middle of the night.

Fast forward a couple of days to Easter weekend. I left Atlanta straight after work, heading to my parents' house in East Tennessee. About four in the afternoon, with normal traffic conditions and typical weather, it's about a four-hour drive.

The drive was normal as traffic goes. At some point, it began to get dark. Very windy. I was driving northeast. Normally, the winds and the rains come from the west as they come over the Cumberland Plateau. This weather was coming from the north, so I was driving directly into the strong gusts. I stopped for gas on Highway 60, Exit 25 off Interstate 75 north. The wind was hard. I got back on the interstate and the rain started. Driving in pelting rain, the storm kept up for over two hours. A magical moment happened ninety-three miles further up the road.

I take the exit for Andrew Johnson, Highway 11 East going north. As I'm on this highway approaching the Four Way Inn area, I have the CD playing "Bridge Over Troubled Water." I'm at a literal fork in the road. It's where the two highways split, one goes north, and one goes east. You have to choose to go left or to go right, the traffic flow does not stop. I said, God, you've got to give me a sign. I cannot see which way to go. I'm driving straight into hard rain due to the abnormal direction of the storm. All of a sudden, there's a lightning strike.

The lightning says, "You have to go to your left," by illuminating the left side of the forked road. It was the biggest strike I've ever seen.

Mike
Well, it must have been terrifying.

Leigh Ann
I mean, it was right in front of me, it took up all of my windshield. As I entered the left side of the forked road, the song came to the part where there was that strong musical break and then the lyrics "Sail on silver girl." And the song continued, saying your time has come and your dreams are on their way.

Right then I knew that I was going to be okay. I thought to myself, *Oh my God, I'm going to be just fine.*

The following Monday or Tuesday, I was contacted by the assistant of the Department of Epidemiology, and she said that I would be getting my acceptance letter. That part makes me cry. Even after I graduated, the part about me being accepted makes me more emotional than graduating. I mean, it's weird. The assistant specifically mentioned that my score improved by two hundred and fifty points on my exam. Nobody comes up two hundred points, she added. She said, "We know what you have to offer."

I went through the program and in the final semester of spring 2004, during the exam, "Bridge Over Troubled Water" came to me as I was taking the test. It was my Epidemiology 2 final exam. And I knew I was okay. That's what that song said to me. The song said, "You still must do the work. There's stuff here in front of you that will have to be dealt with, but you're going to be okay." I did the work. I took all the exams and graduated. My girlfriends who saw me taking the exam said they could see the light shining down on me. And I told them I could hear "Bridge Over Troubled Water." They were probably kidding, but I know I wasn't, and I believed them. I swear.

That was, I think, the first big one.

I'll continue reading from my journal entry.

On March 2004, I learned that a friend committed suicide, and the second I heard those words, the song "Angel" by Sarah McLachlan popped in my head. I noticed that songs started attaching to certain events or people. When one of my dogs, Xena, passed away in 2005 I heard Elton John's "The Last Song."

Certainly, when meditating or working with crystals, music and tones can be very powerful. My journals, beginning in 2018, are the record of my fabulous dance with music and tones, memories and remembering.

I believe the foundation of music and tones are very central to my life. When I started with all this, I began two different journals, and I wrote down everything: The date, time, what song I was listening to, crystals that I selected. I've tried to capture as much as I can because I don't know what part of this is more important or is this all confounding? I've come to learn it's everything.

I also do have a story that involves extraterrestrials. It was April 16, 2019. I'm listening to the song "Agnus Dei" by Samuel Barber. I have a metatron cube grid cloth, a rose quartz, a selenite round, and four quartz points. I could sense my clairaudience opening.

It looked like a silvery, light gray rectangular box, shimmering, ringing, vibrating outward, then out my ear canals out into the world to know I am ready to receive—and it happens.

There is a tone in my ears. A frequency. Strong but not overwhelming. I sense Arcturian contact made from my left side [Arcturians are a very advanced extraterrestrial civilization from the Arcturus star system who wish to share their knowledge and wisdom with the citizens of Earth. They are described as other-dimensional, advanced star beings]. Midpoints around the center chest curving around my breast, up my left chin, cheek into the surrounding half of my back, above my left ear and crown, anchored in delightful supportive energy. Arcturian energy came in again. Both times I saw a being with a Boba Fett helmet. The being stepped up to be aligned to me.

In one of these contacts, the beings requested that I put my dogs somewhere else in the house. I just said no. I said no because I knew they're going to act up if I put them somewhere else in the house. My dogs don't want to be separated. They'll make noise and whine. I had no contact with the being for a while. I'm sorry if you want to contact me, I thought, but my dogs are here, they'll stay with me.

In time they finally contacted me.

Mike
And how did they contact you?

Leigh Ann
I was sitting in my dining room where I would meditate with my crystals. I sat at my dining room table, and had the crystals in front of me, along with pads of paper and pens. It was April 23, 2019, starting at 10:25 a.m. but I did not write the song down. I was visited by three Arcturians on my front right, sitting in my dining room chairs. They were in front of me. I was asked to bring them some rose petals into the dining room. I went out to my front yard, and I pulled two blooms off my red rose bushes. I brought them back into my dining room, and then I heard, "You heard us ask for the roses."

My clairaudience was kicking in. I had set intention yesterday to connect with spirit guides, higher vibe beings of light, and particularly my Arcturian guides. I could sense them and see them a little.

They were clear with a grayish shimmer. I could see more of the energetic outline of the three extraterrestrials. They were large, quite tall. It seems they were long, slim, and blueish. They stood a little further back from me, like they tried to keep a distance, but I could see it all.

Mike
Clairaudience is like clairvoyance, but it's the audio version of it.

Leigh Ann
Clairvoyance is seeing, and clairaudience is hearing it, and then the claircognizance is like knowing it. Am I hearing this, or do I know it? I can't tell, but whatever it is, I had stuff coming in and it was like I don't know which one it is. I think I was more claircognizance[52], but I had clairaudience happening as well. Yesterday they were closer, and I could hear them more and see them less, but I could sense and see the beings energetically. I could hear sounds. I was listening to music. There's even more in the music. More tones, notes, circular tones, connected, yet not distinguishable.

Here's the third story. I'm going to give a little background on this. I'll start reading from my journal as this story spans decades. In 2022, I started having this feeling that I was on a starship. I did not tell anyone about this until last year when I shared it with Lorilei. I had this sense that I was mostly here, but I was also somewhere else. I was aware that I was somewhere else consciousness-wise. And in going back in and bookmarking all of my journal entries I picked up where, I don't know if it's a past memory or future memory, but I'm on a starship.

I was on the deck, and I got this sense that I was in two places. It was late summer 2022 that it happened, often when I was in my backyard on my back patio. I felt that I had restraints around me. It was more like a suggestion. Not like you can't do that, but kind of like there are certain things that maybe you shouldn't do. I had the feeling that, for example, I had to stay on my patio. When I was on my back patio it was like I was on an aircraft carrier and a starship.

---

52 Claircognizance is a psychic ability that means "clear knowing" or the feeling of knowing something without knowing how. It comes from the French words clair, meaning "clear," and cognizance, meaning "knowledge".

I was told that my role was to be moral support.

On my back patio, I listened to music. I went out there and hummed and listened, giving a horrible concert. Telepathically, I was told that somebody needed to hear this somewhere. My energy was needed, whatever that meant. And I had some profound things come through when standing on my back patio. I was there, yet I was somewhere else. I couldn't really see it, but I could feel it. There are these beings around me. I then realized they've been with me my whole life.

Mike
I've been told by musicians that when you hit the flow state, the audience is with you. What people report is that they all feel like they're flying together, that there's this thing called the flow state and people feel like they're traveling together.

Leigh Ann
Oh my God, that just makes me cry. That's beautiful.

Mike
I don't mean to make you cry, but I felt it was important to tell you.

Leigh Ann
It's now November 14, 2023.

The urge to write was strong upon waking up at 6:00 a.m. yesterday. I was standing and walking around my back patio. I was listening to "How Great Thou Art" sung acapella by Sam Robson. I started singing and humming along with my body and face pointing north. Then I rotated to the east and then to the south, and I took a breath to continue singing.

I heard, "It is time for all my brothers and sisters to come home, it's time for all my brothers and sisters to come home." I sputtered, I cried, I whimpered my singing, my energy. But someone needed to hear this. I didn't know who it was meant for.

I continued to the west and to the north to close the song.

Let me add a couple more songs before this event. I was told to *keep on singing no matter what*. It was like I was providing morale boosting. My voice was needed to comfort, but also to show the realness of humans. Was I in the command spaceship again? I don't know. I was surrounded by a resting troop, not an aggressive or an active engagement, they just listened to me singing and humming. And something weird started happening with the patio area, now my bedroom was also part of that. There were two to three beings in there with me. They just stood there, observing me. They asked me questions telepathically. I thought, "Am I talking to myself?"

Mike
What questions did they ask you?

Leigh Ann
Let's say that I've had some situations that could be very positive, or very bothersome. They would basically say, "Well, how did that make you feel?" Then I just go on and I talk about that situation and all of this. It's almost like I have the "what if" conversations of, "okay, so if that really upsets you, what would you say to that person? What would you do to heal it, work it through?" It's like talk therapy. It's like talking there, and they ask very open-ended questions just to keep flow, to keep talking. And then I realized that I've been doing that my whole life. I'll show you this picture sometime, but as a little girl, I would lie outside in the yard with my dog and my mom would say, "You are talking to the dog again," and I would think, "Umm, I don't think I'm talking to the dog, okay?" And literally until last year talking to Lorilei about all of this, I'm like, "Oh my God, I've been doing this my whole life, and I didn't even know it." No, really, I didn't realize. Anyway, this story involves me, my husband, and one of my very good friends that I have known since kindergarten.

I have known this guy my entire life, and as a matter of fact his mother and my mother worked together, knew each other, and were decently good friends. He does not live near me now.

He's been in the military, we've kept in contact all these years and I've actually had a couple of dreams about him that were very, very intense while he was over in Iraq and Afghanistan. It was to the point that I would think of emailing him and maybe ask, "Where are you?" Some of these dreams would be very unsettling. And weird.

This entry is dated May 8, 2023.

Last night I was in my house with my husband preparing dinner.

I had headphones in while working and the songs played in order. "Pancake" by Jaded, featuring Ashnikko, "When Love Takes Over" by David Guetta with Kelly Rowland, and "Finally" by CeCe Peniston. I've started writing the songs down when I sensed it starting. I feel like I'm in my house. In the kitchen. But there's also a feeling of others around, and my kitchen looks the same, yet I sense other humans? Humanoids? There in my kitchen space. I have in quotes "in the kitchen space with me." I believe they aren't visible exactly, but like a whisper of a form. I know they're there. They'd come and go. Not creepy, only neutral observing. Protecting too. Back to last night's events: I had a sense that my friend, DH, was there, too.

My friend DH and I have had at least a few other lifetimes where we knew each other and I'm not sensing a romantic connection, but one timeline that stands out is where I am on a starship. Living or passing some long amount of time where I am a special guest looked after, cared for. They don't interfere with me. They listen to me. They watch me as if I'm a special guest and I'm more of a curiosity. I'm not captive. I'm revered, but there are boundaries with whom and what I can say.

Last night I felt like I was in two places at once. Or this kitchen, house property, et cetera. How big does this expand? Was I a hologram? After prep work, I decided I needed to finish the laundry. I opened the laundry doors. (My laundry room is just the laundry closet in my hallway.) I have John Denver's "Country Roads" starting to play. Here's what comes in. I think his dad was a military officer. John Denver was an op. I had a flash of his face.

Then it requested that I stop playing this song because the info here is sensitive. My friend DH appears, and he says, "Hold on, this song is from our time, our culture, our memory." After this statement this song was allowed, but there needs to be less people around so that they don't hear it. I don't know who these people were. As I was leaning into the washer to pull the clothes out and place them into the dryer, I felt a jolt in my mind and my body. I mean, it took my breath away. We had at least a few lifetimes together. Not soulmates. Twin flames? It was like a panic attack, like four or five seconds. But now I'm aware that my friend DH was on a detail assigned around me in the spaceship timeline events.

Now here on Earth, in 2023, DH and I have not spoken since December 2021. We had made plans to have lunch around Christmas time. He never showed, and he's done this to me a few times, and I was done. I cut him off after that. We haven't spoken since then, but last night, May 7, 2023, I realized maybe he is upset, or he's bothered by seeing me happy with my husband in this life because he felt a connection with me there and he also knows me here. And it felt like jealousy, sadness. It wasn't harsh, and it wasn't mean or dangerous, but just lonely and brooding and just put off. And that's that.

This is how the songs come to me.

March 11th, two days before we talked. I'm out on my back patio.

I'm listening to some songs and then I get a notion of another song and it's like I can barely hear the melody and I'm like, okay, I know what song it is. I can't name it. I don't know the artist. Let's wait for it to come in. I'm like, black and white, the video is black and white. Okay, it's a man. I can start to hear, and I start humming it. And then the words I get are, "falling into you, into you." Something like that.

That's what I get. Two days later, I'm on my back patio again and I hear "Howie, Howie." I listen to the song and it feels like this is about me and my husband, and I've always liked that song. I'm fond of it, but I guess I've let it go, but I'm listening to the lyrics and it's like, yeah, that's a beautiful song. And then my friend pops in.

His initials are DH. Nickname that he has is Howie. I have never called him that name. To all his other friends and everybody in the military, that was his name.

He popped in again, and then I'm looking at the date. March 13th.

March 13, 1993. During the storm of the century, I almost got snowed in with him. But that song came in and like somehow you [meaning Mike] connect in with that with the collide part.[53]

There's something about the collision part.

And that's all I have of that.

But there's a connection there, and that's how that works.

Mike
Well, we collided into each other, you know, in a way. Through the music. These are all powerful, profound, and I think it's kind of a centerpiece of what will be in the book.

---

53 Collide means "disparate things coming together" in Leigh Ann's lexicon.

UFOS IN MEXICO, 1974

Becky Johnson's Story

I met Becky Johnson, also known as "MrsBlueGrass," through the Peter Rowan Appreciation group I started on Facebook. As with many folks from that group, we've become friends. The group has brought people together from Japan, Slovakia, Australia, Italy, the United Kingdom, and all over the United States.

Becky is originally from Concord, Massachusetts, one town over from Wayland, where Peter Rowan was born. Becky's cousin went to The Fenn School in Concord, a private school that Peter also attended. The connections run deep.

Becky is a bluegrass broadcaster. She began her career as a volunteer at WMMT, 88.7FM, followed by five years at WCOM, 103.3FM in Carrboro, NC. Since 2016, Becky has hosted a weekly live bluegrass/classic country music show, *Panhandle Country* on Hillsborough NC's Community Radio Station, 104.7FM.

In 2021, she emceed an event at the International Bluegrass Music Association (IBMA) Bluegrass Live! festival in Raleigh, North Carolina where was asked to introduce Peter, who was doing a showcase for the event.

It was packed. When she went to the microphone to introduce Peter, he said, "Becky, hold on a second." She stopped. "Introduce yourself," he added, smiling.

Turning back to the audience, Becky said, "Hi, I'm MrsBlueGrass," which was met with laughter and applause.

A resident of Durham, North Carolina since 2013, she is also a vocalist, bassist and professional photographer. In 1998, Becky published a book of her work, *Inside Bluegrass, 20 Years of Bluegrass Photography*.

I'm blessed to see her colorful and imaginative artwork posted on Facebook. She and her husband Art, who is one of the founders of the IBMA, are a treasure to the bluegrass community. Art became their first volunteer in 1986, and their first Executive Directorand served on the board as well. Presently he runs "Art Menius Radio Services" connecting clients to Folk Radio stations in the US & Canada.

The following is a story that Becky related to me in late February 2024.

> In the summer of 1974, I planned to fly alone to Mexico City. However, I spent the night at a hotel since my flight was canceled. I took a horrendous thirteen-hour bus trip! It was awful.
>
> Early the next morning, I was awoken by a full Mariachi Band. They serenaded me for, what seemed like, an eternity.
>
> I stayed out in the country in a hut built by my brother, Sam. It was fun for a few days, but I didn't speak Spanish and I got depressed and homesick. Sam took me to the Zocalo in Oaxaca where Americans gathered and hung out. It was wonderful. I was invited to a birthday party somewhere where a guy had built himself a castle. The castle, small and made of brick turrets, was nearly completed but he had run out of money. It looked a little funny as a result. It stood a story high.
>
> There was spectacular weed passing around. This hippy girl became a happy girl as the night wore on.
>
> Out of nowhere, a line of bright lights caught our attention! The lights were silent even as they got closer to us.
>
> Then, as suddenly as they appeared, the lights were gone! Disappearing into the blackness. We were all freaked! Next, a series of small single lights greeted us, blue and gold. They too appeared to brighten intensely and then zip off faster than anything I'd

ever seen before or since. SILENT! No noise except for us all going, "Far out man! Did you see that?" It was fascinating, eerie, and amazing. It's been cool to watch many shows and documentaries on UFOs—they all say more or less the same things: Faster than the speed of light. Totally quiet!

DUETS IN LOCKDOWN

When COVID-19 devastated the world, we all retreated to our homes. Living in a small Brooklyn apartment in New York City, my wife, Arielle, my younger son, Travis, and I saw the world get very small. It shrank to the size of a box when everything shut down. Stores, schools, and businesses. I have to admit, it was scary.

We had only each other. We were all each other's playmates. We bicycled to Brooklyn's Prospect Park and played football or frisbee catch. Sometimes my older son, Thelonious, now living away from home, joined us. There were other families too, but they played safe distances apart. It all seemed so strange.

At night, we hung out in our kitchen nook, until Travis eventually escaped to play computer games. The nook has benches instead of chairs. They resemble pews in church. We made short films mocking the Trump COVID conferences. We played card games. We talked. And we played music.

As I played guitar in the nook, Arielle and I had begun singing harmonies. Arielle has a gift for harmonies. More often than not, she comes up with pretty harmony parts, whereas mine are basic and unremarkable.

I started venturing into Beatles songs, always an intimidating territory for me until then. Who could match John, Paul and George's sophisticated three-part harmonies and beautiful voices? Who would try?

Singing "All My Loving," Arielle took Paul's part, and I took John's. When the different melodies come together, the two voices sound better, fuller. Without thinking about it, we started alternating parts. Sometimes I took Paul's, and she took John's, then we switched back.

"Let's do another song," I said.

Arielle was a little resistant. She had to be pulled out of her comfort zone.

When our two voices come together, for a moment, our beings become bigger than the apartment. When two voices become one, it's as if something else manifests. Perhaps you can call it the Other. The voices swim into each other, creating a new stream of being. I love making this magic happen and often ask Arielle to join me in harmonies. She doesn't seem to get the same thrill I get out of it. But I know other people do. We sing harmonies in part to please others but also to please ourselves.

During the height of COVID, after a night of singing, I sat in the kitchen nook alone. Arielle and Travis were nowhere to be found; I guess I'd worn them out.

I strummed my guitar, then put it down and picked up the glass of whiskey sitting on the table. In the quiet of the night, I saw my body leave the kitchen and slip into the sky like a bird. High above the trees, I looked down on the deserted streets. I swooped into people's apartments. But these weren't our houses. I don't know where these apartments were. It looked like a universe that resembled ours but wasn't ours.

I saw an old man, wispy gray hairs on his face, sleeping on his couch, spit dripping down his chin. I saw a couple, having just argued, retreating into different rooms in their apartment. I saw a baby in a crib, alone, crying. There was a heavy sadness lingering in the air that I moved in. When I snapped back into my reality, I was still alone at the kitchen table. It was late at night and everyone was asleep.

SPOOKINESS AT A DISTANCE
James Faulk's Story

James Faulk lives in Eureka, California. I met James when I was a guest on his *Neon Galactic* podcast in March 2024. I came on the program to discuss my book *For All We Know*. James and I immediately connected. I told James about my new book project, *UFO Symphonic*, and he said that he had a story to contribute. The following is James's story as emailed to me in May 2024.

> In mid-July of 2002, a group of friends and I were crammed into a small studio apartment in Eureka, CA, all of us strumming acoustic guitars and practicing vocal harmonies.
>
> My friend, Andy Cunningham, is blind, and so to provide extra security for his pride and joy, he had an expensive locking mechanism installed on his Ovation guitar. Basically, it was meant to keep the strap attached and protect the instrument.
>
> At one point, in the midst of a song, this locking mechanism suddenly came loose. He hadn't moved, or shifted, in any way, and he kept the strap on the guitar at all times. Yet somehow it suddenly popped off the body of his guitar, and the tuning head crashed to the floor, snapping the guitar's neck and causing an explosive ruckus.
>
> At the same time, the drapes over the apartment's one window seemed to flutter, though the window was closed, and we all experienced a strange sense of foreboding, which we attributed to the rather emotional loss of a favorite instrument. It was a heavy and sorrowful moment. Afterward, no one was in the mood to continue playing, so we packed up and left.

At the time, I was a reporter for the Eureka Times-Standard, and when I arrived at work the next morning, I was greeted by a frenzy of activity. The previous evening, there had been a murder only two or three blocks away from where we'd been rehearsing.

An older woman had lain in wait for an acupuncturist, Kevin LaPorta, and attacked him as he crossed a parking lot. She shot him once, then followed him into a nearby Chinese restaurant, where she killed him in the kitchen as he begged for his life. LaPorta was trying to win custody of his young daughter, and the girl's grandmother—Diana May Preston—was convinced that he'd molested the girl.

DNA evidence had just that day exonerated LaPorta of the crime, but Preston hadn't believed those results, and murdered him.

As best I could tell, the times matched up perfectly—right at the time that LaPorta was shot and killed, Andy's instrument had somehow come loose from its locked connector and smashed into the floor. I can still remember the awful sound. In my thirty years of playing music, I'd never seen such a thing, and coupled with the palpable sense of foreboding we all experienced, to me those events are inextricably linked.

Can I prove it? No. Is it necessarily supernatural? Not by a long shot. But it was an impactful experience that, at least to me, hinted at a layer of deep and complex connectivity.

Could this be a coincidence? Even James writes that it could be a coincidence. Was it strange? It certainly was. And that's where I'll leave it.

SAN PEDRO

San Pedro, also known as Wachuma, is a sacred cactus native to the Andean mountains of Peru, Bolivia, and Ecuador. Along with tobacco, ayahuasca, and coca, San Pedro has been used for thousands of years to expand consciousness and provide medicinal healing.

With the diaspora of various world populations, these sacred plants have become increasingly available to those living outside native communities. I have friends in California who grow San Pedro in their backyard. Apparently, it is legal to grow San Pedro plants, but it is not legal to consume or distribute in the United States.

Given the legal complexities of San Pedro, I will use fictitious names for the folks involved in the ceremony I'm about to describe.

I have a good friend from Brooklyn, who is a Taíno chief, whom I'll call Carlos. Carlos told me that a family of shamans from Bolivia were coming to New York to hold a San Pedro ceremony. The ceremony would be held in upstate New York, near the Catskill Mountains.

I was informed that the event would start in the evening, last all night, and conclude in the morning. We would need a babysitter for Travis, who was then about eleven years old.

I got in contact with the woman who was organizing the event, whom I'll call Victoria. She asked me if I could take two other people with us in our car.

We arrived at about 7:00 p.m. Since it was summer, the sun was still out.

Dressed in Gap pants and a collared shirt, I felt a bit conservative compared to the other folks, who were dressed in rainbow-colored hippie outfits. None of them looked like Deadheads. Their hip clothes suggested expensive boutiques on the Upper West Side of Manhattan. Most of them were in their thirties; I was an elder in this group.

Everyone was very friendly. Many of them knew each other. Wearing a breezy dress that hung loosely on her very thin body, Victoria greeted me in a lovely Ecuadorian accent.

As the night came on, Arielle worried about Travis. Was he okay? Of course he was, but we had never left him overnight and never to attend a ritual like this.

We met the shamans who would run the ceremony, three brothers—Juan, Benny, and Joaquin. They stood apart from the group, preparing the San Pedro drink and infused berry mix, talking amongst themselves, perhaps to keep a little distance before the ceremony.

At about 11:00 p.m., the ceremony commenced. Each of the brothers had a different task. Juan, thin and handsome, was the main speaker. He spoke in Spanish, phrasing his words like a poet, often holding a tobacco leaf and stroking it as he soliloquized. Benny, who translated from Spanish to English, had bushy hair and was chubby. He had a permanent smile on his face and was very funny. Joaquin, who was stout and bearded, maintained the fire all night, sometimes with help from others. The dynamic between the brothers was fascinating. They sat in the center of a circle the rest of us formed.

The ceremony began with the pounding of drums. There were different kinds of drums and sticks used to bang on the animal hides that covered them. The drums were hit with rapid and thunderous thuds.

The drumming was then accompanied by singing and chanting. Some of the chanting was in an indigenous language, some of it was in Spanish. One of the singers, a woman who I learned later was not indigenous, sang in beautiful harmonies.

Juan spoke. "We are family. All of us here. We are here to learn from the sacred plants. They are our teachers. We are only the students," he said, running his index finger and thumb along a tobacco leaf. As he spoke, he sometimes smoked the tobacco, then blew the smoke towards the circle, moving the air around with his hands. Benny translated all the while.

"This tobacco is sacred. Our family has cultivated this tobacco for hundreds of years. It has acquired the wisdom of the soil. The wisdom of our people. We bring it to you to share its knowledge." He added that this tobacco was given to Carlos, who would now cultivate it in his garden in upstate New York.

After the blessing, there was more chanting. Complete darkness swept in. Sitting in the folding chairs we were told to bring, Arielle and I sometimes held hands and smiled at each other. If we had to pee, they said, do not go too far away from the circle. There were bears in the area.

The rhythmic drumming continued. It was beginning to get very hypnotic. Joaquin continued stoking the fire, moving the burnt embers off to the side. Sometimes he got precariously close to the fire.

Now the San Pedro drink was handed to us, the way a catholic priest hands you the wafer in church. Except the San Pedro was administered in paper Dixie cups. Juan continued. "Now, I ask you to hold in your mind a picture of the earth. Think of the mother who takes care of us all."

Benny translated, adding a quip that it wasn't just your mother; it was the mother of all beings. The lightness of his humor was greatly appreciated. With bears potentially a few feet away from us, the beach chairs that we brought now getting a little uncomfortable, Benny's quips gave Juan's lofty poetic speeches some levity. Arielle and I drank the San Pedro. It tasted like soil mixed with berries and tobacco, like a smoothie made of earth.

"Make sure to drink everything in the cup," we were told.

As the drumming and chanting continued, we were each handed clumps of San Pedro in a napkin, which was more solid than liquid. I ate as much as I could. Again, it wasn't easy to imbibe and get down. I did the best I could.

We were told to keep napkins nearby as we might vomit. After about three rounds of administering San Pedro, I began to feel a shimmery presence. The Other. Or was that just me? The Other looked like a ball of luminous light. It was white, with purple and reddish color. It reminded me of pictures of nebulae from the James Webb Space Telescope.

Meanwhile, Joaquin, using a poker, pushed burnt embers to the side, adding new wood to the fire. He was crying, tears rolling down his face. I was certain that the flames were burning his skin.

With San Pedro in our blood, Arielle started to choke a bit. She was getting nauseous. Other people were throwing up. There was a lot of regurgitation and choking all around us. Somehow, luckily, I wasn't vomiting or nauseous. In the darkness, I continued to see orbs of light floating around me. I began to feel very emotional. I was thinking about my in-laws. The fact is, they hadn't been very welcoming to me in the thirteen or so years since I'd been with Arielle. The Other was asking me to forgive them. I was also thinking about my sick mother, whose cognition had deteriorated. The plant emphasized compassion and love.

The night continued with Juan's eloquent speeches, Benny's comic translations and Joaquin's intense crying while he tended the fire. I was certain now that he was getting burned by the flames, but I didn't see any burn marks on him. His behavior seemed like an act of penance. While Juan dwelled in the elevated world of wise words, as Benny smiled and delivered jokes to leaven his brother's heady wisdom, Joaquin suffered for us all. It reminded me of Dante: Paradiso, Purgatorio, and Inferno. All of this played out while the drumming and chanting continued. Fortunately, Arielle's nausea lifted.

She and I went about thirty feet toward the trees to pee. As I stood there, a gentle breeze blowing across my face, I hoped I wasn't going to be mauled by a bear. Arielle crouched a few feet away.

Back in our beach chairs, the San Pedro in full steam, I followed the rhythm of the drums taking me on a journey. It wasn't quite like the psychedelic experience I'd had on mescaline or LSD. It was gentler. And with Juan's wise words, I was taken to the center of my heart, where I felt an abiding love for all things.

When the morning came, with light suddenly flooding the camp, we were all in various states of consciousness. Some of us were coming out of the journey, some of us were still there. Birdsong swelled around us welcoming the day. Above the chorus of voices, one of the birds made a sound like a laugh. We all laughed. It was as if the bird was poking fun at us. *Silly humans.*

We all then went to the river to freshen up. Everyone was in bikinis or speedos. As most of the people there were young and slim, they looked sexy. The near nakedness was a little flirtatious. I wished I hadn't worn boxer shorts. I felt a little corny and was almost tempted to take all my clothes off.

Later we returned to the camp, cleaned up the site, and drove home, first dropping off the two men we had brought with us.

ALIENS LIKE BLUEGRASS
Mark Turner's Story

With the publication of my book *For All We Know*, I began to hear from people who wanted to share their UFO narratives. Some of the contacts were suspicious. I trusted my gut to decide whether to respond. It's not that I didn't believe people's stories. When people have contact experiences, they are often traumatized, sometimes previous to their experience.

After posting something about *For All We Know* on Facebook, Mark Turner reached out to me saying that he had a "music contact story." I realized I'd seen his name on a documentary called *Encounters*, which features contact accounts in direct interview format. Mark and I met on a web call. The following is the transcript.

Mark Turner
I have had a lifetime of experiences, a lot of which I sort of discounted I guess, until about this one time ten years ago. I faced something and was fully conscious realizing, okay, this is not something I've been dreaming of. It's not been my imagination. This is actually happening, you know.

I think that it was like over eight or nine months, I guess, where things kind of progressed in this particular case where I came to the realization that I'm an Experiencer and I've been interacting with these other beings. Since you're talking about musical slant, this actually happened at a musical event. I was deeply engaged with the festival. This was Raleigh's very first year of hosting the International Bluegrass Festival. This is September 2013. There are open stages scattered downtown. Tons of people. People were coming from all over to see these great musical acts and everybody was just vibing really well. You know, it was a really fun day and towards the end of the night, some of the headliner acts were getting ready to play in the Red Hat Amphitheater, which I think has about a 5,000-seat capacity or something like that.

We sat down at the very top of the amphitheater, the grassy area, as there weren't even many seats left.

We're sitting there, it has been a beautiful, sunny day. It was now a bit windy with really high overcast clouds. Like there was a weather front sort of passing through, I guess. We're just slightly right of center of the stage.

The Steep Canyon Rangers and Steve Martin were performing and they were either on stage or getting ready to play. My wife suddenly noticed something just off to the right of the stage and pointed to it, showing me. I'm looking over there and there's at least a half-dozen of these amber orbs that are just kind of dancing just above the horizon, going from right to left from where we were. That would be north to south, I guess, in a real direction.

And I look at them and I'm going, that is really odd. You know, I don't know why there would be that many planes flying in a weird formation like that. And I started to think, okay, well, it's not planes. Are they flares? Is it, you know, helicopters? Or maybe Chinese lanterns?

I told my wife that those aren't aircraft. That's something very unusual and I think that as the show went on that they sort of went out of sight, but it stayed in the back of my mind obviously and I was very curious. So, I wanted to run down all the potential explanations. The next day I called up the city's 911 center and I asked, "Did anybody report any weird lights in downtown Raleigh?" The dispatcher said, "No, we haven't had any reports like that." I called the fire department because they had fireworks that night, after the concert. I asked, "Did you launch any flares before you did the fireworks?" And the representative said, "No, we didn't." I was a very avid blogger at the time, and so I posted something on my blog about flares in downtown Raleigh just to see if anybody had seen those too. And nobody ever actually stepped up. But of course, when I made those calls, I knew for sure that they weren't flares. I couldn't think of anything explainable, but I didn't want to freak people out right away. I wasn't as comfortable talking about this stuff back then as I am now!

Fast forward a couple months. I think it was January, one Saturday morning. I'm going off to meet my family for breakfast downtown. I pull up to this one intersection. It was about 8:00 o'clock in the morning. As it was January, the sun didn't come up until later (though it was already fairly light), but I'm sitting here at this traffic light. I'm realizing that directly in front of me between these houses is a fiery red sort of light behind them. I notice that there is a kind of cylindrical object above the light? It's almost like The Bean sculpture in Chicago. That really shiny sort of thing, and it was very mirror-like at the bottom. I could see that it was super shiny but on the top it was glowing fire. I checked the time and I realized that the sun had not yet come up and I couldn't really explain why that thing was there. It was almost over a local historical cemetery which is right behind that neighborhood. But again, I kind of tucked that in the back of my mind and continued on to my breakfast 'cause by that time I was late, like I normally am.

Moving onto March, March 28, 2014. I was watching some videos on YouTube that day and there was one sequence showing all the scenes that Christopher Walken has been in. It's a whole collection of them. And one of those was the scene he did from Whitley Strieber's film *Communion*. He's dancing there with aliens.

I think it stayed in my mind. But you know, I went on with my workday and went to bed sometime after 10 p.m. And then that night, I think it was about 1:00 a.m. I'm not honestly sure about the time, but it was a hot evening as far as March goes. I think it was like 60°F outside. It was a little misty, and we still had the comforter on our mattress. I'm lying in bed. I'm very hot, the comforter is not really needed that night. At some point in the evening, I become aware that there's something in the bedroom with us. I'm wide awake. I realize I cannot move anything but my eyes and about six feet away from me towards the door was this dark shape. Now it was a dark room. I couldn't really make out a ton of features—people have asked me. What did I see? It was a creature, or being, about 3 1/2 feet tall, and it had a light-bulb-shaped head that I could make out in the dark and really big black eyes. At that moment my wife is sleeping right next to me. I can hear her breathing and all I wanted to do was to give her a shove and say, "Hey, look, I'm not making this stuff up," right? I need her to see that these things actually exist, but try as I might, I could not move. I wanted to shout, just to say, "Hey, do something" and all I could muster was a whimper.

Just a really pathetic sounding whimper.

That's the only thing that my throat could do. She kept sleeping, but I recall distinctly the sound of my whimpering echoing through the bedroom in a way that convinced me that I wasn't asleep. I did actually make that noise. At that point I realized that it's just me and it or him or her or whatever it is. And as I recall the story, I like to say that it was one of the loneliest feelings I've ever had. This thing somehow got into my house, past my alarm system, past my dog, and did not wake me up until it was in the room. I didn't understand how that happened. I've got some ideas now, but I felt very lonely at that moment and the next thing I know and all this sort of gets a little fuzzy at this point, I went somewhere with this being. I think I actually went through my bedroom wall. I have scenes of sitting in a chair, their faces above me. They're doing some kind of operation on me, and they are working on my spine, my lower spine, and something they did to me caused searing pain. I couldn't forget that part.

First, I'd like to describe the feeling I had when I was in the chair. It's very much like when you go to a dentist or a doctor and they're doing stuff and you're kind of compliant, right? You don't necessarily pay a lot of attention. It was almost like you self-hypnotize and you're just sitting there daydreaming while they do their work. That was the feeling I had, but when I felt that pain, whatever hypnosis or trance or something that I was in just ended right away. And that pain brought me right out of it. And I start cursing at him. *What the hell are you doing? You know you're supposed to be these masters of the universe and my dog has more empathy than you do. You know,* I said, *how did you know that didn't hurt? Why couldn't you know that would hurt me.* But even before that, I telepathically told them, *You're hurting me. Please stop.* Then I did the cursing. Somehow, I knew that they would hear me in my mind, and afterwards I was thinking about that and asked myself, *How did I know that would work?* Maybe this is not the first time this kind of thing has happened, but to their credit, whatever they were doing, they stopped right away, and I don't think they were trying to hurt me.

I had other visions where they were poking me with things I didn't like. I remember some kind of pencil-sized fiber optic thing that I don't really understand and all this imagery sort of came rushing back to me when I woke up in the morning. After they brought me back into bed, I just went back to sleep like nothing happened. You would think that if I've had a terrifying nightmare, or a terrifying experience—either one—that I would have been wired and bouncing off the wall, but it was just like it was no big deal. And the next morning, I'm sitting around the table with my family, and I was like, I think I got abducted last night and everybody's like, *Yeah, sure Dad,* you know, *Can you pass the grapes* or whatever? So I didn't really know who to talk to about that, but it was definitely undeniable. And that was one of my first tastes of the stuff that I think I've kind of been "dreaming," you know.

Mike
Was it scary? Were you terrified?

Mark
That's a good question. In the morning when I was writing all this down in my journal, documenting as much as I could, I re-

alized I was far braver than I actually was when it was happening. Before I realized that it was just him or me, and my wife wasn't gonna be able to help me. I remember saying to myself over and over again, "I don't want to see this! I don't want to see this!" and I think I was terrified. I don't think that fear carried through. Whatever happened that night, I think by the time I was in the chair, I was fairly willing to let them do whatever they needed to do. I felt calmer until that pain hit. And then that kind of snapped me out of stuff. And then I just got mad. But I'll be the first to say that I was probably terrified.

Mike
Interesting that you had events leading up to the Bluegrass festival. Can you tell me about what events or what was happening leading up to that?

Mark
It's not that I've been really focused on UFOs or anything. The incidents that preceded, I think, were a kind of preparation, letting me know that they were in the area and that I should expect something to happen. I've had ten years to reflect on this. I think that they don't often just show up out of the blue. I think they will leave clues a day or two before something happens to kind of let me know that they're going to be around. It could have been that they were just kind of fishing, seeing who would be curious about what they were doing. But many people have noted the consciousness aspect of sightings, whether it be UFOs or ETs when people are observing them. And certainly, there is telepathic communication. When that being was in my room, I felt like my mind was an open book. That is very frightening when you are not used to having people invade your mind like that. It's a very weird feeling.

Mike
I can imagine and that's a ubiquitous thing, this telepathic communication and the sense of intentionality. So, this thing, it seems to be in communication with the Experiencer.

Mark
Thinking about that in some of the dreams I had as a kid and some of the things that I thought I might have seen, it all seemed to be like they had a very long-term investment in me. And this probably goes back until at least I was seven years old. Perhaps when the familiarity sort of hit when I was in the chair, maybe that part was more of a familiar experience to me because perhaps I've dealt with some of those particular beings in the past. But I was still just pretty much frightened.

Mike
I could see that being frightening and the way you described it is very much like the face on the *Communion* book cover and the big eyes.

Mark
You know, it drove me to realize that it wasn't just my imagination, that I kind of had the Hollywood view previously about what aliens looked like, and I expected them to be tall and spindly, almost like 5–6 feet tall. And to find something that was short and yet that powerful.

Mike
Have you read Kathleen Marden's book *Forbidden Knowledge*?

Mark
That's one thing on my list.

Mike
It's quite good and you will relate to it as she and her friends are in communication with this council of beings, beings who have different levels of energy, different vibrational levels. The most powerful one is exploding with energy, you can't even be near him because it's too hot. People feel sweaty in their presence. Electrical things stop working.

Mark
I had a previous sighting in 2006. It was December 26th, the day after Christmas. I was sitting in my den one day reading Ingo Swann's book, *Penetration*. I had downloaded a copy off

the Internet. I was fascinated by it. I'm still not entirely convinced that everything happened the way he described it. But it's a book about aliens. It was about 3:00 p.m. Beautiful, sunny day. Wind was blowing strongly. I had been taking pictures that morning of this hawk that had been hanging out in my backyard. I had my camera out. The hawk was probably 20–30 feet behind my house in the trees and I just thought it was really cool that we had this nice bird that was visiting. I put my book down as I got up deciding I would go refill the bird feeder that was on the window. Maybe because I thought the hawk needed to eat or something. I don't know, but I went outside and the feeder was on the upper part of a window well above my head, and so I had to get this pole out in order to unlatch it and bring it down. I'm sitting there at my window in my backyard, looking up at the feeder as I'm trying to unhook it. All of a sudden I see something floating straight toward me right in my field of vision, and I kind of stopped with my bird feeder, and I'm looking at it.

And then I went through the list again of things that I can rule out. Are those birds? No. Is it an airplane? No. It's flying too slow and it doesn't have the same shape. Helicopter? Balloon? No. I went through my list of stuff and eventually I said that's a UFO. It had drifted behind the trees and I couldn't see it anymore, and at that point I just beat myself up because my camera with my telephoto lens is just 25 feet away, and if I'd had enough time I could have snapped some pictures of that thing. But it was weird. I wanted to call it like a flying squirrel. It had several points to it, like a blowfish or something. It was charcoal colored and didn't make any sound. I think it was probably 500 feet off the ground. Afterwards I'm thinking about the odds that I'm reading a book about ET and UFOs and all this, and then one flies right over my house in a position right where I was destined to see it. And I thought, that can't be a coincidence. It just honestly can't be a coincidence. I've seen similar kinds of craft in several UFO videos. I found that they fly over Mexico on a regular basis. In Colombia, there's a famous video by a cargo pilot. Specifically flying over the city of Medellín.

He's a 737 pilot. He's videoing this black sort of beach-ball-looking thing. Almost charcoal. And I was like, that is exactly what I saw flying over my house. I'm not alone I guess in that and again it had the points to it like it was a, it was a blowfish or an old World War II mine, you know that has all the different points around the sphere. That was interesting, but I thought why did it want me to see it? And from that point on, I started to think, well, you know, they want me to know that they're around.

Mike
Do you know Mike Clelland, by the way? He's a writer and he wrote a book on UFOs and owls, and he has collected stories from people all over the world. In your case it was a hawk.

Mark
At my house, it was kind of rare that it was there, so that was kind of interesting, that something I don't really see was there and it got my attention.

Mike
It was calling you.

Mark
Probably so.

And I do have a theory that I've been thinking about that maybe people who are caring for wild animals like putting out bird feeders, taking care of gardens or whatever might be more interesting to the visitors. Maybe just filling in my bird feeder wasn't just a convenient excuse to get me outside and look out in the sky. Maybe that's something that they look for.

I also had some other experiences after the 2006 one. I had a series of dreams. I called them dreams because I know that I didn't actually go anywhere, but they were almost like lucid dreams in that I was awakened and aware of them. I was in these circular rooms.

It was almost set up like a classroom, and there were beings there that were teaching me how to do things, like telekinesis. I was trying to move something with my mind and watching it go around.

You know, whatever room I was in I remember turning to somebody next to me and asking, "You need to tell me, is this something that I can do in the daytime?" And they said yes.

And of course, when I woke up, I'm like, that's just a stupid dream and I haven't actually been able to do any kind of telekinesis, but it certainly seemed real at the time.

So it happened for several nights and I recorded all those in my dream journal, there's some interesting information in there. Another thing they tried to do to work with me was overcoming fear. They would put me in situations where I would have to trust them and worked with me over and over again.

After the sighting, I had a bunch of alien dreams that followed.

I had something recently about maybe two to three years ago that was very interesting. It ties back into my whole music connection with UFO sightings/experiences. That morning, it was in the early spring, probably about this time of year, maybe April. My wife helps organize these conferences for her work and she travels the state, and she goes to various hotels and sets these up for a couple of days at a time. She had one at the North Carolina coast that she was going to go to. And I was able to work remotely and so I decided to join her. I'd go hang out at the hotel while she did her business meetings, and then we would come back to Raleigh. It was about a two-hour drive from Raleigh down to the North Carolina coast. It was a beautiful morning. Actually, before we drove out there, we were rushing to get out the door because she had a ten o'clock appointment. It's probably like, I don't know, nine o'clock or something. And we're really in danger of being late. She's in the other room. I'm in the kitchen. I turn on the light switch as I'm walking out the door and something weird happens.

We have these recessed lights in our kitchen, like a lot of homes do now, and there's five of them on this circuit. But I flipped the switch and only two of them came on. And I said to myself, wait a second, put the switch on again. Same thing happened. I'm kind of an amateur electrician. I've done a little bit of wiring in the house. I know how electricity works and I could not explain why I would flip a switch and only some of the lights on this circuit would come on and the others didn't. So I flip the switch a few times; sometimes a different pattern of lights would come on, which absolutely didn't make any sense.

But I'm looking at this and by this time we're already late. I don't have time to troubleshoot. I was just hoping the house wouldn't burn down while we were gone. So we went to the hotel. She's inside talking with the staff. I'm sitting out on the patio facing the water. It's a beautiful day. There are people around. There's a cafe nearby, people walking back and forth in front of me. At one point I look up and I notice there's a very strange, very odd-looking person who I took to be a woman walking in front of me. And there's one of the hotel staffers, a big guy. There didn't seem to be anything unusual about him. He seemed to be helping her along. She was wearing what looked like a 1980s-era jumpsuit, almost like parachute pants kind of thing. Really sort of like a synthetic fiber kind of hot-pink-looking thing that, you know, you would expect a grandma from the 1980s to wear. This was really odd. She was about five feet tall or something and had an unusually shaped head. But more than that, she was wearing a bicycle helmet. She didn't have a bicycle, nor did she have a walker. I'm not sure why she was wearing a helmet, but she also had on really big dark glasses that covered up most of her face. And she's shuffling along directly in front of me. And I thought afterwards was that helmet for real or was it maybe hiding a funny-shaped head or something? And why was this person wearing this crazy outfit that is so horribly outdated? And then I thought back to that morning and how the lights in my house were malfunctioning and it made me wonder, maybe these two things are connected. Maybe I'm looking at somebody who isn't necessarily human.

Right after that happened, I got a phone call. At that point, I had started doing these karaoke songs during the pandemic because I wanted to have some outlet for my creativity. I had put my hat out there looking for a band that I wanted to join and that morning I got a phone call from the people in the band saying, *Hey, would you like to come and*, you know, *audition for us?* And so that also happened that morning. And I think all three of those things were connected.

Afterwards when I rehearsed, I would set up a camera during our rehearsal to record the songs and try to figure out how we could make our music better. And I kept noticing these orbs flying all around the room while we were singing, and I thought there's something there that is paying close attention to what's going on. I can't say for sure, but it seems to me that I was encouraged to take that step. There's a lot of life lessons you get when you're a musician and you put yourself out there, getting in front of a crowd. You know, trusting that things are going to go right. As a kid I was very shy. I didn't want to stand out at all. Here I am lead singer for a band and a lot has changed and it's been very, very helpful for me. But that's a very strange morning, and I have never before had those lights act up the way they did that morning, and they've never done that since. And I cannot, today, explain how all that happened and why it just happened to be that morning.

Mike
Based on what you described about the garden, I thought of Jack Hunter, who's written many books on the Phenomena. One is called *Greening the Paranormal*. He's become a friend. Jack writes about cultivating gardens to invite nonhuman beings into your domain. They may come as the fey people. They may come as angels or spirits. These things often change according to our culture and who we are, and we see them through the lens of our cultural bias and context.

Mark
You're taking care of nature. I think they like to see people who take care of nature.

Mike

And there is that connection. People often say that there is a communication to the effect of *You're ruining the planet. Take care of the planet.* They're intervening. They're coming to help make us aware of that.

Mark

I've continued to have some visits. I've had neighbors who filmed strange lights over my house about the time frame that things have been happening with me. And the music thing is interesting. I think another thing that caught my attention was a post on Reddit. In some of their UFO forums, there was some guy who I think had the username of Throwaway Alien, but he posted something about aliens and one thing he mentioned was something about how aliens like bluegrass music and that caught my eye. Because one of the major sightings I had was at a bluegrass festival. I reached out to him. I said tell me more about this whole bluegrass connection. He's like, *Well, you know, I was just kind of making a lot of that stuff up.* But I was like, *Well, that's possible, but it did catch my attention* and I think intuitively that they do a lot of things with sound. And I think there's a lot of interesting things that can be done with sound that they know how to do. And so it would not surprise me if they didn't appreciate music in some way.

But that's just a hunch. There's only so much I remember from my experiences, and I'm sure there's a lot more to it, but it is just a nice little theory to hang on to. I think that we probably are some of the rare people in the universe—we who make music. Maybe that's something that attracts them. I would imagine that you don't find that very much in the rest of the universe. Maybe I'm wrong. Who knows? It's a big universe.

Mike

The book I'm writing is about the ubiquity of sound in the universe, that there's vibration and sound, you know, from pulsars, to oceans, trees, birds, and insects rubbing their limbs together. That the universe is just kind of noisy. What humans do is create structured sound. We structure notes in time, and it conjures emotions in other people. Not to mention the synchronicities that occur from music. You saw something at a bluegrass festival and that became pivotal for you. Not to mention that bluegrass is just great music.

Mark
I know what some of these bluegrass musicians can do. So I've got a lot of respect for them. And music helps unite people, right? If you play in a band, you are having to think with your other musicians and everybody kind of locks into sync in that way. Music can stir emotion in people. It can bring us to tears. It can make people happy. Or angry. Then there are binaural beats, like what the Monroe Institute does with Hemi-Sync[54]. Sound can put you in a different state of consciousness, so there's a lot that that music and sound can do for you.

Mike
And I've been exploring binaural beats, and I've been going to this gong therapy, gong yoga thing, and then there's other things like sound bowls and all of that. Robert Monroe was having communications with people with his nonhuman intelligence who were saying much of what you talked about, for example, taking care of the planet. And they even had a sense of humor the way Robert Monroe describes. Once you start investigating what the binaural beats are and gongs and sound bowls, they bring you somewhere.

Mark
Yeah, hard to say, but they definitely have an effect. They can elicit a response from you.

Mike
Music, sound, gives us access to these dimensions that suffuse our own. There's something in music in that matrix. I think there's an Intelligence. Music changes our emotions, connects us.

---

54 Hemi-Sync is short for Hemispheric Synchronization, also known as brainwave synchronization. Monroe indicated that the technique synchronizes the two hemispheres of one's brain, thereby creating a 'frequency-following response' designed to evoke certain effects.

When I play with another musician, that's a form of telepathy. How do we know what each other is going to do and we have those flow moments. We all know when it happens. The musicians, and the audience knows it. Nothing's better than music.

Mark
Can't get any better, yep. Well, I'm excited about the project. I can't wait to read it.

UFO VISIONS
Massimo Teordorani's Story

I met Massimo Teordorani through a series of shared Facebook connections. Some of these relationships spawned from my writing for the Psychedelic Press, a publisher based in the UK through which I've gotten to know many people in the UK and around the world. Although Massimo and I had been "friends" on Facebook, I read about Massimo's UFO data work in Ryan Sprague's book, *Somewhere in the Skies*.

From what I'd read about him, I knew that Massimo is a scientist, with a degree in astronomy and a PhD in stellar physics from the University of Bologna. From his website, I learned that Massimo had published several informative articles on quantum physics, atomic and nuclear physics, astronomy, astrophysics, bioastronomy, the physics of anomalous atmospheric phenomena, human consciousness, and aerospace subjects. He's also a musician.

A few weeks after I did the deep dive into his website, Massimo posted a link to an original electronic piece he had composed called "DMT Shining," which I loved. It was like the phone was ringing, Massimo was calling me, and I had to answer. Like picking up signals from a distant star or UFO.

Massimo's compositional style was influenced by the Berlin School of classical electronic music, an offshoot of Krautrock, which is often described as "spacey," "dreamy," or "psychedelic." Some of the pioneering Berlin school musicians had their musical roots in '60s psychedelic rock. Massimo uses the pseudonym Totemtag to publish his electronic music.

There were too many roads leading me to Massimo. I had to reach out to him and ask him if he would talk about how the UFO Phenomena relates to his music. We arranged to meet on a video call.

It was early December 2023. Sitting at his desk, wearing a knitted sweater, Massimo looked like Umberto Eco. His perfect English made it unnecessary for me to stumble through my poor Italian. However, he wasn't familiar with the non-standard Neapolitan dialect I heard growing up. In Italy, the north and the south are like two different countries.

"In Bologna, we have our own dialect too," he admitted.

As we spoke, I scanned the wall behind him. I couldn't help but ask Massimo about the photos above his desk.

"This is called the Witch's Nebula because it looks like a witch. And this one," he said, pointing to the other photo, "is called the Pillar of Creation. These are from the Space Telescope. Today you can get much better pictures from the Webb Telescope."

The Pillar of Creation shows stars forming within dense clouds of gas and dust. The three-dimensional pillars look like majestic rock formations but are far more permeable.

"And what about those dolls to your right?" I asked, referring to the fifteen or so twelve-inch dolls, sitting on the shelf next to him.

"Those are from my wife Susan's collection. She also makes dolls as well." Susan Demeter is a scholar, author, artist, and witch. Laughing, he added, "Some of the folks from the Galileo Project asked about these dolls, wondering about what kind of science I do."

As a researcher at the Astronomical Observatories of Bologna and Naples, and later at the INAF Radio Telescope of Medicina, Massimo has been involved in research on many types of explosive stellar phenomena such as supernovae, novae, eruptive protostars and high-mass close binary stars—and, more recently, in the search for extrasolar planets and extraterrestrial intelligence within the Search for Extraterrestrial Intelligence (SETI) Project.

"Could you tell me a little bit about the work you did at the Naples Observatory in Italy?" I asked.

"That was two years after I got my PhD from Bologna University. The university wanted to send me to Russia to the Caucasus Observatory, but in 1992 Russia was collapsing. It was absolute chaos. There was no possibility for me to come back, even at Christmas, so I decided not to go to Russia. Then I learned of the option to go to the South of Italy. I also had a friend who was working there from North Italy. I wound up staying in Naples for about three to four years. I was working in the beginning on specific kinds of stars, called protostars. It's the very beginning of the birth of a star. They are infants. They're like small babies that are only about 50,000 years old. They do everything: they vomit, they shout, they scream. Children do the same things. They explode all the time because they are not yet stabilized.

"I was studying the way in which their dynamics develop in several wavelengths: optical, infrared, ultraviolet and radio. I used the International Ultraviolet Explorer (IUE) space telescope. I had been using a lot of telescopes and also making some interpretative physics based on shockwaves. For my master thesis I worked on the dynamics of supernova explosions and the fact that they create shockwaves in the interstellar environment. I studied the Alamogordo experiment at Trinity and all the calculations that were done to determine the effect of a shockwave on the environment. I scaled up all this on the supernova situation. Then I brought this knowledge to my PhD thesis about close binary stars," said Massimo.

"Then I became involved in the Hessdalen project in Norway," he continued.

The Hessdalen lights are of unknown origin. They appear both by day and by night and seem to float through and above the valley.

They are usually bright white, yellow, or red and can appear above and below the horizon. The duration of the phenomenon may be a few seconds to well over an hour. Sometimes the lights move with enormous speed; at other times they seem to sway slowly back and forth. Yet, on other occasions, they hover in mid-air.

"I was brought on to take physics measurements of all the strange light phenomena that are seen very often in the Hessdalen valley of Central Norway. I was planning research and after that I met the people there and I went back several times to do research and I got some measurements mostly in the optical and sometimes also in the long wavelength. I have published many papers, some of which were peer reviewed in serious journals. At the present time (2023), I am deeply involved in a new research phase of Project Hessdalen, of which I am the main scientific advisor and science planner. My life has been working in parallel between studying these Phenomena, astrophysics and also electronic music. Since I obtained my master's degree, I have been collecting synthesizers here and there."

"Did the idea of the UFO, or other aspects of the Phenomena inspire you to start writing music? For you, is there a relationship as to how and why you compose and perform music and the Phenomena?" I asked, curious to hear Massimo's response. The Phenomena includes mystical visions, telepathy, precognition, bilocation (being in two places at once), time travel, synchronicity, psychedelic experiences, dreams, near death experiences, visits from the beyond, visits from nonhuman intelligences, and more. The scope of the Phenomena is beyond the range of human knowledge and comprehension.

"It has happened in both ways: some musical soundscapes that I create seem to have triggered themselves from some 'UFO visions.' Conversely, some of my pieces have been indeed inspired by some of my previous hypnagogic visions and by some real sightings. Correspondence with the Other has been wholly one-to-one," said Massimo.

"You've said to me that you have visions of UFOs on the screen of your mind through music, have you had a UFO experience in normal waking life?"

"Yes, I have. I cannot deny this. Especially when doing my missions in Norway. Most of the time they were just light balls similar to lighted orbs that are moving and blinking, very spectacular. But twice, maybe three times, we saw something structured in the sky. In August 2000, there were five of us, two scientists in one place and three other scientists who were about two kilometers [0.6211 miles] away. It was a triangular thing that we saw, with three lights at the vertices. It came over us, literally. It was a machine, no doubt. But I don't know. I cannot say if it was alien or manmade. Or Skunk Works [a project developed by a relatively small and loosely structured group of people who research and develop a project, often with a very large degree of autonomy, primarily for the sake of radical innovation]. But it was a machine. I could see it very well because I could see the fuselage. There was some residual light due to the aurora borealis. And in summer there is quite a lot of light during the night so I could see quite well. I aimed a laser I had in my backpack, and I pushed the laser, signaling to the thing overhead, asking it to land. But nothing happened and these three lights very gradually turned off. It literally disappeared over our heads!"

"Did it have exhaust or a trail?" I asked.

"No exhaust, no trail, no noise, nothing like that. And three or four days later, I was with my colleague and his wife and suddenly there was a little light. In this case, it was like a giant firefly elliptical object. I know the dimensions because the day after I went there and calculated them: it was about three feet wide in diameter. It arrived, floated over our head and then stopped about 200 feet away from us, close to a fir tree at the height of a man, six feet high or something like that, and it stayed there for ten minutes. My colleague was scared to death. I tried to approach the object, getting about one hundred feet near it, with a camera and tripod, wanting to identify the spectrum of the phenomenon, but there was no time to put the spectrographic filter on the camera. I was only able to take a photo of this giant firefly that stayed there for a long time.

"In addition to the spectacular sights witnessed in Norway I had a closer-to-home, synchronic mind experience. I was at my countryside house, lying on top of my car, smoking a cigarette. Thinking of nothing. My mind was empty. All of a sudden, something told me: Look here—and I looked in the sky and I saw a star-like light that suddenly started to move erratically in a random way, just like a firefly.

"This thing happened three or four times. Always from my countryside house and it was beautiful. Absolutely beautiful. I also had an experience during my childhood, but it's nebulous and I am not clear. Something happened, I just don't remember what."

"Do you have UFO dreams?" I asked, having had many myself.

"Yes, I've had them many times. However, in the last fifteen years I almost never dream about UFOs. I dream about things like other dimensions. Like I am in my city, but it is completely different from waking life reality. It's like a version of my city in that dimensional realm."

"I read in Ryan Sprague's book, *Somewhere in the Skies*, that you were doing data analysis work with UFODATA. Was that related to the Hessdalen project or are those two related?" I asked.

"Not really. I had been working with Mark Rodeghier, Alex Wendt and Ronald Masters on the UFODATA project. My role was to choose the instruments, perform tests and then decide on strategies. I was tasked with being in charge of how to use the instruments and, above all, testing a new spectroscopic apparatus that I was using at my home and doing the calculations at that time, but that was not directly related to Hessdalen. But Erling Strand, who is the chief of the Hessdalen project, was also involved in the

UFODATA project. So, in some way it was related, yes."

"What I liked about what I had read is that scientists were collaborating to apply scientific methods to analyze data that governments are ignoring. Governments, including the United States, are not pursuing a study of the data, so this is an independent consortium of scientists of which you are a part," I said.

"Indeed, it was independent, but it was composed of a body of very competent PhDs, some were renowned, like professor Hakan Kayal, in Würzburg, Germany. But we were not associated with any university department. I had been working for only one year, but very intensely, with the Galileo project, led by Professor Avi Loeb. I don't work with them anymore because there were some disagreements with a few people. However, I totally support the project. They are a team of fantastic engineers and scientists. In this case, the Galileo Project is based at Harvard University and the funding has been obtained by Avi through several sources. Unlike UFODATA, The Galileo Project is university funded."

"Avi's work is very mainstream?" I asked, not wanting to disparage Avi, but to call out the differences.

"Avi is highly intelligent. I recognize that absolutely, his work is clearly logical, and he doesn't say that whatever we see in the sky are aliens. He admits that it could be some natural phenomenon: manmade, Skunk Works, etc. All of these things he admits but is interested in the possibility that we have been visited and this idea came when he analyzed the data regarding Oumuamua, which was very strange. People thought, in the beginning, that Oumuamua was a comet inside the solar system, but it was behaving in a totally different way than a comet or an asteroid. The object had a fast acceleration, so this enabled us to deduce that it was coming from another stellar system. Also it didn't have a tail. There were several aspects that were particularly strange, and so he did several calculations which he published in peer-reviewed journals, stating the possibility that it could be a relic of a gigantic alien spacecraft."

I had to clarify something with Massimo regarding Avi's work. "I accept the fact that when we see anomalous behavior in the skies, it could be unexplainable by our current scientific knowledge. So you see an orb in the sky. It could be something that our science cannot yet account for. However, there seems to be a psychic element to it. Like you said, when you were lying on top of your car, smoking a cigarette, you received a telepathic message to look over in a particular direction. There's some kind of telepathic aspect to this, or something else going on," I said.

"Absolutely yes, I have to admit. As a scientist, it's like we're priests. We cannot blaspheme. Instead, my duty, which is an ethical moral duty, is to take note of everything, even things that are scandalous, although always maintaining a rigorous approach methodologically.

"In the past I had come to know the work of Professor Harley Rutledge. The study was done between 1973 and 1980 in Missouri. At some point there was a so-called UFO flap in the area. People were seeing UFOs every day, practically. Being a professor of solid-state physics, he decided to use his own PhD students to take measurements of the Phenomenon. He was not able to take good measurements, unfortunately. But in his book *Project Identification*, Professor Rutledge stated that often, when he was preparing an instrument, zooming a lens or activating something like a laser, it seemed like the Phenomenon knew what he was doing. And there was a synchronicity of several kinds, not only between the Phenomenon and him, but also between the Phenomenon and his colleagues in the study. I have to admit there is something here that has to do with our consciousness. Professor Rutledge is a man like me who calculates. And like Avi. But Professor Rutledge admitted that there was this strangeness in his observations. Avi would never admit that, and in that sense, he's absolutely mainstream, you're right."

I interjected. "This is noted in many cases. For instance, like some of the navy pilots who had the Tic Tac sighting. According to Commander David Fravor, the Tic Tac accelerated with intentionality, catching up to the pilots and zooming past them, playing cat and mouse. Also, pilots have a term called a cap point. In aviation parlance the cap point is agreed upon before a mission. It is something that only they know, like a strategic triangulation point. At one point, after rapidly accelerating past him, David Fravor saw the Tic Tac object move to the cap point, which was like the Phenomena saying: *I'm reading your mind.*

"Could this science have something to do with our consciousness? Could there be some other kind of science that we don't have a word for yet?" I asked.

Massimo folded his hands and spoke very seriously. "I am very interested in the notion of quantum entanglement, which is incredibly similar to telepathy or something like that. It happens between particles, but a very similar thing seems to happen in our mind. We are not able to record it because we cannot demonstrate it, but it happens. The problem is not that our science is wrong. Although being very accurate, our science is very narrow in its focus, as it should be. But our science isn't holistic. As such it leaves something missing. The problem is that the matter of our study is totally separated from our mind. It's the Cartesian paradigm: *res extensa* and *res cogitans*, the thought is here and the matter is there. It might be wrong because it could be that consciousness is able to affect matter and therefore, we would enter into the realm of the paranormal. As in the case of the quantum entanglement mechanism between particles, our mind could be entangled with another mind. It could also be entangled with an object and if it is entangled, the two things that are entangled are describable by only one wave function, using the terms of quantum physics. As if we are only one thing.

"According to David Bohm, quantum physicist, the universe is completely united. Bohm says that there is another level of reality which he calls *implicate order* and in which things are connected—by what?—apparently, by a feeling, which is not a quantity but rather a quality. The glue of this connection is a sort of animal emotion. It's a feeling, and our science is not able to quantify this because it doesn't include those things."

"Have you ever read John Keel?" I interjected.

"Yes, in the ancient past."

Keel wrote that future science might be more like shamanism. In preparing to write this book, I reread Susan's essay "Through a Magikal Lens." In that essay she writes that Aleister Crowley defined magic as "the science and art of causing change to occur in conformity with the Will." Perhaps more highly developed beings can transform space and time at will, traversing incredible distances, changing the basic structure of things, and penetrating other dimensions. As the Russian scientist Nikolai Kardashev proposed, regarding the types of advanced civilizations we might find in the universe, a Type III civilization is able to extract energy and raw materials from their galaxy. It is capable of intergalactic travel via wormholes, and able to use intergalactic communication and perform galactic engineering.

Sounds like magic to me.

"My wife," Massimo continued, "Susan Demeter, wrote a book called *Cosmic Witch*. Susan points out that witches are scientists, too. Their magic is based on nature and nature is exactly what we're studying. What if the aliens have developed their own technology? Not from science, but from magic. What would have happened if magic had not been crashed down by the church? What if magic had continued to develop its course? Imagine the technology that would have come from it. This is a big interrogation mark that is pestering me all the time."

"John Keel proposes that future science is similar to what you're saying. That it includes magic," I said.

As Keel wrote in *The Eighth Tower*, "The world of tomorrow

will not be a world of wall-to-wall television and spaceships in every garage. It will be a world of oracles. We may be able to accurately forecast the future and avert terrible disasters. We may be able to levitate ourselves and great blocks of stones so we can build pyramids in our backyards. If we can just develop ESP on a practical level, we can drive the telephone company into bankruptcy."

"This is an interrogation mark because magic assumes that mind and matter can interact together. Contemporary science says absolutely no," said Massimo.

I thanked Massimo, having tremendously enjoyed our conversation. This was just the beginning. I knew we'd be speaking again.

We've all been swimming in the same waters for a long while.

Before I had read Susan Demeter's essay "Through a Magikal Lens" in *Deep Weird*, Susan and I knew each other through Facebook. We were mutual friends of UK-based writer Anthony Peake. Both Susan and I had been guests on Anthony's *Consciousness Hour* show.

But I must peel the onion to get to the heart of the synchronicities here.

I wrote to Anthony after coming across his book *The Hidden Universe*, saying that my book *Falling from Trees* seemed to have been inspired by his, although I read his book after I wrote mine. Uncanny. Anthony replied that when he was reading my book on a train to his aunt's house outside of London, he read the chapter "The Three Bridges" as he pulled into the Three Bridges station.

As Eric Wargo writes in his book *Time Loops*, the more we pay attention to synchronicities and precognitions, the more we notice their occurrences.

MUSIC AS A FORM OF TELEPATHY
Joshua Cutchin's Story

I have been studying ufology for some time now and it has changed my life, forcing me to think about how I think and what I know. This has happened in large part thanks to reading the writings of researchers and scholars in the field (some with whom I've been in contact). As my wife would tell you, I have stacks upon stacks of books to prove it. One of the greatest gifts I've been fortunate enough to receive from this adventure has been the friendships that have developed with many smart and wonderful people in this community. Joshua Cutchin is one of those people. Joshua and I connected after I read his book *Ecology of Souls: A New Mythology of Death & the Paranormal*, and then his essay "The Projectionist Booth" in *Deep Weird*. We got to know each other the old-fashioned way: writing back and forth. In our correspondence, we each shared our work, relevant articles, and thoughts.

In addition to *Ecology of Souls*, Joshua is the author of seven critically acclaimed books: *A Trojan Feast: The Food and Drink Offerings of Aliens, Faeries, and Sasquatch* (2015); *The Brimstone Deceit: An In-Depth Examination of Supernatural Scents, Otherworldly Odors & Monstrous Miasmas* (2016); *Thieves in the Night: A Brief History of Supernatural Child Abductions* (2018); and *Where the Footprints End: High Strangeness and the Bigfoot Phenomenon, Volumes I & II*, with Timothy Renner (2020).

The year 2023 saw the release of both his curated essay collection *Fairy Films: Wee Folk on the Big Screen* and his first work of fiction, the novel *Them Old Ways Never Died*. In 2023, Joshua also released *The Ufology Tarot* with Miguel Romero, Greg Bishop, Susan Demeter, and David Metcalfe, a magical art project celebrating the discipline's prominent thinkers. Joshua provided several card descriptions and served as editor and layout designer for the accompanying art book.

Joshua's work has been very influential in the modern UFO Phenomena community. Scholars like Jeff Kripal, Diana Pasulka, and others often mention Joshua's name in their writings and presentations. There is a good reason for this. Joshua is creating a new, more cohesive narrative, marrying his knowledge of folklore with the UFO Phenomenon. Like Jeff Kripal and Diana Pasulka, Joshua is helping others to tell their stories, to weave connections between the various threads of this mystery.

"Did you notice the influence of your work on mine?" I wrote to him after he read my book *For All We Know*.

"Of course," he replied.

My mother's recent death was a key theme in the book—that death is always present, that we perish back into the earth, disintegrating into the elements from which we are made. That death challenges our tidy preconceptions of consensus reality. Anyone who has lost someone they love knows this in their bones.

When I learned that Joshua was scheduled to be a featured speaker at the NYC Anomalous Conference in December 2023, I couldn't wait to meet him. Joshua was the first featured speaker. At about 10 a.m. on a Saturday, people were still waking up, drinking coffee, some having come from across the country to the conference. Joshua took the stage, opening with, "This has something to do with what we call "death." The audience took that in silently.

"That's one way to start the morning, isn't it?"

Everyone laughed. He had kick-started the day with exactly what people needed. UFO conferences are often very serious—a little humor goes a long way.

Joshua continued. "My initial entry point into the UFO Phenomenon was examining the similarities between fairy folklore and encounters with humanoids, which I still find quite fascinating. The correspondences seem, to me, undeniable (if they are true). Jacques Vallée's landmark 1969 work *Passport to Magonia* proved—again, to me at least—that, beyond a shadow of a doubt, there is some sort of connection between older fairy folklore from across the world and the modern UFO contact experience. (Sorry, I'm old-fashioned. I'll be using 'UFO' and even "flying saucer" alongside 'UAP' today.)" Joshua had everyone's full attention.

"What my work *Ecology of Souls* hopefully accomplishes is putting these disparate contact modalities in dialogue with one another. To me, the gestalt seems to suggest that our final transitioning, death itself, undergirds most, if not all, paranormal phenomena...including UAP."

Although Joshua's presentation was a tall act to follow, the day continued with a series of excellent lectures from other speakers. I finally got to meet Joshua in person after his presentation. Standing at six feet four, he is a big man, especially next to me at five feet eight. Broad shouldered, like a football player. Despite his towering stature, Joshua is a gentle person. He is quite smart and easy to talk with.

After the conference, Joshua and I spoke via a video call. He has a very scholarly demeanor. His reddish, Hobbit-like beard starts from the sideburns and covers the lower portion of his chin. He has a fitting look for a scholar of folklore.

"Joshua, where did you grow up?" I wanted to go all the way back to the beginning.

"I grew up in a small town, a little bit north of Charlotte, North Carolina, on Lake Norman. And I guess I can get into why and how I got into music. My sister got pulled into the color guard for the high school marching band, and I had seen the level of camaraderie. I had noticed just how weird band kids were, which really resonated with me as someone who was kind of a weird kid. I made a lot of friends and saw a lot of the leadership that was involved and it was really inspiring. I knew that I wanted to be a part of it in some capacity.

"My school district started music kind of late. Down here where I live in Georgia, these days they start kids in a band at around sixth grade. My district was around seventh grade. Young kids can be put into a Suzuki violin class because there's equipment appropriately sized for them. There are physical limitations when someone is learning standardized wind instruments. We try to start children a little bit later on brass instruments simply because they need to have adult- sized lips," he said smiling, his bright blue eyes sparkling, even on video.

"Also, not everyone can comfortably hold a tuba," I said.

"I don't think that's addressed enough," he said. "It isn't the case that everyone can play any instrument. People with certain body types are better suited for certain instruments. I'm a good example. I've tried to play the trumpet and my lips are just too big.

"I also had an incredibly supportive set of parents. I can't emphasize that enough because tubas are not cheap. I ended up at an intersection of something that I both enjoyed and was good at. I didn't have to be told to practice. By the time I got to high school I was making decisions of whether or not I would hang out with my friends or practice. I really tried to make the most of the support that I was getting, and was trying to make the most of the opportunities I was being given. I attended the University of Wisconsin in Madison for my undergraduate degree. If they have the opportunity, I encourage students to continue their studies in a certain tradition of pedagogy. It's important that a music student has consistency in the teaching style and approach. It enables you to develop further on the building blocks that you've been handed down.

"After getting my degree at the University of Wisconsin, I was invited to come to the University of Georgia on a fellowship with the school Brass Quintet, where I had the opportunity to work for a year or two under the direction of Fred Mills. Fred was one of the founding members of the Canadian Brass. It was a great experience up until my chops failed. There has been this condition running through the brass community, especially through the low brass community, of focal dystonia, which is a repetitive motion injury.

"Whenever I would form an embouchure, I would have less control over my movements than I wanted. This is devastating when you're twenty-two and you've been working at this since you're twelve. But, as I've often said, the best thing about the worst thing you can imagine happening to you is that it is the worst thing you could imagine. It's all uphill from there, or all downhill from there, depending on how you look at it.

"Through the advocacy of the tuba professor at the University of Georgia at the time, David Zerkle, I was able to parlay my fellowship into a different capacity and was able to turn my, what was supposed to be a performance master's degree, into a music literature degree. A kind of a musicology-light degree. What I perceived at the time as being a tragedy of being knocked off of the classical musician route, directed me to doing what I wanted to do all along. I'll never forget it. I was talking with David Zerkle. I said, 'The one thing that I never really got to do was put together a New Orleans style brass band.' And he looks at me. He says, 'The problems that you're having aren't noticeable ones. No one's going to notice in that setting, and if they do, they're not going to care.' And that was my first trip in putting together a band in learning how to write music."

Joshua began describing his foray into forming New-Orleans-style bands.

"That was around 2008. And as luck would have it, I was playing a lot. I was playing way too much once you factored in private lessons, personal practice, and the many ensembles I was playing in. It wouldn't be out of the question to say that I was playing six to eight hours a day. On some days that's a long time to subject your face to that kind of abuse. I was forced to take time off, which helped heal the issues I had. And now I don't have those problems anymore. And in the interim, I have worked on and fostered a career doing commercial jazz and commercial styles. It's gotten to the point where I'm allergic to self-promotion, but I think I can say with some degree of certainty that I have become the first call jazz tuba player here in Atlanta.

"I ended up in a place where I couldn't be happier in terms of the opportunities that I have and the types of stuff that I'm playing. I don't get calls for symphonies. I don't get calls for quintets. On the other hand, I've subbed for a bass player in a rock band. I've even performed with polka groups. It has been tons of fun, playing in really diverse settings. It has been an absolute blessing."

"What kind of things do you think people would be surprised to know that you play on the tuba?" I asked.

"The brass band that I'm currently in has an arrangement, we don't do it very often, of 'Free Bird.' I've also played some Charlie Parker tunes on tuba. It's always fun to walk into a room with an instrument that has a reputation for being clumsy and not very nimble. If you put in enough effort, you can make it almost as nimble. Also, I rarely have a greater honor than for somebody to say, 'The bass player is sick, let's call Josh to play it on tuba.'"

"I heard a version of Jimi Hendrix's 'Machine Gun,' played by the jazz flutist Robert Dick. Dick's jazz ensemble has violin, cello, drums, flute and even a banjo contributing to replicate all the dynamics of Hendrix's guitar playing. The percussiveness, string bending, the wah-wah effects, and distortion. I thought that was super interesting and creative," I said.

"Exactly," said Joshua. "There are certain instruments that have a chip on their shoulder. When it comes to being a square tuba, flute, or bassoon player, it really elevates the level of musicianship that you see coming out. There are tuba players now with six-octave ranges, doing all these extended effects that are just fantastic to hear. And I think that there is fantastic musicianship at all levels and across all instruments; I think that some of the most innovative stuff is really coming out of the tuba-euphonium community."

Agreeing, I added, "There is so much innovation, so many interesting musicians doing great work. Maybe we're not hearing about them. In previous times, jazz was popular. And in other popular music, rock, country, etc. boasted great songwriting and musicianship. Not so much anymore in the popular forum. But there's great music being played now if you want to go find it.

"In late 2023, I went to see the Sam Bush Band at Symphony Space on the Upper West Side of Manhattan. You might call them bluegrass, but they are undefinable. The Sam Bush Band plays a mixture of bluegrass, rock, jazz, and chamber music. They are all great musicians. His banjo player, Wes Corbett, doesn't play traditional banjo, arpeggiating the whole way. He uses a different picking style that allows him to play melodically. Sounds like he's playing piano. Folks like Bill Keith innovated that style, and players like Béla Fleck and others brought it forward. But Wes Corbett is doing something completely original. No pedals, no nothing. He's mastered a way of playing that is completely different.

"I'm a musician. I study music, I write about musicians. But I'm also very much interested in the study of the Phenomena. How did you find yourself on that trail?" I asked.

"I've always had an interest in these things, and I grew up in a household where being interested in these things wasn't discouraged at all. Everybody was just glad that I was reading, I wanted to be a lot of things when I grew up. For instance, I wanted to be a zoo vet and eventually that got superseded by playing tuba. I remember distinctly at one point asking my parents if I could be a cryptozoologist. My dad said *That's not an occupation. You can't feed your family being a cryptozoologist.* But it's always been in the back of my mind. But let's face it, to associate yourself with these subjects, as much as it's become destigmatized, it is still a point of departure. It has to be a deliberate choice to go publicly with the subject of the UFO Phenomenon."

"It can drive people away sometimes," I said, knowing that some people think I'm nuts because of my interest in the subject.

"Let me backfill the other part of my story," said Joshua. "After I finished my musicology degree, my chops hadn't recovered as they have today. I then realized that I never wanted to be a musicologist. What do I do with this master's in musicology? I decided to go back to school and get a master's in journalism. My idea was to do arts criticism, but I ended up applying to public affairs jobs associated with the arts. I got a job as a public affairs director at the University of Georgia and stayed there for three years. At some point it became apparent that I needed to leave that position. I had a commute of about an hour each way. On a good day. And that's when I started listening to paranormal podcasts again. And really rekindling a lot of that interest.

"Around the same time that I decided to write *A Trojan Feast: The Food and Drink Offerings of Aliens, Faeries, and Sasquatch*. I started thinking about the barriers of entry to write a book like that and realized there really weren't any. I know how to write. In fact, the only person who was encouraging me to go into music was my band director. All my other teachers were encouraging me to write. I wrote *A Trojan Feast* during that period, and it all coincided with me leaving that job. Then I wrote and played music. At that time, I distinctly remember a job I was interviewing for in Nashville. I made it past a couple of rounds, I got like four or five calls back. Then I guess they finally decided to Google my name and saw my book *A Trojan Feast*. I'm pretty sure that's why I didn't get an offer for that position.

"Musicians are a peculiar bunch to begin with. Even with classical musicians there are characters that you'll encounter, and these topics get discussed more frequently in the green room than you would expect. Also, my education had an impact on my work. Getting two master's degrees makes you appreciate citations, endnotes and footnotes, and going on the research quest. So that's probably the biggest influence that my background had on my work today."

"Is there a way in which your interest in the Phenomena influences your music?" I asked.

"I go to a UFO conference and people ask, 'You play the tuba. What's up with that?' And then I go to the gig, and they ask, 'You write about UFOs. What's up with that?' I feel like an outcast everywhere. Living in the in between. But it's also a conversation point wherever I go, and many musicians ask, 'What do you think about all this?' I've been in pick-up groups and before we get together at the gig some people say, 'I think I heard you on the *Coast to Coast Paranormal Radio Program*. Musicians coming home late from gigs are probably a solid thirty percent of the *Coast to Coast* audience. Many of us listened to the *Coast to Coast* show on the way back from gigs to keep us awake.

"It doesn't happen every time, but it happens often enough that I think it's worth mentioning. It feels like music is a direct vector to the Phenomenon. I don't experience that while I'm writing music. Some people probably do, but I do in the live setting. I've experienced it with a band that has played a lot together and, in some instances, even when a band hasn't played together a lot. It's fascinating how players can shift on a dime and we all follow along. Or when a player presents an idea, then I'll start doing the same thing, almost instantaneously, and the entire feel of everything we're doing changes, and the synchronicity magically lines up. I'm sure part of that is a function of playing with people and knowing their tendencies, but I've experienced those other times where it feels like it's a form of group telepathy. Unlike a traditional rock band, brass players don't have our mouths available to us, except for the drummer. Who signals the change? No one. We're just listening. Someone makes a change, and everybody picks up on it.

"This is partially a sense of awareness and partially an affinity for the people that you're playing with. But I've also experienced it when it just happens suddenly and locks in so instantaneously that it does feel like it's bordering on something a little bit uncanny. I could be playing and give a look and we all align to the exact same thing at the exact same time. I don't know what that is, but it feels like a neural networking morphogenetic field kind of thing. Sometimes I take a solo or, in my case, take a walking bass line, and when I go back and listen, I have no idea where that idea came from. You enter a flow state.

"There might be something we would call paranormal going on in those moments. Because you do feel a certain dissociative quality and you feel a bit more like a third person observing what's happening as opposed to making conscious decisions yourself. Occasionally the music comes together, and you notice it, especially in the improvisational styles, like New Orleans Jazz."

"Interestingly," I interjected, "consciousness researcher Robert Monroe, in his book *Far Journeys*, described one of his Hemi-Sync induced out-of-body experiences as tuning into a flow state. He envisioned an immense machine, infinitely complex, swarmed with beings climbing all over it, turning a knob here, a valve there, synchronizing the flow of the overall system. Monroe stated that, 'Their concern was the flow of energy through the human experience.'[55]

"Music connects," I added. "It taps into the flow state you mentioned. That's why we use music at ceremonies. Perhaps this has something to do with the origins of music." But as notes don't fossilize, we can only observe the behavior of primates and extrapolate from there. We can only speculate. We don't have definitive artifacts that go back to the origins of music.

In his essay "Origins of Music and Speech," musicologist Peter Marler writes, "Both chimpanzees and gibbons are close relatives

---

[55] *Far Journeys*, Robert Monroe, Page 100

of humans, and vocalizations of both are considered proto-musical."[56] Marler adds, "Rather like birdsong, [pant-hooting] is used as an affective, non-symbolic display in many situations, especially during intergroup encounters, when excited, after a prey capture, to assert dominance, and, often in chorus, to keep in touch in the forest."[57]

Interesting to note that, in Joshua's book *Where the Footprints End: High Strangeness and the Bigfoot Phenomenon, Volume I*, he observed that many bigfoot witnesses describe flesh-and-blood creatures whose behavior closely corresponds to primates. Eyewitness reports include descriptions of a being with "pursed, hooting lips, piloerection (hair standing on end), bluff charging, conical heads."[58] When I came across this connection in my research, I froze at my desk.

I asked, "Where do you think music comes from? We don't need to do music. It is not essential for evolution. Humans might have gotten by with just words, with shouting. But why do you think it exists even though we don't need it? We desire it so much. It's a part of all the major aspects of our funeral traditions. You know, weddings, revolutions, openings of ceremonies. I've read that 'Our distant forebears might have been singing hominoids before they became talking hominoids.'"[59]

"Remember the hippie drum circle and how it has become something of a joke? And that's unfortunate because there is something about the way that human beings synchronize," said Joshua.

He continued, "There have been numerous studies about the effects of music on our hearts and our blood pressure, etc. Not just

---

56 Nils L. Wallin (Editor), Björn Merker (Editor), Steven Brown (Editor). *The Origins of Music*. Cambridge, Massachusetts: MIT Press, 2000
57 Nils L. Wallin (Editor), Björn Merker (Editor), Steven Brown (Editor). *The Origins of Music*. Cambridge, Massachusetts: MIT Press, 2000
58 Cutchin, Joshua. *Where the Footprints End, High Strangeness and the Bigfoot Phenomenon*. Joshua Cutchin, Timothy Renner, 2020
59 Nils L. Wallin (Editor), Björn Merker (Editor), Steven Brown (Editor). *The Origins of Music*. Cambridge, Massachusetts: MIT Press, 2000

in terms of frequencies, but in terms of rhythms. One of my teachers told me there has been an overemphasis in the Western tradition on harmony and I think, when you get down to it, rhythm is the most distilled form of musical expression. You can convey so much with just rhythm. Making fun of the hippie drum circle or writing off some indigenous drumming and indigenous music as "primitive" because it doesn't have Western harmonies is reductive and, quite frankly, harmful because rhythm is so elemental."

In his essay "Gibbon Songs and Human Music," musicologist Thomas Geissmann wrote that, "The beat may help larger social groups to participate in a song, to coordinate it. A well-coordinated song may be a more effective display than a cacophony of voices, and other social groups are less likely to attack or threaten well-coordinated groups."[60]

Joshua continued, "Our conversation here today crystallized the possibility that music serves a synchronous function. It's akin to the use of entheogens. Music generates an altered state of consciousness on demand. I mean synchronization in terms of shamanic drumming, getting you into the right headspace. Think of music in indigenous traditions, the ecstatic trance. If you want to look at it a bit more grotesquely, consider how trumpet calls synchronize people on the battlefield. That's a very sort of similar thing and quite frankly, you know, continues to a certain degree through the New Orleans parade tradition. Many of those brass band tunes start with the tuba. It signals everybody to know what tune we're doing next."

"It's like a calliope."

"Exactly," Joshua said. "I think that the synchronization and the unification aspects of music are a big part of it. To be able to have emotions on demand. I've heard people who have used music to pull them out of dark places. And then there's the number of people that I've spoken to who have written some of the most

---

60 *Origins of Music*, Page 199

upbeat songs when they're in some of their darkest places. I don't know if that's 'The Other,' reaching down to them and pulling them out of the depths or if it was a conscious or subconscious decision. But the fact is that music cannot only pull you out of or into these states of being in the moment, but it can also transform the bad into good in times of darkness. I think it is related to telepathic communication. Perhaps this is why we 'music.'"

"Certain entheogens can help you tap into those deep places of synchronicity, making people feel like they're all having the same experience. Like at a Grateful Dead show," I said, thinking of the relationship between human and primate vocalizations and rhythmic drumming that I'd been reading about in my musicology research.

"I think there's an important clue in that sort of additive quality of these psychoactive substances and music, like there's some sort of synergy there, which I think is crucial to understanding both," said Joshua.

Confirming, I replied, "While on LSD, I've had incredible insights into the nature of reality, especially when listening to music. I've seen hyperdimensional worlds and dazzling geometries. My friend Paul and I had a profound experience watching a tree's branches swirl out of control, then slow down to a creeping halt. We were invited into the inner life of the tree. No joking. The music guided us into a trance state. I remember thinking just by taking these little pieces of paper with suns on them, I can see the secrets buried in the matrices of the music. Like I was initiated into the society of experiencers."

Joshua said, "These states allow us to freeze our emotions in time. With music you have the capacity to put an emotion into a time capsule. Not only a heartbreaking emotion, but also the emotion of a moment. If I took an audio recording of just a crowd at a party, it would sound normal. But if I took an audio recording of a live concert, it also captures the emotion of that setting."

"Like rock concerts, or people at events in stadiums. How it can whip people into a frenzy, even in a dangerous way," I replied.

"For better or worse," said Josh.

Changing the subject, I asked, "Have you had a UFO experience?"

"I've never had a UFO experience. I've had some bigfoot-adjacent experiences, that's what I call them, and I've had some ghost stuff that's happened, but it's never really been in conjunction with anything musical other than those moments of neural networking that happened in live music."

"Do you feel there's some similarity, like when you've had a bigfoot experience? How did it feel to you?" I asked.

"There have been a couple of moments in my life that I can remember in certain performances, where it feels like you go right up and touch the divine," said Josh.

"Do you have UFO dreams?"

"I do from time to time. I don't dream of flying objects often, maybe once or twice a year. I have recurring dreams that involve a being. In our old house, I used to call the old house 'the tree house' because the bottom floor was a small starter home. The kitchen, living room, bathroom and then all the bedrooms were upstairs on top of it. It felt like anytime you were going to turn in for the night, there was a real dichotomy between upstairs life and downstairs life. I rarely have dreams that are in my home. Usually, they're on a planet made of peanut butter or something completely surrealist.

"But in this dream, I woke up from my bed in the middle of the night, and I went down to the bottom of the stairs. There was a tall blurred-out gray figure. I couldn't look at her directly; I only saw her out of my periphery. Then I saw that she had wrap-around gray eyes. I bowed down and said something to the effect of 'my queen,' which probably reflects the way that I think of these things as being related to fairies. You know, fairy queens and such. And then she walked me back up to my bed. I got into bed. I felt the pressure of her getting on the bed as well. Then I woke up and it was a bit disturbing simply because it was something that took place in the actual space that I was familiar with as opposed to being somewhere foreign. I rarely have dreams where you can plot a narrative or anything like that. And in them I'm not even really myself. But I think that was just a dream."

This last bit made me think of Joshua's presentation at the Anomalous Conference in New York City. He respectfully, but very accurately, imitated Terrence McKenna's voice, quoting him.

"This is an important point to make, which the 'flying saucer people' are forever misunderstanding...Saying that the flying saucer is a psychic object does not mean that it is not a physical object...the realm of the psychic and the realm of the physical meet in a strange kind of Never-Never Land that we have yet to create the intellectual tools to explore."

The imitation has everyone rolling with laughter in the audience. It was that good. And the point he made was profound.

Then Joshua went on to say, "In short, our consensus conceptualization of physical versus non-physical represents a false dichotomy. The UFO is both. It is physical and psychic. Perhaps it is a bit like ourselves. Humans are embedded in the physical realm with a component of the psychic; maybe the UFO is embedded in the psychic, with an important aspect that is physical. I would take this a step further and argue that the UFO blends the boundaries between fact and fiction, between reality and storytelling, but that is a topic for another time."

Later he added, "Oftentimes, these doubles are death omens. They signify a weakening of the bonds between body and soul that heralds death. And, as luck would have it, many cultures, from indigenous America to western Europe and beyond, have long treated anomalous lights as death omens."

I was reminded of what I'd read in Robert Monroe's book *Far Journeys* conveying his out-of-body experiences and interactions with the Other. Monroe wrote, "I was escorted frequently to what might be loosely described as another kind of class, in that there was an instructor and there were students, including me. Here, freely translated, there was a brilliant white, radiating ball of light that was the teacher. I could detect radiation of others—presumed students all around me, but nothing beyond that, no form, or any indicators as to who or what the others were. Instruction consisted of a seemingly sequential bombardment of packages of total experience information to be absorbed instantly and stored through thought balls, whose actual name cannot be translated into a word."[61]

At the conclusion of his presentation Joshua said, "Consider these themes in regard to UAP, which already presents substantial connections to the dead. Ufology is a transportation-obsessed discipline: Where are they from? Where are they going? How did they get here? Where are they taking me? The flying saucer serves the same function as a psychopomp's boat: it transports humans to another world."

Like the UFO Phenomena, music is transportive. It takes us back in time and place. To other worlds and dimensions. Being exposed to a combination of instruments and vocal notes, we can vividly recall the most impactful memories of our lives. Originating in our ancestral animal ability to make pant-hoots and shouts, music has transformed in humans. Perhaps due to our specific brain and vocal anatomy we now have the ability to better communicate, to visit places in our emotional worlds that are precious to us and to experience more fully what it is to be human.

Like the brightest scholars in ufology, Joshua maintains an open mind. I admire the process of discovery he admits to in his writing. In *Where the Footprints End*, he writes, "Finally, a word to the reader: each chapter should be treated as a thought experiment. The number of truths in these volumes may be few-to-none.

---

[61] *Far Journeys*, Robert Monroe, Page 95

Topics overlap between chapters in unruly ways; some chapters may directly contradict others. As inelegant as this method may be, it is where we must go if we hope to discover further insight into the bigfoot enigma. We must travel beyond science, into the realm of folklore."

Joshua will appear alongside coauthor Timothy Renner in the documentary *I Believe in Bigfoot*.

I'm thrilled that Joshua is reading my writing as I faithfully read his body of work and look forward to staying in touch with him.

MAKING MUSIC IS PARANORMAL ACTIVITY IN PUBLIC VIEW
Sebastiano De Filippi's Story

Jeff Kripal introduced me to Sebastiano De Filippi, an Italian Argentine music director and orchestral conductor who has received awards from the Music Critics Association of Argentina and has been praised all over the world for his musicality and expressive intensity.

I spoke with Sebastiano at his home in Argentina via a video call. Almost immediately, I felt comfortable with him. Being of Italian descent, he looks like he could be my cousin. While serious about the subject matter, we can both laugh at it, and ourselves as well.

In addition to being a conductor, Sebastiano is also a writer and philosopher. I have watched presentations of his work at the Rice University Archives of the Impossible conference with Jeff Kripal. Along with one other writer, Sebastiano wrote "The Other Toscanini: The Life and Works of Héctor Panizza," which won the Certificate of Merit for Best Historical Research in Recorded Classical Music 2020 Association for Recorded Sound Collections Awards for Excellence.

Mike
Can you tell me a story that connects the Phenomena with music?

Sebastiano
I don't have a concrete life story to tell you, but I do have quite a few thoughts that may interest you, even if they are not narratives.

I would subdivide this idea or system of thought in two big units. The first one would be the process of bringing to life, in the present material world, music that was composed and written by someone in the past. This you may want to compare with a kind of mediumship, but one that you have to work hard to achieve!

Take a composer that may well be dead years, decades and certainly centuries ago, this would constitute my first section, my humble offering to you. I like to be prudent and talk only about comparison in the process of studying a score by a deceased person, a deceased composer. Note that this treasure map of music notation is a dead thing in itself. You try to connect to the thoughts and imagination from the world of sound with a person you don't know and many times you cannot know because they are dead. But you want to get into his head and try to understand what he meant by what he wrote and why he wrote it that way and tried to as a musician, as a performer. Because I'm essentially a performer.

It's a way to have a conversation with a person you don't know. A person from the past, a person who is dead and not only that, but you should be able to connect with this deceased person's mind and actualize, in real sound, and in real time, in our present what he had in mind. You don't push down the piano keys and reproduce each note—that's not making music.

You must have, first, a very complex theoretical and technical study of music, the score itself, the context, the composer, and its time and place.

Of course, there's this first step, which is a huge step of being able to do that, which is I would say mechanical, almost a scientific process. This technical process, as you well know, to make music and especially what they call classical music, orchestral music or whatever, it's a hugely complex process to write, read, perform, and understand.

I'm not saying that this is an easy or just intuitive and inspirational and spiritual and mumbo-jumbo process.

This first step is very difficult, very time-consuming and very energy-consuming. Once you do that successfully, if you are looking for high-level musical understanding—and performance and interpretation—there is a further step. It is not easily described, nor is it something you are taught, or which you can easily explain.

And it is when you get to this point, if you do, that something may happen. But, of course, there is no guarantee you will reach that.

You have this "eureka" moment and say, "Oh, I got you!" [to the composer]. "This is what you meant. This is what you had in mind. This is the sound. This is the atmosphere. This is the feeling. This is what you were aiming for."

Of course, this is extremely difficult to express in words, because if you have something that can be expressed in words you don't write or perform music... that's the whole point of it, right? Music speaks. Through music, you express things that you cannot express through the written or spoken word, and vice versa. Of course, if I have to explain to you some geographical details about my city, music just won't do. But, if as a composer I want to inject into your mind a little bit of my soul, and not explain my feelings verbally but make you feel the same feelings, now that's when a miracle and metaphysical things can happen.

In that sense I do not have a real weird paranormal story about music, but I do believe high level music making is metaphysical and hardly explainable in precise terms. There is this first chapter in which you have to work very hard and know a lot about music and technique.

But then, once you have that under your belt, your world opens up, and if you do it again with another score from the same composer, this process as a person who reads scores from deceased people gets, in a way, easier. You understand what I mean. Perhaps, however, I wouldn't say "easier," but once you repeat that process, which always has its first part which is technical, and then if you get lucky this second part which is more metaphysical, every time you encounter yet another score from the same person the process may deepen and may be sped up a bit, and you start to have a relationship with that composer.

This is something I believe every high-level musician does. Perhaps most of them.

Maybe they do not stop and think about it, and certainly not in these terms, but it happens.

I do not think it's something I've discovered or anything like that, far from it.

I'm just the kind of person who tries to think outside the box about this kind of process, but of course I have to tell you, and I have to admit it, I do feel it when it happens.

I mean, once I take up a difficult and long score, like for example a Mozart opera (which may very well be three hours of music) with vocal soloists, with text, with a libretto with all the staging, with an orchestra, with a chorus, maybe 500 pages of a score—the first step is that I need a month just to read the notes and make sense of them.

But after that, there's a relationship building, you may say that you, as an interpreter and as a musician, build a relationship with the score itself. But let's not forget that the score itself is just a book. Pages, pieces of dead paper. It's just a treasure map, not the treasure itself.

Musical notation is a very limited way to try and write down, and I emphasize "try," what this composer had in mind in terms of sound. This is how you write down sound, in a very poor and limited way, because you know very well that a C is a note, for example, but it can be tuned higher or lower depending on many factors.

When I see a note, say a quarter note, this has a meaning only in terms of proposition with other note values, it's not absolute: you don't know how long the note really is. And if that note has a staccato dot, you know that it's meant to be shorter...but how much shorter, and shorter how? And if you see an accent, yes, there's an emphasis, but how much emphasis? What kind of an emphasis? And of course, all this is just with one note, and then you start building phrases and bigger musical structures.

Then you start exploring the vertical writing, the harmony and the counterpoint. And after all that, you start to get something out of the score—or, at least, you should. Not only sound, but meaning: colors, atmospheres, feelings, and that is very hard to describe or explain in normal everyday vocabulary. It's like some sort of magic, really. So that would be my way to try and describe this first part.

I've discussed this with Dr. Jefffrey J. Kripal and others: when we think about this kind of mysterious process and we use the word "Phenomenon." We have such a huge mess with terminology. I got to a point in the last few months in which I just say "Reality" with a capital R. Reality, because in the end it's a matter of ontology: of what it is, what we are, everything is so ontological in the end. I try not to use the word "paranormal."

My opinion is we will never fully understand Reality because we are not equipped to do so. We are only equipped to pose questions, which is already a big deal. Yet, I'm a strong defender of this—I would say—almost "proud ignorance," in the sense that we are just homo sapiens; we have very interesting yet limited intellectual equipment. Perhaps we are not just like ants or cats, in the sense that we can ask questions, we can defy mysteries and think about them. But, in the end, we are like ants, cats or dogs because we don't get the answers, we may only get some glimpses. And they're always extremely subjective in form. They are always culturally affected and culturally related, I would say culturally filtered. As I sometimes joke with Dr. Kripal, it's obviously not a coincidence that millions of people in the world, in the present and in the past, have religious experiences, apparitions, visitations and epiphanies. But on the other hand, it's also not a coincidence that you don't get the blessed virgin Mary in India, and that you don't get Shiva and Ganesh in Portugal. To me, both these elements are factual. I would not discard any of those two in favor of just one. There is a deeper reality we are not fully aware of, even if we live within it. And sometimes we perceive things out of our daily "normal" range of perception. But then we must be very prudent in not interpreting and reaching conclusions which are somehow comfortable to us, because Reality always appears culturally related.

Mike
I'm focusing just on music because I feel like I have something to talk about, something to say. I'm a musician and, as a music journalist, I've talked with musicians, and no one has answered the question 'where does music come from?' Perhaps it's not answerable.

Sebastiano
There's one thing you said which I would like to comment upon. You said your book about music would be highly speculative. I believe when writing about musical processes you have the chance to write about something which is very concrete and happens each day to a great number of musicians. In other contexts it may seem "out there" and speculative, weird and pseudo paranormal, in fields like the arts it's our daily bread.

Mike
I have books on musicology, and no one can adequately talk about the leap from language to music. Some researchers think that singing came before talking. They think this because the anatomy of singing is related to the anatomy for laughter.

Sebastiano
You've talked about it just now when there is magic that man-

ifests, something happens. We all communicate with the audience. Sometimes something happens that you can't force to happen, but when it happens it is transcendent and powerful. This is why we do the hard work—to be gifted those moments of transcendence.

Yes, and sometimes they happen. You have to work your butt off to get to a point in which you "let go" and something like that may happen.

Mike
Would you say this is a form of telepathy? I don't think it's a hard stretch to say that you're communicating in real time in some unconscious manner.

Sebastiano
Well, that would be the second part of what I meant, as I alluded to earlier. The first one, if we want to assign it a title, would be studying a dead composer's score, which is something you may want to compare to mediumship. If you succeed, I mean. If you get to a certain point, you may succeed in feeling something like what is described in certain kinds of mediumship. That would be the sum-up statement.

The other thing, as you well said, may be somehow related to telepathy and to something called egregore (from the ancient Greeks *egregoros*), which is something materializing out of many minds, not only the performers necessarily, but also—in the best of cases—the audience.

In traditional esotericism, an egregore is a group thought-form. It can be created either intentionally or unintentionally and may become an autonomous entity with the power to influence third parties. A group with a common purpose like a family, a club, a political party, a church, or a country may be able to create an egregore, for better or worse depending upon the type of thought that created it.

I have a daily basis experience around it because I'm not only a performer, which is already something, but I'm a very specific type of performer, a conductor.

A conductor is almost a kind of "extraterrestrial" music performer because he's the only one who doesn't make a sound while making music.

In the interpretive process of a conductor, you also have all the initial steps, which are very concrete, very mathematical, and very scientifical. Hard work and hard study.

Then when you rehearse with your colleagues you have a workshop situation, where you rehearse, you stop, you correct. You go on through the music again, you ask things, you specify things. You try to draw from the performers how you think the music should be performed. Perhaps you explain why you want something done in a specific way, you may sing a phrase in order to exemplify what you mean. That way you go again on the same stretch of music, you repair what you have to repair until you get what you are looking for. You indicate which player or singer should be listening to which part at each instance, so it's a workshop situation.

We could also say it's a study group situation after each one of us has had his individual study work. Only after that can you have this communal stage of studying and working together, of practicing and perfecting the performance as a group of musicians.

But, if you did your thing at home, if they did their thing at home, and then if we all did our thing together the right way, something special, something extra could start materializing. Something which is above the rational, the linear, the describable, the common, and the normal. You are not only connected to what you are playing, singing, and conducting. You are totally connected, like plugged in the same sound world, fully immersed in what the others are playing and singing. That constitutes an upper echelon in music making: to be really connected in real time.

But that may only be another step in the process and not the last one. There may yet be another leap, one forward or upwards, in which you start to feel, at least in part, not only like the individual you are, but also with your fellow musicians like a bigger unity: one person, one mind, one spirit, one soul, one consciousness.

Here again we have the terminology problem. We become like a body made up of several bodies and several minds, a kind of octopus. A Chimera. When this huge musical octopus materializes—I'm talking metaphorically of course—other things start happening. Very subtle things, perhaps. We have read, studied and rehearsed something on a piano dynamic, and now we do it a bit differently. Phrasing nuances start to change, to evolve without anyone noticing. You notice a small ritardando that you didn't plan or expect, and it's like the music itself decided for you, in real time, during the performance. A little accent there that appeared out of nowhere with no intention, no conscious intention anyway. Something starts materializing, like you become a conduit of this music and not an individual interfering in order to perform it.

This may happen not only in the relationship between an orchestra and its conductor, but also in chamber music.

It may happen with a singer and their pianista, in a string quartet situation, with a woodwind octet, in a small choir, you name it. But if you reach that point of "technical independence" in which you have control over the score and you let it go, then the score seems to take control over you, and a whole different kind of music materializes. On the right set of variables, this weird combination of mediumship and telepathy may arise and engulf the performers.

And if it's powerful enough, this egregoric octopus may extend its tentacles and embrace the audience too.

Which is what it's all about, in the end. Because we don't write, study, play, sing or conduct music for its own sake and even less just for our own sake: the whole idea is to reach, to embrace, to communicate, to share.

Words fail me to try and further describe this process, and it's okay, because no words can be put in lieu of music (or vice versa); they are parallel universes. Let's just say that a special, nonlinear, not easily explainable and not easy-to-analyze thing happens—and it happens almost daily.

I'm not saying it happens daily to me in my music making (far from it!), but you can be sure that each day somewhere around the world this is happening. And it's a very concrete thing.

And you know what's amazing?

Up to a certain point, certainly not 100% but up to a certain point, it may even be captured in recording. Listening to the recording, you may say, "Yes, I hear it, something happened." It's not the same, not by any means: you can really experience it live. But you can recognize that something special happened when listening to a recording.

Mike
The listener has to participate...

Sebastiano
There's no real music without real listeners.

I recognize, sadly, that most people are not listening anymore, not to orchestral, choral, or chamber music. And they're the same with opera, or jazz and folk music for that matter. Of course, listening gets more difficult when the music is more complex, and the stretch of music is longer. Now, this is a very serious problem for music, for the arts and for culture. People tend to have short spans of concentration and get distracted. They do several things at the same time. And what does this say to us in broader terms about what we are now as humanity, as a civilization?

What does this say about us today, our spirituality, our inner world, our consciousness? To me it's really tragic. People are not listening any more or they are listening less and less. We are engulfed in this technological world. I have nothing against technology *per se*, on the contrary, but the day we stop listening we stop connecting and stop understanding.

Mike
Without a human mind, there would be no universe...

Sebastiano
I wouldn't put it in those terms, although I think you have a point anyway. In any case, what's the big issue with a thought like that? I mean, we already know that our internal reality, our mind reality, it's not a separate or lesser thing than the material reality in which we live. We build everything we can touch from our mind, actually. So, yes, the cosmos also materializes from our minds, and not only the other way around.

Recently, when I was invited by Rice University in Houston to deliver an address on these subjects, I said something on these lines: it's funny to see all these people interested in extraterrestrial life, aliens, spirits, and the voices of dead people, while showing no interest in learning a second language to read authors from other countries. Why don't we start speaking to each other, right here and right now, and try to understand each other a little bit more before we look for beings from other dimensions?

There's a lot we can get from studying ourselves first and not just labeling things as "normal" and "paranormal." I think good music making is a paranormal activity in public view, on a daily basis.

But then so many things in our lives may be considered paranormal (and normal at the same time); everything may be magic in a way.

Mike
There are things that lure us out of our ego. Dreaming, music, and prayer gives us access to the larger world of the collective unconscious, or whatever word you want to use.

Sebastiano
I tend to agree. I remember in a recent interview, right when we were finishing it. It was for a radio show and the host asked me: "Tell me, Maestro, if you could be a superhero, which superpower would you like to have?" My world as a teenager was populated by Marvel and DC comics, so I was well aware of what they were asking about.

I responded, "I'm already a superhero. I move my hands in the air and music comes forward."

Of course, you have to get this quote right, with the amount of humor it was said, with a grain of salt and not in that ego-centered way, which would be something completely alien to me. We already discussed how music making and conducting are not like that, not at all. And I'm no superhero of any kind.

Again, it's a very long, very complex, and time consuming process.

But in the end, when I'm conducting in a hall before, let's say, a hundred musicians and a thousand spectators, I raise my baton and—lo and behold—suddenly out of the silence there's music...and I'm not producing a sound! That's a superpower. Or, even better, that's magic for you.

Mike
Magic is made daily all the time, and many of us know what it is. But we live it unconsciously. Most of us live in a fantasy world. Even the most rational people: they're watching Disney movies, they're watching fantasies, but they're pretending that's just blowing off steam. But those worlds are real too.

Sebastiano
Nothing is more real than that kind of magic! So much so that it produces money and creates jobs! You live as a music journalist, I make money as a musician, people get paid to work on movies and to write fiction. I mean, there is a very concrete way in which the pseudo normal and the pseudo paranormal live together and are, in a way, one and the same.

This reminds me of another idea I would like to pass on to you. It's nothing new, of course, it's just yet another thought I like to play with.

Among people who study reality (or Reality), you usually have two battling parties, right?

The rational, materialistic and science-inclined people, and well, the other sort, whatever you want to call it. I don't think you can be fully human without the two of them combined. There is little value in being a gullible and not cultivated person. The other end of the spectrum, lacking fantasy and imagination, may also be very limiting and uninteresting.

It's not only a matter of meditating or praying or doing rituals or believing something, in my view that alone is not enough, as it's not enough to read and study without any inner conscious search. Take Helena Blavatsky as a possible example of this false dichotomy: you may like theosophy or not, but that woman researched, wrote and published thousands of pages, she was not just sitting down chanting "om." I mean, you have to work for it—and also meditate, quite possibly!

I think music is a wonderful example of this combination of hard work and letting go, of theory and practice, of science and magic.

In the end, one may reach a point in which magic is science and science is magic. As Arthur C. Clarke said, "Any sufficiently advanced technology is indistinguishable from magic."

YORK CATHEDRAL

In the early spring of 2023, Arielle, Travis, and I visited England. After spending a few days visiting London, we jumped on a train to York, chugging through the verdant rolling hills of the English countryside. For as old as England is, I wondered why it looked so clean from the train window.

When we arrived at York we headed straight to the cathedral. York Cathedral, or York Minster as it is referred to, is towering, reaching a height of 235 feet. Approaching the cathedral from the side, we encountered a large building attached to it. That alone was impressive. But as we walked around to the entrance, we beheld the imposing spires that soared way above the smaller building.

That night we attended Evensong service, which is performed daily at the Minster. It is a church service traditionally held near sunset focused on singing psalms and other biblical canticles. The service of Evensong is unique to the Anglican church and is derived from the older Roman Catholic service of Vespers (or evening prayer). Its structure and wording are contained in the Book of Common Prayer, which dates back to 1662.

Upon entering, we were greeted by armed police, which seemed a little odd at first.

During the service, we were not allowed to record anything, take pictures, and so on. Police roamed the church floors, issuing commands, telling people to put their recording and photographic equipment away. The Minster is tightly guarded, like they are protecting the Pope.

As the procession of singers floated past us, as if in a dream, some holding relics, crosses, ancient texts, they each sang a harmony part. As it was live, we heard each voice distinctly, as they walked in procession. The ages, sizes and sex of the singers varied, creating a wonderful combination of sounds. The voices blended beautifully, bouncing off the walls of the Minster.

Looking up at the vaulted ceilings and beautiful stained-glass windows, I felt like we were in a spaceship traveling across space and time. The Evensong music cast me into a dream. Listening closely, I could hear how the band Yes had incorporated the polyphonic choruses into their music. I thought to myself: I could die here and be completely content. Even Travis, then twelve years old, was quieted by the experience. The profundity didn't escape him.

I asked Travis to take sneak pictures during the service. He surreptitiously held the camera and waved his hand with it, camouflaging the picture taking. A dutiful father, I figured better that he gets in trouble than I. Later in the day, I learned that it was only during services that taking pictures or recordings was not allowed. This was to preserve the sanctity of the service.

Meanwhile, I was entranced by the sweeping distances inside the Minster, rendering me speechless. My eyes scanned the flying buttresses, rows of arches, and dazzling colors, trying to take it all in. It seemed like an endless labyrinth.

Unbeknownst to us, the day's service was in celebration of Ascension Day. Since I couldn't record it or take out my phone to write notes, I scribbled some notes on the handed-out pamphlet.

The liturgy was delivered in a somber but poetic English voice. Here is what I remembered.

> *Wherever prayer is said, wherever peace is proclaimed, we get a glimpse of the stars. We get a taste of the sky and can bring heaven to earth.*

> *The Ascension empowers us to come back to earth with a purpose.*

The speaker said he was quoting Da Vinci, but the quote actually came from a 1965 film about da Vinci, titled *I, Leonardo da*

Vinci. It was likely John Secondari, the screenwriter, who actually wrote the words, but wrote them for Da Vinci to say.

When once you have tasted flight, you will forever walk the earth with your eyes turned skyward. For there you have been, and there you will always long to return.

He continued.

As we see Christ ascend, we are inspired to gaze toward heaven, being called to look up and out of ourselves.

After service, we took a walk along the Roman era wall that weaves throughout much of the city of York. On one side of the wall, the City of York spreads out, dotted with churches, stores, ancient, medieval, and contemporary architecture. On the other side are quaint homes, surrounded by lovely gardens. It's very quiet and separated from the noise of the city.

As we were walking along the wall, we spotted a raven. Sitting on the edge of the wall, the bird appeared to be guarding the path back to the Minster. He looked menacing.

Approaching the raven cautiously, asking if we had permission to pass, I noticed that it had a feather clutched in its talon.

We didn't budge, wondering what the raven might do next.

The raven stared at us, as if wanting us to read its mind. Finally, it lifted its claw in a gesture of peace, offering me the feather. I didn't take the feather, but assumed it was meant to be a sign that we could proceed.

"Okay, let's go," I said. "We've been given permission."

We glided past the raven and sauntered back to the Minster. We were all slightly struck by our communication with another intelligence. The experience was so rewarding, we attended service again the next night.

CREDO

ANGEL VOICES
Julie A. Colton's Story

There are now thousands of people in the Peter Rowan Appreciation Society Facebook group I created, but I connect with only a few of them directly. You've met several already; another was Julie A. Colton, a musician and music fan. I became acquainted through her Facebook posts and our subsequent interactions.

Born in Nigeria, Julie has spent most of her life in Sheffield, England. Julie and I have been in contact, sending messages back and forth. I've gotten to know Julie a little better chatting on FaceTime. The miracles of modern technology. Julie and I share interests beyond music. Though neither of us maintain a specific religious practice, we are both curious about the uncanny.

After we discussed the concept for this book, Julie sent me the following story, written in the third person.

Tentatively, she approached the sooty, black polluted church.

"How do I get in?"

Huge, knotted doors, a barrier. St Anne's Church—how long had it been since she'd entered a church? A good number of years and counting!

Observing a tiny gap, she pushed gently—and was in!

A surge of smells infuses her! The fragrant fustiness of flowers dying, old books; an image of fingers (long dead), thumbing their way through crumbling hymnals. She remembers it well!

Tiptoeing to the farthest pew, this beautiful, but broken woman, heart swelling in her throat, already feels a little hope, a little comfort at this return.

Observing for the first time, a tall man in robes, pale but with kindly lines, speaking soft words toward expectant listeners—fledglings, looking silently up, to be fed. He draws an image that she will carry for the rest of her life: a delicate flower pushing its way through the car park tarmac; a tiny symbol of resilience imprinting on her retina. A dazzle of yellow hope swirling into her brain. Then, the organ promptly speaks of "All Things Bright and Beautiful"—casting her back over the years.

As she begins to sing, she remembers Nanny saying she had a voice like a little silver bell; just like her great grandma of generations before.

She takes this as the message—maybe, just maybe, she could join the choir? Once planted, the thought grows. She scans the noticeboard on her way out—choir meets every Thursday at 7:00!

***

Thursday evening. Cold, miserable and dark. She nearly didn't go. Somehow, the door pushes her out onto the street, snapping the impatient latch shut behind her—don't come back until it is done!

A half run-walk, face stinging in the rain, she finds her way around to the back of the church—the vestry. This is it then… placing her foot onto the scooped-out lichened step, she enters for the first time—the first perhaps, of many more to come, a gentle voice inside her says.

In the vestry, a time-capsule! Fuzzy black-and-white photos of choristers many decades gone. Robes are crammed in the porch. A strong, yet not unpleasant scent of fust, envelops the place. "Fust and fervor!" she thinks, books and scores strewn everywhere! She walks quietly, a little out of breath towards a row of gray plastic chairs. She is asked to meet with the choirmaster for a short audition. Hearing an echo of footsteps from within the church, she braces—and then, there he is. Diminutive, ruddy, again, those kindly creases around the eyes. His tension and nervousness surpass her own fears. A brief shaking of hands—why is he so wired? No matter; she is just here to sing.

"Now then, what do you sing?" She's a little confused, so states that she can sing both high and low—there are words for that, but at this moment, she cannot quite recall.

Passed an enormous, tattered book, she nervously warbles *a cappella* on a hymn. Curtly nodding, he ushers her toward the piano. Playing notes; she emulates; echoing pitches through the scale—higher and higher—when does this stop?

Again, tension and excitement as he quietly mutters "perfect pitch! Perfect pitch!" She sees music is everything to this man and that he too is excited! She feels reassured; a little more confident in her task.

Jumping off his stool, he declares, "Sops! Yes, Sops, I think!" (That was it! Alto and soprano, she remembers it now!) Come back next Thursday to meet the rest of the choir."

"It is done then, it is done!"

"You did it!" A quiet whisper inside her ear.

Already lifted, she runs home excited, through the cold, sleety rain.

The music of her story is about to begin!

***

Whose idea could this possibly be? Madrigals on the tower? Our gentle, intense choirmaster Alwyn—never missing a trip to King's in Cambridge, to watch live, the recording of their famous festival of lessons and carols.

Always scaling the heights of English tradition; yearning for the return of those sleepy English spires. Each year a higher descant written—top C, Alwyn? Really? Who amongst us can do that? "Jesus Christ the Apple Tree"? Are you joking? Even Liz will struggle, they think!

***

It's 6:00 a.m. on a clear, fresh May morning, a clattering of feet on well-worn steps. Giggles turning into seriousness. Scaling the tower, for madrigals at dawn. Top- notch harmonies to caress sleepy residents awake.

***

Confused sleepers speculate, "What is this I'm hearing? Are these voices for real?"

"Such sweet ghosts are nudging me awake!"

***

Until of course. The Egg!

A clumsy foot, a shuffle too many? It's quite tight up here, isn't it? Then, a soft popping sound—the smell, oh the stench! How do you sing harmonies when holding your nose? Not quite the experience expected, but together, they had tried!

***

The years pass, midnight masses, evensongs, funerals and weddings come and go. "Beware the parallel lines!" Frank warns young couples from his pulpit—train lines running side by side, never meeting!" She must always stop herself from mouthing his words! "Jesu Joy" on repeat at five pounds a pop—thank you kindly—only the third time today!

The terror of the solo, legs trembling, but "Oh!" such euphoria in its wake!

The incredulity finding out at his funeral, that Mr. C, the grumpy old verger from the Bass line was running daring missions behind enemy lines for the Special Ops Executive—never spoke a word of it—no one had known!

An uncontrollable fit of giggles, one sunny Easter morning. So infectious no one could stop! Frank's sermon faltering! A slightly bewildered congregation!

At last! Promotion to lead chorister with a surprise medal presentation. This made her feel important and a little bit proud to at last be processing from the front! She is rising!

The young woman blossoms and grows into her fullest self. Her heart is mended with the magic of music.

The angel voices calling a little louder, with the passing of the years.

She is thankful for their call. Her great grandmother gently smiles.

SPACES OF OTHERNESS
Tim Bragg's Story

Tim spent his early childhood in Birmingham, England, and later lived near Warwick. He went to the University of Warwick. Tim studied music in London, later lived in the Czech Republic and currently resides in France.

I met Tim Bragg through my friendship with UK-based writer Anthony Peake.

As with many of the relationships in this book, there's a randomness to how I connected with Tim. I guess you can say that's how life works. Like chemicals, we tend to bond with some and not others.

After Tim had posted some of his music, we interacted via Facebook messenger, eventually getting on a call to talk. Tim and I realized after about an hour that we could talk for the next few hours. But there was laundry to attend to and other household chores.

I bought Tim's excellent dystopian novel *The Mirror* and he purchased my book *Mescalito Riding His White Horse*. Our correspondence only increased. It's like we grew up in different places together. More than being friends, we have now developed a creative collaboration, sharing writing projects, drafts, and ideas. Tim put considerable effort into reviewing the *UFO Symphonic* manuscript. It's unusual for two friends who have never met to have made such a strong bond. I feel like I've known Tim all my life. I am very grateful for the miracle of our friendship.

Here are Tim's two stories and two poems.

One of the few times I took a psychedelic substance—in this case LSD—it corresponded to me playing a new drum kit with my first-ever band. I'd started music late and I was twenty when I got my Maxwin kit, budget Pearl drums in fact, but nevertheless magical for me. The sheer physicality of the drums and cymbals was inspiring. I hadn't grown up playing an instrument, though music was inside of me. My first "trip" experience took off as I began playing. I can still vividly recall how my body melded with the kit. When I pressed down on the bass drum's pedal it was as if my leg was entering into the drum itself. The drum skin giving way to my body and merging with me. Fascinating! At the same time, I recall tapping the ride cymbal. I bought this cymbal in London with my best friend Paul. When I struck the hand-hammered metal I saw layers of color unfold. A whole range of them seemed to hang in the air. I'd never seen sound before. At the time I seemed to accept these sensations almost matter-of-factly despite also being aware of their oddness.

The "trip" played out as one might imagine. We were young men in a rambling old house in the middle of winter with a crackling fire providing our only heat. Looking into the flames of the fire I could see a host of scurrying, emberfied insects and animals. At one instance a dog suddenly leapt from the flames. In one particular room the air seemed to contain hidden partitions, "spaces of otherness," as if I knew that by turning into one of these I would be transported in both time and space. But all was well, for the most part, though there was one chap (not in the band) I instinctively didn't take to and who wasn't tripping.

After jamming we decided to go outside. Snow was falling. Each flake was a tiny fairy or pixie parachuting down onto the ground. It was wonderful. A gun shot rang out and I could trace its sound across the bare wintry sky. The problem was we weren't dressed adequately to be outside. Thus, a part of my mind began to "communicate with me" through metaphor. A black-branched tree suddenly became laden with skulls. My mood was turning. Quickly I went back into the warmth and sat down on a settee. I must have been shivering and I could feel my insides—even where the base of my tongue connected with my throat. The chap who wasn't tripping put on "Be Careful With That Axe Eugene" by Pink Floyd. Not a very sensible choice. I don't think I've listened to this song since (perhaps once) but I heard screams that were either in the track or in my mind. Things took a turn for the worse.

Being able to feel the inside of one's body was bad enough but now I felt as if I were losing my mind. Again, a part of my mind conjured imagery to help "me" and "it". How strange is that? Looking back, it was as if there was me—the mind and body experiencing—but also the same mind split further into two—one side, if you like, was being lost and the other side was communicating with "me" to save it. The mind that was aware of itself being lost presented me with the sensation of being on top of a coach—a stagecoach. It could have been from Victorian England or the Wild West. I was seated high at the front and there was a team of muscular horses. They were galloping wildly, and I was certainly not in control. But it was down to me to wrestle them back. Now, of course, the imagery is obvious—but then, it was real, and I knew I had to save the coach (my mind) from overturning and worse. I had to save myself—my sanity!

I managed to gain control using the reins, though how exactly has now become a mystery. I'd had no experience of horses other than to mount one once at my uncle's small farm and dismount immediately. Now I was just about in control of my mind. I'd brought along a copy of the album Vagabonds of the Western World by Thin Lizzy. The artwork on the vinyl's cover is by Jim Fitzpatrick and has both Celtic and futuristic imagery along with the three members of the band at the time. There were Celtic inscribed stones, planets, a rocket and a city in the distance. Putting the record on, I sat back and listened. In fact, there was a scratch which meant that a song played and then the needle lifted, returned and replayed over and over. With the cover in front of me and with the soothing wave of music collapsing and gathering again, I stared intently at the art. My vinyl copy of this album is stored somewhere in a box of records but with the internet I can easily rediscover the art. And yet. This is not what I saw back then. The band members had become "comic-book" cartoon characters and were climbing the great rocks of the planet (maybe our planet?) and were waving at me. These little figures, animated in design but also with their arms gesticulating wildly, were calling to me from far away. Far away in another dimension on a planet of rock, or a barren piece of Earth, on a vinyl record cover I was holding and utterly connected to. Phil, Brian and Eric saved me. It was Brian (Brian Downey, the drummer with Thin Lizzy) that I can see now, his long flowing locks—his cartoon self as alive as I was.

A year before Vagabonds was released, the opening guitar notes on Lizzy's version of "Whiskey in the Jar" (a traditional Irish song) had grabbed me. I was a child, a youth, when it came out in 1972. I was meant to be enchanted—and I was. Later I began drumming and rapidly improved over the years that followed and at age 21 I was given a flute as a birthday present by the band I was playing with. I hadn't a clue what to do with it other than logically fit the pieces of the tube together and see if I could get a note. Thus began my relationship with melody. The first task was to make a sound by blowing over the mouth hole—creating one's embouchure. I learnt this word much later. What did you do with your fingers? There was a printed sheet with the flute keys and blacked-out notes to show where the fingers and thumbs were to be placed. I had no idea of scales or keys. Playing along to heavy rock mainly, including Hendrix and Thin Lizzy (of course), I began a strange journey into mind and music. Without realising it, my mind was again split. There was me who was playing naturally to what I was listening to and there was a part of me that must have been listening and making note (pun unintended) of which notes were working. Such a long process—and a process that continues to refine to this day.

Paul was mentioned above. My best friend and a classically trained guitarist. I have his guitar now—he was killed out in Africa. He was doing Voluntary Service Overseas—working with blind folk, growing crops up in the mountains not far from

Nairobi. Though I had sold my Triumph motorbike to buy my very first drum kit (not the Maxwin which came soon after, but a mixture of makes), Paul definitely wasn't a biker. He'd been given a small bike by VSO but was constantly asking for a Jeep. During the night before he was killed, he awoke from a nightmare—having witnessed himself being consumed by flames (I think this the case though this is doubly-unsettling as I visited a psychic some years later and he said he saw a friend consumed by fire!). His girlfriend was with him at the time—he definitely had a nightmare, maybe a precognitive one. He had to go to Nairobi in the morning. That's when a matatu (bus) did a U-turn on the motorway and he was wiped out. Tragically the cheque for the jeep he wanted arrived that very day. An untimely and tragic twist of fate.

I told you Paul was with me when I bought the Zildjian ride cymbal back in London. We played a lot together, mainly him on guitar and me on flute. I realise now how generous he must have been—I was a beginner. You know how children whistle tunes just producing one note but thinking they've got the melody? That was probably me on the flute back then. An interesting ability of our minds—to trick us into thinking we're singing, playing or whistling a tune accurately. We used to smoke cannabis and I'd get lost in the sound of the music. Again, there was a sense of a split mind—the part of me that was playing and that other part that was looking on. Though it was many years ago I can still see the imagery I created—the decreasing circles of music, the flute sounds weaving between those of the guitar. I can sense a snake, a serpent coiling the flute. But definitely a dance between wind and strings. This is a mystery of music—this opening up of our consciousness. Just as with performance being enabled by technique but having its own "life," then also this "life," this other element, seems to come through us. Work solely on technical detail and you'll kill a song idea or play rigid scales and you'll deaden a solo. But rather open up to possibilities and ideas will flow in. You can't take full credit for this creativity because there's another dimension at work. It's as if we're communicating with an external world, consciousness, or reality at a very subtle level. An otherness has to enter freely and lightly. No rigidity. As with those beautiful moments when the group acts as a collective, a whole—and rhythms and harmonies change as if by magic—it's like a spiritual experience. Maybe we are connecting with spirit. If we're "channeling" then there's been a lot of hard technical work gone into its preparation. The final act is surrendering to the music. Letting the drums talk, letting the flute soar, letting the body act as if independently.

Well, I have no idea what Paul and I sounded like back then. I do recall once taping him on guitar with me on drums after having smoked quite a lot. We thought we'd been playing at some crazy breakneck speed but on hearing it back we were both astonished by how slow it sounded! Maybe our minds were clouded. But there were times of pure joy. Times when the Spirit of Music had taken hold of our humble forms and made us dance.

Paul got killed the same year as Phil Lynott died. (Thin Lizzy's frontman, bassist and songwriter.) I'd seen Thin Lizzy play in 1975, after Eric Bell had left the band and another Brian (Brian Robertson) had joined—forming their renowned twin lead guitar sound. Thin Lizzy weren't the first, the Allman Brothers and Wishbone Ash had been pioneering this, but it became Lizzy's signature sound. After that first concert I told Phil that I preferred his "early stuff" and in his deep Irish brogue he'd responded, "Ah but you can't always be living in the past now can you?" He could have reacted badly, but I caught his generous and gentle side. Later I saw them again and then managed to get an "All Areas Pass" to see them play in Birmingham, the city I had grown up in as a younger child. We caught them on Friday night and had gone backstage and agreed to meet the following morning for breakfast—we were staying at the same hotel. A late breakfast, of course! We (I was with a friend who knew the promoter) were invited to the pre-gig sound and light check. Brian kindly allowed me to have a go on his drums—with Phil and Scott Gorham playing and a Super Trooper zooming in and out.

Everything seemed to come full circle when Paul and Phil died—more so as I recall this now. I've carried on playing both flute and drums and learnt other instruments. It's still possible for me to "lose" myself in the music, almost—if not actually—achieving a trance-like, other-worldly, state. I play flute naturally by ear—which I think extends back to not knowing or having any expectations or preconceptions when I first started playing. Now I know what scales and keys are (technique) and I can read music—but when I improvise, I can lose all sense of this and allow emotion and creativity to flow. With the drums too, basic technique allows me to free another part of my mind—again there is the split between the observer and the player—but also the creative driver. Me holding the reins but allowing those wild horses to gallop freely! At its most sublime I am immersed in music. With a band of great musicians, the whole ensemble can take flight as if one. This is music's essence—it runs deep within us—deeper than our conscious mind. As deep as time itself. And music is time, after all. Through music our minds connect to deeper, inner layers of consciousness or extend to a greater external consciousness.

In the beginning wind rustled reeds and moaned in caves; birds tapped at bark and animals howled. Life was rhythm and sound. Our minds grew and we learnt to imitate those sounds. Music brought us into altered states. And we discovered new worlds.

I wonder now, what might have happened if as a musical novice, I had taken a turn into one of those "spaces of otherness" during my first trip? The spaces of otherness for me now are found in soloing without conscious thought or in the gaps found within rhythmic repetition.

THIN LIZZY & FREDA
Another Tim Bragg Story

My mother died at 5.40 a.m., 12th March, 2008. I stayed with her in her room at the hospice until 4.00am and then, because of my exhaustion, coupled with her unsettling rhythmic breathing and the strange, ethereal piano music emanating from the next room, told her I had to go. She was asleep, or unconscious. I left her room and went up the corridor to where the nurses' station was. I explained that I was worn out and just had to go but they said I could stay in the room(s) reserved for patients' families.

Stretching out on top of the bed, I soon went to sleep. At some point I awoke as if a bolt of electricity had passed through me. It was a force of visceral energy, like lightning, shooting up my spine. Turning over I felt cold – outside it was a wild, windy night. There were gales in fact. Sometime soon after, I don't recall how long, one of the nurses–Lisa–came to tell me that I should come with her quickly as my mother was about to die. A nurse from Zimbabwe was sitting with my mother in the room. As I followed Lisa, the nurse was saying to my ma that "Tim is coming." As I stepped over the threshold of the room my ma took her last breath.

Later I asked the Zimbabwean nurse whether this was definitely true–I asked over and over again and was assured by her that as she said, "Tim is coming," my mother took her final breath. I thought I actually heard her take these final breaths, though they might not have been "true" breaths. I can only interpret this now as possible post-mortem exhalation. If that exists.

While my mother was alive, I asked her to get a message to me after death if she was able, and that I knew this would have to come in an *oblique* fashion.

On the way back to my ma's house, near Warwick, where I was staying, I accidentally killed a fox. I was about a mile or less from her home. The fox was my ma's favourite animal. She'd told me about seeing a badger after her father died–*his* favourite animal.

When I drove back after she had died, a fox ran across a dual carriageway in front of me. It seemed poignant.

After the funeral we returned to our rented cottage on the Somerset/Devon border, arriving on a Wednesday night. It was also a Wednesday when my mother had died and my wife, Annie, a teacher at the time, had to return to school on Thursday and be there for a Parents' Evening. She would have come back in the interim while my son and I stayed on in the Midlands.

On Friday I was trawling some internet sites and went onto YouTube. I wanted to listen to and watch some bands play, most likely to soothe my soul, but only watched Thin Lizzy. Furthermore I listened to *Whiskey in the Jar*. This was in the afternoon and took place within an hour or so *at the most* from when Annie was travelling back home from school. When she arrived she said she'd been listening to Radio 2 and that I wasn't to think her mad (unusual for her to say this!) but there had been a request from Freda and friends for *Whiskey in the Jar* - Freda is my ma's first name, it's unusual. It also seems that my wife had only just tuned back into the radio when the request came on. [I also strongly recall her telling me that though she always listened to the radio when traveling to and fro this was the *first time* she had tuned in since her initial and subsequent return.]

For the record my ma was also a fan of Thin Lizzy's music—which always impressed me. She died just nine days short of being eighty-two.

FLUTING CONSCIOUSNESS—
Tim Bragg

    I blow breath across the flute's mouthpiece
    Inspiration filling my soul
    Intention escaping pursed lips
    My fingers lengthening and shortening its silver body
    High and low notes
    Stave off restlessness

    My thoughts extemporize without control
    And yet their grammar is the scales
    Falling from fingertips
    Do we listen to the still small note or turn the key?
    High and low notes
    All seems recklessness

    There is a connection between these elements
    Flesh, air, metal and mood
    Between sight, even if blind
    Following ornament, or eyes closed listening inside
    High and low notes
    Ad-libbing relentlessness

    Consciousness let loose and free
    Spirit, mind, body to flute
    Language learned between rests
    What directs my fingers and soul to sound
    High and low notes
    With unbidden resourcefulness?

MUSIC IS A LANGUAGE—
Tim Bragg

>Music is a language
>Unlike any other
>Its vocabulary is
>Limited
>And yet
>Its expression boundless
>
>Music plays through us
>But cannot be held
>Against its will, we can
>Guide
>And channel
>Yet its source is mysterious
>
>Metal tubes, valves
>Strings tightened, plucked
>Skin stretched
>Tapped
>Breath controlled
>All bring this mystery into existence

Thin Lizzy & Freda

Everyone understands music
Even the deaf can feel
And be touched by its
Vibrations
And yet
It lives only when played

Music cannot be grasped
Curious symbols try to contain
But its soul is
Free
It is
Conjured from another realm

Is music within us
Or does it flow from without
Is it natural or supernatural
Transcendent
Or worldly?
We are the mediators of its spirit

Music is a language
That can be played with
Brought into being
Conducted
For all
From the beginning to the end of time.

DOORWAYS TO OTHER REALITIES
Tim Kaney's Story

I watched the documentary *Encounters* on Tubi, one of the video streaming services. Along with other candid interviews, the director, Bill Howard, visited Tim Kaney to discuss Tim's repressed memories of alien encounters. In addition to the content conveyed, what struck me about these interviews is how unrehearsed and raw they were. The interviews weren't edited, except for sound and color corrections. What you see is the discussion they had.

After I watched the video, I friended Tim on Facebook. As with other "UFO" folks, we had over a hundred common friends. Months later, when my book *For All We Know* came out, I was surprised to see Tim commenting on how much he liked the book. This emboldened me to reach out to him. During our conversation, Tim mentioned that he's working on his book, then sent me the manuscript to review. Tim's book is an important contribution to the catalog of first person testimonial accounts. Tim also mentioned that he had music related themes in his anomalous experiences. Tim's stories follow:

> After a friendly call with Mike about this book and our experiences, I was asked to share a few notes or lines on sound, music, etc. and how it relates to my own experiences and the Phenomenon. Well, I never really considered that it did, honestly. Only when I thought deeply about it did I realize just how prevalent it features. Kind of.
>
> Before coming to the recent, I must relay what sound meant

to me growing up. Our family bonded early over movies, TV shows, and cartoons. We all developed a type of photographic memory of the soundtrack and lines of dialogue. I especially seemed to imprint on the sound design of movies. Soon after watching, we could have conversations based only on movie quotes. Later in life, if I heard the soundtrack or music, I could tell you exactly when in the movie it was or what was happening. I am transported back to times of happiness, peace, and feeling connected to family and friends when I watch these movies or hear their music again. This also goes for video game soundtracks. Composers like James Horner, John Williams, and Hans Zimmer were the orchestrators of many youthful memories that have never faded. When I see these films again, my mind is here and also there. The past and the present—at once. Two signal inputs. A very in-between space.

Music is responsible for my friend and I witnessing a cat die. Let me explain. About the time we were in middle school, we were doing kid stuff on his old Toshiba PC, hunkered down deep in his basement which was carpeted in blood-red shag. Suddenly, a horrible scuffle rang out behind us. We spun around and saw his cat in the throes of a terrible fit, flailing about. I ran to the animal's aid. It had stopped moving, and I placed my ear to its chest. The heartbeat was light and slow. My friend was frozen in his chair. I relayed what I heard. Listening again to the heart revealed a lack of thump-thump. Shocked, I told my friend my suspicion. One more time listening, confirmed it was no longer in the land of the living. And now to the point: we both dropped our jaws when we realized what was playing on his computer. Metallica's "Die, Die My Darling" was the soundtrack of that poor cat's death. Our minds were always puzzled over that. We speculated as kids that music killed his cat.

Music also has a deep, positive meaning for me, as I used it often to fall asleep. It helped drown out my anxious, racing thoughts. It brought calm and peace to my mind. What's more is that metal bands seemed to be the most effective at quelling my teenage angst. It would take about three full CDs on my stereo to finally get me to fall asleep. But it did work.

In 2010 or 2011, I had what I call my triggering event with the Phenomenon. It started with a low, droning hum that I felt in my bones more than I heard upon waking. I was not able to move and could not open my eyes. Moments later, it stopped, and I shot upright in bed. I am bathed in silence and it is deafening. I felt a presence in my room. I see a shape flit out our window. That sound will always haunt me. I can never forget it. It transformed my life.

My thinking and later research suggests sound and vibration acts as a type of transfixing or control avenue for whatever happens to us during these times. We are not supposed to be aware of it, but it does happen.

I regard certain music as transformative or transporting devices. It was used to induce me into hypnosis. Further, sound from memory extended that induction by literally placing me in a time of my past, where I felt no pain and no stress. There was a tree I used to lay under. It was the most beautiful thing to lay under it and listen to the fall leaves rustle and crackle while blowing in and around it.

Another type of music at a certain frequency enables one to enter a specific type of sleep, allowing for lucid dreams and a type of astral travel. For a while, I did this to get to the bottom of my own experiences. Sometimes I had memory fragments come back to me in dreams that needed to be pieced together. Or dreams which produced sudden revelations.

So, what does it mean? For me, it means being able to sleep. It means being able to go back to a happy place in time and space. It brings on good feelings of energy and hope when I work or drive. Furthermore, it also has a more esoteric effect when I hear music close to that used in my hypnosis sessions. There is also a piece to it that is not so positive, but yet must have been part of my own evolution.

In the end, music is a type of sound. Sound is nothing more

than vibrations. Vibrations are heralded to open doorways to other realities. These vibrations could even alter the physical realm around us. Maybe it means it is the universal transmedium device that allows for the connection of consciousness to other signal inputs. Likely, it is a method for putting our mind and body in the place between places. All we need to do is take that final step and we will see the unseen.

Music and sounds are to me the key to unlocking the door to the vestibule of figurative and literal liminality, a space and time adjacent to the here and now.

Sometimes it is good. Sometimes it cripples me.

YUNGCHEN LHAMO

There are some singers who invent a genre to suit their uniqueness. Yungchen Lhamo is one of those artists. Born in Lhasa, Tibet, Yungchen crossed the Himalayas to Dharamshala, India, with her son strapped to her back. She then moved to Australia, where she recorded prayers of meditation. This collection developed into her first CD, *Tibetan Prayer*, which won the Australian Recording Industry Award (ARIA) for best world album in 1995.

Performing throughout the world, Yungchen was signed by Peter Gabriel to his recording company, Real World Records, through which she released her second CD, *Tibet, Tibet*, in 1996.

Yungchen has since performed at Carnegie Hall with luminaries such as Philip Glass, Michael Stipe, Natalie Merchant, and others. Yungchen also performed at the 1997 Lilith Fair festival with Natalie Merchant, Sarah McLachlan, Sheryl Crow, and Jewel. Around this time, she was invited by Laurie Anderson to perform at the Royal Albert Hall in London, sharing the stage with Sir Paul McCartney, Annie Lennox and Lou Reed.

I had the privilege to talk via Facetime with Yungchen at the end of March 2021.

"How did you learn to sing?" I asked.

Dressed in a traditional yellow Tibetan robe, holding prayer beads, Yungchen described her earliest recollections.

"Where I grew up, life was extremely hard for all of us, especially being raised by a single mother back then.

"We prayed all the time. One day, as I was singing a prayer, my grandmother asked me, 'Where did you learn that song?'

The conversation went something like this.

"What song, grandmother?"

"The song you're singing," my grandmother said.

"I just made that song up."

Surprised, she asked "Do you want to be a singer?"

"No, I want to grow up quickly and become either a nun or a man," I said. My grandmother's jaw dropped upon hearing this.

"Why do you want to become a man?"

"I want to be able to carry firewood and water, and help the elderly," I said.

"If you want to help people, you must sing. This is your gift," my grandmother replied.

"Then one day, I was singing 'Ari-Lo,' which would be a song on my second album *Tibet, Tibet*."

"How do you know this song?" my grandmother asked.

"This is a song I made up," I replied.

"My grandmother and mother were now both in tears. This was a very moving and magical moment for all of us."

"You need to sing to the world," my grandmother said.

And singing to the world is what Yungchen has done.

"Where did you meet Peter Gabriel?" I asked.

"I met Peter in London after I toured Australia when I was performing for the Dalai Lama. I hadn't yet made an album. But I was told that I needed to make a CD. I didn't have the concept of singing something to then sell it. Even now, I don't believe myself to be a singer. For me, singing is an offering. A prayer. However, listening to my manager, I quickly made the album *Tibet Prayer*, which, to my surprise, won the equivalent of the Grammy in Australia for Best World Music album. But this also meant that now I had to travel the world to perform. I would be representing Tibet and bringing our music to the world. And so, I went. And since then, it's never ended."

"Why did you decide to go with Peter Gabriel's label?" I asked.

"I chose Real World because Peter insists on having music from around the world. Because of him, people know about other cultures. Peter looks beyond the music, to the culture, and the story behind the song. He cares deeply about the world. Not just about making hits. And Peter's a good friend. He's made the impossible possible. I had every obstacle in front of me. I am a woman, I don't speak the language, I don't have a big band, I perform spiritual songs and I don't have a stage show. But Peter believed in the music, and this has made all the difference."

"Do you consider yourself a Tibetan artist?"

"There are two main types of Tibetan music. The first is the traditional Tibetan folk songs and operas, which I learned when young, but my own music is not Tibetan in that sense. The other type is the Tibetan Buddhist chanting of prayers and mantras and my songs tend to reflect something of that tradition," she replied.

"The industry labeled you world music."

"You know, when I first heard this term *world music*, I thought it sounded silly. Isn't music something that's meant for all the world?" added Yungchen.

"It's a term that describes how narrow the music industry can sometimes be," I said.

"I hear everything in your music. That's what makes it so special. I hear blues, jazz, classical and folk. Yes, I hear prayers too, but sung like I've never heard before. Besides, isn't all singing a form of prayer?" I asked.

"I sing for the world—not just Tibet. I don't look for the music—sometimes you make connections—you make creative contacts. I play with people, not just the instruments or styles from which they originate. I mostly sing *a cappella* but since I've worked with musicians from other cultures, each of my albums after *Tibet Prayer* has a different feel. For instance, on *Coming Home*, I worked with French producer Hector Zazou. My fourth album, *Ama,* was produced by Jamshied Sharifi, an Iranian American. My third album, *Tayatha,* was produced by Anton Batagov, a Russian pianist and post-minimalist composer. And finally, on my current album, *Awakening,* I worked with Spanish producers Julio Garcia and Carmen Ros. No doubt each album reflects the culture and musical traditions of the different producers and musicians that have worked on them," she replied.

"How did you meet Peter Rowan?" I asked, having seen a video of Yungchen performing with him. As a bluegrass fan, I was very interested in this connection. I told Yungchen that I've been a huge fan of Peter Rowan since his collaboration with Jerry Garcia, David Grisman, and Vassar Clements on *Old & In the Way.*

"I met Peter Rowan in 2015; we were playing on the same bill at the Leaf Festival in North Carolina. Peter then asked me if I wanted to play with his bluegrass group at the Lake Eden Arts Festival, also in North Carolina. The Lake Eden Arts Festival is traditionally a bluegrass *only* festival, I was told. 'They might resist something new,' Peter said. I must tell you; we were a hit. People gave us a standing ovation. Then that autumn I toured with Peter for his new album, *The Old School,* and we have collaborated on and off since then. I am working with him again right now on a new song and plan to meet up with him in California in April. One can say that Peter sings bluegrass, but his music transcends that category," said Yungchen.

"You're a true world music composer," I said.

We both laughed a little.

"Your new CD, *Awakening,* is spectacular. I love all the spiritual aspects of the songs, but I hear so many emotions and influences. "Home Is Wherever you Are" for instance, reminds me of an Appalachian song. I hear that high, lonesome sound in your voice. It's layered with longing and sadness. What inspired this song?"

"I hear music and it finds its way into my music. I don't try to copy. It just happens."

Perhaps Peter Rowan's influence found its way into the feel of "Home Is Wherever You Are," I thought.

Like all Yungchen's albums, the songs on *Awakening* are incredibly varied. And while the title song, "Awakening," is a prayerful invocation, Yungchen's ribboned voice winding around a violin on the song "Monkey Mind" comes more from the blues tradition.

"'Loving Kindness' has a flamenco influence and features singer Carmen Linares. The song "Sun and Moon" is a sensuous romance. Yungchen's voice whispers through mysterious landscapes, taking you on a visionary journey. As though flung across the globe from closer to Yungchen's roots, the song "Four Wishes" is reminiscent of Chinese music.

Yungchen is like a sponge who takes everything she hears and incorporates it into her music. You will hear her voice sound as delicate as the wind, but you'll also hear her voice boom like it can carry across mountains. At the heart of all her music is prayer. Tuneful prayer.

I asked Yungchen about her One Drop of Kindness Foundation.

"At One Drop of Kindness Foundation, people can volunteer, bringing their specific talents with them. Whether they're writers, designers, or teachers. We're just asking for people to give their time. Elderly people willing to teach Tibetan children. One week, thirty minutes. In the future we will have a place so that children can go to learn dancing, singing and prayer. This is open to everyone. Like the One Drop of Kindness water signature logo suggests, all it takes is one drop of yourself. My wish is that if we human beings appreciate the world around us, this makes us healthy and makes the world a better place. One drop of water accumulates. Many drops of water make an ocean."

Since it was established in 2004, the One Drop of Kindness Foundation's projects have brought music, hope, health, and happiness to many people in Tibet, Nepal, India, the US, and Ireland.

Initial projects included providing single mothers, children, and the elderly in Tibet with clothing, shoes, prosthetic limbs, and educational supplies.

In addition, Yungchen has brought her music to countless homeless shelters, classrooms, retirement homes and community spaces throughout the US, Asia, and Europe. A show in Kingston, NY, "You Are Beautiful, I Am Beautiful," was reviewed in *Newsweek* magazine.

Yungchen also makes jewelry, which she started doing during the pandemic.

"If you purchase my jewelry, it goes towards the foundation."

"What's next for you?"

"While I'm trying to find a label for *Awakening*, I'm working on another album now called *In Grass Valley*."

We talked for a while longer, discussing the importance of trying to do the right thing in life, to be a good person. I really didn't want to hang up. I showed Yungchen my guitar and we even played a song together. It was delightful. I told Yungchen that she's like water and can fit into any shape. If Yungchen is considered world music, it's because her music contains the entire world.

Yungchen and I stayed in touch. She invited Arielle, Travis and me to visit her in Kingston, New York. Yungchen made a delicious Tibetan dinner for us and some others, suggesting we invite our friends in nearby Woodstock to join.

"You have to let me help," I said, as Yungchen brought out the dishes of food.

Although she presents herself as a very serious spiritual person, Yungchen has a great sense of humor and can be silly, too. Later that night, we danced around with her friends, listening to Peter Rowan's "Free Mexican Airforce."

"Do you want to talk to Peter Rowan?" she asked. As a rule, I never ask artists that I interview to introduce me to other people. It's a pride thing. "He's waiting for your call," she said.

MESCALITO RIDING HIS WHITE HORSE—PETER ROWAN

The details of my introduction to Peter Rowan are described in my book *Mescalito Riding His White Horse*. Initially I had intended to write a short article for a music magazine about Peter's legendary career. But, like so many other events and "chance" meetings, a simple offer/question/comment led to something much larger and far reaching.

I was drawn to Peter's music, but there was more. Peter's knowledge of bluegrass and music lore, and in particular his relationship with Bill Monroe, was fascinating to me. Peter related stories about Monroe, sometimes playfully mimicking Bill Monroe's Kentucky accent. He also shared some of the profound philosophical ideas that Bill Monroe imparted to him.

"Pete, when the music's right you will feel like you're flying. And then you can hear the ancient tones," said Bill Monroe, for example. When relating this to me, Peter added, "It wasn't that you hear the ancient tones and so you go and try to make them. You make the music, and the ancient tones emerge. You follow the musical rules, but you're not invested in them. The ancient tones emerge from the application of selflessness."

Receiving the precepts of bluegrass directly from Bill Monroe, Peter interpreted the ancient tones for a new generation. "The veil that keeps bluegrass from being appreciated more deeply is that the notes go by too fast. The fiddle was the only sustaining instrument in a bluegrass ensemble. The guitar has occasional leads, but is mostly rhythm, hidden down in the matrix of counter-rhythms.

When it worked it was transportive,"[62] Peter said.

"Also, Bill Monroe taught me that music is very physical, all the way from trance dancing to crowding the microphone [as they would all huddle into it] to singing a bluegrass duet," he continued.

Peter has applied these ideas to the music in his catalog. The song "Panama Red," for example, is imbued with Peter's alchemical transmutation of the ancient tones. "Panama Red," like many of Peter's tunes, unleashes powers that charge you to dance and sing. That makes listeners want to kiss and embrace one another. Its rapture inspires people to a holy state of pure love and joy.

The ancient tones take us to this place of transcendence or paradise. The word "paradise" comes from the Persian *pairidaeza*, meaning "park" or "enclosed garden." It suggests an intermediate state between incarnation and bliss. The enclosed garden is a primal state, charged with vitality and possibility.

Receiving these bits of bluegrass lore from Peter set my imagination on fire. I began having dreams and visions:

> *I was at a summer home that was also some kind of portal. I could feel the presence of aliens and other beings behind the walls. When I left, someone put an adhesive acid tab on my face, and I started tripping. I ran into Peter, who was a train conductor. When I got on the train, I had to hold on, upside down, as we roared through the subway tunnel—but it was more like a roller coaster. I was laughing and crying, saying I wouldn't want to be anywhere else. Peter told me that I was making too much noise. The subway tunnel became a mall. People were going into shops. The train stopped. My mobile phone was still in my hand. I slid it into my shorts pocket and zipped it. The train took off again.*[63]

Another dream:

---

62 Fiorito, Mike. *Mescalito Riding His White Horse*. London: John Hunt Publishing, 2023
63 Fiorito, Mike. *Mescalito Riding His White Horse*. London: John Hunt Publishing, 2023

I was given a sacred object...by extraterrestrials. The object looked benign. When I looked closer, I saw a likeness of a green and purple Yoda Buddha. But the image could only be discovered by holding the object sideways and upside down. Like the way you might suddenly "hear" the encoded messages in bluegrass. You had to discover the primer to truly "hear" it. You had to come to this realization.[64]

While writing the article, and then the book, my dream journaling became more frequent and intense. The dreams and visions spoke to me powerfully.

I joked with Peter that he had *put a spell on me,* recalling the song by Screamin' Jay Hawkins, but of course it wasn't his doing. While Peter is deeply philosophical and interested in wisdom traditions from around the world, he is very down-to-earth. I sometimes wondered what he made of my dreams. Did he think I was nuts? Perhaps my long familiarity with his songs, the embedding of his music in my unconscious mind provoked a deep response in me. Our communication was potent, magical, triggering emotions and thoughts deep in the history of my mind, penetrating the dimensionality of time. As music does. We are simply not in control.

For this reason, I ascribed to him, as other people have, the qualities of a mystic or shaman.

As Joachim-Ernst Berendt wrote in *The World Is Sound,* the words for "poet," "singer," and "magician" derive from the same linguistic root in Latin and other languages. In Mexico, for example, the Huichol Indians use the Spanish word *cantor* to mean, "magician" or "shaman."

"One can sense the transition that must have taken place somewhere in time: in the process of working magic through primal sounds, evoking metamorphoses through sounds, man musicalized these sounds—he sang,"[65] wrote Berendt.

64   Fiorito, Mike. *Mescalito Riding His White Horse.* London: John Hunt Publishing, 2023
65   Berendt, Joachim-Ernst. *The World Is Sound, Nada Brahma.* Rochester: Inner Traditions, 1983

As Mircea Eliade said, shamans sing in the lost language of the animals that humans once knew.

Peter's fans have long considered him to be a cosmic cowboy or a bluegrass shaman thanks to songs like "The Walls of Time," "Land of the Navajo," "Dharma Blues," "Across the Rolling Hills (Padmasambhava)," and many others.

In interviews and on stage, Peter is sagacious, referencing religious texts and spiritual traditions. He is endlessly curious. And his intimate collaborations with people like Bill Monroe, Jerry Garcia, and Tony Rice have given him deep insights into American music in the twentieth century.

In addition to dreams there were synchronicities.

I sent Peter my book *Falling from Trees* to give him a sense of the direction the book project might take. Peter then sent me a poem he had written many years ago called "Falling from the Trees." This was uncanny. When I told him about an out-of-print Harry Smith documentary I had in my possession, Peter related to me his Harry Smith story: meeting him in New York City, then at the Naropa Institute.

The coincidences only flamed the Peter-Rowan-inspired dreams I was having.

As Terence McKenna wrote, "The shaman is able to act as an intermediary between the society and the supernatural, or to put it in Jungian terms, he is an intermediary to the collective unconscious. Through the office of the shaman, the society at large is brought into close and frequent encounter with the numinous archetypal symbols of the collective unconscious. These symbols retain their numinosity, immediacy, and reality for the society through their constant reaffirmation in shamanic ritual and through the shaman's epic narration of mythic scenarios and his artistic production."

Peter's dreams become the stuff of reality for his fans. In an interview I did with Peter for his album *Calling You from My Moun-*

tain, he said that "The Song That Made Hank Williams Dance," was delivered to him in a dream.

"A tantric goddess approached me in a dream. I was in Texas at that time. Doing meditation practices. Every day I'd go by the Guadalupe River to meditate. Evenings after those meditations, I would have dreams. I think she was an emanation of Tara.[66] In the inner sleeping awareness state, Tara can appear as a dakini [a tantric goddess],"[67] said Peter.

After a pause, Peter added, "In a dream, a dakini said to me *I'm the dance that made Hank Williams sing. I'm the song that made him dan*ce. It was a moment of what I think of as 'mythological immediacy,' when the *so-called* past takes shape in our mind as an enduring moment, a kind of spirit."

The shaman is the conduit to the underworld, or the collective unconscious. Called by many names, the shaman makes the journey to a place where others dare not go. Having healed themselves through confronting the darkness of their own soul, the shaman brings this knowledge to benefit others. The journey is often guided by a song.

"Because the point of this performance is a healing, the shaman dispatches his chief ally down the World Tree to the underworld, where it seeks out the shaman's ancestor spirit who will tell it the nature of the man's illness. The dialogue between ancestor spirit and ally is heard by all since it comes out of the shaman's mouth in the form of screams, grunts and yells,"[68] wrote Mickey Hart.

Apart from being a gifted songwriter, Peter has the ability to lift other performers and audiences alike. At a Grateful Dead tribute show in Ardmore, Pennsylvania, Peter and Kanika Moore sang "Stir it Up," "Rivers of Babylon," "No Woman, No Cry" and "Sit-

---

66 https://en.wikipedia.org/wiki/Tara_(Buddhism)
67 https://atwoodmagazine.com/prhw-peter-rowan-the-song-that-made-hank-williams-dance-video-premiere/
68 Hart, Mickey. *Drumming at the Edge of Magic, A Journey Into the Spirit of Percussion.* Harper Collins, 1990

ting Here in Limbo." As this set was lathered into full gear, Peter shimmied on stage. Although perhaps twice as old as some of the other folks on stage, Peter led the charge. I could tell that Peter was spontaneously introducing call and response with Moore, perhaps surprising her a bit. Then Steve Kimock joined in the conversation, his slide guitar bell-tone notes harmonizing with Peter and Moore's voices. The group was in no rush to end these songs. Rather, Peter lifted the band, taking both them and the audience to soaring heights.

As the call and response increased in intensity, Peter ululated above the music. If you listen to the song *"Land of the Navajo,"* you'll hear exactly what Peter's ululation sounds like. Ululation, from Latin *ululo*, is a long, wavering, high-pitched vocal sound resembling a howl with a trilling quality. It is produced by emitting a high-pitched loud voice accompanied with a rapid back and forth movement of the tongue and the uvula. In some cultures, the sound of ululation is mournful, while in others it is a heartful, even joyful, expression of emotion, praising warriors for acts of valor, for instance. Peter's voice was like a waterfall pouring into the band's ocean of sound. As Peter swayed in the light, I was reminded of how, in the Bhagavata Purana, Krishna performed his cosmic dance on the snake Kaliya (Nāga). Krishna had assumed the weight of the entire universe in his tiny feet and almost crushed the snake to death. But Krishna stopped after hearing the prayers of Kaliya's wives. Awakening from the trance of Peter's spell, I found myself standing in a column of light, reduced to a peaceful silence.

In addition to songwriting and performing, Peter has impacted many people's lives, both personally and professionally. Without going into personal details, I can relate that I was told by Peter about a woman considered to be his "greatest fan." The woman was near death, having been ill for some time. Peter assured her that he would be by her side at the hour of her death, to guide her to the other side. Peter was in Independence, Missouri and she was in St.

Louis, Missouri. With his friend, Leon Milligan, Peter drove multiple hours to be by the woman's side. She held on, waiting for him. When Peter arrived, she passed away. This is the shamanic effect Peter has on people.

Aside from the friendship, I see Peter as a kind of UFO in my life. Our collaboration and friendship have spawned numerous other friendships and relationships with other people from all over the world. Some of them are covered in this book. This all spawned directly from the music. From songs I heard in the Ravenswood Project hallway, ricocheting off the concrete walls on cold winter nights. A message in a bottle sent to me, slowly carried across time and space.

THE GODDESS (ALSO) LIVES ON TINDER
Christopher Henry's Story

While researching my book on Peter Rowan, I came across an interview with him that had been posted on YouTube by Christopher Henry in 2012. Christopher's questions were open- ended and theoretical. For example, he asked Peter, "Where do you think creative energy comes from?"

Wearing an artist's ascot, looking very cool, Peter replied, "Most people see the universe as taking place somewhere. I see it as nothing taking place everywhere," then laughed. I would come to know this laugh very well in my conversations with him. Throughout the thirty-four-minute interview, Peter eloquently extemporized, in his mellifluous speaking voice, answers to Christopher's thoughtful questions.

As I later told Christopher, this interview with Peter influenced my book *Mescalito Riding His White Horse*. In listening to Peter's sixty-plus-year oeuvre of music, I had been struck by the overarching spiritual quest that I observed in his songwriting and performing. Christopher's interview confirmed that observation and emboldened me to ask Peter deeply philosophical questions, trusting that his answers would contain interesting nuggets.

Christopher is a member of the Peter Rowan Bluegrass Band. The band's album *Calling You from My Mountain* was nominated in 2023 for a Grammy Award for Best Bluegrass Album of the Year. He is a gifted musician and educator renowned for his diverse talents as a singer, songwriter, mandolinist and multi-instrumentalist. He has been honored by the International Bluegrass Music Association with nominations for Song of the Year, Mandolin Player of the Year, and Instrumental Album of the year.

Christopher began playing the mandolin at a young age and has since mastered multiple instruments including banjo, guitar, bass, ukulele and fiddle. He is also an excellent singer. Christopher is highly regarded as a mentor to many aspiring musicians and is known for his emphasis on teaching by ear rather than using written materials. Christopher's teaching style focuses on precise instruction, teaching note-for-note, pick-stroke by pick-stroke.

Showcasing his deep interest in South American music, particularly traditional Peruvian healing and medicine songs, Christopher released *Heart Spaces* in June of 2023. The album reflects his extensive study of wisdom traditions and his experiences working with medicine plants in Peru under the guidance of a *curandero* (healer). The songs on *Heart Spaces* feature catchy melodies while conveying profound statements about reality and exploring themes of humility, healing, kindness, and compassion. Christopher describes the genre of the album as "shamanic gospel," while his wife, Brooke Carlson Henry, calls it "jungle grass."

Not only is Christopher a great musician and songwriter, but he also has a delightful sense of humor. While he may come off low-key and maybe even a little shy, he turns on when the camera rolls. Christopher leads a bluegrass ensemble called Razzle Dazzle, through which he has developed an alternate "rapper" persona. Though the music is essentially bluegrass, Christopher introduces the songs in a rapper voice, wearing a baseball cap and gold chains. The juxtaposition of rapper personality and bluegrass musician is hysterical.

I met Christopher in person for the first time at the International Bluegrass Music Awards event in Raleigh, North Carolina in 2022 when Peter was inducted into the Bluegrass Hall of Fame.

Having gotten to know him well, I consider Christopher a friend, and in many respects, a mentor. I've taken guitar lessons from him and subscribe to his monthly guitar licks service.

For this book, I asked Christopher if he had a story connecting music to the Phenomenon. That story follows.

> This was an ostensibly serendipitous revelation that came to me as I was driving one day. If I would have been super safe, I would have pulled over to open the app and see in the old section called "moments," or something like that. I noticed that someone had posted a picture of a radio station playing a song that as I recall was displaying a title that included the word "Goddess."
>
> This was sublime confirmation.
>
> In the Ayahuasca world of Peru, one can get into a lot of trouble if you are not following the rules of the diet. I learned this three times the hard way and nearly ruined my life. After I completed my chuchuhuasi and chiric sanango correction diets, life started getting much better, though it took a good while for the crushing momentum of careless sin to abate.

In Shipibo and other traditions, the *dieta*, or diet, is a practice that invites the spirit of a plant to merge with your body and spirit, and ultimately become a teacher and help you develop the power and knowledge to heal others. Dieting a plant involves fasting both food and water for a certain amount of time. The idea is to have a simple bland diet and be removed from all stimulation so you can meditate and concentrate on the plant spirit and build an authentic relationship with it. This can take a long time and can be very subtle but, in the long run, the experience can be remarkably life changing. It is very important you are aware, prepared, and ready for what you will face. Like a raging forest fire, sometimes everything will need to be destroyed before new life can spawn out of the ashes[69]

---

[69] https://www.ayahuascafoundation.org/blog/

Another important aspect of the *dieta* is the *icaro,* which is a song that is whispered, whistled, and sung by the curandero, or shaman. The word *icaro* is believed to derive from the Quechua verb *ikaray*, which means "to blow smoke in order to heal." As scholar Stephan Beyer wrote, "the *icaro* is given to the shaman by the spirits of the plants and animals, and the shaman uses it to call the spirits for healing, protection...to control the visions of another person who has drunk ayahuasca, to call the spirits of dead shamans, control the weather, ward off snakes, or visit distant planets."[70] As one mestizo shaman said, "You cannot enter the world of spirits while remaining silent."

> One night after finishing teaching at a mandolin workshop being hosted in the Virginia countryside, I realized I couldn't find my toothbrush. I went up the road, bought one and returned. As I was about to pull into the driveway, I saw what looked to be a dead animal in the left lane. In the next moment, I realized it was my mandolin that had been run over by a car or truck. I forgot I had set it on top of my car as I was looking for my toothbrush.
>
> Feeling devastated, I picked up the many splinters and pieces of wood and took them to my parents' house. It was my father's mandolin that he had let me start playing when I was getting serious about music at about age ten or eleven. When I told him, my father knew that I was upset and was just glad I was ok, as was my mom. On my spiritual radar was the possibility that the careless accident was connected to my previously crossed diets.
>
> As I went to work gluing pieces back together, I was uncertain if the mandolin would ever play again. It was my most precious physical object and I was determined to at least try. I acquired some new maple for the destroyed sides and contacted Randy Wood, the luthier who had made the mandolin in 1981. The phone call was made and soon I would go see him and find out if resurrection was possible.

---

70 Singing to the Plants, Stephan Beyer, 2010

The Goddess (Also) Lives on Tinder

That fall I went to Peru and dieted with albahaca, more commonly known in North America as holy basil and tulsi. It was a powerful experience, and I received a lot of deep healing, especially with my inner child. I hadn't really heard from chiric [the plant speaks to people] and I was still wondering about the mandolin.

After the diet was finished, I went to drink ayahuasca with Carlos, the first curandero I had worked with in Peru. When I was imbibed the medicine, chiric told me that yes, he had taken the mandolin as a consequence for my terrible behavior with the diet, and that everything was OK with our relationship now. That was a huge relief!

When I returned to Virginia, I set up the trip to Georgia to do what we could to put the mandolin back together with the new sides.

On the way down to Savannah I stopped in Charlotte for one night and matched with a woman on Tinder. I remember on her profile she had her Mayan Dreamspell sign, something about dragons, and most importantly an interest in icaros.[71] I had certainly never seen that on Tinder before.

I would later find out she had only been on Tinder two days and had not met up with anyone. I had a "little" more experience with that world than she. We made plans to meet for brunch the next morning.

Within five minutes of meeting, Brooke and I realized together that we were both working and learning independently from the same Mestizo curandero in Peru. We knew something unusual was happening.

I continued on to Savannah and we were able to get the mandolin back together. I named her Phoenix Shakti, and I presented

---

71 *Icaros* (Quechua: ikaro) is a South American indigenous and mestizo colloquialism for magic songs. Today, this term is commonly used to describe the medicine songs performed in vegetal ceremonies, especially by shamans in ayahuasca ceremonies

her to my father in newly playable condition on his 70th birthday.

Through the following months I would continue to stay in touch with Brooke. That summer we had some magical experiences that brought us closer together and I moved in with her, her fourteen-year-old son, and their territorial Jack Russell Chihuahua named Boba Fett, in Charlotte. After coming back from my next chiric diet that December, I asked her to marry me, and she said yes!

Before we got married, we did our first diet together in Guatemala with Papa Gilberto Mahua, an amazing Shipibo[72] curandero from the Ucayali River basin in southeast Peru. We dieted noya rao and she helped us get ready for the ride of our lives. We were married the following summer solstice.

On the Ayahuasca Foundation Blog, I learned that *noya rao* means "flying medicine." It is known as the flying tree or in Spanish "palo valador." In the Shipibo tradition, it has been said that *noya rao* is the pinnacle of master plants, and the plant spirit is second only to God. "A long time ago there was a Shipibo community near Pucallpa, that lived around a *noya rao* tree. One day, as happens in the Amazon, the rivers began to flood, and the community was trapped. It was said that the *noya rao* tree, aware of its ultimate demise, began to uproot itself carrying all the land, huts, and people with it and flew them all to safety or possibly another dimension."

> I was following the trail synchronicities from the revelation of the Goddess being on Tinder to the correction of the diets, to being led by chiric sanango, to meeting my future wife on the way to fix the broken mandolin, which was very symbolic of my own brokenness. I write this on a plane with Brooke heading to go see Papa G. I'm going to diet Chiric Sanango. We have

---

72 The Shipibo-Conibo are an indigenous people along the Ucayali River in the Amazon rainforest in Peru. Formerly two groups, they eventually became one tribe through intermarriage and communal ritual and are currently known as the Shipibo-Conibo people.

been married for four-and-a-half years and through all the hard times, we are still very much in love.

As far as I'm concerned, Christopher Henry is a lifelong friend. I'm excited to imagine our future collaborations.

THE MAGIC FLUTE
Frank Serio's Story

I met Frank Serio after writing *Mescalito Riding His White Horse*. Frank had posted some wonderful pictures on Facebook of Peter Rowan from various performances. I wrote to him hoping that I could use those pictures for the book and he not only sent some but we struck up a correspondence, eventually meeting at the 2021 Suwannee Festival in Florida.

In the meantime, I had learned that Frank, who'd spent the last thirty years attending and photographing music events, is also an excellent songwriter, having co-written songs with some very prominent players, including Verlon Thompson, Shawn Camp, Claire Lynch, and just recently, Peter Rowan.

Frank told me that his life partner, Sue Cunningham, a fiddle player, had performed live with Peter Rowan numerous times. She had also toured, played and recorded with Chris and Lorin, Peter's brothers. Her fiddle playing was precise and evocative. Sue made the fiddle cry.

In addition to performing with Peter, Sue had played with acclaimed musicians, including Jim Lauderdale, Vassar Clements, Darol Anger, and others. She also had a PhD in aeronautical engineering. Sadly, after a five-year struggle with cancer, Sue passed away at fifty-seven. She was beloved by all, but especially Frank.

Frank had sent me "Ode to An Angel," a tribute book that he'd put together for Sue. "Ode to An Angel" has song lyrics, some written by Frank and Sue, some written by Frank and other people, along with pictures and anecdotes about Sue. What struck me most were the loving photos of Frank in embrace with Sue. Even though I didn't yet know him well, the tears welled up in my eyes when seeing those pictures. Their two young shining faces, beaming on the page, punctured my heart.

Frank also sent me CDs of Sue's recordings with the Rowan Brothers. I found all of this very moving. From our conversations, I knew that it was hard for Frank to talk about Sue. I held the heaviness of Frank's loss in my heart.

When I learned that his father is Sicilian, as were my grandparents on my mother's side, I sent Frank my book *Sleeping with Fishes*, which he gave to his father to read. After Frank's father read the book, he called me with his father on speakerphone.

"Your book reminded me of my childhood," said Frank's father. His father's words hit me in the heart. This is why a writer writes—to connect, to make people feel. Introducing me to his dad brought me closer to Frank. It was a sign of trust, friendship, and family.

These familial ties made Frank an instant family member to me. And I know he feels the same way. When we call or write to each other, we end with "Love you, brother." This is not something either of us would say easily. Who makes friends like that after fifty? We both come from big families with many brothers and sisters. The connection I have made with Frank is another example of the magic of music. Although invisible, evaporating in the air, music is palpable. It binds people. In the case of Frank Serio and Mike Fiorito, music has made us brothers.

In "Ode to An Angel" I had read about the song "I Love You More Than Anything," written by Frank and Verlon Thompson.[73] Verlon was very close to both Sue and Frank. Sue had performed frequently with Verlon and recorded "Find Your Angel," with him

---

[73] Verlon Thompson is an American singer, songwriter, guitarist, and troubadour from Binger, Oklahoma. He has long partnered with Guy Clark as a producer, guitarist, and song co-writer.

in the last days of her life.

As the story goes, just two weeks after Sue's passing, sitting in his kitchen with Verlon, Frank said, "I don't know what to do… maybe we should write a song." Verlon agreed. Frank told Verlon about something he and Sue often said to each other. When one would say "I love you more than anything," the other would respond saying "I love you more than everything." There were little sticky notes around their house with those sayings on them. Verlon picked up the guitar. Glutted with emotion, he and Frank wrote the song in fifteen minutes, speaking parts back and forth, almost telepathically.

The next day Frank wrote to his sister saying that he and Verlon had hugged and cried, "letting Sue's spirit envelop us. Sue was right there in the room with us as we wrote in the kitchen, which was one of her favorite rooms. We just talked and talked, letting the song write itself."

At the 2021 Suwannee Festival, Verlon Thompson performed "I Love You More Than Anything." When he started singing the lyrics "I love you more than anything, I love you more than everything," Verlon choked with emotion and stopped. There wasn't a soul in the audience who didn't have wet eyes. It was as if Sue's heart was being held by everyone at once.

Since I met Frank, I've been telling him that I want to collaborate with him to tell Sue's story—this is Sue's story, Frank. Now here's a story that Frank conveyed to me about a song he wrote with Peter after the 2021 Suwannee Festival.

> Peter and I were at the 2021 Suwannee Music Festival and after four days of the festival, we drove from Live Oak, Florida down to my place in Jupiter towards the southern part of the state.
>
> The morning after arriving, the festival behind us, we're sitting around, feeling pretty spaced out with festival lag and so forth.
>
> We're drinking coffee, and Pete noticed Sue's flute, which was

sitting in the bookcase. I had never heard that particular flute played before.

Pete said, 'What's that? May I look at it?'

So I brought it over to him. He opened up the beautiful red velvet case and pulled out a silver flute.

It came in two or three pieces. Pete put it together and just began riffing around on it and playing.

One of the things that makes Peter such a great writer is the fact that he's so interested in everything. The flute became central to everything he was thinking about at the moment.

He had me looking up the serial number and surmising this and that. What it could be, where it came from? The whole time he's messing around with it.

I'm sitting and watching Pete play Sue's flute and enjoying my coffee. I decided to tell him a story that I got from a book that I was reading that I really thought would make a cool song. I proceeded to tell him the basic idea of the story. It's about a Lord in the fifteenth century in England who goes stag hunting at midnight.

The Lord leaves his wife at night, venturing out into the woods. He does this three or four nights in a row, returning empty-handed. Meanwhile, his wife starts wondering.

One night she followed him into the woods and, lo and behold, found him in the arms of another woman.

The Lady snuck up behind them without them noticing a thing. Furious, she grabbed the lord, slit his throat and ran away into the darkness through the woods.

When she gets home, she feels like she's in the clear. No one will know a thing. She gets into bed and tries to sleep.

The next morning she's awakened by a banging at the door. The townsfolk ask her "Do you know that the lord has been murdered?"

The Lady goes to the mirror to get ready to come out. She realizes there's a big blood red mark on her neck.

What is this? she wonders.

Evidently, the woman the Lord had been with was a sorceress. The sorceress had laid a curse on the wife.

Shortly thereafter, the Lady realizes she's pregnant by the Lord, her now-dead husband.

Nine months later, the baby is born with a big blood red mark on his neck. Furthermore, this curse carries down through the ages. The family is all born, everyone, with this mark.

I looked at Peter while telling him the story. He never said a word. He just kept riffing around on the flute and staring at me. I wasn't sure if he liked or even listened to the story.

"It would make a great song," I told Pete. "I have written four lines that I think would make for a good chorus," I added. I read him those four lines and he still looked at me and kept playing on the flute.

Then he took it away from his mouth and said, "I just wrote the melody."

So he was paying attention, I realized. He then played the little melody on the flute. And then he just looked at me and said, "Okay, write this down. This is how it goes," and he proceeded to kind of recite the story back to me and rhyming verses.

Then he said, "Here comes your chorus right there and then a little bit more verse story."

The chorus is "No land without a Lord and no Lord without his land."

I said, "Pete, I can't keep up." I began furiously scribbling the verses he recited. Then I took out my phone, pushed the record button and we went right through the song.

Pete had the whole story in his head. So we wrote the verses and I recorded everything. Then I said, "I've gotta listen to this recording and try to transcribe everything, so we can see what we have, Pete."

I sat there on the floor with a giant sheet of paper, listening to the recording and wrote what I was hearing.

We made a few tweaks and changes, and then, voilà, we had this magical song and we're both pretty excited and in awe of what had just transpired. High with the feeling of accomplishment.

Pete sang it a few times and we knew we had something good.

A few days later we were saying goodbye as he was flying back home.

Pete looked at me and said, "Do you realize that after we wrote the song, the flute wouldn't play? I couldn't get another note out of it."

"It just stopped playing?" I asked.

"It only played then, while we wrote the song. Then it went silent."

It was then that it really hit me. I recall that after the big buzz of writing that he was puffing away on the flute to no avail. I was so thrilled and caught up in the moment that it didn't register at the time. Neither of us talked about it at the time.

Then, as we sat there in the car, reminiscing, talking about it and realizing the extraordinary happening, it really hit home for both of us that after creating the song, the Magic Flute did not play. This was absolutely mind-blowing. Did Sue make the flute come to life just to write the song? It was a mystery.

Three or four months later, on Peter's birthday, I ended up giving him that flute.

And now it looks like Peter is back interested in the song. He's going to start performing and wants to bring it to Ireland to play for the folks over there because it's in the style of an English/Irish ballad.

That's the grateful mystery of the magic flute.

Frank's story about the flute reminded me of something I'd read in Dean Radin's *Real Magic*. In his book, Radin, who is chief scientist at the Institute of Noetic Sciences, recounted a story that Michael Shermer reported to *Scientific American* in 2018. Shermer is an American science writer and the founding publisher of *Skeptic* magazine, a publication focused on investigating and debunking pseudoscientific and supernatural claims.

At the time, Shermer was planning to marry his fiancée, Jennifer Graf.

Everything was good, but Jennifer was missing her grandfather, who was like a father figure to her. Sadly, her grandfather had died when Jennifer was only sixteen. One of the few heirlooms that Jennifer kept from her grandfather was a 1978 Philips transistor radio. Shermer had tried in vain to get the radio to play, taking it apart, replacing parts, but never could. Frustrated that he couldn't get it to work, Shermer placed the radio in the back of a desk drawer in the bedroom.

A few months later, Shermer and Jennifer were married. Jennifer was feeling sad that her grandfather wasn't there to witness it. The night after the wedding, the couple heard music coming from somewhere in the house but didn't know where. They eventually traced the music to her grandfather's radio, sitting in the back of the desk drawer, playing a lovely song.

Jennifer and Michael Shermer were stunned into silence. Jennifer told her new husband, "My grandfather is here with us. I'm not alone." The radio played all evening, then went silent the next day and never played again. This experience shocked Shermer, shaking his materialist views to the core.

Do things just stop working for no earthly reason, or are they intercepted by a spirit, or being, that is trying to break through into our dimension? To be heard. To be reckoned. Not understanding a phenomenon does not justify ignoring it.

The origin of music seems inextricably bound up with the origin of consciousness, although we don't yet know how and may never will. Perhaps buried in the leap from pre-human primate to thinking hominid is a song. That song is as old as the universe itself. Comprehending this hidden knowledge is the key to understanding our place in the cosmos.

SEE YOU TOMORROW

Andrea Tarquini's Story

I met Andrea Tarquini through the Peter Rowan Appreciation Group. Originally from Rome, Andrea now lives in Milan. He is an accomplished songwriter and musician. Andrea has played with Peter Rowan in Italy on several occasions. He has great stories to tell when we chat on Facebook. Even though my Italian is not that great, and his English is perhaps the same, we communicate well enough. I used Andrea's surname for the main character in my book *For All We Know*.

Here is Andrea's story.

> It is so rare to experience an otherworldly phenomena. It is even rarer that a person who has had these experiences can then clearly remember them. I have heard of people who, at night, in a large old country house, had heard the singing of a little girl who passed decades before in tragic circumstances. I have also heard musicians telling stories or experiences somehow linked to the afterlife having nothing to do with music.
>
> During the 1980s and 1990s, my father was the manager of a television series department of one of the most important Italian public national television networks. One of his skills, it seems, was to import the narrative patterns of American television series and adapt them to Italian national stories and the domestic television market.
>
> One day a journalist, during an interview, asked him, "Why in the era of X Files and Lost in Italy, do we continue to produce TV series about hospitals, policemen and other public figures?"

My father's response was very clear; he replied: "When we imagine aliens landing on Earth, we imagine this happening on the flat mountain of Wyoming, not in Monteporzio Catone near Rome."

This means that in every nation there is a specific collective imagination that influences people's fears and shapes them. If in the American provinces the arrival of Michael Myers is feared, here in Italy we were afraid of the ancient country brigands who kidnapped and sold children or of the spirits of these brigands. Or especially in the countryside, of some evil gnome.

And everything that is unknown recalls the narrative aesthetics of Andersen and the Brothers Grimm fairy tales rather than science fiction stories like "The Mind Thing," written by Fredric Brown in 1961 and published in Italy a year later.

However, given all this which has an undeniable European flavor, here too for adults and children it is full of stories, fears, imaginaries linked to ghosts, strange presences and contacts with the afterlife.

Personally, I believe that we are certainly not alone in the universe (there is certainly not only one of us!).

As I don't believe in God, when I think about the afterlife, I remember a beautiful song by Laura Nyro and recorded by Blood, Sweat and Tears entitled "And When I Die." In this song, the idea is that, when we die, we return to dust precisely to make room for another child to be born. Perhaps it is thanks to this beautiful way of seeing things that the end of life doesn't scare me. Indeed, it seems to me perhaps the only true form of ecology that humans have not yet managed to corrupt.

As I was saying, however, even though I don't believe in an afterlife, I do believe in energy.

When at the end of Close Encounters of the Third Kind a character says that "Maybe Einstein was one of them"...well, since human thought is an immaterial energy, I think that what we do, what we are and what we have been, leaves traces even after our death. Energy traces.

We simply have not yet learned to measure and understand this energy. We have not understood if and how much of this energy remains after our bodily death. What happens to that energy? Does something perceivable remain? Is it perceptible to some people only?

Perhaps when Einstein said that we only use ten percent of our brain, he was referring precisely to this. Maybe some people can access more of their brain and perceive things that most of us cannot.

But, in order not to go too far off topic, I will tell the only truly relevant episode even if it does not involve music but other arts.

My mother, my maternal grandfather, and I looked very similar to each other physically and I think we had some innate ways of feeling in common.

My parents were separated. My sister and I lived in Rome with my mother.

My grandfather, Pietro, was a very good, but not very successful, painter. After twenty years living in Venezuela, he returned to live near Turin, therefore far from us. However, for me he was very fascinating, every time I saw him, because I knew that I would go to art school where I would learn to paint like him.

It was the winter of 1984; my grandfather, who had smoked hundreds of cigarettes every day for years, learned that he had lung cancer.

One day he was admitted to hospital, as his condition suddenly worsened.

My mother took the first train from Rome and rushed to the hospital in Turin for fear of not having time to say goodbye to him.

My sister and I stayed in Rome with my paternal grandmother.

My mother arrived at the hospital in Turin to find her father still awake and in good mental condition.

My grandfather, who had cursed Jesus in every known language during his life, asked a nun to pray with him because he understood that his life would soon end. In his last days he alternated between moments of consciousness and moments of sedation.

Suddenly, in a shocking moment of clarity, he saw my mother gathering her things and her jacket and asked her, "Hey! Where are you going?"

"I have to go back to Rome, to my children," she replied.

And he said to her, "Okay, see you soon."

One minute later, he died.

In the following months she thought a lot about her father's words, as I later learned from several people, she struggled to understand their meaning. A few months later, in September 1985, she was killed in a scooter accident. The mandatory use of helmet law would go into effect just a few months after.

I was thirteen years old.

Was this what my grandfather meant by "See you soon"? I have always wondered if, seeing the door open to another world a few steps away from him, my grandfather had been able to announce a tragic future event, or was it just a figure of speech?

Certainly the love for the same arts was shared with him and my mother, who wanted me to go to art high school. It was my mother who bought me my first guitar. I never, ever, stopped playing. And the fact that today I am a professional singer-songwriter and guitarist, puts before my eyes a panorama of shared energies and similarities between me and them (starting from the shape of the middle toe) that transcend life and death.

In the almost thirty-nine years that have passed since that tragic event which changed my life, the one thing I have never stopped doing is honoring what my mother and her father would have loved. That is, the daily idea of filling existence with creativity, with that childlike part that we should keep awake within us even as adults, making us think that fairies exist.

Maybe it's also because of all this that I write songs and that I never swear to know fully what is true and what is not true in this complex world in which we live.

THE BRON-YR-AUR SONG

As Patrick Harpur noted in *Daimonic Reality: A Field Guide to the Otherworld*, the stories of alien encounters resemble the accounts of Marian apparitions, fairy sightings, and illuminating orbs in European folklore. As Harpur has said, when the fairies, who lived underground, were banished, they returned from on high as UFOs and aliens. Harpur adds that these sightings fall into two main categories: benevolent and malevolent.

"I awoke to see the loveliest people I have ever seen. A young man and a young girl dressed in olive-green raiment were standing at my bedside. I looked at the girl and noticed that her dress was gathered about her neck into a kind of chain, or perhaps some stiff embroidery...But what filled me with wonder was the miraculous mildness of her face."[74]

By contrast, some visions are ghastly.

"He looked earnestly into a corner of the room, and said, 'There he is—reach me my things—I shall keep an eye on him. There he comes! His eager tongue whisking out of his mouth, a cup in his hand to hold blood and covered with a scaly skin of gold and green,'—as he described him, so he drew him...a naked figure with a strong body and short neck—with burning eyes...and a face worthy of a murder.'"

We recognize both the angelic and beatific visions in UFO literature. And the ghastly too.

All of this is very interesting to me but what I found specifically relevant to the subject at hand is the incorporation of music

---

74 *Daimonic Reality: A Field Guide to the Otherworld*, Harpur, Patrick (xvi)

and sound in some of the Welsh folk tales that I came across in my research.

The story "Llew" in *Wonder Tales of Ancient Wales, Celtic Myth and Welsh Fairy Folklore*, as retold, describes the misery of Llew, born poor and sent off by his family to work for a cruel shoemaker.

Before he is dispatched to the shoemaker, Llew encounters an old man ensnared in a thorn bush. Noticing the kind look on the man's face, Llew sets him free. The old man reveals that he is one of the tylwyth teg, or Welsh fairy folk, meaning "fair family" in English.

The man tells Llew that the tylwyth teg love kind people and hate those who are cruel to others. He tells Llew that whenever he is in trouble or need, he should sing a song, and that the old man's kith and kin would appear to help him.

"And, when he had spoken, he sang a sweet, abiding tune which sank into the lad's heart as the song of the thrush gladdens the traveler in the early spring tide."[75]

This is the song he sang.

Little lad, my little lad,
Sing for your friend,
When your heart is very sad,
My help I'll send.
And wheresoever you may be.
When you sing your friend you'll see.

As the story goes, the shoemaker was abusive to little Llew, prone to hitting and burdening him with impossible tasks. One time, the master left the boy in the workshop insisting that if Llew didn't finish all his work, he would be beaten black and blue.

In his despair, Llew sang a song to the tylwyth teg. In no time, the room was filled with tylwyth teg folk, dancing and jiggling, taking out the shoemaker's tools, vigorously pegging and hammer-

---

75 *Wonder Tales of Ancient Wales, Celtic Myth and Welsh Fairy Folklore (page 4)*

ing with them, making fine shoes.

In the gleeful clang of work, Llew couldn't tell the tylwyth teg apart from each other.

That is, until one of them spoke to him.

"Why didn't you sing before? We cannot come unless you sing," said the old man whom he now remembered. Llew took note of that.

While the tylwyth teg were working, they showed Llew how to make beautiful shoes, downloading their knowledge into his mind. Now the boy would be able to make shoes worthy of a king.

As luck would have it, days later, while the king was out hunting, he tore his boots and needed shoes. The king had heard about the beautiful shoes coming out of the workshop of Llew's master. Arriving on horse, the king visited the master's workshop, demanding to see examples of his work. The shoemaker showed the king the shoes that Llew had made.

"Did you make these shoes?" asked the king.

As the master started to say "yes" a scream instead bursted from his lips. He tried again to speak, but only howls and shrieks would come out of his mouth. As the master tried again, in vain, to answer the king, the tylwyth teg visited great pain upon him. So much so that he finally copped to the truth and summoned Llew to meet the king, who praised the boy for his excellent work.

"This is not the right workshop for a person of your skill. You should come work for me," said the king. He made Llew shoemaker for the royal family.

Having soon become comfortable in his new life, now in his cozy bed, dressed in silk pajamas, Llew heard voices singing to him. The words of the song said that someday Llew would be king.

Years later, when the realm went to war, a voice whispered to Llew that he must "make a pair of shoes as fast as the wind" so he could stand forth as the king's messenger. To help him further, the tylwyth teg provided Llew with a beautiful coat wrought skillfully of gossamer thread so that he would be invisible. Llew used the coat to sneak into the enemy's camp and learn of their strategies, which he then directly reported back to the king.

Proving to be of high value to the king, Llew was named chief minister. Spending time in his court, Llew fell in love with the king's daughter. They were married. When the old man passed away, Llew became the new king of the realm. But he never forgot the tylwyth teg.

"Outside his palace, there was a beautiful garden, stocked with fragrant roses and all the fair flowers that grow in the meadows, or by the river-side. Silvery fountains leapt gleaming and sparkling in the rays of the sun, and little murmuring streams flowed merrily along. People said that sometimes when the moon was silver bright, if anyone peeped over the wall of that garden there might be seen a band of many little folk, dancing hand in hand through the drops that fell glittering in the moonlight."[76]

In this tale, as in many others, the fey people are conjured by song. Also interesting is that the shoemaker's words, when lying to the king, are transformed into screams and howls. Not necessarily music, but sound.

---

76 *Wonder Tales of Ancient Wales, Celtic Myth and Welsh Fairy Folklore (page 9)*

AMERICAN PSYCHIC
Marla Frees's Story

Along with his team at the Monroe Institute in Faber, Virginia, consciousness researcher Robert Monroe developed and patented Hemispheric Synchronization, also known as Hemi-Sync. He observed that listening to specific sound patterns, or binaural beats—two tones with slightly different frequencies—could safely and gently guide the brain into various states ranging from deep relaxation or sleep to expanded mindfulness or "extraordinary" states, enabling us to "escape our ego." Monroe suggested that beyond our consciousness, or deep within it, is a door to another world. A world that is here and now, but invisible to us in our consensus reality.[77]

This notion of accessing "another world" is not singular to Monroe. It may be called something else in a different culture, or by a different researcher, but there are common elements in all of them. By using a method, or tool, we can explore other realms, sometimes communicating with other aspects of ourselves or other beings. Consciousness explorers like Terence McKenna and John Lilly stated that they were communicating with a nonhuman sentience in their research. Of course, indigenous cultures around the world have been exploring these realms for millennia.

Monroe's research caught the attention of the Central Intelligence Agency (CIA). The CIA began experimenting with these

---

[77] Hemi-Sync is short for Hemispheric Synchronization, also known as brainwave synchronization. Monroe indicated that the technique synchronizes the two hemispheres of one's brain, thereby creating a 'frequency-following response' designed to evoke certain effects

techniques in 1978, with the intention of using them to "remote view" missions. The CIA's remote viewing research would come to be known as Project Stargate. In 2017 the CIA declassified previously unreleased details about Project Stargate.

As Monroe wrote in *Journeys into the Mind*, "Thereafter, during active out-of-body-experiences, I tried many times to communicate with these presences, single or plural, to no avail. Correction: I thought I received no reply because no words were forthcoming, only pictures, sensations, and actions. The change came about when I dimly began to realize I wasn't speaking their "language," as it were. Review of my early notes supported this, for the most part. Words and language, as we know them, are strictly human. My deflated ego rose somewhat with the realization that whatever my communication method was, a response was coming from these nonhumans."[78]

Monroe goes on to say that when he let "them" do the driving, his practice got deeper. "They knew the territory far better than I," he adds. In his continued dialog with the Other, Monroe reports that they came to him to provide guidance. That humans are on our way to achieving a high level of consciousness but are still chasing shadows.

"You are presuming a complexity which in our reality is very direct and simple. It is the distortion of time-space illusions that causes this in your consciousness," said the Other to Monroe during one of his sessions.

According to Monroe, he was communicating with a higher intelligence. Call it astral projection, telepathy, clairvoyance, interdimensional travel—the techniques that consciousness explorers share have an underlying framework.

In an interview on Kelly Chase's podcast, *The UFO Rabbit Hole*,[79] Dean Radin, chief scientist at the Institute of Noetic Sci-

---

78 *Far Journeys*, Monroe, Page 92
79 https://uforabbithole.com/podcast/ep-31-an-interview-with-dean-radin-on-consciousness-psi-phenomena-and-real-magic/

ence (IONS), echoed Monroe's theory of the Other. Radin said, "We use labels like telepathy or clairvoyance but underneath there's a growing consensus that there's probably just one underlying phenomenon. It is something like interconnectedness, for want of a better term." Monroe reported what was spoken to him by the Other during one of his Hemi-Sync sessions: "It is the distortion of time-space illusions that causes this in your consciousness." Radin added that separateness is merely an illusion.

The nonlinear forms of quantum mechanics explore the possibility that information can be transferred instantaneously—from here to there, via "spooky action at a distance,"[80] a term coined by Albert Einstein. In other words, quantum mechanics is confirming that all phenomena in the universe are connected in some way that we do not yet understand.

Marla Frees

Marla Frees is a psychic, author, and lecturer. She travels across the country and internationally, offering interactive group audience presentations called, "Messages of Love with Marla," where she works with audience members offering divine insight about any aspect of their lives and messages from deceased loved ones. She also works in private sessions and small groups.

Most recently, Marla participated in YouTube teleconferences, discussion panels, and the International Cultural Connection Tour with physicist, author, and consciousness expert Tom Campbell, sharing the science behind Marla's work making the paranormal, normal.

Marla is a popular radio guest on George Noory's "*Coast-to-Coast AM*," and dozens of other radio programs and podcasts, including "*New Thinking Allowed*" with PhD parapsychologist Jeffrey Mishlove.

---

80 https://www.astronomy.com/science/what-is-quantum-entanglement-a-physicist-explains-einsteins-spooky-action-at-a-distance/

I wrote to Marla after I read her book *American Psychic: A Spiritual Journey from the Heartland to Hollywood, Heaven and Beyond*. Her book *American Psychic* depicts Marla's journey from small-town girl to successful TV and stage actress, a career she left in 2002 to surrender to her calling as a gifted psychic.

I wrote an Amazon review of *American Psychic* and shared it with Marla. She was very appreciative. Later I learned more about Marla's various projects, podcasts, and radio appearances.

As a thank you for my book review, Marla offered me a psychic reading. To be honest, at first, I was a little intimidated. In *American Psychic*, I had read about Marla's work with law enforcement. That she'd pick up an object of a crime victim and would see images, enabling her to help detectives to solve crimes. Inviting someone to peer into your soul can be a little scary.

Marla and I connected almost instantly while on our call. Marla is not a shy person. She can be a little brash in her language, which I found fun. Our conversation was a mix of intellectual talk, personal anecdotes, and rapid-fire exchanges about our mutual interests.

Marla was gentle in her reading with me, saying that people would be receptive to the stories in my UFO book-in-progress. She urged me to be honest and vulnerable in my writing. I took her insights to heart and made sure that I incorporated them.

When I texted Marla about writing a book that connected music to the Phenomenon, she responded promptly. We spoke the next day. I asked her to talk about this connection.

My conversation with Marla opened me to do more experiential research in binaural beats, gong yoga, and sound baths. It occurred to me then that my project wasn't just about music but about sound in general.

What follows is my transcription of a conversation with Marla:

Marla
One of the things that I think is important to remember is the

idea of the stimulation of both hemispheres of our brain. Many of us have been using binaural beats to access other levels of consciousness. Of course, you know we go back to the drumming, to the indigenous cultures. All of that has been going on for many years, giving us an opportunity to have altered states of consciousness without the use of drugs.

And I've been very interested in that. I've been working with Tom Campbell for the last fourteen years. Along with Bob Monroe, Tom was instrumental in developing the Hemi-Sync program at the Monroe Institute. They were finding out how by stimulating both sides of the brain and holding your brain in a stasis, gives you the opportunity to experience altered states of consciousness. I've been exploring that. Last year I ran into gong master Lou Maurer, who has a gong and yoga studio here in Los Angeles, and we traded services.

The first time that I was in one of his private sessions was in some ways overwhelming. I was tapping into one of his deceased loved ones and I could feel even more than I usually feel when connecting to the dead. The vibrations of the gongs, I thought, opened another door. I was really surprised when I started going to these sound baths where Lou was joined by another talented gong master or someone with singing bowls or other sound frequencies. It was a cacophony of information and I started having parallel life experiences.

Most recently (during a session) I went out and sat on the rings of Saturn. I found myself oscillating between Earth and the sky and the stars. Then I found other energies that would start to merge with my body and offer information.

This is a nonphysical matter reality coming to me while I am in an altered state, all happening because of this sound bath. I also had the experience of not being me but being in the body of a lion. Then being in the body of a robotic kind of consciousness...and, of not being a woman...but being a baseball pitcher for the Cubs.

I am interested in experimenting with and understanding how the stimulated brain works. My father had Alzheimer's and Parkinson's disease, and this has made me interested in the science and experiential aspects of the stimulated brain.

During one of the sessions with Lou, I found myself in the dirt. I became an entire webbed root system, underneath what was growing aboveground. I didn't realize until after this experience, that the day before the sound bath I had taken a lion's mane mushroom supplement for brain support. I researched mushroom supplements (not psilocybin) and found mycelium, a root-like structure of a fungus consisting of a mass branching and there I was in this sound bath merging with an ecosystem under the ground.

Mike
How did it feel?

Marla
To be honest, I didn't know what to do with it all, but I have continued to have the most amazing experiences.

So I can actually say sound baths are now a transformational part of my work. I'm working on my second book now, looking at the science of this phenomena and exploring what is going on.

Clearly Hemi-Sync and sound manipulation help us to navigate inner space. I wanted to dive in with both hands to directly experience this phenomenon.

GONG YOGA

Marla introduced me to Lou Mauer, who runs the Astro Gong Yoga studio in Los Angeles, California and was willing to talk to me about the effects of sound meditation. Born in England, Lou moved to Los Angeles in 2019.

Not too far off in age, Lou and I hit it off right away. We both are bespectacled men with gray hair, have been married more than once and, despite our shared interests in esoteric matters, we remain a bit skeptical of people's authenticity at times. And we don't take ourselves too seriously. I was hoping I could get a sense of how Lou discovered Gong Yoga and get a demonstration over Facetime.

"I've always been rightly skeptical about these things. In the United Kingdom there are many who profess to be, but who are not quite, authentic. Despite my skepticism, I've always been intrigued because I believe there is an energy that some people have. That's how I felt when I met Marla. I knew she had something special: vibrational energy is a universal energy that connects everything. When I'm teaching sound training, I pick up on things from different people, like their energy and emotions. I often see what's happened to someone's trauma world," said Lou.

I noted that there are a lot of charlatans in the spiritual community. "There are a lot of tricksters," I said. "And sometimes the tricksters have something of value to offer, too. It's an interesting spectrum. Not all psychic people have their shit together. And some people are just trying to make a buck off other people's suffering."

"Are you a musician?" I asked. "Did you study music?"

"No, I'm certainly not musical in any way, shape or form," said Lou. "I can't read music. I can't play any instruments musically. And then that's part of the reason I enjoy playing gong and American flute and drums and things like that because it's all intuitive and there's nothing actually to read. There isn't anything for me to read or follow, other than the energy and flow of the vibrational current of my surroundings."

"Gershwin didn't read music. Nor did Jimi Hendrix," I said. "Errol Garner, the guy who wrote 'Misty,' didn't know how to read music, either. And that song is perfect. How did you come to discover the gong?" I asked.

"I've always been a tree hugger, talking to animals and connecting through things like that, from about six years old. My mother always frowned on it, thinking I was a bit strange and weird. Now, I'm sixty-three and I still haven't grown out of it, so."

"You've grown into it," I quipped.

"I've grown into it even more," he said. "My wife at the time wanted to do yoga. There was a yoga center that was about forty-five minutes away from where we lived. The truth is I didn't want to go. My wife went and enjoyed it. I thought I was off the hook. Then my wife said that there would be a sound bath the following night. *Do you want to come to that?* she asked. *Oh my God, that's even worse.*

"She said that I'd be able to lie down and have a cup of tea. For ten pounds I could sleep for an hour? Now that sounds like a deal. I went and had all manner of experiences. I had visions. I heard opera singers. I heard cannon fire. I heard shouting. It was just totally confusing to me. I had eye patches over both my eyes, but I saw colors. I couldn't open my eyes to see where it was coming from. The instructor, Mark, who is my gong master, asked if I would like to talk about my experience after the session. There was no way I wanted to share what had just happened. The following night Mark said he was teaching Kundalini yoga with a gong relaxation after. I went along the following nights and basically just got hooked into everything."

"When you hear these things like the opera singer or the soldier shouting, where do you think that comes from?" I asked.

"I believe it's all part of the vibration. I guess it depends on your belief system. I believe that gong vibration helps you access the Akashic records. But it's not a given that it will happen. It depends on the student's receptivity. Gong can take you far, but only if you're open to receiving."

The Akashic records are believed to be the repository of every thought, word, and deed of every living being, good, bad, and awful, in all times; past, present, future. It's a compendium of knowledge of all life forms and entities. But those familiar with the records report that there is no judgment or implied penalty in the records—they are said to simply be a record of each soul's journey through the infinite.

Lou continued, "I believe that every bit of information, every sound, every noise, and every thought has already happened and it's out in the universe, like all connected in the matrix. When the brain calms down and quiets the monkey mind, it allows the mind to harmonize with itself and come into focus, which then allows thoughts to come in and sounds and visions and things like that. I suppose these things come from other dimensions. But really, I don't know."

"Are there things that come back, an entity, a human, or non-human sentience that you have a continuous relationship with?" I asked.

"Not so much. However, I certainly have had angels that return. I did a sound bath with Marla and, in exchange, she did a psychic reading for the studio. Seems we've got a spirit here at the studio and we've got a vortex in the cloakroom. Other people have experienced this spirit as well. I wanted to find out whether that was one of my two ex-wives, or what," said Lou, chuckling.

He continued, "Marla didn't know anything about my exes, but she was on point with everything she said. But we all want to have proof, right? It was interesting that she also picked up on energies, saying that she didn't think it was my ex-wives. We had another psychic come in to give his evaluation. He said 'No, no, no. This is not your ex-wives; this is an angel. This is *your* angel. Why do you keep on trying to push it away and deny it?'

"We have often seen at the studio, not always, identifiable forms. I have seen things, more than a few times, in my peripheral vision, going into our closet. Things moving, lights changing, lights coming on, going on and off," said Lou, adding jokingly, "I realize not all of the electricians in Los Angeles are equally as good.

"Where my girlfriend lives, in her apartment, I've seen lights turn on and candles, electric candles turn on and off. There's constant evidence that those other energies are there. As I go about my life, I often see people's auras literally shining and shivering. Sometimes their hair starts shining out of nowhere."

"Do people often have repeat experiences?" I asked.

"Not very often because as soon as they've experienced something, they go back in and say, *I want to do that again*, but can't. It's like having a dream. You're on a beautiful desert island, and you're being served by all these beautiful half-naked girls, bringing you cocktails and everything else. And you go, *I wanna go back into that*. Never happens, right? No matter how hard you try, you'll never go because of the expectation. Things like this often happen with sound healing. People have a phenomenal experience to start with and then try too hard to recapture it. And men are interesting in this way. Certainly in the United Kingdom men come to these things, asked along by their wives. They come with no expectations, thinking it's a load of rubbish, shaking their heads. *I just wanna get to the bar*. When they walk out all sort of bleary-eyed and a little bit out of shape they know that something has happened that they don't understand.

"Sometimes coming with a clean slate makes you fully open," said Lou.

"I looked at the site and checked out a few things. Can you talk a little bit about the importance of ritual and setting and how you utilize that in a session or ceremony?" I asked.

"Yeah, there are different kinds of thoughts within ritual. Of course, it depends on your belief system. I use ritual to a degree within the sound healing because it gets people into the right space. Because sound healing is based on vibration, it goes into the body. No matter how stubborn or obstinate you are. A lot of the ritual for me is to help people relax and to get into this space. So they feel that they're being held and cared for and respected, and the energy is changing. Some of the old shamanic methods, using sage, for example, help clear the energy. I believe, in part, it's clearing the energy of the people, the participants, because something like eighty percent of the sound healing is done through intent. Intent has been proved scientifically to be a great factor in sound and natural healing. But if you're a Buddhist, for example, then the ritual is important. So much of it is people's acceptance of what's going on and how much they intend themselves to be healed and cared for within that space. But if people start off by saying *this is rubbish* now you've got a hard job ahead of you, right? Because they're not relaxed and they're not willing to participate and give it their all. There are certain elements that certainly do work. The amount of and different kinds of lighting and things like that and placing of feathers in a certain way, can have an impact. It's a little bit of showmanship, to a degree."

"Do people use gong yoga mainly for healing or for consciousness exploration?" I asked.

"They use sound healing as a form of connecting to other realms. The whole thing about sound healing is that it's not me healing people. The whole point is to sync the vibration of the gongs with our own frequency. Sound healing teaches our body and mind how to be in harmony with their natural state. This is beneficial because we're often out of balance. It helps us to hear ourselves. It doesn't have anything to do with me waving a magic wand or anything. It's just allowing our natural healing ability to take over. Sound healing literally relaxes the whole body, relaxes the mind and gets everything to a state where we can experience other things because it quietens us."

I found Lou's acknowledgement of humility very moving. I can see why he's effective.

"I noticed too that you incorporate astrology into your practice. Can you talk a little bit about that?" I asked.

"We infuse astrology within most of the things we do. Tonight, for instance, we have a moon time which will have specific gongs. I play planetary gongs. They are scientifically tuned to the planets. The planetary tuning information was gathered from NASA and given to a guy called Hans Kusto, who actually used a very old Greek formula to calculate the frequency of the different planets. And then Paiste, a Swiss company with factories in Germany, hammered the various tones into different frequencies. Emily, who's my business partner, is an astrologist. She'll say, for example, 'Tonight you're using the Jupiter and New Moon gong,' depending on what's happening up in the astros."

"I saw that you work with drums and flutes. Do you use them for different purposes?"

"No, not really. I do a journey that helps people experience sound healing. I'll play drums, use crystal bowls, rattles and singing bowls, and chimes and things like that. But my main instrument is the gong."

"How do you think rhythm plays into your approach?"

"Shamanic beats connect to the heart, and the associated brain waves. Rhythm can be super important when it comes to drums. And I know some didgeridoo players who use different rhythms to connect to certain states, making people feel comfortable. If you have fast rhythms, you start getting into war tones and so forth. Too loud, too thumpy. Like the African tribes used to signal battle. It's a bit more frightening and gets the adrenal gland going, which then doesn't put you into a good state to do sound healing."

Music has that power, I thought. It could inspire you to revolution or ecstasy. Music is a form of instant telepathy, communicating information to people who might be three or fifty feet away. Ululations, which people use in war and at funerals, can also be used to express ecstasy, intense feelings, or heightened spirituality. Those things are deep within us. We must be careful how we use them.

"Nothing works for everybody. Within music alone, you know, some people love heavy metal, and other people hate it," said Lou.

"But everybody loves disco right now?" I said, kidding. "I have two older sisters. I can dance disco."

"I was always the one standing at the bar," said Lou.

"Is there a kind of a standout experience, something that you could share? Something that was just so unexpected and transformational that it shocked you, or the individual themselves?" I asked.

"I only do one-on-one gong training. I've had a lot of situations where the students had experiences within ten or fifteen minutes of playing the gong and discovering traumas they had repressed.

"I had a doctor who came for a twelve-hour training. She played the gong for an hour and had the profound revelation that her father had abused her sexually. Big, big stuff comes up for people. Ninety percent of people end up in tears at some stage because it goes so deep."

Like all music, gong takes you to places deep in your unconscious. Sometimes it takes you into the even deeper well of the collective unconscious, where you go into the transpersonal realm.

"Even people who say *I won't need those tissues*, are gushing with tears ten minutes later at times. The practice gives them permission to do it especially if they're one-on-one with me, connecting with and looking after themselves. It's all about the space and the energy we create."

Trying not to exhaust Lou, I asked, "This is available to everyone and works with everyone. Are there certain people more prone to it or prone to accept it or be receptive?"

"One hundred percent. Sound healing is eighty percent intent. My intention is to heal and to hold people and keep them in safe places to heal, sending them love and compassion. But if the person comes in and they are totally unwilling, there's nothing I can do about it. Some people leave in tears and then they never come back. Because they're expecting just to lie down and be really chilled and really relaxed. But you know, sometimes it goes far deeper, and people feel these uncomfortable feelings and don't know what they are. And they aren't prepared for them. Everybody in their own time and their own space. It's not up to me to control them."

"And it's their responsibility to address it," I said.

"Absolutely. For instance, penicillin heals ninety percent of people, but it also kills people."

To prepare for my second FaceTime call with Lou, I put my headset on, folded my hands and closed my eyes. Sitting on a cushion, Lou had gongs on stands arranged around him. Banging the gongs with the mallets he held in his hands, the sounds swelled and gushed, even over the wire. As Lou hit the gongs, in my mind's eye I saw newborn stars forming, emerging from the cradle of emptiness, felt their quaking, thundering sounds, like a violent storm, rumble in my chest. The images shifted to oceanic waves, as if heard from the hull of a ship at sea, groaning and creaking. I didn't feel threatened, I just didn't expect these things to come into my mind.

Then Lou showed me the flume that he used sometimes instead of a mallet.

"This has a different sound," he said, waving the flume. It resembled a thin poker used to stoke a fire, except that the flume had a curved silicone shape atop it, which looked like a seahorse. Unlike the mallet, the flume made a singing whale sound. It was less shimmery and thinner. It reminded me of a violin bow.

"The flume drives some people nuts," he said. "And some people love it."

"I like it," I said.

"No one hears these sounds the same way," said Lou.

As mentioned, the gongs are tuned to frequencies that are mapped to planets. Depending upon the astrological configuration of a given day, specific gongs are chosen. The Sun Gong is tuned to a B note and resonates at 128 megahertz, which is achieved by a center strike. That being said, gong notes vary, according to different factors such as atmospheric pressure, humidity, and so on.

Paiste, the Swiss gong manufacturer, says of gongs on their website:

> Since the depths of time, they have had a deep psychological meaning attributed to them. In music, gongs with their indescribable sound colors, have always played a prominent role.
>
> Gongs belong to the oldest and most important musical instruments of South East Asia. Their origins may be traced back to the second millennium B.C., but it is assumed that the Gong is much older. In Chinese history Gongs are mentioned in the Tang dynasty around 660 A.D., attributed to the Western region called His Yu thought to be between Tibet and Burma during the reign of Emperor Hsuan Wu.[81]

Historic research provides us with four main regions—Burma, China, Annam, Jav—that gave rise to at least seven gong shapes and sound structures. Only a few families knew the tradition of gong making as it passed from generation to generation. The art of making gongs was veiled in a sense of magic. Gong makers believed

---

81 https://en.unesco.org/silkroad/knowledge-bank/
western-regions-his-yu-under-tang-empire-and-kingdom-tibet

that a gong could only succeed with the help of higher powers and that they were exposed to such forces more so than ordinary humans.[82]

Lou told me that, like the didgeridoo and the conch shell, you can't write a tune on a gong. Consequently, you can't play it the same way all the time.

"I'm just a conduit," said Lou. "If I've had a bad day, I have to step aside and let it go so as not to project bad energies and intentions. Otherwise, people curl up in fetal positions, wincing when I strike the gong." He said that musicians are the hardest people to train to play a gong. They're used to playing something predictable and repeatable. The gong forces you to let go, letting your unconscious do the work. The gong leads and you follow.

After speaking to Lou, I sought out local sound healing centers in New York City.

---

82 https://paistegongs.com/history.php

THE GROUND WILL PROTECT YOU

Inspired by Marla and Lou, I visited the OHM Center in Manhattan for a sound bath session.

The OHM Center offers sound baths, crystal sound baths, meditation, Kundalini, Reiki, hypnosis, and other classes.

Having arrived just in time, I was directed to the back room to lie down on my back, with my head on a pillow. There were maybe six other people in the room. The walls were adorned with Buddhist paintings and other spiritual imagery. It felt very welcoming. There was a time when New York City had more venues like this.

The OHM Center uses sound bowls and chimes instead of gongs or binaural beats. The singing bowls produce sounds that center the frequencies of the physical body and mind. Hearing these bowls played has also been said to cause the left and right sides of the brain to better synchronize, facilitating meditation.

Upon first lying down, I was a little uncomfortable, maybe because I had rushed to the studio. While the instructor, Kevin Brown, provided a guided meditation, trying to relax the class, I started hyperventilating. Was I out of breath or feeling pressured to relax? Like going to the bathroom, meditation doesn't come to me as easily nowadays. When I was younger, I could sit cross-legged and meditate for forty-five minutes, achieving periods of deep breathing and what I perceived to be moments of samadhi. Now fifty-seven, I had a harder time relaxing and centering the breathing in my stomach. Somehow, I expected older age to be accompanied by increased wisdom. Older age, it seems, is more related to the depreciation of organs and other bodily functions. Hey wisdom, waiting on you.

Kevin introduced the bowls to guide the meditation by playing them lightly.

"Leave everything behind for now. You are here now. You are here to work on yourself. You deserve to be happy. We all deserve to be happy," he whispered.

While these phrases sounded cliché, the authenticity of Kevin's voice was comforting. This is not just about banging bowls with a hammer. There is a real compassion and an overall feel that the guide must be provided by the guide.

Occasionally, Kevin struck a bowl unexpectedly loudly, which set off fireworks in my spine, shooting up and into my brain. At times the oscillations of one bowl harmonized with the ringing of another. Although I couldn't see him, I heard Kevin walking around. There were about twelve bowls scattered around, varying in sizes. Some were glass bowls. Some were made from metals.

My body began to relax, my breathing deepened. Like Lou had told me, the vibrations are going to have an effect whether you're trying to meditate or not. Soon I felt like a mummy in a tomb. Fifteen minutes in, I was taking long deep breaths. The sounds triggered images in my mind, reminding me of the hypnagogic visions I've seen while drifting off to sleep on a train. Since I was lying down with my eyes closed, I couldn't write them down, but here are some of the images that drifted into and out of my mind, like capers in the night. These visions came without my intention or effort,

I envisioned an older woman, resembling an Italian *strega*, or female witch, yelling at me, her words unintelligible. Then the cartoon figure of an old man materialized. He wanted to argue with me. Yet, like the witch, I couldn't understand his words. I didn't think of it at that moment, but later mused that I must be a difficult person, arguing with conjured beings buried in my subconscious. However, none of this was unpleasant. The visions just flashed before my mind without me trying to make anything happen. I didn't even realize it was happening until I realized it was happening. The bowl sounds directed the flow of my thoughts and I let them take me wherever they would.

My hands on either side of my body, knuckles down, were cupped and receptive. I felt someone holding them, then moved my fingers to see if there was another hand in mine. I imagined it. No one was holding them; my hands were made numb and warm from the sound of the bowls.

In fact, my entire body became heavy, as if weighted to the ground. I couldn't have gotten up quickly if I'd wanted to.

Kevin changed the speed of striking the bowls and the strikes came unpredictably, with an element of surprise. Some of the tones cut right through me, like a laser beam ricocheting inside my skull. Some of the tones were warm and inviting, like gentle summer clouds floating above me. This made me think of the term "skull-shining" breath, or *kapalabhati,* that I had heard in meditation classes. *Kapalabhati* is a compound word. *Kapala* means "skull," *bhati* means "to shine or to be lustrous." This practice is said to "make the skull shine" by cleansing the nasal passageways and sinuses, and ultimately supplying the brain with a fresh supply of oxygen-rich blood.

Breathing heavily now for over thirty-five minutes, the sound bowls having a hypnotic effect on me, Kevin moved over to the chimes. Unlike the sound bowls, which have a regal quality, as if announcing the arrival of a king or queen, the chimes made miniature, almost childlike sounds. They reminded me of songs I had heard played on twist-up porcelain lullaby figurines. Very delicate. Having brought me to a state of deep meditation, the chimes felt like tickling. The smallness of the sounds recalled fairies in the woods playing pan flutes, frolicking. The gentle, tingling sounds tapped vague memories of being loved—how my mom tucked me into blankets in my crib. I had the general feeling of being cared for and protected.

At some point, I noticed that my exhalations had become long and slow, I forgot that I needed to breathe. It wasn't a panic moment. It was an observation: Oh, I'm not breathing. The floor had dropped from beneath me.

Breathing resumed, my belly filled up with oxygen until the air moved up into my chest, slowly inhaling and exhaling. This was relaxing but more so in a way than relaxing.

On another night, a woman walked in the studio while I was awaiting a sound bath. She wore fancy sparkling pants.

"What kind of bowls do you use?" she demanded.

Elisa, one of the administrators, replied, "Kevin uses many different kinds of bowls."

Fancy pants asked another series of rapid questions. I wasn't listening. I just noticed the overall tone of *I paid money and you are here to serve me as I please* from this woman.

When I laid down on the mat, Fancy Pants walked in behind me.

"Are these clean?" she asked, pointing to the pillows. Before Elisa could respond, she added, "Were they washed today?" I'll admit that I had thought that before, but I hadn't asked the staff, and certainly not in such a rude manner.

Kevin began with his usual guided meditation.

"Trust that the ground will hold you," he said, hitting the sound bowls. "You are loved. You are lovable," he added.

The woman sighed. I heard her saying "Jesus Christ." We've got a live one, I thought to myself. Kevin continued.

"Is there talking during this session?" she asked abruptly. There were about four people lying down on their backs, eyes closed.

"Is there talking?" shot back Kevin. "Trust that there will be silence," he said, trying to be polite, but also trying to shut her up.

"I asked a yes or no question," she asked.

"Yes, there is talking. I'm talking now. Then it will mostly be the bowls playing."

"Good," said Fancy Pants. It sounded like *fuck you*.

I was smiling, even as I was deep-breathing, trying to get into the rhythm of the session. It's enough to arrive from busy Manhattan streets, after traversing trains and all the rest.

My mind drifted with the ringing of the bowls. Unlike sitting meditation, sound baths unearth latent beings in our minds and take us on a journey, I suspect, due to the vibration of the bowls and chimes. You have no choice but to follow where they take you.

I had a premonition of someone standing over me, then lying on top of me. It wasn't violent or worrisome. There was a presence around me which quickly disappeared as other personae drifted in and out of my mind. I can't remember all the details.

Meanwhile, I followed the ringing of the bowls, their tones oscillating, sometimes rapidly, colliding with the other bowl tones. The chorus tones reminded me of Palestrina's masses: long legato notes that drowned you in oceanic waves. In fact, the singing bowls recalled to me the feeling of being in church, the way parts of the mass are signaled by a triangle or a chime, followed by singing voices.

Do this in memory of me, followed by a ding, as I heard in Catholic mass.

Emerging from the meditation room, I peed, put on my warm coat and hat, and left the OHM Center, trying to escape confrontation with Fancy Pants.

On another night, I lay down very close to the bowls. The ringing of the bowls seemed very personal now, like they were ringing just for me.

Now knowing what to expect, I again struggled with hyperventilating, trying to control my breath. Reciting *om mane padme om* and trying to hold my breath lightly at the top of an inhale, I managed to slow my breathing. Soon I was in a deep state of calm. Images flashed before my mind: a person, standing on a ladder, placing a star on a tree. People coming and going, zipping through my dream state. Again, my inhale and exhale were very long and even now; I realized at one point I wasn't breathing, or that my breathing was very shallow. I didn't plan this, it just happened from the breathing and the sound vibrations ringing in my body.

I left the studio that night feeling meditative and peaceful. Of course, a few minutes on the wily streets of Manhattan would challenge even the Buddha's state of mind. But the point is that I learned another way to penetrate the presence of the Other, who seems to occupy the deepest realms of our being, if only we find the right doors to open that perception. The knocker on some of those doors is a chime, a gong, or a musical sound that can lead us into an otherwise hidden dimension.

CALL ME GUIDO

When I was a kid, my father played Jimmy Roselli and other Neapolitan singers for me. Back then I hated it. He took me to the Italian novelty store, E. Rossi & Company, on Grand Street in Little Italy, as if to impress me with the Neapolitan music they played. It was too Italian for me, too narrow. I wanted to see the world, not be imprisoned in our family heritage or a national identity.

Despite this, twenty-five years later, I've amassed a collection of recordings of Neapolitan singers and read many books and articles on the subject. Now, I go down to E. Rossi & Company to play guitar with Ernie, the owner. I look through his record collection, searching for a Neapolitan singer I don't know or an album I don't have.

I've become obsessed with the topic. I'm searching for more than information. I'm resurrecting my father, communicating with him across time and place. When I write these pieces, I'm writing them for him first. To delight him. To share my enthusiasm with him. I know my father would have loved to read them.

When I learned that the first six-stringed guitar is said to have been made in Naples, I wished I could have visited my father. The conversation may have gone something like this.

"I have some interesting news for you, Dad."

"I'm listening," he'd say, not yet looking up from his crossword puzzle, tapping his foot, snug in its slipper.

"Have you heard of Giovanni Battista Fabricatore?"

"I may be dead, but I'm not stupid."

"Fabricatore, a Neapolitan luthier, made the first six-stringed guitar," I respond, proud to have discovered this fact. To share it with him.

"Listen kid, I always told you the Italians were the first in many things. And especially the Neapolitans. Do I have to give you a list of our accomplishments?" he says sternly, then smiles. A joke was always a breath away with my father.

"You know I'm learning this stuff for you?"

He stops being facetious now, his face softens, and his bright eyes suddenly beam. "You know I'm busting your chops. This is just like you. You become obsessed about things. It's one of your strengths. To be honest, it drove me nuts sometimes."

He notices that I've taken a bit of offense to what he's just said. He adds, "But it doesn't now." He's my father and yet he's also a wise angel. A spirit. A being who sees it all, who is above it all.

And he tells everyone else, when I'm around, what I'm writing about. He takes copies of my books, essays, and stories with him wherever he goes, in this universe I'm now dreaming.

My father's teasing was his way of saying he liked you. If he teased you, it meant he felt you could take it. I saw him do it with some of my friends. It was an honor he bestowed. The difference with me is that I teased him back. We poked at each other. The joking was mixed with honest criticism. It was never bitter and never went too far.

To tease me, my father told me that he wanted to name me Guido when I was a kid. Guido would have been the worst name possible for a kid from Queens. A "Guido" was a guy who talked funny, wore gaudy clothes and drove a Camaro. This was the entire point.

"I love the name Guido," he said.

"It's stupid, I hate the name Guido," I replied.

"Why, it's a great name. You should be proud of it. It's Italian."

"A Guido is a guy who slicks his hair and wears white shoes."

But some of the greatest Italians were Guidos. Among them was Guido d'Arezzo, who invented modern musical notation in approximately 1025. Guido d'Arezzo wrote *Micrologus*, a guide that helped singers learn and remember Gregorian chants. *Micrologus* is considered the second most widely read medieval treatise in Europe after the writings of Boethius.

In the eighteenth century, the control of territories and regions passed between the hands of kings. Naples was under the rule of the Spanish king. And being devout Catholics, the Spanish monarchs opened music conservatories to teach church music to young children. If nothing else, the church was always a patron of the arts. Spanish control of Naples, however, was short-lived. In 1806, Napoleon marched into Naples, claiming it as his own. Napoleon's rule opened conservatories to commercial interests; composers now wrote concertos and compositions in his honor. And despite the turmoil that Napoleon created, music remained central to the culture of Naples. Perhaps because it was the stomping ground of multiple nations, Naples acquired various influences. It is said that Neapolitan music developed a light melodic quality. The Neapolitan musical dialect became a signature of musical styles for the rest of Europe.

Another interesting development at this time, specifically in Naples, was the emergence of the guitar as a serious instrument. With kingdoms and courts came the appetite and the resources for cultural and artistic development. There was an explosion of music conservatories in Naples. And this profusion of major music conservatories drove an industry of instrument production techniques in Naples as well. The making of stringed or bowed instruments, such as the violin, the cello, the mandolin and the guitar, flourished in and around the city. In addition to Fabricatore, there were other well-known luthiers of the eighteenth and nineteenth centuries in Naples, such as Vinaccia, Filano, Calace, and Alessandro Gagliano. Gagliano was an apprentice of Antonio Stradivari in Cremona and was largely responsible for transitioning violin making to Naples.

Some of the Neapolitan guitar makers migrated to America, bringing centuries of luthier techniques and traditions with them. Among these was John D'Angelico, who opened D'Angelico Guitars in Little Italy in 1932. D'Angelico used the same techniques he learned from his uncle, an expert violin and mandolin maker, to design and build some of the most beautiful guitars the world has ever known. In 1952, D'Angelico then apprenticed Jimmy D'Aquisto in his shop. Some consider D'Aquisto to be the greatest electric-guitar maker that ever lived. Thus, the lineage of guitar making can be drawn directly from Cremona to Naples and on to New York City's Little Italy.

Italian guitar players were of course influenced by the Neapolitan composers, players, and luthiers who shaped the legacy of the instrument. Although better known as a violin player, Paganini was said to be a dazzling guitar player. Paganini preferred to give guitar performances in intimate settings. His rapturous style must have been spellbinding. According to contemporary accounts, Paganini performed like a possessed madman. Like a modern rock musician, he lived a flamboyant and reckless lifestyle. He was known to exist between bouts of gambling, drinking, and fiery performances. Paganini wasn't the only major composer to compose for and perform on the guitar. Even Vivaldi wrote compositions for the guitar. There is a litany of other players, of which I'll mention a few. Ferdinando Carulli (1770-1841) was regarded as the leading Italian guitarist of his day. Though from Naples, he lived and settled in Paris and enjoyed great success as a composer, performer, and instrument maker. Carulli wrote the first complete classical guitar instruction book and composed over 400 works for the guitar.

Another well-known guitarist from southern Italy was Mauro Giuliani (born in 1781 in Bari, died in Naples in 1829). Giuliani was originally a cellist but took up the guitar and emigrated to the north, finally settling in Vienna, where he was considered the world's greatest guitarist. He eventually returned to Naples, composing and performing for the royal house of Naples. Giuliani was also a prolific composer, turning out about 200 compositions, many of which remain standards for guitar repertoire. He composed concertos for guitar and orchestra, fantasies and several sonatas for violin and guitar. He also wrote a guitar instruction method.

Why did these composers and musicians leave Naples? T. F. Heck, in "The Role of Italy in the Early History of the Classic Guitar," cites some potential reasons, among them: political turmoil caused by Napoleon, too many guitar players in Naples, the emergence of opera, and the lack of Neapolitan music publishers. In leaving their home of Naples, composers exported the Neapolitan sound to the rest of the world.

This history found its way to the United States, specifically to New York City's Little Italy. As I walked the streets of Little Italy with my father when I was a kid, I had no idea that I was strolling in antiquity. When we went to E. Rossi & Company, where our family friend Eddie Vecchione worked, I had no idea that the store was once a publishing house for Neapolitan composers from Italy, Canada, America, and Argentina. I didn't know that Eddie was the uncle of the current owner, Ernie Rossi, or that our family history was intertwined with the history of Neapolitan music.

So now I talk to my father in the form of essays and stories. I've taken a grand tour of the world, having missed the things that were in front of me for most of my childhood. But there's still time for me to do the excavation. And in this process, my father's voice emerges. I hear him talking to me even as I write this.

JUST A GIGOLO

Life comes full circle when someone I don't know writes to me about my piece in the *Red Hook Star Review* on Louis Prima. That someone, my new friend Charlie Diliberti, tells me that Louis Prima's son, Louis Prima Jr., tours the country playing New Orleans-style jazz, like his father. In fact, he knows Louis Prima Jr., he says. Would I like to meet him? Charlie also tells me that he speaks Sicilian. We correspond about our Sicilian origins.

I'm going to pause here for a moment to connect the time travel elements of all of this.

The piece that Charlie has read was inspired by me thinking about my dad's musical interests. He was a big fan of Louis Prima. And by writing the piece, I am connected to the future, to new friends.

A few weeks later, Charlie writes to say that Louis Prima Jr. and the Witnesses are playing at The Cutting Room in Manhattan. Would I like to meet him there? Of course, I say "yes."

When I get to The Cutting Room, Charlie has filled three tables with friends and family. He introduces me and my twenty-three-year-old son, Thelonious, whom I drag along. Everyone is friendly, talking and having fun.

Like in Spinal Tap, when Prima Jr. and the Witnesses take the stage, their set starts at volume eleven. Not ten. Eleven. From the first note, they erupt on the stage, bucking and kicking, stomping and romping, never missing a single note. They are smack on. Meanwhile, the room is eager, but they haven't caught up to the high velocity of the band. They're still eating, having only had a few drinks. Prima Jr. is hopping around and singing, like his father. The band follows his antics, bouncing on one foot in unison, while playing their instruments with incredible accuracy.

And like his father, Prima Jr. has a lead sax player and a female vocalist. Marco Palos, lead sax player and arranger, also writes some of the songs. Kate Curran, like Prima Sr.'s vocalists, can hit the high notes making it sound easy. And she too plays the onstage theatrics. She's the steady to Prima Jr.'s wild gymnastic performance. She's shapely and exotic, hand on hip like Bettie Boop.

The band then plays a few songs written by Marco, Prima Jr. and A. D. Adams from their two albums *The Wildest* and *Blow*. The songs recall Prima Sr.'s style, but they are new and fresh. Marco is impeccably dressed, tall and handsome. He is debonair, expertly playing his sax like it's a walk in the park. Meanwhile, the whole band is singing harmonies. And they are all stomping on one foot now, as if trying to tilt the stage. I imagine that even the street outside The Cutting Room is on a slant, parked cars rolling down the street. I hold on tight to my beer, so it won't slide off the table.

The sound level, now at twelve, threatens to blow the roof off the venue. As Louis and the band bounce and hop around, the venue is hot and humid. It's a rainy and sticky night. Somehow there isn't enough air-conditioning flowing into the room. All the players are mopping their faces with rags. I'm sweating too, yet I'm not running laps like they are.

Four songs in, the audience is now warming up. The band's intoxicating energy is infectious and the audience is no longer just passively watching; we are part of the show, most of us out of our seats. Some are whipping napkins over their heads. This is a party. *This ain't no foolin' around.*

I get up to go to the bathroom. When I come back, I'm grabbed by the hand and spun by a woman I don't know. Now I'm dancing, too. Even my son Thelonious is bopping around in his seat. He winces at me dancing with a stranger, as if saying *Dad, how could you? You look ridiculous.*

After a break, the band comes back on, taking turns singing songs. They are all excellent singers. I now notice that Prima Jr. has slipped behind the drum kit. Everybody plays every instrument in this band, it seems. They perform lively versions of songs like "Born on the Bayou" by Creedence Clearwater Revival and Elton John's "Saturday Night's Alright for Fighting," revealing their rock-music roots.

The crowd is now almost all out of their seats. It's pandemonium. Fully lathered up, Prima Jr. returns to the mic, singing a few of Sr.'s old hits like "Just a Gigolo" and "Buona Sera." The audience is now totally wild, singing along with every lyric, punching their fists with every stomp and stop. I see two guys in the audience fall to the ground while dancing drunkenly. This scene has become an orgiastic Mardi Gras.

After their last song, Prima Jr. comes off stage. He has basically just run a marathon. Still wearing a fancy Vegas performer suit, he walks toward me. I ask him if I can take a picture. Even though he's been running on stage for two hours, in the picture I take, he looks cool and relaxed. I, on the other hand, look haggard, like I've run into a Mack truck.

After the picture, I thank him with a hug. I think to myself that we're about the same age. Our parents would be about the same age. It's as if our fathers introduce us from the past. Wait, how could that be? I leave The Cutting Room thinking about how things come full circle, how little gestures or events can change the future, how life can be so ironic. I'm looking at a picture of me and Louis Prima Jr. I wish I could show my dad—mainly because he's responsible for all of this. Sometimes life just makes sense in some way that can't be explained.

AGNUS DEI

MUSIC MATTERS EVEN IF MUM CAN'T SING

Dianne Porter's Story

I met Dianne through the Peter Rowan Appreciation Group. Dianne lives in Canberra, Australian Capital Territory. We've never actually spoken but we have shared ideas and notes. She's become a good friend in the way that you become friends on Facebook with people you'll never meet.

This is Dianne's story.

> Preamble: My Mother was not a singer. In life she sang nursery rhymes to me when I was a child but that was it. Her excuse for not singing when I challenged her on this issue was that she was tone deaf. Her name was Helen Byrne; she was 81 in June 2010 when she died of terminal bowel cancer, in Clare Holland House, Canberra, Australia. The title of this article is the name of a chapter in a memoir I wrote to honor her life and the life of my father. It was called My Mother's Way of Dying Well.

> Imagine my surprise when I heard my mother singing clearly to me in a dream a few weeks after she died!

> "I heard the voice of Jesus say, come unto me and rest.

> Lay down thou weary one lay down, thy head upon my breast.

> I came to Jesus as I was, weary and worn and sad.

> I found in him my resting place and he has made me glad."

At the sound of her voice, I was abruptly alert in my dream, even though I was sound asleep at the time. I listened intently to the timbre of her voice till I was certain it was hers before I focused on any message it may convey.

The tune had been playing in the background of my mind in my awake life for a while. It slowly became louder and louder till I finally heard it clearly in this dream. In my own heart I was certain the song Mum was singing was the message she wanted to send me. I was amazed she had chosen music to do so as it was the language my father Geoffrey Byrne and I shared.

Dreams fade soon after we wake up so I hummed the tune as I was waking and immediately wrote notes of the music and lyrics on my computer to try and catch as much detail of this dream as I could. Humming the tune helped prompt my word recall as the words my mother sang faded from my mind in the light of day.

I kept humming the tune as I picked up my guitar. I tried to find the notes of the song. I made notes and scrawled anything I could on paper so I could get the tune back if I lost it in the days to come. The few words I could recall guided my internet searches that proved fruitless at the time. I had a hunch I knew the tune already but could not recall its name.

When my husband Michael woke up, I hummed the tune to him to see if he recognized it. Together we worked on the tune till we had a basic composition that was enough to keep the sound of the melody in a form our memories could use to recall it at will.

Weeks went past but I still could not find the source of the tune.

I was at a prayer group of ladies my mother's age some months later when I had the idea to share my dilemma with them. I hummed the melody hoping they could help me identify it. They immediately burst into song and sang a hymn they all knew well. At last, I had enough lyrics to do an internet search and found the tune. It was called "I Heard the Voice of Jesus Say

Come Unto Me and Rest" but the words my mother sang to me were not exactly the same as the song they knew.

My internet search revealed the song my mother sang to me was actually a composite of a song and a hymn. The two parts to the song were my mother's answer to the questions that bothered me after her death.

My questions were—What did Mum feel as she crossed from our world into the world of spirit? What did she learn on her journey toward the afterlife that enabled her to just let her body go and trust the journey she would take as she died?

My mother's gift to me of newly arranged lyrics to a tune already known was an amazing comfort to me. I sang the song over and over for hours at the time because it gave me peace. The sound helped ease the feeling of dread in my heart. Singing the song gave me a chance to allow my mother's voice to ease my sorrows and comfort my soul the way she did when I was a child. It helped me recall my happy memories with her so I could keep something of who she was in my heart. During a grief counseling session, I learned we grieve in the child mode. Music matters to me because it is a comfort my inner child connects to. Music transcends my adult self's boundaries in a socially acceptable way.

When I sing, I can be a child. That is why I sing and play music. It helps me remember the good times in my life, especially when the sad times seem overwhelming.

THE ANGELIC ORCHESTRA
James Iandoli's Story

I met James Iandoli in October 2022 at the *Inquiry Into Anomalous Experiences and The Phenomenon* event in New York City. Along with Jay Christopher King, Kelly Chase, Pricilla Stone and others, James gathered an amazing panel of experts to present their research on UFOs and related phenomena. Among the panelists were folks like Leslie Keane, Joshua Cutchin, James Fox, Jeff Kripal, Diana Pasulka and many others.

When I first met James at the Helen Mills Event Space and Theater, I think it was Priscilla Stone who said, "You UFO guys are really tall." Standing maybe an inch or two over Jay Christopher King, James is about six foot three.

I have since been to all the conferences that James and his team have hosted in the New York City area. Since each conference has had seven to ten speakers, they tend to go all day. And despite the length of the events, I remained riveted from start to finish. The presenters come from a variety of backgrounds: ufologists, anthropologists, journalists, philosophers, folklorists, and more. Sitting in my seat, I'm usually furiously taking notes, trying to capture as much as possible.

I have enjoyed these conferences immensely. There is no doubt that my thinking has been opened and transformed by those attending these events.

Because of this, I am grateful to include James's story in this book. I can honestly say that *UFO Symphonic* was born when I read Jeff Kripal's *The Flip*, but accelerated and deepened by attending the *Anomalous Conferences*.

The Angelic Orchestra

James is currently writing a book about his experiences. I'm looking forward to reading more about his experiences and ideas about the Phenomenon. In the meantime, with James's permission, I excerpted and slightly modified the transcript from his appearance on the *Vetted* Podcast in June 2024. Here is James's story.

> At twenty years old, because of the earlier events, I was already investigating UFOs and psychic phenomena. Anything kind of strange caught my attention.
>
> One day in 2007, I was at work, doing an overnight shift. My coworker, a steward, was cleaning the area. The steward was a porter. He didn't know that I was interested in UFOs and the Phenomena. He said, very casually, "Hey how are you doing? How's the family?" Then he added, "Did you hear about the UFOs in Mexico?" This was weird because he and I had never had a discussion regarding UFOs.
>
> Later that morning, I drove home and went to sleep. I dreamt that I was driving and I saw an electric or plasma orange UFO, maybe twenty feet above my car. In my dream, I was driving down one of the old streets where I had previously lived. I began to feel electrical pulses emanating from the orange UFO that was still hovering right above my car. Feeling reactive, I tried to evade it. But, speeding up, I still couldn't seem to lose it. The UFO stayed with me the whole time. Escaping seemed pointless.
>
> Then I snapped out of my dream and woke up. I said to myself *wow that was freaking weird*. At this point I wasn't thinking about what the porter from work had said. I hadn't connected the two at all until one of my family members later said "hey, did you hear about the UFOs in Mexico" and then it hit me. *Something's going on here.*
>
> I left my house and drove down the street to a Chinese takeout where I often go, especially after the gym. It was spring, maybe early summer. The sky was a clear blue. It was between 3:30 p.m. and 4:00 p.m. I had only driven about four hundred feet at this point. I looked up in the sky and, right in front of me,

was a stationary fireball hanging in midair. I thought to myself *that's a UFO!* And, as soon as I thought that the fireball started moving. Freaking out, I was also very excited. The fireball wasn't just an orange orb. It had an organic or living quality to it. From my car, it appeared to be about one-third the size of a dime. It was maybe a few hundred to a thousand feet from me. There were no flames coming off it; it was completely contained. The fiery orb glided across the sky, while I tried to chase it in my car. The orb moved slowly and finally flew over the horizon past the trees, obstructing my view. It wasn't moving fast but I had to negotiate the streets and buildings to keep up with it, while it moved in the sky unrestrictedly. Then it disappeared.

Two months after that sighting, I got into a car accident.

I didn't realize this for many years, but I got into the car accident exactly where I had the fireball sighting! It gets even weirder. After the car accident, I had a trauma induced out-of-body experience.

Because I was exhausted, while driving, I fell asleep at the wheel, crashing my car. When I awoke, I was face-to-face with a being of light. The being's "body" was tapered down. It had arms, a neck, a head, and a chest, but I didn't see any feet. It was a whitish blue. This experience was different from everyday reality. I was conscious and aware the entire time. I knew it wasn't a dream. It was more like I suddenly woke up *out* of a dream and was now face-to-face with this entity.

Then I heard an amazing crystalline-like angelic orchestra. Suddenly, I was above the scene of the accident, looking down at the whole thing. I saw an ambulance and my car. I thought that I was dead. I didn't feel like I was in my body. However, I was totally relaxed. I didn't feel any regret or panic. In fact, I felt complete equanimity, like I was in a meditative state. A few moments later I was back in my body. Then it occurred to me that I was looking down at the accident from the vantage point of where I had seen the fireball. I started to think. *What if the fireball was a being from another dimension, or my conscious awareness from the future?* Perhaps we present ourselves to other

The Angelic Orchestra

beings, or even to our future ourselves, as a fireball in another realm. The experience generated a thousand questions.

There was a part of that experience that never left me completely. I felt a buzzing that stayed with me for many months after.

The next day, I got out of the hospital without any serious injuries. I thought that maybe the buzzing sound was coming from the concussion I had because of the accident.

And while falling asleep at the wheel and almost dying was terrifying, I was grateful to literally walk away from it. I felt lucky to be alive. That I'm privileged to experience the miracle of life every day. In all the vast space of seemingly barren planets out there in the cosmos, here I am alive and sentient. I have the capacity to love, to have a family and enjoy life. What a gift.

The next day, cleaning my room, I was feeling thankful to be alive. Pondering the miracle of existence.

Suddenly I heard a voice echoing through my body saying *come outside*. However it communicated, it felt telepathic, generated within my mind and throughout my body. The moment that I heard the voice I also knew exactly what was going to happen. I saw an image of two human-looking entities in a spacesuit. They had blond hair and blue eyes, that kind of complexion.

I went outside and as soon as I got out the door, I looked up into the sky. I knew that I was going to see a UFO. I heard a low hum *vom vom vom*; it was very bassy. I felt it throbbing throughout my body. I was locked into the consciousness of these beings. Like I could feel their feelings. I was having what I now know to be a Kundalini Activation[83] experience. I was happy, excited and

---

[83] Kundalini activation is a transformative experience that involves awakening a primal energy, known as Kundalini, that is believed to be located at the base of the spine. When awakened, Kundalini is said to rise up through the central nadi, or sushumna, and activate the seven main chakras along the way. This process is thought to lead to different levels of awakening and a mystical experience, culminating in a profound transformation of consciousness when Kundalini reaches the top of the head, or Sahasrara chakra

almost giddy.

Getting past the trees that were blocking the way, I looked up and saw a metal craft. Almost like a hexagon except the edges were not straight, they were rounded off. The craft was mounted with a completely square white light fixture that had different color lights bleeding around the edges in a circle. *My God, this is the most amazing thing I've ever experienced.* I was elated. Following it, I ran trying to make sure that I didn't trip. The craft was not far above the trees. Then, suddenly, it started moving along and disappeared and then reappeared maybe like a thousand feet away over a man-made lake that was across the street. While I was thrilled, I'm also thinking that maybe I hit my head so hard the day before in the accident that I was imagining this.

Meanwhile, the beings were emanating a loving connection directly into me. I was receiving a download.

I ran into my house and told two of my family members to come outside. They came outside and they were watching these crafts along with me. At that point there were three crafts, and they were moving across the sky with the lights going around them for some minutes. I thought that other people must have seen this because it was maybe 9:30 p.m. at night in the summer. *Is this disclosure happening right now?* Were the beings announcing themselves to the human race?

The crafts moved through the sky for over twenty minutes, one disappearing, another one appearing and so forth. At one point, there were two of them going towards each other in the sky as the lights were going around their perimeters, blinking. As soon as they were about to make contact, thinking that they were going to crash, they made contact and disappeared. Like the show was over. Like the TV was turned off.

QUESTIONS ON SCRAPS OF PAPER
Christina Marrocco's Story

I met Tea Marrocco in Chicago at an Italian American writers' conference. I was on a panel with Tea, along with two other writers, Karen Trintori and Susan Llyod Caperna. We all became instant friends and have since presented again at a conference in Pittsburgh.

The following is Tea's story as emailed to me.

> The backs of my thighs have adhered to a wooden pew at the Wonewoc Spiritualist Church. On my left, Grandma, her red hair faded with age and permed into a hundred springs, presses an embroidered hanky to her forehead. On my right, Yvonne Crighton, my friend and bandmate from home, black eyeliner smudging in the heat. It's the summer of '81, and it's not just the Amish who go without A/C in Wisconsin.
>
> A Stevie Nicks doppelganger wafts up and down the aisle, passing out scraps of paper and golf pencils. Everyone in the pews writes down one question for the medium along with their first initial, for identification. Up in front, a man toots out Greensleeves on a wooden flute, barefoot. Grandma nods to people in various pews.
>
> *This is my granddaughter,* she mouths to a few, motioning to the top of my head. I am not a forthright girl, and yet I manage to compose a forthright question:
>
> "Who will I fall in love with?"
>
> Grandma and Yvonne scribble away as well, everyone does. A

woman with a guitar makes her way to the front of the chapel, joins Ian Anderson up there, and strums her first note. A rescuing wind dances in through the open windows. We all lean into it like tallgrass in a breeze. And sway for a moment.

It must have been the wallowing on her nubby green couch days before, my admiration of the picture box pinned with exotic butterflies above it, the way I gnawed Bubblicious and read my way through her odd bookshelf, that convinced Grandma to bring me up to church. I'd rapidly devoured her books: Many Mansions, The Bridey Murphy Story, Chariots of the Gods.

Yvonne and I were also likely allowed this unusual day because my mother and aunt just couldn't stand us anymore, fourteen and as one-minded as two mules in the same harness.

Well before the trip to Wisconsin, Yvonne had burned Ray Valenski's name into her forearm with a pencil eraser, rubbing until she took off skin there. This meant she loved him and had no access to tattooing tools. It was in this same era that we formed our band, an up-and-coming concern we dubbed Blind Daze. Certainly, we were ripping off Blind Faith—imitation being the sincerest form of, well, imitation. Yvonne and I spent hours in front of my bedroom mirror, practicing stage poses. She did something very Roger Daltry, lots of bicep flexing despite her role as drummer. I dangled an unlit cigarette from my bottom lip, held my beat-up guitar low—challenging without a strap—grimace-smiled, while shaking long dark hair into my face. I was entirely indistinguishable from Jimmy Page.

In further preparation for fame, I'd signed up for lessons at Sandpiper Used Books, darting across four lanes of traffic to get there every week, guitar held high above my head. Every cent of babysitting money found its way into the cash register at Sandpiper Books with its heady combination of guitar lessons and historical romance novels. The sort where any female protagonist is either an inmate of Bedlam Asylum or imprisoned under similarly horrific conditions elsewhere, waiting to be shipped off to a penal colony. I'd arrive for my lessons hours early and

Questions on Scraps of Paper

lurk among the stacks of books as if hypnotized, inhaling the heady smell of them, feeling as well, the homes they'd come from.

Joyce, the store owner and guitar teacher, was calmer than any adult I knew. All that guitar playing must have sedated her. Joyce wanted me to begin my tutelage with Martha and the Vandellas' "Dancing in the Streets," a song I had absolutely no interest in playing. I wanted to start with "Stairway to Heaven." Joyce promised that if I mastered her choice, we could move on to "Stairway."

Yvonne, however, was not preparing for our futures. She'd taken not a single drum lesson. Nor did she have a drum set. And she wouldn't be getting one either, not any time soon. Because what she did have was a mother who forbade drumming and other "noise" in the house. She wouldn't have approved of the medium either, but she never would find out. When we practiced, Yvonne wore shorts and slapped out a rhythm on her bare legs.

Not all will be answered, Grandma whispers to us in the pew, and as she does, the flute and guitar players both come to a stop; it must be time for readings. I've never been to anything like this before, but I'm certain Stevie Nicks must be the medium or psychic or whatever it's called. I'm wrong. Another woman comes in, at least as old as Grandma with big round glasses and a cane. She takes her seat, faces the congregation, closes her kindly eyes. Her small hands reach into the basket, unfolding a slip of paper. She reads my insipid question, aloud.

T, she says, T is a young person, a girl, a man with a guitar will be the one you love. I see you surrounded by music, and I also feel I must tell you to watch your headstrong nature—do not let it blind you.

Headstrong-schmedstrong. I'm going to have a guitar-playing boyfriend! He can join the band. I rejoice. There's this one guy, Jack Lister—I've seen him waiting for lessons at Sandpiper. I suspect he, pigeon-toed and a year ahead of me, is already playing "Stairway."

By comparison, Yvonne does not get a satisfying message, not at all. The medium sings out something about being kind to her mother and slowing down things she's rushing. Yvonne sighs. I chew the ends of my hair, fan myself with a pamphlet.

When school resumes in the fall, I'm far too shy to speak to Jack Lister, so I just stare when I see him at school or waiting for his lessons. Pick at the blisters on my fingers in a way that makes sure he can see them. This goes on for months. Until I have no choice but to settle on someone else, a kid from another high school, a frizzy-haired, skinny blond guy Yvonne and I meet outside a kegger party. He does all the talking.

What draws you to a lover at fifteen? For me, it was no more than a floppy leather hat like the one Stephen Stills wore during his Buffalo Springfield days. This guy doesn't even know who Stephen Stills is, but still...the hat.

The result of any relationship is life-altering. For me, what would follow was extreme: a teenage pregnancy, leaving high school, quitting lessons, all the shame that accompanies all of that: an early marriage, a second child with childhood cancer, a divorce, a remarriage, domestic violence, two more children, finally attending college in my late thirties, a second divorce.

Three decades later, when I follow the impulse to return to camp, I'd love to drive up to visit Grandma first, wallow on her sofa and return to her books. But she's gone. But the message I received by her side three decades earlier still floats in once in a while, and I wonder—or believe I know—I chronicle all the things I've done to cheat myself out of that guitar-player and the love he would have given me and mine. I load up my car with a cooler, overnight clothes, bring along my two youngest boys, fourteen and fifteen, bring their harmonicas and guitars, too. Though I'm weak with exhaustive stress, having just completed my graduate degree during that second divorce, we drive.

Camp is up high in the driftless zone, atop a bluff; the car strains up the hill. We park and head for the gift shop to check in when a blue swallowtail lands on my bare toe—sandals will allow that. You can't bring a butterfly into a gift shop where it could get trampled so I veer away and instead walk the oval path of the camp, carefully. I inhale the piney sweet of the air, sunshine on my face then my back, sense the gravity and fragility of the simple medium's cabins that dot the circle, holding to the bluff as they have done since the Victorian era.

There's nothing as gentle as the lick of a butterfly proboscis on your toe, nothing as real as the pinch of its tiny feet holding on. Michael and Matthew walk a little behind me, lost in their own conversation, two mules in the same harness. Talking music of course, the perennial conversation between them.

And that's when it hits me.

The message has been true all along.

And I've cheated myself out of nothing. All their music lessons I'd budgeted for, delaying electric and gas bills. Not to mention all the driving to gigs at county fairs and Veterans of Foreign War halls, all the scrimping—for an amp, a guitar for Christmas, the tuba—all the music in the kitchen with my kids, records and CDs spinning. Heck, I'd been in love with guitar players the entire time. And I'd been loved by them as well, just not in the way my fourteen-year-old self had assumed it would be. Thanks, Grandma, I breathe into myself. The butterfly lifts off and we walk to the gift shop for cans of cold Coke, lean against a few pines and glug them down.

This summer I know exactly how deer approach the cabin doors, nibbling impatiens from the window boxes, and picking their way along the circular path. I laugh as the fox charms psychic mediums out of old eggs near the kitchen building. I've returned for good—it's where I am during the summer. Where people have been for a very long time: it's common knowledge that the Wonewoc Spiritualist camp overlays grounds that were, beyond memory, a meeting place for the Ho Chunk people, for peacemaking, for council. After the Ho Chunk came the Victorian ladies in bustles and men in suits—they departed the steam train in the town below and climbed up stone steps set into the side of the bluff, bought a ticket at the booth and came into camp. They still do, in residual ways.

It's been a very long time since I sat with Grandma and Yvonne here, even a somewhat long time since my boys came up with me and the butterfly rode my toe. Time slips as a breeze and reveals new selves. This most recent summer I traveled with my unruly cattle dog, Jolene and a parlor guitar I bought for myself—new. A Loar. This is the third summer since my lovely daughter died—cancer kept coming—and this is a pain that brings everything home. Breaks a person open like an oyster. I suppose we all diverge from our truths and return to them in some way.

Between the readings I give in my cabin, I step out the back door onto the sandstone bluff. I gaze down at the roofs of houses and steeples in town, muted greens and browns, whites and reds. Another world. I sing a wordless song.

Many nights when the visitors have gone home and we have done all the dishes in the communal kitchen, I rest in the back room of my cabin, pick up the guitar, and teach myself. I think about my children, living and gone. About dreams and realities. About meaning. I hear the carpenter ants chewing at the roof.

Some nights there are also the sounds of drum beats, chanting as well. And none of us who work here have a drum. We welcome those beats, talk about them over breakfasts of bacon and eggs, the fox hoping to be thrown an egg, half-hiding near the birdbath. No one doubts that the drumming and chanting comes from beyond the veil. On special nights, in my cabin at the edge of the woods, I try to play along with it, and sometimes my guitar weeps. Sometimes I am keen. The drums have power, sorrow, joy. Sometimes I cannot tell when a beat ends and a melody begins.

I'm not sure I'm a musician, but I'm certainly in a band these days. We all are.

BANDS!
Janice Aubrey's Story

I wrote an article about the previously mentioned E. Rossi & Company in Little Italy for the *Red Hook Star Revue* a while ago. Sometime later, I received an email from someone who'd read the article and felt strongly enough to write to me about it. That person, Janice Aubrey, told me that when her mother visited New York City, she used to go to E. Rossi & Company to buy music, religious statues, and other Italian specialty items to take back to Pennsylvania with her. She wrote that the article reminded her of her Italian upbringing and added that she wanted to send me a book called Bands! which her brother, Joe "Jody" DeVivo, had written.

The book *Bands!* centered on music in New Castle, the small town in Pennsylvania where their family was from. The book was never officially published for the mass market but sold on Amazon for a while. She'd be thrilled, said Janice, for other people to read it, especially someone like me, who was interested in the history of Italian American music.

I wrote back saying that I was moving and maybe now wasn't the best time to send it. I looked up Janice's name; I couldn't find any information on her. Not on Facebook or anywhere else. To be honest, I was also a little concerned about giving my address to someone I didn't know. Janice replied saying that Jody had recently died; she was disappointed she could not share his book with me. This hit me right in the heart; I immediately asked her to send the book.

When I received *Bands!* I was completely surprised. It was not at all conventional. It was broken up into small autobiographical stories about New Castle and the DeVivo family. The stories were hysterical and the illustrations were wonderful.

Bands! is about a section of New Castle known as Mahoningtown, which at that time consisted of mostly southern Italian immigrants, nearly all of whom, or so it seemed to Jody, were spectacular musicians. Everyone except for poor young Jody.

As I read the book, I realized that Janice was mentioned as well. I wrote to her and asked, *You're a musician too?*

She replied saying her career was winding down now, but she'd been a pianist, music director, and conductor for over forty years. This was getting interesting; I arranged to speak with Janice.

"You come from a musical family?"

"Yes, my father played the guitar and mandolin and sang; and he was the choir director at a large church in New Castle. My two older sisters had studied piano and many of my cousins and uncles were good musicians. Jody played the clarinet and sax; but not very well (as he admits in his book)."

"Where did your father come from?"

"My father, Joseph DeVivo was born in Cese, Italy in 1903. Then he moved to the U.S. with his family in 1912."

In those times, like many other southern Italians, her grandfather had first traveled alone to New Castle to work on the railroads, leaving his family behind. But as soon as he made enough money, he sent for his wife and children to come join him.

"Was your mother a musician?"

"No, but my mother loved music. She loved to listen to the Italian music programs on the radio and would order the sheet music she heard on those shows from E. Rossi & Company. Then I could play the songs and help my father learn them."

Janice paused. "My parents met when they both sang in the church choir as teenagers. My mother fell in love with the way Joe could entertain everybody with his music," she added giggling. "It didn't hurt that he was very handsome; he looked like Al Pacino."

"You're a good pianist, but you also mentioned that you have strong sight-reading skills. How did you learn to sight-read?"

"I started to study the piano in the second grade. Since my older sisters had studied piano, we had stacks of music in the house. I sat for hours playing through the piles of sheet music. I didn't realize that by doing this I was developing my sight-reading skills. It soon became evident that I could learn music faster than most. I also have to admit that I was also a little bit of a showoff. When I would sit at the piano to practice in the summer, I purposely left the door open so everyone in the neighborhood could hear me. I guess I was getting in touch with the fact that it feels good to be able to entertain an audience."

"What happened when people discovered you were a good pianist who could read music so quickly?"

"I was asked to provide accompaniment for instrumental lessons in school and that continued all the way through high school—music competitions, choral concerts, etc. When I sat down to play a new piece of music, I could easily see the music in my head and anticipate the way it should sound. But it wasn't only about playing notes. When I played, I tried to communicate what I thought the composer intended for the audience to hear. That instinct seemed to come naturally. I guess this is why some people 'play instruments' and others 'make music.'"

"This is where your music career started?"

"I started to work with performers at a college in Youngstown and also with local theater groups. Then, one summer day I got a call from a girl I had worked with who was working for a brand-new summer stock company in Warren, Ohio. It was called the Kenley Players, a professional theater company that presented hit Broadway shows to 'the hinterlands' using New York singers and dancers with popular movie and TV celebrities in major roles.

They needed a rehearsal pianist so I auditioned and that began what would become an almost twenty five-year association with the Kenley Players. The Kenley circuit grew in popularity and expanded to become a four-theater circuit: Warren, Dayton and Columbus, Ohio and Flint, MI, then later in Akron, OH.

"The people I worked with there would be very influential to my career and many remain friends to this day. I think my first show was 'Bells Are Ringing.' It was the early sixties; I was paid $100 a week, which was a lot of money for me. (Imagine—I was being paid to do something I loved and would gladly have done for FREE!) With Mr. Kenley's support I eventually became an assistant musical director (AMD) and then was asked to become one of his conductors. Being a woman conductor was something very new in those days.

"By this time, I had married and moved to Youngstown, Ohio and was raising a family. I was then hired to be music director at the Youngstown Playhouse where they mounted two major musicals during a season. I also was hired by a local Jewish temple to play for their annual Broadway musical. It was there where I became assistant music director to the music director, Shy Lockson. Shy owned a tailor shop, but he had toured with his own dance band in the 1940s and was active in the local musician's union. When he learned how much the Youngstown Playhouse was paying me, he sat me down and taught me how I needed to ask for more money. This was an especially important lesson for me since I was never particularly good at asking for the money I deserved. Music was always too much fun!"

"Does a good pianist or sight-reader necessarily make a good conductor?"

"They're related and those skills do help but being a conductor involves far more. You need to be able to communicate to the musicians using your hands, arms, and body. There are plenty of conductors who can beat time and hold things together; but others, like a Leonard Bernstein, can inspire their players to play their best by using their entire body and personal energy. A good conductor looks out from the podium at the sea of musicians' faces and determines how to cue them to play in a way that will help them create the most beautiful sound at just the right time. The conductor tries to do this by making the musician feel safe, so that they can play their absolute best. And this all happens in *real time*."

"You also toured Europe?"

"I began touring in Europe in 1997 after I had visited my husband David Shoup in Zurich. He was working for a production company based in Berlin and at that time was playing guitar for an *Evita* tour. I knew the musical director of *Evita* from the Kenley Players and he asked me to join this tour as his assistant music director. The German producers liked my work and when *Evita* was about to close, they asked me if I would like to go on a year-and-a-half tour of *West Side Story*, which would begin rehearsals in one week. This then was the start of another over twenty-year association with this German-based company.

"When I joined *West Side Story* I was hired to assist another conductor I'd met at the Kenley Players. The tour traveled to many cities in Germany, Switzerland, France, Austria, and Italy. Many of those cities I would revisit in the coming years and they began to feel like home. The whole company, band included, traveled by bus. After *West Side Story* closed, the producer mounted a production of *Grease, das Musical,* which became extremely popular and was his biggest money maker. At some point, the *Grease* conductor was fired, and I was asked to become the conductor. The producer particularly liked the way I could work with the singers to offer them vocal help—teaching them to relax their throats or show them how to reach notes they thought they could not; helping them to give their best musical performance. I was a vocal coach of sorts."

"Have you ever worked in New York City?"

"I didn't have too many connections in New York City, but I conducted lots of tours that emanated from NYC and then headed out across the country. I was what many call a 'road rat.' While I was living in Cleveland, where I'd been music director for a small opera company, I was invited to conduct one of the earlier National Tours of *Annie*. After that tour, my husband and I moved to New York. More tours followed, including more productions of *West Side Story*. The most recent professional job I did was at Westchester Broadway Theater. It was *An American in Paris*. The conductor was a good friend and he asked if I would play the keyboard. Little did I realize when it closed in November of 2018 that this would be my last foray into musical theater. Enter Covid 19."

After my conversation with Janice, I brought Arielle and Travis to Brooklyn Heights to meet her and David. After a long lunch, we went to their house to continue our conversation. I was a little worried that Travis would be bored, but Janice seemed to know just what to do. She invited Travis to sit down at the piano in her living room. Miraculously, he started to play. And his playing sounded good. It wasn't the usual clunking of keys that kids do. He played actual melodies and chords that he invented, and the sounds were pleasing.

"I'm surprised," I said. "I didn't think he would take to the piano. He takes guitar lessons, but he kind of drags himself through them."

"Something told me that he might like to sit down and play," said Janice. "If you'd like, I can hear that he's musical and I'd be happy to give him lessons."

And I thought to myself, *and this all happened from writing a piece in the* Red Hook Star Revue. Not only is our story yet to be continued, but Jody DeVivo's story now has a new life.

WHILE MY GUITAR GENTLY WEEPS
Marilyn Brannon's Story

Like other folks I met on this journey, I met Marilyn Brannon through the various UFO-related connections I had made. When I posted that I was writing a book about the connection between music and the UFO Phenomenon, she wrote to me. Marilyn sent me this story via Facebook messenger.

> I began to have what I now call a reawakening to the ETs in 2008. I say a reawakening because I began to remember being contacted as a child.
>
> I was not immediately thinking that I was seeing UFOs. I was questioning my sanity because it was happening so frequently. I mean most nights they would appear. It continued in this manner until around 2013 when it subsided a bit.
>
> I had moved to a little country town north of Dallas. One day I was going to the city to spend some time with a good friend. I had a strange small red airplane seeming to fly along with me as I left home.
>
> At my friend's house I went out on her porch to smoke as she took a phone call. I was looking at this one cloud that had appeared in a cloudless sky. It was so unusual since it was shaped like a heart. Then out of it came a white cylinder-shaped craft. I was seeing this type of craft frequently. I thought that maybe they are the Arcturians, as I was reading a book about them the night before. I thought about the twin Arcturians described in this book. As I had this thought the cloud splits into two hooded figures. I was just stunned in amazement. So much so I didn't

even think to call my friend out.

We hung out discussing Edgar Cayce talking about the Arcturians in a book of his that she owned. Afterwards, I left to drive home.

This was Valentine's Day, and the radio station was playing a bunch of sappy love songs. But then suddenly they played a song that seemed way out of context to the others. It was "While My Guitar Gently Weeps." I had heard that song a million times but at this moment I heard its real meaning for the first time, and I knew that the ET had played that specifically for me. The deeper meaning I was hearing was extremely profound for me. I was crying by the end of the song. When it was over more sappy love songs continued for the rest of my ride home.

VISIONS OF TRUTH
Max Wareham's Stories

Max Wareham is the banjo player for the Peter Rowan Bluegrass Band and was featured on the Grammy-nominated album "Calling You From My Mountain." Max is also Peter's cousin.

A few years ago, Peter had suggested that I talk to Max when he had published his first book *Rudy Lyle: The Unsung Hero of the Five String Banjo*, chronicling the life and music of early bluegrass banjo master Rudy Lyle. In this unique book, Max presented never-before-published transcriptions and analyses of every break Lyle recorded with Bill Monroe, the "father of bluegrass." The book also includes interviews with banjo legends and members of Rudy's family. There are also intimate portraits of each interviewee alongside several never-before-published photos of Rudy Lyle. Max's book is an important artifact of bluegrass history.

On a personal level, Max is one of the gentlest and kindest people I've ever met. He has a calmness about him that makes me feel calmer. And he's a patient musician. I've seen him play with Peter in venues around the country. Peter often improvises during performances. Max is an excellent listener, he never loses a beat when Peter changes course. Max remains keyed into Peter's playing, moving with Peter's changes, supporting him and the group.

In addition to being a great banjo player, Max is a gifted guitar player.

I was lucky enough to spend some time with Max when he played with Peter at a venue in North Hampton, Massachusetts. After the performance, I was invited to stay with Max and Pete at a place where the former was house sitting. That night, when we arrived, we played guitars and sang until the morning hours. At breakfast, Max conveyed two stories to me. After a few weeks, he wrote them down and sent them to me.

Here are Max's two stories.

During the summer of 2014 I set off on a pilgrimage to find my musical hero, guitarist Norman Blake. I had heard that he lived in Rising Fawn, GA, in the northwest part of the state, so I set my sights and started driving. After many days on the road with adventures and detours (mostly tent camping and visiting with friends), I arrived in a very hot and humid Rising Fawn and walked into the local music shop. I talked with the guy behind the counter for a while before asking if he ever sees Norman around. He told me he had been in just the day before buying strings. He gave me the number of a friend of Norman's.

... *ringing*

"Hello?"

I returned the greeting and explained the mission I was on and asked if there was any way that I would be able to meet Norman.

"Well... Norman doesn't really *like* meeting people he doesn't know."

After we had talked a while longer, he said, "Well... you're in luck because Norman only plays a couple of times a year, and tomorrow he's playing up at the Mountaineer Folk Festival on the Cumberland Plateau in Tennessee. I'll introduce you."

The next morning, I drove up to Tennessee and then slowly up a hill that was the beginning of the plateau. Up and up the road ran, until finally it leveled off. I expected a view of a valley below, but above the trees there was only more sky. After many winding roads I arrived at the festival. It was a real Appalachian event. They had lots of pieces of mountain folk culture, including hand-carved wooden tools, paintings, quilts, an old horse-drawn corn mill. There was an old canon from the Civil War that they were firing off at regular intervals of about twenty minutes. Norman began playing and I studied his every move. His songs were quiet, his picking slow and beautiful, his voice feebler and wiser than the earlier recordings I had of him. Then...*BANG* sounded the canon. As the reverberations of the shot faded into the distance, Norman's guitar playing came back into focus as he chuckled.

I was introduced to Norman after the set, and we got to stand around and talk for a while. It was great to get a sense of his world, to shake his hand and pay my respects.

That night I camped out on the plateau above a huge waterfall. I had a dream that felt like more than a dream—it was so vivid that my waking life felt more like a dream compared to this. In the dream, I was being guided through a hallway with many doors. My guide explained to me that behind each door was a vision of truth. He asked if I'd like to see my own story. Then he opened one of the doors. I looked through and saw my entire life unfolding, starting with a rather uncomfortable image of my parents having sex and my own conception. I watched my birth, my childhood, and everything that came after until I saw my own gravestone. I can recall everything that led up to that present moment, but I wasn't able to remember anything that had occurred in the future. The guide then said that I can open any other doors I'd like to, which I proceeded to do. They all contained some cosmic vision of the human experience. I learned many secrets about how the universe works. The only catch was that I wouldn't be able to understand any of that information once I woke up again–almost like hearing something in a language you didn't understand. And I woke up right from that dream and looked out on a sunny morning. I felt more well-rested than I ever had in my life.

By late 2015 I had grown disillusioned with trying to pursue a career in music. *If not music, then what?* Archaeology, naturally–the number one most popular second career. I found a website database of active archaeological digs that needed volunteers, and on January 1, 2016, I found myself back on the road, headed for Tennessee again. The dig was through East Tennessee State University, excavating an old Cherokee settlement from the sixteenth century along the Nolichucky River in what is now Washington County. While the dig was mostly ETSU students, there were a couple other volunteers like me—we all became fast friends. We were staying in a house just over the border in southwest Virginia, driving the rental car to the dig each morning.

I got my hands dirty. The most common find was a shard of pottery. I did have the fortune of finding a small blue glass bead, which the professor leading the dig explained to me had been made in Italy during the Renaissance, traded to the Dutch, who then traded it to the Spanish, who then traded it to the Cherokee, where it then fell into the ground. I'll never forget the feeling of washing the dirt off the bead and holding it up to the sun, watching the light illuminate the blue glass.

I spent a month down there. Sometime during the third week, I found a shard of pottery that seemed big. As I continued to remove dirt from the edges, I started thinking that this is a pretty large shard, and there's a small chance this isn't a shard at all, but rather a complete piece of pottery. I mentioned this to a couple people digging near me and a small crowd had gathered around the hole in the ground, looking at what they could see of the pottery. The professor walked over. I explained to him what I might have found and suggested that someone with more experience in archaeology take it from here.

"Well, you say you're a musician. You're supposed to be pretty good with your fingers, right?"

He handed me his trowel.

I continued digging, this time with greater care and patience. People watched as more of the pot revealed itself from under the dirt. After a couple hours of gentle scraping away of dirt, I pulled it from the ground and held it in the palm of my hand–a small round pot with a tiny opening at the top. I showed it to everyone gathered around and handed it to the professor. One of the people on the dig, who was part Cherokee, pulled me aside and said, "Do you know what that is?"

"An old pot?"

"It's a medicine man's pot. And you didn't find it—it found you."

At some point during my stay in Tennessee, word had gotten out that I was a banjo player, and somebody insisted I go with them to a jam happening in southwest Virginia. We drove along in the dark, windy roads, up into a holler, and arrived at a luthier's shop, where many people from the community gathered every Friday night. There was a stage and the audience sat in church pews. They saw my instrument and immediately asked me to get up on stage. I had a great time that night, playing for and with the kindest people. It was actually a real education for me. There I was—a Yankee out of his element. I had learned that music was something you could be good at, or better at, but this night helped me realize that music can't be separated from people or its culture. This music is what all of these people do on a Friday night, whether playing or listening. It was their community. Prior to this, I think I had been viewing music from the head, rather than the heart.

I returned to the north reinvigorated, with a deeper understanding of my purpose in the music. Was there any connection between the journey of deepening my relationship to music and the discovery of the medicine man's pot? I think maybe so—the meaning in life is that which we give it.

SEASONS THAT PASS YOU BY[84]

It is 1978. Squid and I start smoking pot. Our music listening becomes deeper. We don't yet realize how perceptive we are, that we are rejecting the bullshit world of the status quo. That we are consciousness pioneers.

Now fourteen, Squid and I pass a joint back and forth in Squid's bedroom, gazing out the window. We're recovering from a traumatic event: I've just had a gun put to my head. We live in a tough neighborhood.

Living on the sixth floor is like being on top of the world. From Squid's window we see the distant rooftops of other project buildings. At this moment, it seems as if our project complex is a chunk of Earth floating out in space, surrounded by a million years. The trees have a bright green shimmer as they sway in the gentle summer breeze.

We're listening to Yes's *Close to the Edge*, one of the many albums lined up on the shelf near the window where the record player sits. The title song blares out of the speakers. Squid's brothers listen to music at full volume, so this isn't unusual in his house. My father would probably call the police on us if I played music this loud.

Close to the Edge opens with the sounds of birds twittering. The music conjures up a distant world: we're on another planet, sitting in a valley between mountains, spaceships flying overhead.

In the sky on this planet there are two suns and a gigantic purple-red moon, visible during the day. Suddenly the band's music blasts from the speakers, like a titanic UFO is crash-landing on our

---

[84] Fiorito, Mike. *For All We Know*. Baltimore, MD: Loyola Press, 2024

project building. The room shakes as the music screams out of the walls.

"Yes is my favorite band," shouts Squid over the music

"They're my favorite band with Bill Bruford as drummer," I say, leaning into his ear to be heard. It never occurs to us that we can lower the music.

"I know, I know. You like Bruford."

Squid likes the Yes configuration with Alan White on drums.

Bruford is more of a jazz drummer, he plays wonderfully unpredictable, offbeat rhythms. White is more of a straight-ahead rock drummer. Squid likes the live Yes albums and I prefer the studio albums.

Squid and I have this discussion for hours while smoking weed. We talk about the worlds that Yes weaves with their music. Worlds of bucolic beauty. Mountain landscapes floating in space. Visions of a future in which humans have become spiritually and socially advanced. But Squid and I don't use words like bucolic. We don't know those words, though Squid writes reams of poetry that he sometimes shows me. But we're drawn to the poetic lyrics in Yes's songs. And we're fascinated by the interesting sounds of the instruments: mandolins, church organs, harpsichords, pedal-steel, nylon and twelve-string guitars. There are also a lot of futuristic sounds in Yes's music: Moog synthesizers, Mellotrons and Hammond organs. The mix of ancient and futuristic makes Yes's music sound timeless. That, along with the legato singing and polyphonic harmonies, make it seem as though their vocals are sung by all the angels and saints in Heaven.

We may not know what we're doing, but we know in our bones that we're connected to the most important journey of a human soul. That music can transport you. Deliver you. That music is a form of time travel.

Squid's mother bangs on the bedroom wall, shouting over the music, asking us to lower the volume. She must have been banging for a while. Squid turns down the knob on the stereo.

"Thank you," we hear from the hallway. She doesn't sound angry; she practically sings her thank you. The music must have been at rock-concert levels.

"I can't believe what happened last night," says Squid in a hushed voice.

"I know, I totally freaked out."

"Why didn't you hand him your radio?"

This is not an easy question to answer. Sure, I panicked, the black-metal gun to my head made me go blank. But there was much more to it than that. I had begged my dad for months to get me the radio. It's a Panasonic with a cassette player. I saved up for months to get it; he gave me half. Then he insisted I keep it at home so it wouldn't get stolen. But this little plastic box with knobs brings voices from another dimension. It tunes into frequencies on the electromagnetic spectrum that only initiated beings can hear. Beings from anywhere in the universe. It can communicate in two ways. They can hear us, and we can hear them. Who are they? I don't know now and I didn't know back then.

"I mean, just running away like that from the kid with the gun, that was crazy," says Squid, lighting up the joint again. The song's chorus rings out over the speakers. I know Squid knows what I'm thinking. Despite the events of last night, the music calls to us. We're just kids, unable to explain that the music transports us to a safer, more beautiful place. A place less dangerous than the projects. Not as filthy. No dead steel factories or abandoned buildings in this world. In Yes's music we journey to places with mountains, rainbows, and rivers. Some of these places are right here in front of us. Sometimes, they are scattered across the galaxies.

"This might be my all-time favorite album," Squid finally says.

"Even with Bruford on drums?"

"Maybe," he draws out slowly. He's patting his head with his fingers. "I might put *Yessongs* on the same level as *Close to the Edge*."

I nod along with him, pleased.

"Do you think that guy would have shot me?" I ask.

"What?" Squid replies. He always says what when he's not sure. There is nothing bitter or mean in Squid. He loves the crazy shit I do, but he wouldn't be the person to do that crazy thing. And he doesn't want to upset me.

"Do you think that guy would have shot me?"

"But he didn't shoot you."

"He put the gun up to my head."

"But he didn't pull the trigger." Squid smiles. "Maybe because he knew you were a sick motherfucker."

"But he was one click away."

"He was." Nodding, he adds, "It would have been over in one second."

It's Squid's quick answer that gets to me. I picture how my body would have looked, splayed on the concrete, a puddle of thick red blood gushing from my head like gas from a busted fuel tank. I shiver for a second, but Squid doesn't notice.

"But you, you were a madman, running away like that. I mean, the guy would have shot you if you simply flinched." He waits a few beats. "You must have known that, right?"

I don't have an answer for him. The joint between my index finger and thumb has gone out. I light up again. Squid adds, "I'm just glad you're here and we can listen to music together. No one else hears music like we do."

I'm choked up by his words. We both know how close that call was. Close to the edge. I take a pull on the joint and pass it back to him. We try to avoid looking at each other's watery eyes.

Then Squid reaches over to make the music louder as the final chorus plays on the stereo. The refrain on the title song, "Close to the Edge," reminds me of how I traversed the border of life and death, at one instant being both dead and alive. I hear the ghost echo of a gunshot in my brain. My blood feels cold and still.

KING DIAMOND[85]

I'm not a heavy metal fan. But Joe insists we see King Diamond. It is 1980. "This is great music, man," he says. "They're amazing musicians. It's not just guitar shredding."

"What's the band's name again?" asks Squid.

"King Diamond," replies Joe with a straight face. Squid and I laugh.

"Trust me," pleads Joe, shaking his head to underscore the seriousness of the band and his opinion of them.

But Squid and I are doubtful. Our love of heavy metal music stops at Black Sabbath and Deep Purple. Joe is deep into groups like Megadeth, Iron Maiden and Motorhead. He has the albums, wears their T-shirts. Squid and I are more into progressive and psychedelic rock, not just Yes but Jethro Tull and King Crimson. Psychedelic groups write songs about other worlds, about the love of the universe, of knowledge. That kind of crap. They transport us out of drab Long Island City with its factories and project buildings,[86] sending us into fantastic new realms. The album covers are fairytale-like. A chunk of earth floating out into space. Extraterrestrial creatures. And the instruments they play, and play well, include mandolins, acoustic guitars, and Moog synthesizers. Spacey far out shit, somewhere between *Lord of the Rings* and *Star Trek*. This is where we want to be. Lost in the cosmic swirl. Not stuck in the dismal shithole of the projects or the satanic hellhole of heavy metal.

---

85 Fiorito, Mike. *For All We Know*. Baltimore, MD: Loya Press, 2024
86 Public, subsidized housing.

Joe persists. He begs. Let's face it, he doesn't want to go alone—all the way to L'Amour in Bay Ridge, Brooklyn, from Queens—and he wants us to *like* his music, too.

We take the train to 62nd Street in Brooklyn. To make the long train ride bearable, Squid and I smoke a joint in-between the train cars. We hold onto the train handles, passing a joint with our free hand, swaying with the stopping and starting of the train. The great thing about riding between train cars is that you can do anything. You can smoke cigarettes, pee on the tracks, or vomit into the rushing air if you must. This is the NYC subway system in 1980. There are no rules. It is a lawless land.

Before we head back into the train car, Squid and I each pop a hit of mescaline. Joe never takes drugs. He just watches us as we slowly devolve into idiots.

Sitting in the train car, we laugh and joke. The train moves slowly, creaking its way to Brooklyn. There is garbage swirling around the train cars and graffiti on their walls. As littered and filthy as the train car looks, it begins to glow and shimmer.

By the time we get to our stop, the mescaline and weed have fully kicked in. Walking down the street the neon signs speak to me in some secret electronic language, luring me into the stores over which they hang. Maybe aliens hide behind the counters in the stores.

From the outside, L'Amour looks like a humdrum bar, but when the door swings open, the bright velvet curtains and ornate chandeliers give the impression we've stepped into a medieval dungeon. The mescaline is now fully pumping through my brain. Colors are sharper, sounds more articulated. I hear wind in the drumkit's cymbals and radar signals in the guitar notes.

There are at least three floors inside the club and little alcoves with couches where you can make out or smoke weed in a more private place. Since the band hasn't yet started, we wander around the club, exploring its hidden chambers.

The castle-like atmosphere is enhanced by the chalky white-faced zombie fans who sashay through the venue. The dead look in their eyes is a little ominous. Along with the thundering guitar sounds and heavy bass riffs pounding the walls, it feels like we are being led into a slaughterhouse. Machines blow curls of smoke that twirl and twist in the arena lights, taking on the changing colors. Lights flash and blink to the music. The only things missing are lightning and rain.

Style-wise, Joe, Squid and I are completely out of place here. We wear simple dungaree pants and T-shirts. We don't have gothic outfits, makeup, or long purple fingernails. And our hair is short and coily, not straight and long.

Suddenly all attention turns toward center stage. It becomes dark and silent. The zombies gather around us; I wonder if they will try to eat us in a savage frenzy. Lights flood the stage. The band, materializing out of nowhere, begins playing. The music sounds like the groan of an enormous metallic whale chained to a cage in Hell.

As the thick smoke from the stage clears, a studded coffin emerges from the blackness. I hear grunting from the zombies around me. Are they alive, or are they dead already? Mouths open, hands extended, they eagerly await the moment their leader will tear into them like a devil, ripping open their stomachs with his fangs and claws.

Joe frantically points to the stage. He's whispering to me and Squid, but we can't hear him. We want to laugh but between the mescaline and the weed, we are scared out of our wits. I swear I see bats flying around us. This is getting serious now. The coffin slowly opens. The leader of the dead zombies, King Diamond, steps out. He sticks his tongue out and makes threatening faces, opening his mouth wide, pushing his eyeballs out of his head.

As soon as he starts singing, the zombies begin shaking their heads in unison with the thudding rhythms, as if their long hair is clapping to the music. Shaking their skulls, turning their brains to pulp. We stand in awe, hands by our sides, hearts beating rapidly.

Singing into a microphone shaped like a human skull, King Diamond's face is painted with blood, as if his zombie worshippers had chewed into his cheeks. At some point, King Diamond spins and whirls to the music, the stage a vortex where demonic wizards and spirits swim in an embryonic cell. Their bodies liquefy and ooze in the placental walls, their essences melting to the hypnotic rhythms and screaming guitar frequencies. This is way beyond just music. This is a consecrated transfiguration. We are witnessing the beating heart of the universe, everything that has ever lived and died. All existences metamorphosing into a single blood cell that pulses and pumps. It is nothing short of a possession.

Goblins and demons follow us home, some of them disguised as ordinary subway passengers. We move to different cars to escape them and because we can't stop laughing. Every time we do stop laughing, we get serious, concerned that some evil spirit will attack us with spikes and toss our severed limbs to other flesh-eating fiends. We aren't sure if the train is going down into Hell or just west and north back to Queens.

Somehow, we make it home at almost four in the morning, stumbling back to the Ravenswood project building, where we live. A pink silver streaks the sky, suggesting that the world will once again be wrested from the demons.

SOUNDS IN THE SKY[87]

One morning I wake up to the sound of a loud boom. I run to the window in my bedroom. The sky is bright blue. I can't see a single cloud. My eyes fix on a squadron of gigantic metallic spaceships zigzagging across the sky in formation. Outside, looking up alongside my neighbors, I can see that the ships are black triangles enclosed in translucent spheres. The edges of the triangles push up against the spheres. The ships are massive, like mountains or gods. They move effortlessly and without sound.

A woman taps me on the shoulder. "Do you know why they're here?" She has red hair; her blue eyes are wet with excitement.

She might be wild, I think to myself.

"No, I don't," I reply calmly.

"They've finally come to take over. They've been watching for thousands of years. They know who we are," she says.

"How do you know this?"

"They've always come to me in dreams. We've fucked up on this planet and now they want to remove us and secure Earth before we make it uninhabitable."

The heavens are exploding, clouds billow and grow. Bright lights stream down on us. I'm not sure if they are from the spaceships or what.

On the street it's pandemonium. Cars have stopped, people have gotten out of them to gaze into the illuminated skies.

"We didn't take care of Mother Earth," the woman says.

"We've been too focused on greed and plundering the bounty

---

[87] Fiorito, Mike. *For All We Know*. Baltimore, MD: Loya Press, 2024

we were given."

"Is this a punishment?" I ask.

"It is a reclamation," she says.

I look down and notice that I'm in my underwear.

The sky has become pitch black. Lights flicker and blink.

Despite what this woman is saying about the end of the world, the whole thing is beautiful. I feel joyous. At least we'll all die together, I think. Isn't that the best way for us to go? In one fell swoop.

The black fold of night is on fire with erupting stars. The light is so great it shines like it's day.

I start to run and bump into Mickey Ness and Squid. Wait, how old am I? When is this happening? I have slippers on, too. Underwear and slippers. I must be dreaming. So I launch myself into the sky, grabbing onto one of the spaceships. Inside the sphere, the black triangle is marked with hieroglyphics that resemble transistors. These are poems about the distances between stars, about the formations of life that have occurred throughout the universe. They are very personal. Reading them, I feel the individual lives of unfamiliar beings coursing through my body. My heart beats with many hearts. I hear music like I heard as a kid in church. The light, sound, and frequency sing in unison like a billion angels in a million heavens.

I've been having this dream all my life.

FROM LANGUAGE TO SINGING

As I wrote in the beginning of this book, some research suggests that singing precedes language. There are also cultures that use musical and other forms of speech for specific reasons, instead of using spoken language.

Daniel Everett, an American linguist and author, lived among the Pirahã, an indigenous people of the Amazon Rainforest in Brazil, studying and recording their language. Everett's book, *Don't Sleep There Are Snakes*, describes his twenty-five-year relationship with the Pirahã people.

As a Christian missionary, Everett's ultimate goal in learning the language was to translate the bible into Pirahã and convert its people. Instead, in the process, Everett endures a spiritual and intellectual transformation. The Pirahã were not interested in his message. The Pirahã relegated Everett's "preaching" to peddling in superstition. He learned that the Pirahã were practical, grounded people, in contrast to the people of Western Civilization, with our consumerist obsessions and world weariness. They didn't have a notion of sin. They accepted things as they are, including sudden death by snake bites, other predatory attacks, or disease. They didn't fear death. Death was around them all the time. It was accepted that life is a hardship. That children die if they aren't careful. The Pirahã maintain a faith only in themselves. There is no word for "worry" in their language.

Everett's book is both a treatise on linguistics and a very personalized account of his and his family's experience with the Pirahã people. What struck me in Everett's account is how various forms

From Language to Singing

of speech are used to communicate different moods and states of mind. This is not singular to the Pirahã people, but musical speech is less common among world civilizations and, as a result, Everett's book caught my attention.

The Pirahã use whistle speech, hum speech, musical speech, yell speech and of course, normal speech.

Hum speech can "say" the same things that can be said with consonants and vowels, in words. "Hum speech is used to disguise either what one is saying or one's identity."[88] It is often used for private speaking. In some respects, it is like whispering and is conducted at a very low volume. It is often used by mothers when talking to their children.

Yell speech is commonly used on rainy days when the rain and thunder render normal speech ineffective. It is also used to communicate at long distances. Yell speech can occasionally be in falsetto.

The Pirahã use musical speech by "exaggerating the relative pitch differences between high tone and low tone, and changing the rhythm of the words and phrases to produce something like a melody."[89] The Pirahã call musical speech "jaw going" or "jaw leaving." It is often used to communicate important new information and to communicate with spirits. The Pirahã say that musical speech is also used by the *kaoaibogi*, or spirits, themselves. Everett notes that musical speech is often used when people are dancing. He adds that women seem to produce musical speech less self-consciously, although he admits to not knowing why this is the case.

Whistle speech, which the Pirahã call talking with a "puckered mouth"—the same way they describe sucking a lemon. Whistle speech is used to communicate during hunting and in aggressive play between boys.

Everett recounts an experience he had while hunting with the Pirahã.

---

[88] Everett, Daniel. *Don't Sleep There Are Snakes*. New York: Vintage Books, 2008
[89] Everett, Daniel. *Don't Sleep There Are Snakes*. New York: Vintage Books, 2008

"I heard the men whistling to one another. They were saying, 'I'll go over there; you go that way,' and other such hunting talk... The whistles carried long and clear in the jungle. I could immediately see the importance and usefulness of this channel, which I guessed would also be much less likely to scare away game than the lower frequencies of the men's normal voices."[90]

Everett offers one example of musical speech, or singing, and how the Pirahã interact with what they call *bigi*, or beings in the various layers of the universe, which are believed to be visible to the naked eye. The Pirahã claim that the *bigi* walk about their jungle and see their tracks on the ground. They see the *bigi* lurking as ghostly shadows in the jungle darkness.

It should also be noted that the Pirahã encounter *bigi* in their dreams. They believe that dreams are a continuation of everyday experience. And that these otherworldly beings traverse their dreams.

One morning, Everett chronicles, as most of the Pirahãs were sleeping, one of the group, Xisaabi, suddenly sat up and started singing about what he had just seen in the jungle, in his dream, saying, "I went up high. It is pretty," referring to an upper layer of the universe.

The next day, Everett asked Xisaabi about his dream.

"Why were you singing?" Everett asked.

Xisaabi replied that he was singing *xaipipai*, what is in your head when you sleep.

Everett eventually comes to understand that *xaipipai* is dreaming but is classified as a real experience. According to the Pirahãs, dreams are not fiction. "You see one way awake and another way while asleep, but both ways of seeing are real experiences."[91] Everett adds that Xisaabi had used musical speech because he was recounting a new experience, recalling what I had stated earlier.

90 *Don't Sleep There Are Snakes, Page 188*
91 *Don't Sleep There Are Snakes, Page 131*

From Language to Singing

As in all other cultures, singing, chanting, humming and the use of incorporating sounds into our experience enables us to manifest the mystery of life. Music, singing, and sound offer pathways to the deepest parts of ourselves that may go unnoticed or unexplored.

ENCORE

PAUL'S DREAMS OF JOHN

I dream of you often nowadays. I must admit that when the Beatles broke up, I was mad at you. We had spent far too much time together. Like brothers, we slept in the same bed sometimes. We were boxed into hotel rooms, having to take refuge from a world that wanted to steal a piece of us. We wrote songs together. We sang songs together. We ate together. What didn't we do together? The truth is, I needed room. We needed room. And maybe we shouldn't have both flung ourselves into relationships and pitted ourselves against each other right after the group broke up. But we were kids. Kids who were spellbound by unimagined success.

It's hard to explain to other people, but I'm just a guy. I'm that same kid from Liverpool, even though I look like an old man. Can you believe that John? I'm an old man. And you are forever young. Always the one to get the last laugh. *You left me standing here a long, long time ago.* Ok, I know, you'll say, there I go again promoting my own songs. But we both did that from the day we met. We both pushed our own songs. We pushed each other. But I was your greatest fan, John. Always. You gave me something that I can't quite put into words. It was more than inspiration. It had meaning, purpose. Focus. We made each other better.

Let me tell you something, John. Remember the excitement we all felt when we recorded "I Want to Hold Your Hand"? Especially you and me. That was something else. I'll never quite get over it, really. What stands out most about that song is that we wrote it together in an almost feverish way. It was as if we couldn't contain the flood of ideas that came over us. And when I listen to that song now, I hear your voice sometimes in the foreground and sometimes I hear my voice. We didn't plan that. It just happened that way. We were like one mind. One mind wrapped around each other. Our voices trailing one another, one overtaking the other, both voices lost in the singularity of one voice. Like a Bach fugue, it's hard to tell when the foreground voice steps back, and the background voice becomes primary. It's hard for me to untangle our voices today. Of course, there were songs before "I Want to Hold Your Hand." But that song was our announcement to the world. We are here. The Beatles have arrived. It might be one of the greatest pop songs ever recorded.

I won't go through the many other songs. Songs we wrote together; you wrote a part, and I wrote another part. But again, like one mind flowing into another. There are some songs that I hear today, and I honestly can't tell who is singing which part. We sometimes sounded like each other, our voices often blending, sometimes becoming indistinguishable. There are voices implied in our harmonies. Many voices, one mind. When does that happen between two people? Never again with me, and not with you.

Then you were taken from us. From me. Ripped from my soul. Imagine the pain I had to endure, not even being able to articulate what I was feeling. I was still reeling from our split. But I was somehow thriving on the anger. Our egos clashed. Who was the real force behind the Beatles? Who wrote what? And blah blah blah. But, of course, it was all of us and let's face it, it was you and me especially. And then you left me. For Yoko. *You left me*. But let's not go into that.

And now, I dream of you. I dream of you always. It's as if my mind is searching for itself and finds you. It is the dream that dreams the dreamer. But then you're gone. You're there and then you're gone. Then I'm not there. *I am he as you are he as you are me. And we are all together.* See, one of yours. We're playing in one of the bar halls in Berlin and my bass melts while on stage. Then we're playing on the Ed Sullivan show for the first time and, suddenly, you vanish into thin air and I'm still playing, bobbing up and down. But I'm alone and all the world sees me. It's as if the entire world cries because we're not together. The whole world misses us, John. Not me or you, but us.

It's not only that I miss you. I miss the me I was with you. We were something else. Something that, together, was greater than each of us. *Something*, one of George's. When I hear the songs, or see the videos, I know I'm not watching me; I'm watching the us we used to be. Maybe I'm the one who died and you're just dreaming of me.

Two of us riding nowhere. Yours again. Two as one.

And so, I'll dream my way to you. Until I see you again. And smile into your eyes and sing the way we used to. The way we sang as kids in Liverpool and as young men in the Beatles, in a way no two human beings have ever sung.

> *Two of us wearing raincoats*
> *Standing so low*
> *In the sun*
> *You and me chasing paper*
> *Getting nowhere*
> *On our way back home*
> *We're on our way home*
> *We're on our way home*
> *We're going home*

And so, I'll dream my way to you. Until I see you again. And smile into your eyes and sing the way we used to.

BIBLIOGRAPHY

Books

Angelucci, Orfeo. *The Secret of the Saucers*. Zinc Read, 2023

Beyer, Stephen. *Singing to the Plants*. Albuquerque: University of New Mexico Press, 2009

Berendt, Joachim-Ernst. *The Third Ear, On Listening to the World*. New York: Henry Holt, 1985

Berendt, Joachim-Ernst. *The World Is Sound, Nada Brahma*. Rochester: Inner Traditions, 1983

Chaudhuri, Amit. *Finding the Raga, An Improvisation on Indian Music*. New York: New York Review of Books, 2021

Cutchin, Joshua. *Where the Footprints End, High Strangeness and the Bigfoot Phenomenon*. Joshua Cutchin, Timothy Renner, 2020

Diallo, Yaya and Hall, Mitchell, *The Healing Drum: African Wisdom*. Destiny Books, 1989

Dunbar, Robin. *Human Evolution*. New York: Penguin Group, 2014

Everett, Daniel. *Don't Sleep There Are Snakes*. New York: Vintage Books, 2008

Harpur Patrick. *Daimonic Reality: A Field Guide to the Otherworld*. Pine Winds Press, 1974

Hart, Mickey. *Drumming at the Edge of Magic, A Journey Into the Spirit of Percussion*. Harper Collins, 1990

Henderson, Bernard & Jones, Stephen. *Wonder Tales of Ancient Wales, Celtic Myth and Welsh Fairy Folklore*. Chicago: Kalevala, 2010

Fiorito, Mike. *For All We Know*. Baltimore, MD: Loya Press, 2024

Fiorito, Mike. *Mescalito Riding His White Horse*. London: John Hunt Publishing, 2023

Gallimore, Andrew. *Alien Information Theory, Psychedelic Drug Technologies and the Cosmic Game*. Strange World Press, 2019

Jung, Carl. G. *Flying Saucers, A Modern Myth of Things Seen in the Sky*. Princeton University Press, 1978

Jung, Carl. G. *Memories, Dreams, Reflections*. Vintage Books Edition, 1989

Kripal, Jeffery, *Esalen*. Chicago: The University of Chicago Press, 2007

Karel F. and Heda Jindrak. *Sing, Clean Your Brain and Stay Sound and Sane: Postulate of Mechanical Effect of*

Vocalization on the Brain. City: Publisher, Year

Khan, Inayat Hazrat. *The Mysticism of Sound and Music.* Boulder: Shambhala Publications, Inc., 2022

Mack, John E, M.D. *Passport to the Cosmos.* United Kingdom: White Crow Books, 1989

McKenna, Terence. *The Archaic Revival: Speculations on Psychedelic Mushrooms, the Amazon, Virtual Reality, UFOs, Evolution, Shamanism, the Rebirth of the Goddess, and the End of History.* New York: Harper Collins, 1993

McKenna, Terence. *True Hallucinations.* New York: Harper Collins, 1993

Monroe, Robert. *Far Journeys.* New York: Bantam Doubleday, 1985

Nils L. Wallin (Editor), Björn Merker (Editor), Steven Brown (Editor). *The Origins of Music.* Cambridge, Massachusetts: MIT Press, 2000

Pasulka, Diana. *Encounters, Explorations with UFOs, Dreams, Angels, AI, and Other Dimensions.* New York: St. Martins, 2023

Strassman, Rick. *DMT: The Spirit Molecule: A Doctor's Revolutionary Research into the Biology of Near-Death and Mystical Experiences.* Rochester, Vermont: Park Street Press, 2001

Wallin, N.Merker, Bjorn and Brown, Steven, Editors. *Origins of Music.* London: MIT Press, 2000

Vallée, Jacques, *Dimensions: A Casebook of Alien Contact.* Anomalist Books, 2008

Online Resources

https://youtu.be/4HIELWKbKSw?si=_ChdVKHEb_frzu7z (Behind Greatness podcast)

https://www.nytimes.com/2019/05/26/us/politics/ufo-sightings-navy-pilots.html

One Earth (Oneearth.org)

https://en.wikipedia.org/wiki/Beat_(music)#On-beat_and_off-beat

https://en.wikipedia.org/wiki/Tara_(Buddhism)

https://atwoodmagazine.com/prhw-peter-rowan-the-song-that-made-hank-williams-dance-video-premiere/

https://www.ayahuascafoundation.org/blog/

https://uforabbithole.com/podcast/ep-31-an-interview-with-dean-radin-on-consciousness-psi-phenomena-and-real-magic/

https://www.astronomy.com/science/what-is-quantum-entanglement-a-physicist-explains-einsteins-spooky-action-at-a-distance/

https://en.unesco.org/silkroad/knowledge-bank/western-regions-his-yu-under-tang-empire-and-kingdom-tibet

https://paistegongs.com/history.php

ACKNOWLEDGEMENTS

This book was made better by all who read iterations of it before my work went to the publisher.

I'm grateful to the many reviews and inputs that I received from my wife, Arielle, and my friends, Susan Kaessinger, Sam Mastandrea, Bill Bernthal and Pete Rowan. Special call-out to Angela Welch for her multiple readings and invaluable insights. And thank you to Tim Bragg, who not only contributed chapters to the book, but also provided close readings of the manuscript in progress. I am also grateful to MK Barnes for her thoughtful reviews of the book. A great bow of gratitude to Jeff Kripal who encouraged me to bring this project to fruition. And thank you to the contributors who shared their stories. I am forever honored by the trust you showed in conveying your stories to me.

ABOUT THE AUTHOR

Mike Fiorito is a freelance journalist and author. His books include *For All We Know*, *Mescalito Riding His White Horse*, *Falling from Trees*, *The Hated Ones*, *Sleeping with Fishes*, *Call Me Guido*, *Freud's Haberdashery Habits*, and *Hallucinating Huxley*. *Mescalito Riding His White Horse* received the 2024 Independent Press Distinguished Favorite Award in Spirituality. *Falling from Trees* received the 2022 Independent Press Distinguished Favorite Award in Short Stories.

Apprentice House Press is the country's only campus-based, student-staffed book publishing company. Directed by professors and industry professionals, it is a nonprofit activity of the Communication Department at Loyola University Maryland.

Using state-of-the-art technology and an experiential learning model of education, Apprentice House publishes books in untraditional ways. This dual responsibility as publishers and educators creates an unprecedented collaborative environment among faculty and students, while teaching tomorrow's editors, designers, and marketers.

Eclectic and provocative, Apprentice House titles intend to entertain as well as spark dialogue on a variety of topics. Financial contributions to sustain the press's work are welcomed. Contributions are tax deductible to the fullest extent allowed by the IRS.

To learn more about Apprentice House books or to obtain submission guidelines, please visit www.apprenticehouse.com.

Apprentice House Press
Communication Department
Loyola University Maryland
4501 N. Charles Street
Baltimore, MD 21210
Ph: 410-617-5265
info@apprenticehouse.com • www.apprenticehouse.com

Printed in the USA
CPSIA information can be obtained
at www.ICGtesting.com
LVHW020849111224
798824LV00002B/2